A Gate to Somewhen Else

L. J. Hutton

ISBN: 9798757597126

Published by Wylfheort Books 2021

Copyright

The moral right of L. J. Hutton to be identified as the author of this work has been asserted by her in accordance with the Copyright, Designs and Patents Act 1988.

All characters in this book are fictitious, and any resemblance to actual persons living or dead is purely coincidental.

All rights reserved. No part of this publication may be reproduced, stored in a retrieval system or transmitted in any form, or by any means, without the prior permission in writing of the author, nor to be otherwise circulated in any form or binding or cover other than in which it is published without a similar condition, including this condition, being imposed upon the subsequent purchaser.

Acknowledgements

This time around I have to give special thanks to Dr Mary Ward for her eagle-eyed intervantions. She is an amazing copy editor and picks up all the little glitches that have slipped through the other editing processes. Also thanks are once again due to the academic members of staff at Birmingham University who taught me so much about the Anglo-Saxon era and the culture of that time. Any mistakes are mine alone and no reflection on their teaching.

And as ever, thanks also to my husband for having a mentally absent wife even if I was only in the other room. Also to crazy Dirk, and the marvellous Mr Matty – gentleman greyhound of the highest order.
This is dedicated to the memory of our beautiful lurcher Belle, gone too soon.

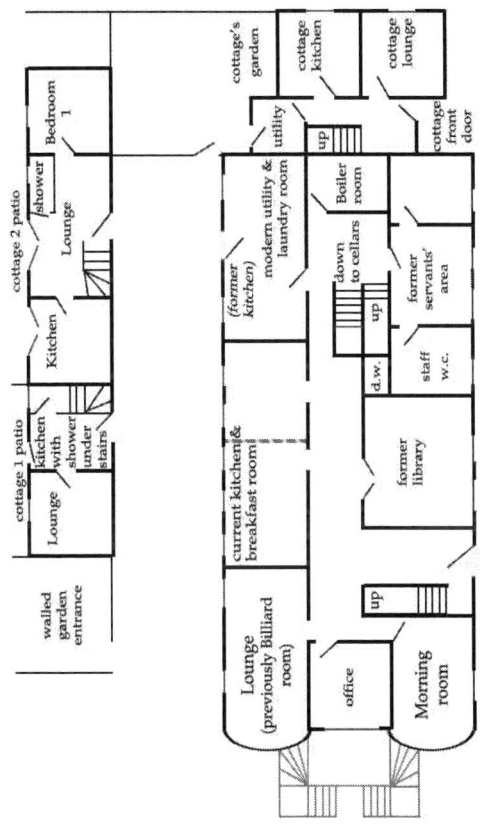

Fownhope Priors, ground floors of both the main house and cottages

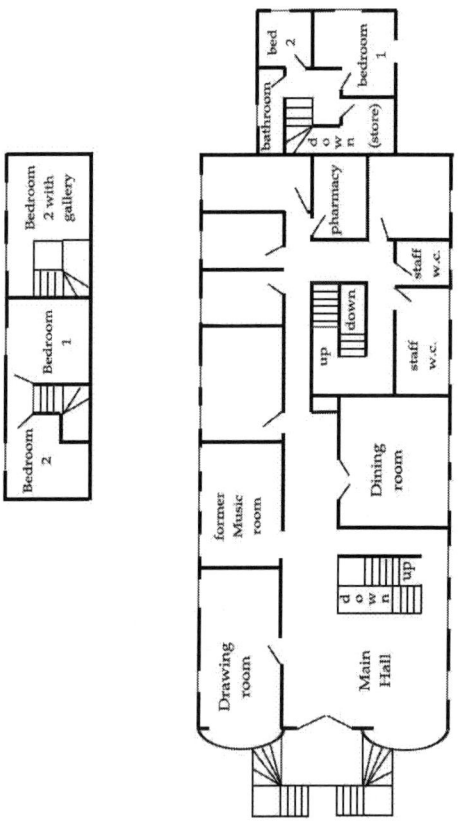

Fownhope Priors first floors of both the main house and cottages

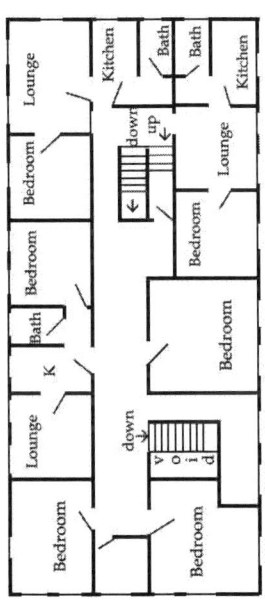

Fownhope Priors top floor of the main house

Chapter 1

The annoying voice was at it again, echoing around the railway station's void like an irate magpie's crowing.

"Catherine! Catherine! Over here!"

Whoever the hell 'Catherine' was, Kat really hoped she would show up and silence this irritating relative. It was bad enough that she'd had to get up at some ungodly hour to catch the train for a commission which, in truth, she really didn't want, but in her current circumstances couldn't afford not to take. That was what you got for having briefly had a boyfriend with light fingers where your business account was concerned, and Kat sighed deeply. Well Peter and his dodgy fingers had been dumped at speed and locked out of all of her bank accounts – though how on earth he'd found her passwords was still a major frustration considering how careful she'd been – but it meant that her interior design business was still several thousand pounds short on its operating budget. And so while the police investigated wretched Peter, she was forced to take whatever was on offer in the way of jobs.

She looked around her. Where the hell was her lift? If the damned client wanted her to come

A Gate to Somewhen Else

out into the wilds, the very least she could do was show up as promised, and it was then that she saw an older and very rotund woman with wild grey hair storming up to her.

"Catherine, why are you ignoring me?" the woman demanded belligerently.

Blinking in surprise, Kat answered as civilly as she could, "I'm sorry, I think you have the wrong person, my name's not Catherine."

"Oh!" snapped the other woman. "Then why are you standing there with all those cases of samples for us? You are the interior designer, aren't you?"

Kat felt her own anger rising. How presumptuous of Mrs Hawkesmoor to use what she thought was her given name. Until they'd been properly introduced it would have been professional, not to mention polite, to call her Miss or Ms Newsome.

"My name is not Catherine," she said coldly and with as much calm as she could muster, as Mrs Hawkesmoor began making shooing gestures towards a mud begrimed Land Rover parked at an erratic angle on the train station's car park.

Mrs Hawkesmoor sniffed and gave her an odd look. "Oh." She managed to invest that one syllable with an awful lot of disdain. "Are you one of those people who like to go by funny shortenings? I think if your parents give you a proper name, you should use it, not go chopping it about."

Valiantly suppressing the growl she wanted to make by thinking about the bank balance, Kat ground out, "If you must know, my proper name is Ekaterina, but since most people can't spell or pronounce that *properly*, I choose to be known as Kat."

Mrs Hawkesmoor halted in her tracks and looked Kat up and down. "You're not one of those *foreigners* are you?"

Peter, I'm going to wring your wretched neck, Kat mentally snarled, then with very forced politeness answered, "I suppose it depends on how far away you class as foreign. I was born over the border in the West Midlands." *There you miserable old witch,* she silently tacked on, *stick that in your prejudicial pipe and smoke it!*

"Oh, so you are English," Mrs Hawkesmoor sniffed. "That's good, because if you weren't, you could turn around and go back! I've already sent two other designers packing because they were foreigners masquerading under English trade names. We have a prestigious old *English* house, and I want someone who understands *English* design – not some Rajah's boudoir or an Italian brothel!"

Kat immediately revised what her quotes would be for this job, not simply because of Mrs Hawkesmoor's revolting prejudices – although she was clearly mistaking Greek for Italian – but because she instantly knew from those summations who those two designers had to be, and what they charged as a matter of course. If Mrs Hawkesmoor could afford to go to them first, then Kat certainly didn't need to trim her services to the bone to get this job. *Keep taking deep breaths and think of how much you can screw the charges up if she can afford Marina Stelakis, or Neena Ramesh-Southcote's basic quotes as a starting point*, she told herself firmly, and forced the smile back on her face.

What a bloody time for my car to develop engine problems, as well, she mentally groaned for the umpteenth time, as she loaded her cases into the back of the Land Rover. One was obviously her laptop, but another was a proper artist's case with her portfolio in it and had been unwieldy on the train, while the third was filled with examples of fabric and wallpapers and was damned heavy. *Just when I can't afford to get it fixed until I've got more cash coming in. And why did it have to happen when I'd just finished what was on the books because I'd been planning a much-needed holiday? ...Which I now can't afford to take, thank you very much Mr Peter-bloody-Erdington!*

Then, it suddenly dawned on her why she had been so taken aback by the dreadful Hawkesmoor woman. Whoever it was who had spoken to her on the phone hadn't had those broad Yorkshire vowels. Northern, yes, but not so very distinctively north Yorkshire. And in that case, who was this woman she was with now?

"Mrs Hawkesmoor," she began, only to be interrupted with,

"I'm not Mrs Hawkesmoor," although it came out as, 'Aaahm no' mussis Haarksmaar.' But before Kat could ask who she was in that case, the older woman ploughed remorselessly on with. "I'm not having our Jeanette being taken advantage of by the likes of you. If that idiot husband of hers can't be bothered to watch where the pennies are getting spent, then someone has to."

Kat inwardly cringed. God in heaven, this was the bloody mother-in-law! And how badly was she stirring the pot? The Mrs Hawkesmoor who'd phoned her had sounded positively reasonable compared to this harridan, and without even having met Mr Hawkesmoor, Kat's sympathy was all with him. What on earth had he done to deserve a mother-in-law like this?

She forced herself to ask, "And your name is…?"

"I'm Mrs Underhill," the frumpy woman said with considerable pride. "There've been Underhills in the Dales for centuries, I'll have you know."

"That's as maybe," Kat riposted with more chill than she would have done to the actual client, "but this commission is here in the Midlands, and I have to state most firmly, Mrs Underhill, that I will be taking my instructions from the person paying my bills, and *nobody* else."

She could have sworn that the woman chose that moment to start the rattling old engine of the Land Rover, as under her breath she muttered, "We'll see about that!" thinking that Kat wouldn't hear her.

You can 'see' all you want, Kat thought firmly, *but if you think I'm some newcomer to this game, then you've got me all wrong. I'm not getting caught in your domestic bickering – or God forbid, all out war. I either work for the one with the cheque book or not at all!* She'd seen other designers come to grief by going along with who they'd mistakenly thought was the dominant partner in a relationship, only to find that the money lay elsewhere, and then found that person subsequently refusing to pay the bill for work they hadn't wanted done in the first place.

However, it still didn't explain why the woman who had phoned her had been so cagey about the size of the job, nor clear on what she wanted done – hence the case of samples. It seemed very likely that this client might also be someone who just couldn't cope with computer images, but needed to see stuff off-screen. Mercifully there weren't many like that these days, but sometimes the most technologically challenged were the ones who'd pay for the biggest jobs, which was why Kat was lugging all this stuff with her. Several times Kat had asked how many rooms were involved, and she'd yet to get a straight answer. Was that because Mrs Hawkesmoor was as penny-pinching as her mother? Or was there some other reason why she'd not been told? Whichever it was, it had made costing the job an absolute nightmare, and the best Kat had been able to do was to give Mrs H. a very rough estimate per room, and that was not the way she normally liked to work. All of which had her again cursing under her breath the day Peter had ever been born. That man had a lot to answer for, and it stiffened Kat's resolve not to cave in and let him walk away even more, though it had hardly been needed to continue to press charges against him, despite all of his wimp-like pleading.

Kat had been forced to take the train from Worcester, where she lived, to Hereford, which was the nearest station to where the Hawkesmoors' property lay. And as Mrs Underhill flung the rickety Land Rover around the tight country lanes at a speed which Kat would never have deemed safe, she was mentally adding money to the bill at every bend. This was danger money, nothing less! If Mrs Underhill had ever passed a driving test, then she had surely forgotten everything she had been taught during the intervening decades, because she drove as if she owned the road. All Kat could do was pray that they didn't encounter a farm tractor coming out of a field, because there was no way that this pile of rust would stop in time if they did. As for airbags, they'd probably not been invented when this vehicle had come off the production line.

So it was with considerable relief that she saw the sign for Fownhope Priors flash by, and realised that at least they were now in the hamlet where the house lay. She spotted a few red-brick 1930s former farm labourers' cottages as they careered past, and then with something little short of a hand-brake turn, Mrs Underhill threw the aged Land Rover into a driveway, and Kat felt as though she could at least draw breath again. Even so, the long curving drive was filled with potholes which ought to have required a more leisurely pace in order to avoid them, and Kat found herself bracing herself with one hand up on the roof of the vehicle, and another on the seat, if only to save her spine from the battering it was taking from being thumped down into potholes you could have lost a pig in, and then accelerating out of again with a massive thump.

In fact she was so busy bracing herself that she completely failed to notice that they had come out of the tree-lined drive, and onto an open turning circle in front of the house itself. Only when Mrs Underhill slid to a jerky halt at what she presumed was the front, did Kat properly focus on what was outside. A horseshoe set of steps swept up to a grand front entrance of two French doors which bypassed the ground floor altogether, and went in at first floor level on what was almost a double bay-windowed frontage. It had undoubtedly been designed to impress, and even probably two centuries on from its construction, it still did. And the fact that its lovely honey-coloured stone was backdropped by mixed woodland, which showed it off to its best, did nothing to lessen the impression.

"What a beautiful house," Kat found herself spontaneously saying out loud, although given that she'd just got out of the passenger side, and Mrs Underhill was slamming the driver's door noisily at the time and therefore didn't hear her praise, was probably a good thing given the woman's ability to take offence at everything.

To then find herself facing a much younger, taller and slimmer version of Mrs Underhill coming around the corner of the house, was something of a shock. The woman, who couldn't have been much older than Kat herself, and therefore in her mid to late thirties, would have been almost pretty except for the supercilious sneer on her face. Bleach-blonde and heavily styled hair framed regular features, but if this was Mrs Hawkesmoor, then Kat thought she needed a good skin-care routine considerably more than the heavy make-up she wore in an ineffective attempt to hide her terrible complexion. Also, looking back at Mrs Underhill, Kat could see the family resemblance. At the moment, Mrs Hawkesmoor was just about winning the war with age, but if she let go for an instance, Kat could see that she would slide swiftly into her mother's hard features.

Sighing to herself, Kat smoothed the trousers of her professional suit and walked towards Mrs Hawkesmoor, hand held out to shake.

"Hello. I'm Kat Newsome."

"Hello," Mrs Hawkesmoor said with a noticeable lack of enthusiasm.

God, this is going from bad to worse, Kat thought, and in a desperate attempt to save the situation said, "You have a wonderful home here."

"It's not *my* home," Mrs Hawkesmoor snapped. "*My* home is in Yorkshire, not this bloody dump!"

As Kat gulped, not knowing what on earth to say next, any awkward silence was avoided by Mrs Underhill piling in with. "This is her husband's next project." Not 'my son-in-law', Kat noted. "Last lot in here were a nursing home. Place reeks of old people and piss! God knows why he thinks he can make something of it. It wants a bloody miracle, not an interior designer, if you ask me." And then as Kat started towards the sweeping horseshoe steps up to what she presumed was the front door, "No! Not that way! You won't get in up there. This way! Tradesman's entrance is this way."

Tradesman? Kat nearly threw the sample cases on the ground in affront. What century did this damned woman think she was living in? Did she think she was going to turn this place into some twenty-first century Downton Abbey, and with the hired helps knowing their places and staying out of sight?

Luckily the other two women were stalking off ahead of her, and so she didn't get to speak to them until they had rounded the corner of the building and she saw more of it. At that point, things became a bit clearer. For a start off, this house was far bigger than she'd realised, for the entrance she'd seen was actually on one of the short sides, and making the best of the glorious view. But the full length of the building, which was around the corner, was easily twice that of the other side, and there was another grand and porticoed doorway going in on the ground floor in the middle of this long side. Not quite as grand as the staircase to be sure although still far from tradesman-like, but considerably easier for anyone carrying bags or just a bit unsteady on their feet.

Biting her lip, and feeling a bit annoyed that the two other women hadn't as much as offered to carry even one of the cases, Kat lugged her wares in their wake, and then was even more surprised when they continued past the door and turned into what had obviously been one of the servant's cottages back in the house's heyday.

"There's this, and then some more cottages in what used to be the stables," Mrs Hawkesmoor said in a faint voice. "Only bloody part worth living in at the moment. ...Positively exhausts me just traipsing around the place." She gave Kat a sideways look as she waved her towards an uncomfortable looking chair, and flopped onto the chintz-covered sofa. "My doctor says I must be careful of my nerves, you know. No stress, he said. So what does my husband do, eh? Takes on this crumbling heap and drags me miles from home." She adopted what she no doubt thought of as a long-suffering expression. "I shall do my duty, of course, and support him."

"You always do, my darling!" Mrs Underhill barged in with. "He doesn't deserve you. After all you've been through, to put this on you – it's a disgrace, that's what it is!"

"Oh, Mother, don't carry on," Mrs Hawkesmoor said in the kind of weary tones that belonged in some Victorian melodrama. Then she looked despairingly at the case of samples and the portfolio and asked faintly, "You don't expect me to look through *all* of those, do you?"

Kat's blood was beginning to boil now. "Well if you had given me more of an idea of what it was you wanted to do with the place," she said through gritted teeth, "then I could have narrowed down the possibilities. But as it stands, you said nothing on the phone of how the finished house is to be used. If you had, I could probably have been a little more selective in what I brought along. However, from what little you gave me, I was led to believe that it would be a family home, which is a much broader commission than say an office suite. Yet you've already said now that this *isn't* your home. So what is it, then?"

"Her husband's a property developer," Mrs Underhill said, as though he was a sewer cleaner, or some equally filthy job. "Bought this place on some whim when he should've been at home looking after his wife. Left her all alone at her lowest point, he did! Disgusting behaviour. He should've been by her side day and night, not gallivanting about the country looking for his next project."

"Oh Mother, don't bring it up again, I can't bear it," Mrs Hawkesmoor pleaded, and for the first time Kat could see some real distress there. Clearly there had been some sort of family tragedy, so maybe she should give them some leeway for odd behaviour.

However, Mrs Underhill sniffed. "*Hmph!* Expecting you to help him after all you've been through. Unreasonable doesn't even come close. What your father would have said if he'd been alive I do not know."

Clearly not the death of said father, then, Kat mused, because that sounded as though he'd been gone a while, and there was no renewal of the Oscar-worthy performance from his daughter at the mention of him.

"Look, I'm sorry to press you on this," Kat sighed, "but I honestly need more to go on. Is this going to be a business property, then? Are you turning it into a hotel? Or is Mr Hawkesmoor going to carve it up into flats? Or do you just want it renovated so that you can resell it at a better price?

"And I'm sorry if you find this trying, Mrs Hawkesmoor, but how many rooms are you expecting to consult me on? Just looking at this side of the building we've walked past, I can see that there are a lot more rooms than I thought there would be. Do you want me to deal with all of them, or just the reception rooms? Because I have to say that this is not the normal way I do business. I don't know what the interior designers you've used in Yorkshire are like, but this opened-ended way of doing things is not normal practice, and I cannot possibly give you a proper quotation until I know more specifically what it is that you want me to do."

Whatever answer she was expecting, it wasn't Mrs Hawkesmoor's shrill riposte of, "It's not my fault! I've never done this before! Scott said it would be good for me to do something to take my mind off *things*. He said he would go with what I want. But when I said just do it white all the way through, he said some very..." and she descended into sniffles without finishing.

"It's his project," Mrs Underhill said savagely, "he should bloody-well choose! He shouldn't be putting any sort of decisions off onto you. He's the man of the household, for God's sake – or would be if he had any spine! So you go off, Miss whatever your name is, and have a look at this rotten pile of bricks. And if you think you can do anything with it, give us a quote. He'll have to pay and like it."

"I'm afraid it doesn't work like that," Kat said firmly. "I need signed contracts for specific work." Then saw that Mrs Underhill was building up a head of steam for a full blown argument, and conceded, "However, I will go and have a look around the building since I'm already here. At least that will give me some idea of what we're dealing with, but then I am going to need some decisions from you."

Chapter 2

She got up and walked out, relieved beyond words that neither woman followed her outside. Leaning against the cold bricks of the cottage wall, she looked up at the three floors. Was it really worth it? Could she survive if she didn't take this commission? No, not least because she desperately needed to get the VW estate back on the road or replace it, and either way that wasn't going to be cheap. On the other hand, she couldn't think that any other designer in the area would touch this with a barge pole, so that would give her a bit more leeway to push for what she wanted contractually. How many others had already turned Mrs Hawkesmoor down just at the phone-call stage? It might be worth a few calls of her own once she got back home, if only to find out just how desperate the Hawkesmoors might be.

With a sigh she pushed off from the wall and went to the front door, relieved to find that it was unlocked and she wouldn't have to go back and ask for any keys. Inside, she found herself in a short hall with what looked as if it had been the main staircase in front of her. Then looking up, she realised that the reason why it wasn't as dark in here as she'd expected was because there was a skylight at the top of the stairwell, and a certain amount of natural light was coming in that way even though it was far from a bright day.

So should she start with the reception rooms, or go upstairs? Something about those sweeping outside steps nudged her to go up at least to the next floor, because she had a funny feeling that there might be reception rooms up there too. But it was as she got to the top of the stairs that she smelled it – cigarette smoke. Someone was smoking up here.

Then she remembered that down on the driveway there had been several skips filled with random detritus. Old bed-frames, and bits of obviously rotting wooden moulding, had been in amongst a substantial amount of ratty carpets and some general rubble. So no doubt there was a workman up here somewhere. That might not be a bad thing, though. If this man could give her a better idea of what was happening with the building, it would help her considerably.

And so literally following her nose and the scent of the cigarettes, she turned left and found herself in the room with the double French windows at the top of the steps. It had beautiful wood panelling, some wonderfully ornate plaster coving, and had clearly been the centre-piece of the old house, although probably of late had been the nursing home's main lounge. There, seated on the sill of one of the side windows was the man, dressed in well-used jeans, a pair of builder's boots, and a plaster encrusted fleece jacket. He was staring out at the view as though he had nothing better to do, but as Kat got closer she could see the tension-lines on his face, and she wondered whether he'd been on the receiving end of one of Mrs Underhill's rants. If so, she could hardly blame him for taking his time. After all, she herself hadn't been offered even so much as a cup of tea, and so it was probable that the workmen weren't treated to such basic hospitality either.

"I wouldn't let Mrs Underhill catch you slacking," she said with a smile, then saw him jump in shock. "Sorry. I didn't mean to creep up on you. I always wear soft soled shoes when I'm inspecting a job – much safer than risking marking anything with heels. I'm Kat Newsome, by the way. The interior designer – or will be if I can ever get a firm decision on what I'm supposed to be quoting for," and again she held out her hand to shake.

This time the man made an effort to get to his feet to come and shake her hand, but saying, "You don't have to warn me about Flora Underhill, I've been saddled with her my whole married life. I'm Scott Hawkesmoor."

"Mr Hawkesmoor? Oh! I'm so terribly sorry. I was given the impression that you weren't here. I do apologise."

Kat felt mortified. What a mistake to make!

Luckily Scott Hawkesmoor just gave a wry smile, saying, "I think those two are hoping that if they ignore me, I'll finally vanish. As far as Flora's concerned, I've been absent for the entire twenty years I've known them."

Kat winced. Good grief, there was a lot of bitterness there. What on earth had gone on between these people? And Scott certain didn't sound Yorkshire. If she wasn't mistaken, there was almost something of a hint of Welsh in his voice. Then she pulled herself together. The most tactful thing to do was not to pry in this man's private life, but to do the job she'd come for.

"Well I'm very glad to meet you Mr Hawkesmoor..."

"...oh please, call me Scott..."

"...Scott. So can you tell me what your plans are for this building? I'm afraid your wife has been more than a little hazy over everything. I'm not even sure what it is I've come to give a quote on. The impression I was given was that you were planning to convert something that was in a rough state into a home. But seeing the size of this place, and hearing some of what Mrs Hawkesmoor said, clearly you aren't looking for me to decorate your own home here."

Scott gave a bitter laugh. "No, not my family home." He looked back out of the window and as the light caught his face, Kat could have sworn she saw tears in his eyes.

"Mr Hawkes... Scott, are you alright?"

He fished a packet of tissues out of his pocket, retrieved one, and blew his nose, turning away from her in the false hope that she wouldn't see him wiping his eyes. Then he turned back to her and sighed.

"You might as well know. God knows I wouldn't blame you for turning this job down.

You see a year ago we lost our two sons in an accident."

"Oh my God! I'm so sorry!"

He grimaced. "And to some extent it was my fault." As he paused and dragged in another deep breath, Kat thought that this explained an awful lot about Mrs Hawkesmoor too. What she was half expecting was for him to say that he'd been at the wheel of the family car when it had been in some sort of crash, but to her shock he carried on with,

"You see they'd badgered us and badgered us to let them have motorbikes. I'd said no. They were too young. Kevin was only seventeen, and Martin just fifteen." He sighed deeply. "But they were always good at getting their mother and grandmother on their sides. And so I had the four of them hounding me at every turn whenever I was back at home. ...No excuse, I know. I should have stood my ground. ...Well I did in a way. I refused outright to buy them bikes they could take onto the open road – and Martin was too young anyway. But I finally caved in and bought Kevin a quad bike for his seventeenth birthday. I told him quite firmly that I was *not* going to license it for use on the road, and if he got his mother to do it for him, then I would take it back off him and sell it.

"I think he believed me over that. I've always been the one who stood my ground with the boys – meant what I said and stuck to it. It was so easy for them to get around their mother that nothing she said to them made any impression anymore. But I told them, they could ride it around the fields we had as long as they wore proper helmets, *and* if Kevin had lessons before he took Martin on the back."

He didn't have to say any more for Kat to know that that hadn't happened. Clearly Kevin had gone out with Martin on the back and something dreadful had happened. So she was just trying to think of something consoling to say, to save Scott from telling it all over again, when he continued,

"Actually I'm glad to have someone to tell this to. I've had to keep everything bottled up inside for so long." He had to use another tissue, but then said in a firmer voice. "You see, Jeanette and I were only kids ourselves when she got pregnant — or rather, when I thought she got pregnant." He shook his head and sniffed. "To this day I don't know whether it was a total fiction, or whether she really did get pregnant and lost it early on. Christ, I don't know if that one was even mine! After I'd been practically frogmarched up the aisle by her father, I found out that Jeanette had been something of the village bike. That's what you get for being the good-looking lad working on her father's building site."

Bloody hell, no wonder he's bitter! Kat thought sympathetically, and dared to say, "I can hear that you're not from Yorkshire."

For the first time she got a genuine smile from him. "Me? God, no! My folks were from Cheshire, right on the Welsh border. Farm workers my lot were, but by the time I was old enough to go out to work there wasn't much of that sort of work going, so I went and got an apprenticeship in the building trade and began working my way up.

"I think old man Underhill must have had a bit of a guilty conscience about forcing me into marrying Jeanette, because after a year or so he started paying for me to go to college. In the end I'd even got basic architect's skills. Oh, I couldn't design a building from scratch, I'm not that good, but I could handle restorations where I just needed a sound understanding of where the key walls and supports were, and stuff like that. So when he had his first heart-attack, he signed the whole company over to me."

There was another of the bitter, short laughs. "He knew if he put Flora or Jeanette in charge, the firm would be bankrupt within a couple of months. But in the few years he lived on, I took the company to new ground, specialising in renovations and repurposing old buildings, and we made good money out of that, too. So when he died five years ago, with him having endorsed every decision I'd made for the previous four and been openly been delighted with what I'd done, the two downstairs couldn't really argue that I shouldn't stay in my position as MD.

"But of course, those sorts of projects don't turn up on your doorstep very often, and I worked away from home a lot of the time. To be frank, I was only too glad to as well. Then once Charlie – my father-in-law – had died, there was nobody in the house I could even have a civil conversation with anymore. The boys had been too much in their mum and gran's care to ever see me as anything but the enemy. God, they weren't even sorry to see Charlie gone! I think they thought he took too much of the attention away from them in his last illness. All they could keep going on about was how, when Kevin turned eighteen, he'd be the one to take over running the company."

Scott shook his head. "Would never have happened, mind. It's now a registered company, not some backstreet family builders. There are accountants and solicitors, and also shareholders, and they wouldn't stand for some lad who flunked all of his exams telling everyone what to do. ...And that was another thing I was the devil incarnate for saying. I told Kevin that either he went back to college and retook his exams, or he went out and got a job. I wasn't going to pay for him to sit around at home playing *Call of Duty* and *Grand Theft Auto* all day. And when I found that Jeanette was giving him money, I cut what I put into her account and put in a standing order for the local supermarket to deliver to us on my account. Were there ever rows about that! But I said straight, 'you teach the lad to be responsible and I'll change things back to the way they were,' but I wasn't going to have him running riot behind my back."

Kat was feeling more and more sympathetic to Scott. "I think there are a lot of parents these days who struggle with that – kids not understanding that they need to work for what they want, I mean. I've got a couple of old school friends whose kids are in their teens now, and they're practically tearing their hair out whenever

I speak to them – and they don't have money to throw around in the first place. You're far from alone in that."

"Well I sure felt it. So much so that Jeanette and I were in the process of starting divorce proceedings. But then I was up in Carlisle, finishing converting a big old house into a hotel, and I got the call. Kevin had been coming home drunk, and this time he'd really overstepped the mark. He'd punched his mother and Flora had thrown him out of the house to sober up.

"She's a hard old besom, but for once I can't hold it against her. Apparently she whacked him out of the house with the broom, because he was turning into a big lad with a lot of weight behind those fists when he turned ugly, and she thought she'd locked him in the garage. It has an upstairs space with a bed and a wash-basin in, you see – a hangover from when Charlie was at home and liked tinkering with his old cars. Flora and Jeanette wouldn't let him in the house in his oily overalls, so he had somewhere made where he could clean up and have a midday nap in peace.

"So Flora wasn't being that evil to Kevin, and she needed to get Jeanette to A&E, because they thought he'd broken her nose. Off they went to the hospital, thinking Kevin was safe and sobering up. They couldn't have guessed that Martin would go and let him out, and that they'd decided to run away together."

"Oh no! How did you find that out? ...I mean, it must have been obvious that Kevin had been drinking when they did the..." she managed to stop herself before she blurted out the word 'autopsy'. Reviving memories that his son would have been carved up on some pathologist's slab wasn't kind or tactful.

"They left a note. Or rather, Martin did." And now all the hurt was back, written large across Scott's face. "The things they said about us, and about me and Charlie in particular. Awful. No parent should have to hear that. Especially as it was hardly true. I did care. I did love them. It was just so bloody hard when every move I made was undermined by someone else in the family. And with Martin I have to include Kevin in that. God, but he was a bad influence on his brother. If Kevin had put even half the effort into studying as he did into getting around me, he'd have come out of school with top grades all round. But instead, he made sure that Martin followed his lead.

"Martin was more like me in temperament, a lot calmer, but he didn't stand a chance with that lot around him. I was even going to start taking him away with me as soon as he turned sixteen and could leave school. I thought if I could get him away from the others, I might be able to straighten him out. But of course I never got the chance."

Scott turned and walked to the French windows, flinging them open despite the stiff breeze that flew in, going to stand out on the top of the stone stairs and dragging in the sharp country air like a man who had been drowning. After a moment he looked back over his shoulder at Kat.

"They went tearing off over the fields in the bloody dark. Stupid, stupid thing to do. And they weren't wearing helmets. Turned out the ones I'd bought them had never been used. ...And then they found the edge of the old quarry."

He didn't need to say any more. Kat could already picture the quad bike sailing out into the void, and the long drop down. No wonder neither boy had survived, and she wasn't going to ask if the quarry had been like so many she knew of, with a deep pool at the bottom, yet that question indirectly got answered.

"Took the police two days to find them. The bike had gone to the bottom of the pool, taking them with it. ...And then there were all the enquiries. Why had they been there? Hadn't they known to wear safety gear? Why had Kevin been drinking when he was under-age?"

He came back inside with a shiver that wasn't just to do with the cold wind he shut the doors on. "I may have hated the sight of Jeanette by then, but I wouldn't have wished any of that onto her, not ever. I got off lightly. It was accepted that as the bread-winner, I was working away a lot. But Jeanette and Flora came in for a lot of criticism, and the bloody local rag got wind of it, and they were like sodding dogs with bones."

He gave a snort of disgust. "Of course it might have helped if Flora hadn't stamped all over half of the local villages beforehand. There was precious little sympathy from anyone there for either of them, especially as the pair of them had been very quick to shove the blame for

Kevin being drunk onto some other local lads. Turned out these lads hadn't got the money to go out buying that much drink, and it had been Kevin who'd been the ring-leader in their boozing exploits. So you can imagine how that went down with their mums and dads. Poor buggers were probably having nightmares and thanking their lucky stars that it hadn't been their kid on the back of the bike. You couldn't blame them for being outraged at Flora trying to shove the blame back at them.

"But that was when Jeanette had her breakdown. For a couple of months she was completely out of it on antidepressants and sleeping pills. And that was when I came up with the idea of us just getting away. Away from Yorkshire. Away from Flora. I wasn't expecting to have some romantic reunion. There hadn't been enough romance there in the first place for that. But I couldn't leave her there like that, either. So I thought that if I was going to have to look after her for the next few years, then at least we could do it without her practically being spat upon every time she wanted to go out for a pint of milk and a loaf of bread."

He turned and looked about the room. "Bloody fool that I was, I started looking around for somewhere new to renovate. I handed the company on, took my handsome pay-off, and thought of getting back to my roots and doing some hands-on stuff again. But I bought this place after a mad flit down here, and after just an hour's viewing. Christ knows what I was thinking. Wasn't really. I was just bloody desperate to get away.

"And then we came down here and bloody Flora came with us – or rather, we'd been here all of a day and Jeanette was screaming down the phone begging her to come and rescue her. Didn't help that I'd had an agent in up in Yorkshire to look at putting our house on the market. The two of them then spent days shrieking at me that I had no right to sell 'their' home, as if I'd never even lived there."

He waved a vague hand at the room. "And it hasn't helped that since I've been here I'm completely revising what few plans I had for this place."

"What did you want it to be?" Kat asked tentatively.

"*Humph!* A conference centre! ...Down these lanes? This far from a motorway? What the fuck was I daydreaming at?"

Kat went and put a sympathetic hand on his arm. "I think you were doing your best in an impossible situation," she said gently. "The house does have a lot of potential, you know."

He looked down at her, and this close to Kat could see that in his youth Scott must have been almost male model handsome. The years hadn't been kind to him, though, or at least the last one hadn't, and that wasn't helped by him clearly still having a lot of guilt and self-loathing going on inside.

"Potential?" he barked despairingly. "What do you think I could do with a mansion with at least eight reception rooms, God know how many bits of servants' stores and office spaces, and three cottages and a stable block – not to mention cellars a vineyard would be proud to have? I've paid one and a half million for this to start with, and at this rate it's going to bankrupt me!"

Chapter 3

"One and a half million?" Kat gulped in shock. For a moment she thought she must have misheard. Then the number of rooms sunk in. Feeling horribly guilty for taking advantage of the moment, and of Scott's misfortune, nonetheless all she could think was, *if I can make something of this it'll solve all of my problems*! After all, to be the designer behind a beautifully renovated mansion house would be something that would bring her in bigger commissions in the future. But that meant that she was going to have to come up with a blinder of a good idea of what to do with the place, because it was clear that Scott wasn't in any state to do so.

"I know," she heard Scott saying. "Barmy, eh? To pay all of that and not have a single room habitable except in the cottages. And I can't even let those out as holiday cottages because the rest of the place is going to look like a building site for ages."

"Is the roof sound?"

He blinked and looked at her in surprise. "Good God! You're the first person to ask a sensible question. Erm, yes, actually it is! That was the one thing the old folks' home had to pay for. In fact, I suspect that the cost of the new roof to industry standards for that kind of place was probably what drove them out of business. The roof isn't much over three years old, and the place has been empty for eighteen months."

Kat smiled at him. "Great! Then at least it's water-tight. Why don't you give me the guided tour? I can't help you until I've seen what you've got here."

Scott's harassed air seemed to lift a little. "Okay. Where would you like to start? Top or bottom?"

Kat thought for a moment. If this place was to have any kind of life as something like a hotel, the upper bedrooms had to be of a decent quality. If they weren't, and ready to just be touched up, then she would have to come up with something a lot more creative.

"Let's start in the attics," she said with a smile. "I presume that the staff lived in the cottages, but there must be something up under the eaves?"

"Attics it is," Scott declared. "Come on then, follow me."

He led the way back to the main stairs and upwards, but then going off to the back of the house to where a small and cramped staircase was hidden behind a narrow door.

"Back in the day they no doubt had the poor housemaids tucked away up here," he said, as he had to stoop his six-feet-two height to get through the door, something that Kat at a good eight inches shorter had no trouble with. "No sign of any window up here now, mind, but then why would you put even Velux windows in for something that was only going to be a storage area?"

He had reached the top of the stairs, and going through another narrow door, Kat heard him click a switch and then the attic was revealed in the light of a couple of bare bulbs. At least someone had put decent strength bulbs in, she thought, because although the stark light made the cross-beams of the roof trusses cast strange shadows, she could see that the attic had been properly floored. That was good. So many places she had been up into the roof space of required a delicate balancing job walking along the joists, or risk sticking a foot through the ceiling of the room below.

"Well at least you have usable storage up here," she said, determined to give him something positive. "The slope of the roof is nice and high, as well, so although you won't necessarily want to do any conversions up here until you've got the rooms below in good order, this space does have potential." In fact, the high roof was making her revise the age of the building. She'd been thinking it might be Georgian, but no Georgian or Palladian mansion had this kind of steeply sloping roof. "What age is the house, do you know?"

Scott looked at her with some surprise. "You'd care? I thought most interior designers were more bothered with how many walls they could rip out than restoring the original shape."

Kat laughed. "Oh dear, you've not met the best of my profession, have you! But that wasn't why I was asking. I was thinking more about whether the house has any history you could exploit?"

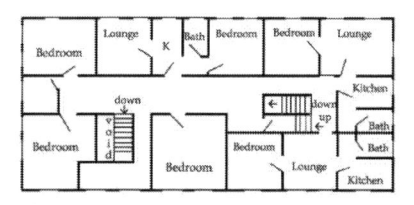

His eyes opened wider. "Oh! Now that was something I hadn't even started to think about." His enthusiasm swiftly waned, though. "But I'm afraid that this place only goes back to the 1890s. If you're up for that kind of investigation, I have the deeds here, locked away safely. They might give you a clue. But all I can remember at the moment is that this was once something to do with one of the major churches around here."

"Hey, you never know what we might find," Kat persisted, keeping her tone optimistic. "However, I think we've established that the roof will hold – given all the rain we've had lately – and that there's nothing we can or need to do up here. Let's go down to the bedrooms."

Shutting up the attic space, they went down to the first floor, and it was here that for the first time Kat got a feeling for just how big this house was. At the back of it were four self-contained apartments. Not just bedrooms, but actual one bedroom apartments, each with a lounge as big as the one she had in her tiny one-bedroom house. Indeed each apartment probably had more space in it than her house did. They all had their own small kitchen and bathroom, which had been made out of what had once probably been an original bedroom. Then the apartments' lounges and bedrooms were what had been the other bedrooms towards the back of the house. Better still, these apartments were all in relatively decent repair.

"Do you know, I think these must have been for the nurses at the home," Kat mused. "Honestly, Scott, it won't take much more than a skim of plaster over the ceilings to repair where the roof leaked and the old plaster's surface got damp. And in truth, I've seen ordinary houses with far more rain damage than this which have still been habitable. The only thing I would say is that you'll need to make a choice between removing the loose bits and skimming, or having sheets of plasterboard put up – and with those joists we've seen from above, I don't think the plasterboard is a no-no."

She turned to look at him and was gratified to see the stress almost visibly falling away from him.

"Yes," he agreed with alacrity. "Yes, of course! Plasterboard would be my choice. Quick, relatively cheap, and easy to put up."

"And I wouldn't worry too much about trying to put these rooms back to the old shape of things, either," Kat said. "Whatever you decide to do with this place, that back staircase which the servants must have used gives you the option of having quite separate access to these flats. You could easily rent these out as holiday lets, you know. Lots of people love coming to this part of the country, and the remoteness from the main roads will be a plus, not a minus, for them. I've worked on another project where three small flats each brought in the best part of a grand a month in season."

Scott's eyes lit up, finally beginning to see that he might just get some return on this investment after all.

"I'm telling you now, you've got this commission if you want it," he said gratefully. "You know, I'd totally failed to take into account that, even when I was the boss, I never decided on a project without first taking my key men around a place with me. And I should have remembered why. It's too easy on your own to miss something – especially when you've got some eager agent with his commission in sight wittering in your ear! I've always had someone to bounce ideas off, even if at the end of the day I disagreed with them. And that's what's been wrong here. I can't talk to Jeanette. I hoped that getting her away from Flora, and into a new place without all of the bad memories, would spark some life …some interest in her."

"And that hasn't happened, has it," Kat sympathised. "Even I can see that in the few minutes I had with her. All she can talk about is getting back to Yorkshire." Then seeing him nod with a pained expression on his face, dared to say, "Then why don't you let her go?" Then had a panic-stricken moment wondering why she'd opened her mouth like that? Talk about going in where angels fear to tread! Poking her nose in was just inviting to get booted off the job.

He looked at her with surprise, but not as angrily as she'd half expected. That emboldened her to say,

"If you were going to get any sort of reconciliation, surely it would have happened by now? And what you said about her calling in her mother before she'd even given you a chance …well that sort of tells you all you need to know, doesn't it? You've got to give this your best shot, but you don't need to do it with your wife and mother-in-law cutting you and everyone else to shreds before you've had a chance to get things started. And that's just talking from some of what I experienced this morning! Mrs Underhill had the cheek to have a go at me for not answering to a name that isn't mine anyway."

"What?" Scott gasped, and Kat told him about the whole 'Catherine' incident.

"So you see," she concluded, "I can see that this is someone who makes up her mind on the spur of the moment, and then regardless of what you then tell her, is never going to change her mind. Do you honestly want someone like that around the place offending contractors left, right and centre? I know the average builder isn't a sensitive flower who'll wilt at the first words, but I've known a fair few who would stick two fingers up at her and walk off the job after one of those outbursts. So if those two want to go home, why don't you let them? That would at least give you some breathing space."

Scott sank down on the top steps of the main stairs, burying his head in his hands for a second. When he looked up his first words were,

"I'm so sorry you had to go through that. And you're right, she should have given you the simple courtesy of calling you by your business name, let alone insulting you for your first name."

He sighed and ducked his head again briefly. However, when he looked up Kat could see that he'd come to a decision. "You're absolutely right. I need them to go home to whatever it is that they think they have there. If it's the bloody house, well then they're welcome to it. Since that place is roughly half of my assets, I think if I make that over to Jeanette then the lawyers can hardly say I've done her down. It's up to her and her mother then. They can either sell it, or live on there on what Charlie left Flora – though they'll struggle with that! Most women would make a good home out of half of what Flora gets a month from Charlie's investments, but not those two."

"But then it won't be your problem," Kat pointed out cautiously. "I know what happened to your sons is awful, absolutely dreadful. But as you said, you weren't there to prevent it, and so why should you be taking all of their guilt as well as your own? I know it's not my family and not my choices, but from what I've seen other people go through, and in my own family too, you've got more chance of both of you healing if you're apart. Together, all you're doing is tearing one another to shreds over and over again, and that just isn't healthy – not for you and not for her. And given that the first words she said to me were about how she will never think of this as home, I don't think she's left you much choice. Your only decision is whether you go back with them right now and put this place back on the market – and hope to God you recoup your costs – or let them go and tough it out here yourself, with at least the potential for you to come out of this slightly better off than when you went into it. That doesn't have to be the end of your marriage, because you could still go back to Yorkshire later. But if you do, then it will hopefully be feeling more positive about things."

Scott gave her an odd look, and for a moment Kat feared that she had this time drastically overstepped the mark. What had she been thinking saying such things to a man she had only known for an hour or so? The words had seemed to tumble out of her mouth as if they had a life of their own, but that didn't make it right. Presumptuous didn't come close! *Oh God, please don't let me have fucked this up magnificently*, she prayed. *What was I thinking, opening my big mouth like that? Whatever made me speak out like that? It's none of my business. It's like my mouth is running away with me, and that's not me – it's just bloody weird! Just because I took an instant dislike to those two women, it doesn't mean I can start telling him what to do. Good grief, Kat, get a grip on yourself!*

Mercifully, a life spent amongst plain-speaking, or downright blunt, Yorkshire folk had made Scott far less touchy than most of the men Kat had met in recent years, and to her amazement, he actually seemed to like her honesty.

"Thank you," he said to Kat's amazement. "I think I needed to hear someone else saying that. To be truthful, I'd been thinking something along those lines, although not in quite such clear terms. And you're right. There's nothing I can do now to make things right with me and Jeanette. The moment Flora turned up here that ship had sailed. I don't stand an earthly chance with her dripping poison in Jeanette's ear at every turn.

"And you're right about this house too. I need to be able to think straight about this place, not have my mind half on those two all the while, and what they're doing behind my back. Nothing would please Flora more than for me to fall flat on my face, and have to go crawling back to what I'm sure she still thinks of as *her* company, begging them to give me a job. She can't see that if I go under, then there'll be no alimony for Jeanette. …Not that I would go back to them for a job, because that bridge is burned, for good or bad. You can't go back in instances like that, and I wouldn't blame the company one bit for not taking me on. Too many of the men remember me as the boss, and the new bosses are not going to risk me undermining the middle management, even if they feel bloody sorry for what our family has been through."

He got up and stretched, working out what were no doubt tensions in his shoulders. "Come on, let me show you the rest of the house. Are you staying here, tonight?"

That took Kat by surprise. "Erm, no. Actually I was hoping to catch one of the trains after five o'clock back from Hereford to

Worcester, where I live. My car's out of order, you see, so I had no choice but to come by train. It couldn't have picked a worse time to conk out on me, but that's the joys of car ownership, isn't it?"

He smiled back at her. "Oh, they have a knack of doing that. In which case, depending on what you think of the rest of the place, I might have a proposition for you."

That intrigued Kat, but she wasn't about to press him on that yet. Instead she walked with him through the rest of the top floor, discovering three more generously proportioned bedrooms (by modern standards) before they got to what must once have been the main bedrooms of the house. One of them looked out over the portico of the ground floor entrance, while the front two faced down the valley just as the front steps did.

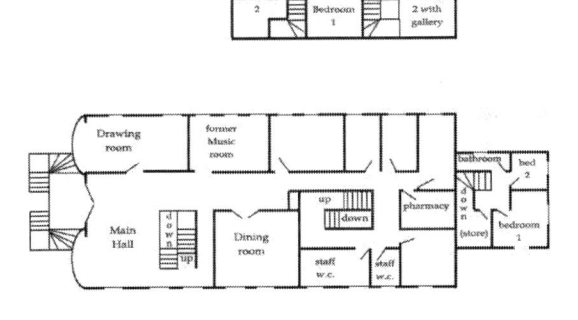

These two rooms were glorious, and although they needed a good makeover, nonetheless they had the potential to be beautiful, light-filled rooms once that was done. Going by the marks in the floor, four beds had occupied these larger rooms in the nursing home days, and Kat couldn't help but think that as long as the nursing care had been decent, these old folk had ended their days with beautiful views from their beds.

Moving on downstairs to what Kat now realised in terms of status, at least, was more of an upper ground floor than a first floor, they began in the room where she had first met Scott. This was clearly one of two principle rooms from the original house, and was the reception hall where they had probably entertained guests. The plasterwork on the ceilings was ornate and thankfully intact, because it would have cost a fortune to restore, and Kat would have felt it a terrible waste to have to remove it for just a few missing bits. The still splendid oak panelling and oak staircase going up and down, which Kat could see a lot more clearly now that her eyes had become accustomed to the gloom inside, was a lovely honey colour and along with the panelling gave the room a warm glow.

"This room is just made for holding receptions in," she said. "You could hire this out to people for product launches and photo shoots without any trouble. All it needs is a freshen up. There's no point in putting anything too fancy in here, because you want that lovely warm, pale oak wood to really show itself off. Honestly, Scott, you don't have such a big job on your hands with this place as you thought you did. Not every room needs stripping back to basics and starting all over again. The main thing is to check that the plaster is sound. After that it's all cosmetic, and a lot of it emulsion at that. We're not talking heritage wallpaper for a lot of the place, and at the prices that commands, honestly we're not."

He perked up at that, and led her across to what had been the other main reception room – probably a drawing room. Here again were the beautiful plaster ceiling and coving, though the walls were covered in what must once have been expensive paper, but which now had seen better days. That would have to come off, and once Kat could see the plaster she'd decided whether to replace the paper or not. Back along the first floor hallway, Scott showed her the equally huge dining room, complete with dumb-waiter just outside the door going down to the kitchen. Across at the back of the house was another room which Scott said on the plans had been a music room, but which was still easily twelve feet by sixteen, and then another room which had clearly been used as the staffroom of late, having a small office beyond it and three rooms of indeterminate use. Beyond them were the staff toilets and an enclosed room which still had a 'pharmacy' label on the door and a very secure lock. These were the first rooms that Kat saw where she thought some serious work needed doing, and she said so to Scott. Clearly this was where some of the rotten wood in the skip had come from.

As they went back down the first stairs Kat had come up, she said,

"Do you know, I think if you don't come up with an idea for this place yourself, once it's straight, I think you could do a lot worse than pitch it to one of those specialist holiday companies. You know the sort. They do luxury breaks for the early retireds. Posh country houses with a choice of B&B or self-catering, and plenty of facilities. The people who use those sorts of places aren't looking to be going out touring every day. They want to stay put in peace and quiet and be pampered for a few days. How much ground does this place have?"

"Acres of it," Scott said with a weary smile.

"Enough to have its own golf course, then?"

He stopped and stared at her. "What a bloody marvellous idea! I hadn't thought of that."

Kat laughed. "Well with the lumps and bumps around here it could be quite a challenging one – but then isn't that what the golf fanatics want?"

He grinned. "So I'm told, though I was never one of those businessmen who did my work at the fifth tee, or whatever they do. Always seemed a waste of a good walk to me."

"And do those woods behind the place belong to here too?"

"Oh yes, or at least some of them do."

"Well then a few well designed paths through them and you've catered to the nature lovers too, because those trees must be home to all sorts of native species, whether it's plants, birds or beasties. All you'd have to watch for was how high the Wye comes when it floods."

"The Wye?"

"The river down at the bottom there. Didn't you know that was the Wye? It rises in Wales, and while it's just picturesque for most of the time, if you get heavy rain in Wales, you can get some quite dramatic floods along here. Not in the house," she added hurriedly, seeing his dismay. "You're way too high up here, even for the worst of the floods. I was just thinking of the golf course. You wouldn't want to pay a fortune for the best turf only to have it washed away in the first winter."

He gave her a sideways look. "You do realise that you're talking yourself into a job every time you open your mouth, don't you? All this local knowledge, it's worth a fortune."

Kat just laughed, not trusting herself to speak. This probably wasn't the time to tell Scott that her maternal grandfather had come from a long line of Siberian shamen, on both sides, and that her private dream had been to open up a country retreat where she could pass on what he had taught her. That level of alternative awareness wasn't something which went down well with everyone. Papa Viktor, as she had known her grandfather as, had been a teenage conscript in the Russian army at the end of World War Two, and had somehow ended up in Berlin at the end of the war. Equally bizarrely, he had somehow managed to leave Potsdam with the British army instead of his own – something he put down to his shamanic abilities to cloud others' perceptions when in desperate need. Kat had never quite believed that story, thinking it more likely that the British army lads had felt sorry for the boy soldier from the far eastern end of Russia, who was picked on by the others of his supposed own side. Whatever had happened, Papa Viktor had ended his war here in England, where he had met and married Grandma Valerie, a girl from the Welsh valleys with more than a touch of Romany in her blood too. That probably accounted for why Kat's mother had always been what her dad had called 'sensitive' to people and places, a gift or gene – depending on how you thought of it – which she'd passed on to Kat.

And right now Kat was realising that she had been running on that instinct ever since she had met Mrs Underhill. The woman's abrasive attitude had set her senses jangling with her first words, and since then Kat's alternative side had been operating at full stretch. That was why she had spoken out to Scott, and it was now why she was wondering why on earth she was getting such a tingling down her spine about this house. Nothing she had seen so far gave her the slightest hint that this was anything other than what Scott had said it was – a late Victorian mansion house, built for some local worthy of the time who had more money than sense, and which now needed a good coat of TLC. So why was it that the further down the house they got, the more this strange sensation was twanging at her nerves? If there was nothing here, why was she now feeling deeply on edge?

Chapter 4

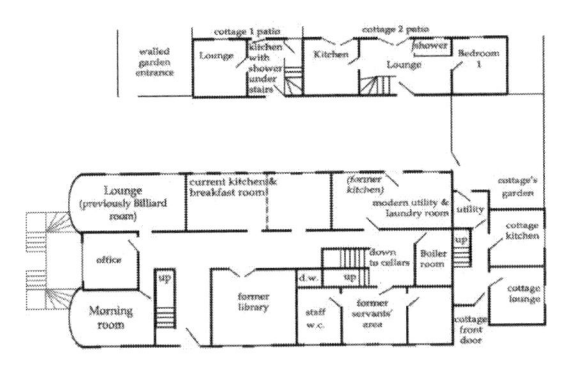

"I don't know whether you'd call this the ground floor or not," Scott said, as he led Kat down to the bottom of the stairs and turned to the front of the house again, then turning right into the first room. "This big room at the front is as big as the drawing room above it, but you can see that the plasterwork isn't as grand. In those days, would the ground floor have been classed as the one with the main reception rooms on, regardless of whether it was actually at ground level?"

Certainly the windows in these rooms at the front weren't as tall. With only two tiers of mullioned glass, and with each not as tall as any of the three tiers in the windows upstairs, you had to conclude that originally this must have been something like the gentlemen's billiard room – a place where the main members of the household come to on a daily basis, but didn't generally entertain in. Unlike the one opposite, which had a full length window on the side, the room on this side just had ordinary windows to the side elevation, possibly because it looked more towards the stable block. The room on the other side – probably the morning room since it partly faced east - also looked out to the front, and had the same side windows as the grand hall above.

Behind these rooms, and facing over the stable yard, was a truly huge and modernised breakfast room and kitchen with the biggest Aga Kat had ever seen, and then behind that, a utility and laundry room which Scott said on the plans had been the original kitchen, and the boiler room. To her amazement, the boiler looked both modern and well-maintained, confirming to her that the owners of the former care home had at least kept it properly serviced. That then meant that the radiators throughout the house also probably worked quite well, even if they were stylistically of the old-fashioned cast-iron sort. But then they would probably be considered quaint and period features given the right treatment, and as long as they worked in the chillier weather, there'd be no complaints from guests.

All that remained on this floor was a former library – or so Scott said it was labelled on the original plan – which had clearly been another ground floor bedroom in the nursing home days, for those unable to tackle the stairs; and then some more staffrooms. Yet it was down here that she really began feeling her skin prickling all over. Yes, there was definitely something down here, but what? It wasn't actually in the kitchen or any of the other rear rooms, of that she was fairly sure, but it was certainly close by, very close.

Forcing herself to quell her inner radar from going off the chart, she talked kitchens with Scott for a while and then followed him out through the laundry room door – the former kitchen door – to the stable yard. Bizarrely, the weird tingling followed her, and that really made her wonder, but it vanished as soon as they got inside the first of the courtyard cottages. These were in slightly poorer decorative condition than the apartments in the house, but even so, Kat had no reservations that it wouldn't take much to turn these into lovely holiday lets. And there were two of them, each giving onto a little courtyard garden on the far side to the main house.

"Beyond here is a lovely old walled garden," Scott told her. "It s a bit of a mess at the moment, but it seems as though someone's been growing veg' in there relatively recently." He took her back through to the stable yard, and now Kat could see that the cottage they had left the two other women in was actually built back-to-back with the end wall of the big house.

"Before we go in there," Scott said, putting a restraining hand on Kat's arm, "I have to ask you something."

"Oh?"

"Would you be prepared to come and stop here for a few nights?"

Whatever she had been expecting, it wasn't that, and her puzzlement must have shown on her face.

"I've been thinking about what you said, you see," he began trying to explain, "while we walked around …about letting Jeanette go home. Only …well you've seen Flora's driving."

"Dear Lord, yes!"

"Well I don't want her driving Jeanette back up the M5 and M6."

"God, no! She's a pile-up waiting to happen! But isn't that awful old Land Rover hers? That wouldn't go above fifty anyway."

"No …or rather, that's not her normal car. She bought it for a song off some old farmer around here who must have seen her coming, but I ended up footing the bill and it's now in my name. She came down by train, you see, regarding anything south of Leeds as 'foreign parts'! But I know Flora, she'll want to drive my Jag' back. So the only way I can make sure that they get back in one piece is if I take them."

Kat totally got that. "And you certainly don't want Jeanette's potential injury on your conscience. That would just be unbearable, I can see that." She didn't dare say 'death', but was envisioning two corpses all too vividly – rather too vividly actually, and which felt worryingly like a premonition.

"Thank you, I thought you would. But I'd like you to start straight away on making some plans for me as to what you think needs doing, and which are the priorities. If you can work some rough costs out for me, that's going to help me make the decisions. So I was going to ask whether it would be too much to ask you to keep driving over here for a few days until I get back, but then you said about your car. And I'm thinking that it'll take Jeanette a couple of days to pack up all of her luggage, so if I give you a lift back to the station tonight, and then pick you up the day after tomorrow, on Wednesday, I can bring you back here, and then set out for Yorkshire the day afterwards which will be Thursday. Hopefully I'll be back during the weekend to get you home for the start of next week. Would that be alright?"

Kat thought for a moment. "I don't see why not. There's just one thing though, Scott. I'm really sorry, but I would need you to sign a formal contract with me before I do that. It may sound hard-headed, but I can't afford for you to vanish off into the Yorkshire Dales, or wherever it is that you've lived, leaving me stuck here, and with potential bills for travelling and anything else I outlay."

She hoped he wasn't going to baulk at that. He seemed like such a nice bloke, and she really felt sorry for him, but then again she'd known a few con-artists in her times who'd tried to hoodwink her, and they'd seemed fine on first meeting. Back then it had been those extra instincts of hers which had warned her that they weren't all they seemed, and sure enough, they'd refused to put pen to paper. And while this time she was getting a good feeling about Scott, whatever it was about this house was throwing up very conflicting signals to her, and she wasn't going to let herself get carried away by him.

Happily, Scott was enough of a business man to be at ease with her request, saying that he'd have been surprised if she hadn't asked for that. And so much relieved, they walked into the cottage to be greeted by a shriek of,

"Have you seen that woman? She's left all of these cases about the place and I can't get my feet up on the pouf! She was only supposed to be looking at the place and she's been gone for *hours!*"

Scott stepped aside, saying, "This woman?" as he gestured Kat through into the lounge. "Honestly, Jeanette, that's a bit bloody rude, even for you. Kat's been talking about the house to me since you couldn't be bothered to show her around." He waved Kat on through a door into what turned out to be the kitchen.

"Put the kettle on!" followed them through in Flora Underhill's strident tones.

"I don't suppose they offered you a cup of tea?" Scott sighed.

"No, and I'll admit that I'm gasping for one now," Kat admitted, gratefully taking a seat on one of the cushioned wooden chairs at the kitchen table.

Rolling his eyes in disgust in the direction of the lounge, where daytime TV was blaring away, Scott went to the sink and filled the kettle. "I don't know about you, but I could do with a sandwich too. Is ham and mustard okay?"

For the next couple of hours, Kat talked him through the broad ideas of different kinds of looks as she showed him the portfolio and the sample design schemes, making it clear which she thought wouldn't do the house any favours, and those which would enhance what it was. Every so often Mrs Underhill would barge in unannounced under some pretext of getting another tea, or putting the evening meal on to cook. However, Kat was well aware that the old besom was really watching for any hint of intimacy between her and Scott, and was getting more irritated with each visit when she wasn't seeing it.

What kind of woman actually seemed to want to see her son-in-law entwining fingers with a woman he'd only just met, and under the very same roof as his wife? That utterly baffled Kat, and the only thing she could think of was that Flora Underhill was desperate for some reason for her daughter to divorce Scott which would put him firmly in the wrong. But even so, surely she ought to have wanted to spare Jeanette that misery? It would be one thing to prove an affair at a distance, but quite another to think he was flaunting random women in Jeanette's face. And in the end, all Kat could think was that Mrs Underhill didn't so much love her daughter as see her as a useful pawn in whatever cockeyed game of mind-chess she thought she was playing with the world.

So when Scott asked her if she wanted to stay for dinner, Kat was quick to decline, saying she would either get something in Hereford, depending on how soon the next train was, or back in Worcester. What she wasn't expecting was for Scott to seize on that to say that he would be driving her, and for Flora and Jeanette to carry on and eat without him. That gave Kat a momentary inner lurch. Was Scott intending to eat with her, and if so, what did that mean?

Luckily, as soon as he'd got her and her cases into the considerable comfort of his Jaguar, he confessed,

"I was praying that you wouldn't want to eat with them. Flora's cooking is bloody awful! She can make a boiled egg taste vile! So you've given me a reason to stop on the way back from dropping you off. Even fish and chips would be bliss after the last couple of days of frozen stodge."

Kat laughed to cover her relief. "Well there are several good pubs in the road leading to the station, and several more within walking distance in the town itself. Believe me, you won't starve there! Just watch out for the real ales – some of them are just too drinkable for safety when you're driving."

"Any personal recommendations?"

"Not really. If it was Worcester I could name you several good eating places and local beers, but Hereford's close enough to home that I tend to prefer to get home and ditch the car first."

"Sensible. But I think if I don't get my teeth around a decent steak soon, I might fade away."

Again Kat laughed with him. That was such a normal manlike thing to say. Her girlfriends would have been hankering for a decent salad or some fish, but clearly Scott was enough of an ordinary bloke that he was dreaming of a good eight-ounce sirloin with all the trimmings. That made for a very relaxed drive back into Hereford, and having exchanged mobile phone numbers, Kat gratefully accepted his help loading the sample cases onto the train, and then half-dozing her way back into Worcester.

Thoroughly drained, she got a taxi to her flat from Foregate Street station, even though she could have walked it, and once home, happily kicked off her shoes, went and got into her baggy jogging bottoms, and ordered a takeaway. After she'd wolfed her way through a chicken jalfrezi, rice and nan bread, she felt more human again, and was just starting to doze on the sofa in front of the TV, when the phone went.

"Well? How did it go?" the voice of her close friend Ruby demanded eagerly. "Have you got the job?"

Feeling rather talked-out for the day, but knowing that Ruby was just worried for her, Kat relayed her exploits.

"Oooh! A soon to be single divorcee!" Ruby declared with relish at the end. "So what's he like? Is he hot?"

"Oh Ruby, no, don't go there," pleaded Kat. "He's a nice guy, okay? A nice guy I feel really sorry for. But after what he's been through, I think it would be a miracle if he ever looked at another woman romantically again. And to be frank, I'm still feeling seriously bruised by my encounter with Peter. I thought I was successfully keeping him at a distance, but clearly not enough."

"Ellen should never have introduced you two," Ruby declared disgustedly, but Kat didn't agree.

"No, it's not Ellen's fault, and nor is it her Tom's. It's not Tom who's to blame that his old school friend had gone off the rails in the years since they'd seen one another. Ellen was genuinely just asking me along when they met up because she didn't want to sit through that meal all by herself, listening to those two harking back to their school days, and laddish stuff like farting contests, or who could pee highest up the wall. Tom's a great bloke, but he's not the subtle type, and he sometimes just doesn't get why he makes Ellen cringe when he gets a bit loud. And Tom may be drop-dead gorgeous, but she's found to her cost that while he doesn't have a malicious bone in his body, sometimes he's more than a bit of an empty vessel, and she was dreading being stuck with two of them like that. She was as shocked as anyone when Peter asked her for my number the next day, not least because she was relieved that he and Tom weren't likely to be having many reunions, and she's been mortified since I told her about what the little shit did to me. No, please don't blame Ellen and Tom."

"Well have you found out any more about how Peter got access to your stuff?"

Kat huffed in disgust. "*I* haven't, but the police have. It turns out that Peter chatted up the cleaning lady who comes in to do the building where my office is. I thought it was such a good idea, Ruby, having her come and do my ground-floor showroom-office as well as the other offices upstairs. You know it's not a big space, but I thought that if I'd been spending the day cutting up swatches for customers, at least I wouldn't have to be vacuuming the carpet before I could have a client in first thing the next day.

"And to be fair, it worked for four years while Mary was the cleaner. It's only since she retired and a contract cleaner has taken over that it's gone wrong. Mary would never have let Peter in, not ever. But the half-soaked lass we've got now was too easily lured by a few quid and Peter's blue eyes. I tell you, though, the others in the building have given that company the elbow! As soon as they heard that my computer had been hacked, and the police came asking if anyone else had had information on their bank accounts stolen, that contract got ended faster than you could blink."

She heard Ruby's grunt of agreement, followed by, "But what I don't understand, Kat, is how he got past your passwords? Surely you weren't daft enough to leave them written down in there?"

"No, I wasn't, but I did use my mum's maiden name. I mean, who would have guessed that it would be Russian, let alone the spelling of it?"

"So how did he get it then?"

Kat winced, wishing that Ruby hadn't asked, but knowing that she had to answer now. "Unfortunately that *is* down to Tom. I gather from what the police have told me that their digital forensic experts found, Peter went into the office the first time and must have tried to get into my computer without success. So then he arranged for a seemingly casual night of a few drinks with Tom, got him a bit the worse for wear, and then pumped him for information. Not that Tom would have known exactly how to spell Artemyev – but I think that it gave Peter just enough that he would have found the name eventually in a decent internet search.

"And, of course, Tom would have given him all sorts of other random bits of information about me at the same time. That's why Peter was so bloody persistent with me. It wasn't that he fancied me to death – he just needed time to work out what was important to me to prioritise potential passwords, and to have an excuse if I came in and found him in my office. Had we already split up, he would have looked very dodgy if I'd walked in late one evening and found him there, and that's why he overdid it when I told him I didn't want to see him again. He practically sobbed for me to give him more of a chance, so I think I was just unlucky that the next time he tried to get into my computer, he hit on the right password, because it would have been the last time he dared try after I'd slapped his face and told him to piss off. By then he already knew I tend to work random hours sometimes, and couldn't guarantee I wouldn't be there in the evening, even if he couldn't see a light on from the road."

Ruby sighed. "What rotten luck. You are still pressing charges, though, aren't you?"

"Oh my God, yes! I can't afford for him to get away with this. And in my eyes as well as the detectives', he's a bloody menace. I'm sure this wasn't the first time he's done this and they agree. I just want to make sure it's the last." *And for other reasons even you don't know, Ruby,* Kat thought with a shiver. *God but he could have caused some trouble for me!*

"Then you'll be relieved to hear that I have good news about the car." Ruby's brother Gareth was the motor mechanic who currently had Kat's VW in his care. "Gareth got called out to a pile-up on the M5, and what should turn out to be the front car but a VW just like yours. The back's a write-off, and Gareth says that the floor is rippled like a pond so it'll never drive again, but the engine is still good. So much so that he's begun taking yours out, and he'll put the other one in as soon as the insurance assessor has said the other one can be scrapped. He hopes to have it back to you for the weekend."

"Oh Ruby, that's wonderful! That's the best news you could have given me. I'll text Scott Hawkesmoor and tell him that, all being well, I'll be able to drive over on Friday. I'll just tell him that something's come up and I won't be able to get back for Wednesday, but if he leaves me a key somewhere, then I'll start work on the house as planned. You can tell Gareth to consider himself thoroughly hugged."

What she wasn't saying to Ruby was that she felt a whole lot better about going back to the house if she had her own car there. Being reliant on Scott collecting her from the station felt too much as though she would be trapped in that odd place, especially with him immediately disappearing off to Yorkshire. How would she have got back, short of a taxi to the station, if he was longer settling Flora and Jeanette than he thought? After all, once she'd taken measurements and checked out things like the light sources and angles in the various rooms, everything else could be done in her studio-office. In fact she would need to use the design programmes she had on her Mac to create mock-ups of the rooms for his approval, and she certainly wasn't going to lug the Mac all the way down there on the train.

So she chatted briefly to Ruby about other things, and then excused herself on the grounds of being shattered and in need of an early night. However, by the time she was soaking in her bath, candles lit, and soft music on, she couldn't avoid facing up to the fact that the house had somehow got under her skin. She would so have loved to just dismiss it for the night, but whatever had set her senses twitching, it wasn't going to leave her alone so easily.

Was it Scott or maybe the two women? She thought not. It was definitely the house itself, but the upper floors had been almost devoid of atmosphere, except for a faint lingering sadness, and that she could put down to the remnants of the old people whose lives had ended there, possibly forgotten by those they thought had loved them. That sort of atmosphere was something she always picked up on. Yet what was bothering her was something other than that.

Something altogether stranger and more unfamiliar. But by the time she snuggled down under her duvet she was still unable to figure out what it might be.

Chapter 5

Scott Hawkesmoor eased the Jag' into a parking space in the city centre and walked into the pedestrian part to find a pub. By the time he was settled in *The Vaults*, pint in hand and a decent meal on order, he was feeling totally relaxed for the first time in weeks. This was a world he knew, the kind of place he was familiar with. Years of living out of suitcases and stopping in Travelodges or Premier Inns, and then eating in the kind of pubs where the food was good but didn't cost the earth, weirdly made this feel more like home than anything since.

He leaned back with a sigh of contentment and took another gulp of bitter. Could he get away with booking himself into somewhere here tonight so that he could have a couple more beers? Maybe complain to Jeanette that the Jag' was making strange noises and he'd need to see a mechanic? Then he shook himself. No, that was just putting off the inevitable row. Yet what Kat had said about taking Jeanette and Flora home had not only stuck, but had felt like a lifeline being unexpectedly thrown to him.

And what a breath of fresh air Kat had turned out to be. Even if in the end she might turn out to be not the greatest designer he could have hired, just her down to earth sensible suggestions had been a refreshing change after the last year. She was the sort of woman he was comfortable with, business-like and intelligent, and it dawned on him now that the reason why he and Jeanette had never been able to make any sort of viable relationship was in part because he had no idea how to handle her endless histrionics. If he solved her petty problems for her, he was accused of being heavy-handed and controlling; but if he let her get on with whatever it was, he got told he was cold and uncaring. There never seemed to have been any middle road, or at least not one that he'd ever found.

And then there'd been the boys. Even now, a lump came into Scott's throat whenever he thought about them, and about Martin in particular. The guilt of not saving at least one of them would be something that might never leave him, because if Kevin had been a chip off Jeanette's block, and somehow genetically doomed to turn out like her, Martin hadn't. There had been odd occasions when he'd been able to get Martin alone and had an almost normal father and son relationship with him. Martin hadn't been academic, but he'd shown a real aptitude for working with his hands, just as Charlie had done, but while he was around his older brother it hadn't been cool to show any interest in anything like that.

With a sigh, Scott rolled his shoulders, feeling the last of the tension knots working their way out. No, Kat was right. Whatever bizarre reasoning was behind it, Jeanette seemed unable to function if Flora wasn't there telling her what to do at every turn. And if he hadn't broken that dependency in twenty years, it wasn't going to happen now – something he should have woken up to before. This move to Herefordshire had been his last attempt to put things even halfway right, so now it was time to admit defeat and do what was best for both of them – although he was far from convinced that leaving Jeanette with Flora could be counted as the best outcome by anyone. Rather, it was the only one left to him that didn't see them dragging him down into their personal hell-like pit alongside them. And maybe that was why he'd been so unwilling to make the final break? He could imagine only too well what a miserable future Jeanette was creating for herself, yet he couldn't find a way to prevent it either.

There'd be rows when he got back and told them, he knew that. They wouldn't let him get away with making any decision without a fight, not even if it was one they wanted. He'd be the bad guy all over again, but at least this might turn out to be the last time he had to face that in person. Once he'd left them in the rambling Victorian pile they called home, he could check that he had everything he wanted out of there and into storage, and then drive down that long driveway which had always felt like the descent into hell every time he'd returned, and never go back there again.

While Kat had been packing her samples up, he'd already called the Yorkshire estate agent and told them to take the house off the market, apologising for messing them around. Then he'd made another call to his own solicitor, again with an apology, but this time with more of an explanation as to why he wanted the divorce proceedings to be started once more. Luckily Drew, the solicitor, was a good friend, and had said right at the outset that Scott was being misguided if he thought that any reconciliation would work; and he was a decent enough man not to say 'I told you so' now.

"Just draw a line under this," he advised Scott in that call. "I think you're absolutely right. The value of the Underhill's heap is enough that I can make sure that you won't be saddled with any crippling alimony if you make it over to them. In fact, depending on how badly you want to be free of them, I'd suggest you sign over that block of shops in town which Charlie bought. They don't bring in much on a commercial scale, but a family court will see the annual income from them as a generous offer on your part. With the farmland they could potentially sell off as another asset that won't force the sale of the house itself, I think you'll be seen as being very reasonable. Leave it with me, Scott. I'll go around to Carl Dobson's office tomorrow and break the bad news to him that he'll have to represent Jeanette after all, because I'm sticking as your solicitor regardless of whether my dad was Charlie's. Dad always said he never understood what Charlie saw in Flora, and I'm sure as hell not having her shrieking down my ear and telling me what I should be doing, especially if what she wants isn't legal."

And that, Scott thought now, was Flora summed up perfectly. She wouldn't even take the advice of a professional on something she knew nothing about. The big difference now would be that she wouldn't have Charlie and his considerable bank balance to soothe all of the feathers she ruffled. At which point it occurred to him that this was another reason why she loathed him so much. Scott had never gone around to people once Charlie had died, having quiet words with them, or making donations to whichever worthy cause would ensure that Flora's blunders didn't come back to bite her. In those years, Scott had been too absent and too busy to take much notice, but now he realised that the virulent ill-will he'd seen on display after the boys had died hadn't come about overnight. Some of that had to have been brewing for a very long time, and both of the women were in for a rude awakening if they thought they were returning to some north-country idyll.

Happily the sirloin steak he'd ordered was good enough to drive any gloomy thoughts away, and as he drove back through Hereford to pick up the narrow road out to Fownhope Priors, he spotted a little corner mini-mart that was still open. Inside he found not only bottles of the local beer he'd enjoyed in the pub, but also a halfway decent bottle of single malt. If nothing else he'd be able to have a stiff drink after he'd broken the news, and he was even contemplating grabbing the cushions off the sofa and a duvet, and decamping to one of those apartments in the house overnight. Without Flora's snoring rattling the roof, he might just get a decent night's sleep as well.

Unfortunately he'd barely got in through the door of the cottage before the two of them started on him.

"I hope you're not expecting me to tolerate that woman working here," Jeanette screeched at him, as Flora snapped,

"Don't think I've saved you any dinner! Ruined, that's what it was! Your share's in the bin, and I'm not starting cooking again at this hour!"

"Shut up! Both of you!" he bellowed over them, and got a stunned silence for once.

Typically it was Flora who recovered first, even as Jeanette's lip began to wobble like a toddler who'd been told off.

"Don't you speak to me…!" she began, but Scott cut her off.

"I said, shut up, and I mean it! I'm taking you two back to Yorkshire on Thursday. Do you understand that? You're getting what you wanted. So tomorrow I would start packing if I were you, because I'm not hanging about on Thursday, we set off first thing."

"Well it's about time you came to your senses," Flora said smugly. "Put this heap back on the market, go and ask for your old job back, and start behaving properly for once."

Scott shook his head, "You really don't ever listen, do you? I said I was taking *you* back to Yorkshire. *I'm* not stopping there. I'm coming back here and making a go of this place."

"It's her, isn't it!" squealed Jeanette. "That woman! You want her instead of me!"

Scott stared at her in disbelief. "Are you mad? I hadn't even met Kat until today. What sort of man do you think I am that you'd believe I'd throw everything away on some torrid affair with someone I'd known for five or six hours? I didn't even know she existed until *you* brought her down here! *You* were the one who commissioned her, Jeanette, not me. I gave you carte blanche to find an interior designer, and she was the one you came up with, so how on earth can you twist that into her being someone I'm having a fling with?"

"You were pally enough with her in the kitchen," Flora bit back.

Scott threw his hands in the air in disgust. "We were talking *professionally*. Or did that not percolate through that revolting web of suspicion you see everything through? If you'd got off your arse, Jeanette, and extended her the least bit of professional courtesy, it would have been *you* dealing with her, not me. But you couldn't, could you? So don't you dare get uppity with me because I've signed a contract with the first person who's come up with workable and sensible suggestions. Kat Newsome is an asset I'm lucky to have coming on board this project."

"*Huh*! And I bet you'll have her onboard in another way too, if you get the chance," Flora sneered, making Jeanette wail so loudly that Scott just gave up.

"Just start packing tomorrow," he flung over his shoulder as he marched into the kitchen.

Forget the cushions off the sofa, he'd sleep on the bare boards tonight rather than spend another night with those two. He took his shopping through to the house via the back doors, and up to one of the apartments up on the top floor. He picked the one on the corner facing out over the stable yard and with a view of the walled garden and the woods. It was peaceful up here, peaceful and quiet, and he popped the top off one of the beers and took a swig. Normally he wouldn't drink from the bottle like this, but just at the moment he was past worrying about finding a glass.

How had life come to this that the prospect of a night roughing it and drinking beer from a bottle seemed blissful? Where had the dynamic company leader he'd been vanished to? It was almost as if someone had taken a paintbrush and emulsioned over his past life leaving nothing but a blank wall where it had been. In his head he could still remember all of the big projects he'd completed, but all the sense of satisfaction, all the pleasure in seeing those old places being brought back to life, all of that had somehow trickled away without him even noticing until now.

He looked out over the cobbled courtyard, and over the stable block's roof to the garden, still just visible in the gloom. It was the end of March and soon the garden would start burgeoning again. He hadn't tended a garden since he'd been a lad back at home helping his dad, but all of a sudden it was as if those generations of farming folk in his blood were calling to him to get out there and get that rich soil in his hands. And suddenly he knew what he wanted. Whatever else happened, he was keeping those two cottages in the stable block. That was where he was going to live, because the garden led straight off their little patio areas, and nobody was getting their hands on that but him. Originally the back wall of the stable block had formed the wall of the garden on that side, but once the stables had been converted into living spaces, the big French windows put into those walls had given them direct access out into the old kitchen garden. Now each one had a dinky patio of its own, only separated from the garden by some tall trellis panels, but the fact that the garden only had one gateway into it would guarantee his privacy, and also make the old garden area his own private space.

Kat would help him come up with some viable use for the main house, of that he was now sure, and he was already thinking of asking her to become a business partner in the venture, even though he knew she didn't have the capital to be a major investor. She thought in the right kind of way, and she knew the area. Yes, Kat would be a useful ally to have this time around, and best of all, after what she'd told him about that bloke skimming her bank account, she didn't seem to be looking for any romantic entanglement. Theirs was just a meeting of minds and interests, and that suited Scott just fine.

He allowed Jeanette and Flora time to calm down, or at least to head off to bed, neither of them being night-owls, and then he crept softly into the cottage and picked up a few things. They had the posh coffee maker, so they wouldn't miss him having the kettle and the tea, and he'd picked up a pint of milk for himself, so that was morning tea sorted. He grabbed one of the frying pans to cook up some bacon on, and along with a plate, a mug and a knife, decided he could make do at that.

A second trip got him the duvet he'd been using while sleeping on the sofa – something he'd been doing ever since Flora had turned up – and he half thought about taking the cushions. But then he realised that if Jeanette got up and couldn't immediately flop full-length on the sofa, that would be giving her another thing to complain about. And so although the prospect of sleeping on the floorboards at the age of forty-two wasn't great, he decided it was preferable to having one or the other of them – and it would most likely be Flora – coming stamping up to his refuge in a temper first thing in the morning. Tomorrow, at least, he would wake up and have time to breathe before he engaged in the battle, he promised himself.

It was almost surreal to wake up the next morning and hear nothing but birdsong. Disregarding the chill in the air, he threw open the lounge window and leaned on the sill, mug of tea in hand, and drank in the view. The old garden was glorious, delicately bedecked with a late scattering of ground frost. Tall skeletal spikes of plants which should have been dead-headed in the autumn, now looked too beautiful to cut down, and he could see a flock of tiny brown birds eagerly harvesting the remnants of last year's seeds from them. Over on the edge of the woods, a bright flash of colour zipped across telling him that there were woodpeckers in there somewhere, probably currently busy feeding the new season's chicks.

God, I've missed this, he thought with a flood of emotion. The last time he'd been anywhere like this had been when he'd gone home for his dad's funeral, and that brought with it another set of regrets. He'd not been able to spend half as much time with his now elderly parents as he'd have liked, and it was his own fault that his sister had told him that he wasn't welcome at her house after she'd taken their mum to live with her. And it *was* his fault, he now had to admit. Somewhere along the line he should have stood up to his in-laws and remembered instead how much his own parents had done for him. It hadn't been their fault that they couldn't afford to support him through college, forcing him further into Charlie's debt. Instead he should have acknowledged and thanked them for doing the best they could; but his mum had always favoured his sister, and once his dad was gone, there hadn't seemed much to go back for.

Shaking the gloom off, as he watched various other birds darting about the place in their spring frenzy of feeding chicks, he made himself some large bacon sandwiches for breakfast, which he enjoyed while sitting on the sill. He couldn't quite believe his luck that he'd not been disturbed as yet. Most likely it was because of some stubbornness of Flora's, her deciding that they wouldn't stoop to come looking for him, and that suited him just fine. After his day with Kat yesterday, he was looking at this place with fresh eyes, and while the feeling lasted, he thought he would like to go and walk around it again before the battle campaign to get them to Yorkshire began.

So he washed his stuff up, and getting his i-phone out, decided to go around this floor first. As he wandered through the apartments feeling clearer headed, he could now see what Kat had meant. These really only needed a good lick of paint in colours that would flatter, rather than the very antiseptic white that was peeling off in places. And she'd been right, too, in saying that while all brilliant white looked great in modern houses, with ceilings this high it tended to make a place look institutional, not warm and welcoming.

The two rooms overlooking the main drive faced approximately eastwards, and now they were flooded with sunshine. *Yes,* he thought, *you were right, Kat, these would make lovely holiday lets. If you took photos of these in the morning, and with the views out to the woods from the windows, you'd have couples queuing up to rent them.* He could just imagine harassed city workers wanting to come here for a quiet weekend break, and that would be his ideal market, he realised. Heavens, Kat really had a sound business head.

He was so taken with the idea that he stood for a while in one of the front principal bedrooms thinking that these two would also make a wonderful lounge and bedroom for another flat. That or keep these two and the third one on the side for B&B. The view out down the valley to the River Wye was now visible in all of its glory, and he knew it would be easy to market these. *Time-share, that's what would work here,* he thought. Give people the chance to have four or more weeks in what they could think of as 'their' piece of a country mansion, and pitched at the right price it could be very viable indeed. A hint of possession would do wonders for ensuring that they left the place in good order at the end of their week, and with travel to other countries all up in the air now that the UK was moving away from Europe, not to mention whatever new legal positions which could arise, that might make this a very attractive proposition indeed.

Feeling positive, Scott swung down to the next floor, and another look at the main two rooms had him wondering whether this might not make a very good wedding venue. There was money in that, he knew. The last but one place he'd worked on was now one, and had an eye-watering annual turnover. That thought had him sending a text to Kat.

> Main rooms as wedding venue? If whole of upper floor made into apartments, potential for bridal suite? You said photo shoot, but weddings need bad-weather alternatives too! Can you bring samples for that when you come?

He hit 'send' and was glad when she immediately replied,

> Great idea! Those stairs are made for group photos! With room for main guests to stay on-site, would be very marketable. Will sort out samples for colours and for bridal suite possibilities. Won't be able to come on Wednesday – discussing with supplier – but will definitely be down on Friday with own car! Can you leave key in safe place?

Scott replied without reservation,

> Of course, not a problem. Will leave a key under a pot by cottage door around the back. That gets you into the cottage. Can leave you keys into the main house under the sink. Will bolt main house from the inside except for old kitchen door so you can open up what you need. See you Saturday with luck!

That would do, he decided, cheered by Kat's instant positive response.

Still not quite able to believe that Flora, at least, hadn't come to have a rant at him, since she'd not been so reticent before, he decided to carry on. The kitchen would do well enough to bring outside caterers in for, he decided, and it would be worth laying out the money for an industrial dishwasher or two, but if the venue took off, then it wouldn't matter if this end of the house didn't get used more. The front of this ground floor was more of a tough one. Scott wasn't sure whether to go with the idea of one larger apartment, or to find some other use for them, and he decided he would have to confer with Kat on that.

He was so absorbed that he didn't notice for a moment that he could hear someone down below him. Who the hell was that? Surely it wasn't Flora or Jeanette? They'd never ventured into the cellars. Yet when he stopped and listened more carefully he was sure he really could hear someone down there.

Hurrying to the cellar steps, he flicked the light on and went down. In the first of the barrel-roofed cellars there was now nothing, he having lugged all the detritus up from there and out into the skips. But the sounds were coming from beyond there in either the middle cellar or the front one. Going through the rough wooden door into the second cellar and switching on the lonely light in there, the feeble bulb just showed rack upon rack of empty wine storage. God knows how much the original family must have planned on drinking, but the cellar was huge and every alcove of the vaults had built in wine racks. Yet that meant that there also wasn't really anywhere where anyone could hide in here, either.

Then he froze. Beyond the next door he could swear he could hear someone whistling. With shivers running down his spine now, he carefully reached for the old door into the front cellar, vaguely registering that the slightly rusted iron handle felt oddly warm. Yet as he threw the door wide open his senses reeled. How could this be? This couldn't be here! This was supposed to be inside the building, but the strange buzzing noise in his head was rising fast, making him feel disorientated and giddy, and as he sank to his knees the last thing he thought was, *where is this?*

* * * * *

"Where's he bloody got to?" Flora demanded rhetorically as she dumped her suitcase in the cottage hall. "If we're going, we're damned well going now! I'm not hanging around until he says we can go! Where is he, Jeanette?"

"Oh Mother, I don't know," Jeanette whimpered. All of a sudden she was feeling downright frightened by the future. Was Scott really planning on leaving her up in Yorkshire with her mother?

She shivered. That wasn't such a nice thought. Their neighbours had been foul to them when the boys had died, and finally it dawned on her that it had been her dad who had made friends with people. Her mother was too abrasive, too harsh to encourage pleasantries and confidences, and the thought of being all alone with Flora in that other big old house was now unexpectedly downright scary. What would her mother be like when there was nobody else to blame for everything that went wrong? And belatedly Jeanette began to realise that the new scapegoat would be her, if only because there'd be nobody else.

Yet when Flora came stamping back into the cottage lounge with a vicious smirk on her face, and said, "Put those bags in the boot," Jeanette was so programmed to do as she was told, that she found herself doing it even before she realised.

Even more terrifying was seeing Flora pick up Scott's car keys.

"Mother! You can't drive the Jag'!"

"Oh yes, I bloody can! Thinks he can order us around, does he? Well we'll see about that. Get in the car. Now! I'm not hanging around waiting for his lordship's pleasure. If we're going back home, we're going back when I'm ready. Let's see how Mr high-and-mighty Scott Hawkesmoor feels when he's stuck here all on his own!"

Chapter 6

Gareth was as good as his word, and on mid Friday morning he drove the VW around to Kat's house, a grin of satisfaction on his face.

"See? I told you I'd sort it," he said after she'd hugged him.

"I am eternally grateful," Kat told him, and meant it. The car was her lifeline.

"So what's this our Ruby tells me about you getting a commission on some big old place over Hereford way?"

Kat grinned. "It's bloody huge, Gareth! Former nursing home, and before that the home of one of those nouveau-rich Victorian industrialists, I'd guess. Okay, the name is Fownhope Priors, but that could just be the village, or some old place once associated with it. I haven't seen a thing which would make me think it goes back before the 1890s, besides maybe the barrelled vaulted cellars, and even then I'd doubt it. But then that means that it's not that antiquated either, and I certainly don't have to worry about it being listed. So I've pretty much got a free hand with it."

She laughed. "I'm sure Ruby has visions of me ending up with the bloke who owns it, but to be honest, I'd be amazed if he didn't sell it on.

He's got a horrific family problem going on – his two teenage sons got killed on a motorbike, and his wife is just a nightmare towards him, let alone her mother who doesn't give him a moment's peace." She grinned at Gareth. "I wouldn't be surprised if the poor bugger didn't become a monk after that. I'm sure as hell not planning on marching him up the aisle the moment his divorce comes through."

Gareth was laughing with her. "Our Ruby's like one of those Jane Austen heroines – always trying to fix people up with one another. Incorrigible, that's what she is. Set me up on a blind date last week," and he rolled his eyes in mock despair. "Nice enough lass, but not my sort by a long way. You stand your ground, Kat, don't let her push you towards someone when you aren't ready."

"I won't," Kat promised, then when he'd left, threw the bags she'd already packed into the VW and headed for Hereford.

Arriving at Fownhope Priors, Kat wasn't surprised to see the place looking deserted aside from the mud-splattered old Land Rover. After all, she knew that Scott wasn't going to let Flora take that back up north. What was rather more annoying was that she searched every pot by the cottage doors, and several others besides, and couldn't find any evidence of any keys having been left there. Of course poor Scott might have been so harassed when he left that all thoughts of keys for her might have vanished in the haze, but it was still irritating to think that she'd come all this way for nothing.

It was only as a last resort that she tried the laundry room door, having expected to find it locked, and then discovered that it wasn't. Good grief, Flora Underhill must really have been in full spate if she'd muddled Scott to that extent, because Kat had him down as a much more practical man than that. Even out here in the depths of the countryside, it was still taking a risk leaving a prestigious property wide open like this. All it would take would be a band of travellers looking for somewhere big enough to take an extended family, and they'd be squatting here and difficult to evict if left unnoticed for a while.

Walking through the ground floor, Kat was even more surprised to find that the front door was unlocked. What had Scott been up to? And what about the cottage? She hurried around the main house and tried the cottage door. That was unlocked too!

"Scott? ...Mrs Underhill? ...Mrs Hawkesmoor? ...Anybody home?" she called as she peered into the lounge.

There were signs as if at least some of them had left in a hurry, but Kat got rather more worried when she went into the kitchen. A bottle of milk had gone sour sitting out on the table, and two breakfast mugs had been left dirty and sitting in the sink, along with what she guessed must be breakfast plates. Yet if this was where the women had been, where had Scott spent his last night down here?

Feeling ridiculous for the sense of growing dread building inside her, Kat found the cottage key still in the inside of the front door and made sure to lock it up behind her. Part of her couldn't shake off the feeling that Flora was quite capable of murdering Scott if the mood took her and, God forbid, if that was what had happened here, then the cottage was a potential crime scene.

The only thing stopping her from ringing the police right now was that she couldn't see anything obvious like blood, and without that she knew she'd look a bit of a fool. After all, she'd known Scott for all of a few hours. How could she hope to answer any questions about what was in character or not if asked? And couple that with any questions referred back to Worcester about her, and she knew that she could end up seeming the kind of flaky woman who dated dodgy men who then committed fraud, if nothing worse. And there was a potential 'worse' lingering in the past which she had no wish to bring back up. No, she would have to have stronger reasons than just her Russian shaman genes screaming internally at her.

Look for where Scott's been, she told herself sternly. *You can't do anything until you know that*. And so she began a systematic search of the house, gradually working her way upwards. Inevitably she got to the apartment he'd used last of all, and again she couldn't shake the feeling that he hadn't meant to leave like this. Unlike in the cottage, his mug and plate were neatly washed up and draining on the side, and things like the milk and bacon were back in the fridge.

But Kat wondered why he hadn't taken them with him? The milk wouldn't last from when he'd opened it – presumably on Tuesday morning – until into the weekend. Indeed she gave it a sniff and decided that it wouldn't last beyond today, although looking in the bin, he'd been sensible enough to buy only small packs of bacon, and had used one up with the other having at least a week's date left.

"But where the hell are you, Scott?" she asked aloud as she tried his mobile number and got told that the phone was not switched on. "Why would you turn your phone off? Or has the battery gone dead? What's going on?"

She was just going back down the main stairs when she heard a car pulling up on the drive, and believing it must be Scott returning, hurried down to meet him. What brought her up short was seeing a policeman getting out of a patrol car.

"Hello," she said worriedly. "What's happened? Where's Mr Hawkesmoor?"

The sergeant seemed almost as taken aback by her words as she'd been. "Can I ask you who you are Ms…?

Kat walked up to him. "My name's Kat Newsome. I'm the interior designer Mr Hawkesmoor commissioned to help renovate this place. I met him here on Monday, but I've only just got back down here because I've had car trouble."

"And you were expecting to meet Mr Hawkesmoor here?"

"Well not exactly," Kat had to admit, and explained about Scott taking his wife and mother-in-law back to Yorkshire. "So you see I wasn't expecting him to necessarily be here on the doorstep, but the house hasn't been properly locked up at all. And I know I don't know Mr Hawkesmoor well, but he came across as the kind of professional who wouldn't be that careless.

"And there's another thing. I wasn't quite sure whether to contact the police, because to be honest I have no evidence of what's happened, but the way Mrs Hawkesmoor and Mrs Underhill left seems, well …just odd. Like they stepped out of the door and vanished. Maybe they were just sloppy people, but stuff like the milk has been left out on the side – as if they were either expecting to come back before they left, or were expecting somebody else to come and tidy up after them straight away."

"Show me, would you?" the man who she now knew was Sergeant Miles asked, and so Kat took him around to the cottage and unlocked the door.

"I locked it up simply for security," she explained, letting him go in alone.

When he reappeared it was with a frown on his face. "I agree it doesn't look like they were planning on going and never coming back. Have you looked upstairs?"

Kat felt a touch foolish confessing. "I didn't like to, beyond calling for Mr Hawkesmoor. Mrs Hawkesmoor is an odd sort of woman. Takes offence very easily and where none was intended, if you get my drift. Mr Hawkesmoor told me they lost their two sons in an accident last year, so I guess she's every right to be a bit of a mess, but I was very glad I wasn't going to be working for her, if that doesn't sound callous. And her mother, Mrs Underhill! Lord, there was a woman who must make enemies wherever she goes! Very abrasive, very aggressive, and used to ruling the roost unless I'm much mistaken."

Sergeant Miles gave her an odd look but vanished upstairs, coming back down looking even more perplexed.

"Well there's no women's clothing up there, but there are men's clothes. Did you say that Mr Hawkesmoor had every intention of coming back here?"

"Oh yes. This weekend if at all possible. But that's why I'm concerned that his mobile seems to be off. I heard from him on Tuesday by text, but then didn't think anything of him not being in touch until now, if only because I thought he'd probably got his hands full with his family. Not now, though. I would've expected something from him by now, even if not a long chatty conversation." The odd looks Sergeant Miles kept giving her were now starting to seriously spook her. "Look, what's going on? Why are you here? Has something awful happened?"

He gave a grunt. "We were contacted by our colleagues up in Yorkshire. They're looking for Mr Hawkesmoor."

"Scott Hawkesmoor? Why? Whatever for? He didn't strike me as some master criminal."

"Well whether he's responsible or not, we need to speak to him because both his wife and his mother-in-law are dead."

Kat felt herself sway and heard Sergeant Miles say, "Are you alright?" as he caught hold of her arm. Why did that feel as though she had known it was going to happen? Why had that feeling of someone having a violent death been all over her ever since she'd come back? The news felt almost physical in its intensity, and she had to swallow hard several times to not be sick.

"Dead? Are you sure? ...Oh God, what a stupid thing to say. Of course they must be sure." Then a terrible thought occurred to her. "It wasn't on the way to Yorkshire, was it? Because Scott Hawkesmoor was definitely worried that if he didn't drive them, then Flora might take his Jaguar; and believe me, going on her driving when she picked me up from the station, she was a bloody awful driver! I was scared to death the whole way!"

"Not on the way there, no. But it was a Jaguar registered to Mr Hawkesmoor that crashed."

"A big bright red beast? Only a year or two old? Top of the range by the look of it, though I'm far from that much of a car enthusiast to know."

Miles brought his phone out and retrieved a photograph which had clearly been sent on to him. "This one?"

This time Kat really did have to go and sit down on the front steps. The Jag' was a wreck. Crumpled and bent, it appeared to have careered off a road and down into a steep ditch somewhere rural. But you didn't need to have expert knowledge to know that nobody could have walked away from that. They'd probably had to cut Flora and Jeanette's bodies out, because no airbag could have saved them from that tangled mess of metal.

"Was Scott with them?"

"That's what we'd like to know. You just called him Scott. Very familiar for someone you only met once in a business setting."

Kat understood what he was implying. "No, sergeant, there was nothing going on between him and me. In fact I've probably still got at least one of his wife's messages on my answer-phone from when she brought me out here. It was just that I felt so bloody sorry for him. Even before I'd met him, those two women had seriously rubbed me up the wrong way. They were so rude, so insulting, and so I suppose I was primed to see him in a good light right from the start. And then when he told me about how his two sons had died, well I just felt that he was taking the blame for something that wasn't his fault."

"Oh really? How come?"

So Kat relayed what Scott had said about trying time and again to modify his sons' behaviour, and to save them from being spoiled by Flora and Jeanette. "I think it was when he said that his wife and mother-in-law shoved all of the blame onto him for the crash that I felt most sorry for him." She concluded. "I don't have kids, but to lose a child must be the worst thing ever, whatever the circumstances. But to then have your wife and mother-in-law washing their hands of any responsibility for supervising two teenagers while he was working away, and shoving all their guilt onto him …that just felt beyond unfair. And him coming here and taking on this project had been supposed to be a chance for him and Jeanette to try and salvage what was left of their marriage. That's why he came all this way."

"He told you a lot in a short time."

"Yes, he did. But to be frank, I think he'd sort of reached bursting point. Does that make sense? I don't think it was me in particular. I think he'd have bared his soul to anyone who was even vaguely sympathetic. Because he'd always been the boss, and had left his post within the company, I don't think the poor guy had any mates left by that stage. Somebody different would have gone down the pub and had a heart to heart with his pals, but between his job and his family, all that had gone for Scott. And so when I started showing some real enthusiasm for this project, I suspect I was the first person in months he'd had even as much as a civil conversation with."

"Poor sod," Miles sympathised. "He does seem to have had a rough time of it. So do you think he's in Yorkshire now, or is he still down here somewhere?"

"I honestly don't know."

"Only you see, we do need to find him, because it looks like the Jaguar's brakes had been tampered with."

"Nooo!"

"Unfortunately, yes. So you see, if Mr Hawkesmoor was down here all the time, then that's one thing. But if he went up to Yorkshire with them, then we seriously have to start looking at him as the man with the best motive to get rid of Mrs Hawkesmoor and Mrs Underhill. After all, he stands to inherit a substantial piece of property as well as investments."

Kat buried her head in her hands. Money or not, somehow she just couldn't see Scott as the murderous type. Then something occurred to her.

"Motorway cameras!"

"What about them?"

"Well Scott Hawkesmoor probably knows the entire country after all the travelling he did, but if the two harridans went back to Yorkshire alone, I doubt they'd have strayed off the motorways. And I'll bet you something else: given the way Flora Underhill drove, she'll have picked up a speeding ticket if not several. Having been in a car with both of them, I can tell you that Scott was a good driver. He said he'd got the Jag' because it allowed him to do long haul journeys in comfort, not because of its speed. I doubt he ever got a speeding ticket in it in his life."

Miles nodded thoughtfully. "Certainly the M5/M6 intersection has plenty of cameras. I'll be sure to pass that information on to my colleagues." Then craftily said, "So you think he's still here, do you, if the women were in the car alone?"

Kat felt her frustration rising, but knew he was only doing his job. "I merely thought that a camera might prove if there was someone in the back seat," she clarified. "With just the two of them, there wouldn't be anyone in the back, would there? But if you can see someone in a back seat, even if it's nothing much more than a shadow, then the chances are that Scott would have been driving – because he certainly wouldn't have taken the back seat himself!"

"Point taken," Miles conceded. "So have you looked all through the property?"

Kat hauled herself to her feet, wishing that right now she could go and have a tot of the whisky she'd seen up where Scott had been. A stiff gin and tonic would have been even better, but something suitably strong and fortifying would be very welcome right now.

"I've covered all of the house except for the cellars," she declared, feeling distinctly shaky again. "Would you come with me while I check them?" She didn't dare say that she was dreading finding Scott's body down there along with some heavy implement.

All Miles did was gesture her to lead on, and that made Kat wonder whether he thought she might have done for Scott? Hell, this was turning into the most complicated commission she'd ever had, and she'd barely started yet!

"Mind your head," she warned him at the top of the cellar steps. "The servants were obviously shorter back when this house was built. Scott kept having to duck until we got into the cellar itself."

There certainly wasn't the same headroom on the cellar steps as those above, and Kat felt vindicated when she heard a bump and a grunt of pain from the man behind her, as she opened the door into the first cellar and found the light on. It could just have been carelessness, of course, but it still bothered her. Then she saw the topmost footprints in the dust. A man had clearly walked through to the other cellars, but she couldn't see any tracks coming back.

Should she say something to Sergeant Miles? *No*, her instinct told her. *If he thinks you keep building an alibi for Scott, he might start suspecting you even more. Stand aside and let's see if he spots that himself.*

She stepped off to the side so that Miles had a clear view of the cellar.

"Good grief, this is a cellar and a half," he said, straightening up and rubbing his head where it had collided with the stair roof.

"And this is only the first one. Wait to you see the wine cellar through the next door." She paused, waiting for him to look at the floor, but although he looked about him, he didn't seem to notice the footprints.

Sighing to herself, Kat led the way, carefully staying to the side of the prints, but then seeing Miles tramp all over them. Maybe he was a rural policeman because he wasn't the sharpest sergeant on the force? Harsh to think, but he wasn't filling Kat with confidence.

She opened the door into the next cellar, and this time Miles couldn't help but notice that the lights were on in here too.

"Were the lights regularly left on down here?" he asked.

"Not that I'm aware of. I was surprised just now when we found the first ones on. That again isn't like the Scott Hawkesmoor I met. He wasn't a spendthrift, that's for sure. I spent a couple of hours talking costs with him, and to me he had his finger on the button all of the time. He's not the type to run up the electricity bill when the house is empty. I'm sorry, Sergeant, but the more I'm seeing, the more I'm worried about Scott Hawkesmoor's whereabouts. You may not see him this way, but I'm concerned he's another victim, not the perpetrator."

They walked across the deserted wine cellar, seeing the door through to the front cellar was open, though this time the lights weren't on. Only as they got to the door did, they spot what was on the floor at the doorway.

"Oh my God, is that blood?" Kat gasped, looking at the red-brownish smear on the flagstones.

"I'm afraid it is, and it looks fairly recent too."

Chapter 7

As Sergeant Miles got on his radio to summon help, Kat stood in the driveway feeling lost. Where did this leave her now? That was a serious consideration, because if Scott was dead, then she was in totally new territory as regards her contract. And yet although she knew she ought to be focusing on that, and not on someone she barely knew – however much she'd sympathised with his plight – something here at this place was trying to get through to her on a whole other level, and it just wouldn't let her focus.

Whatever was going to happen now, one thing was clear – she wasn't going to be spending the night in the house, if only because the police would be horrified at the prospect, and it might make her look even more suspect in their eyes if she asked to do it. So there was no point in her taking her bags inside. Indeed it might be better if they stayed hidden in the boot of the VW for now, because an overnight bag might seem as if she'd been intending to spend the night with Scott. But one thing she had brought with her was a packed lunch. When she'd made the sandwich and the flask of coffee this morning, she had simply been thinking of the practical matter of not wasting time. At the end of the day she'd intended to go and find a pub to eat at, and to pick up anything like bread and milk for her stay then.

But now she was feeling the urgent need for a hot drink, wishing that for once she'd put sugar in the coffee. At least she had some chocolate biscuits with her for a bit of a boost. And so she went over to Miles and said,

"I'll stay out of your way. I'm going to and eat my sandwich in the walled garden."

"Where's that?"

"If you go around the fancy steps at the front of the house and keep going, you'll see an ornamental gate. It's through there."

"Okay." He looked at her ashen face. "Are you sure you're alright, Miss Newsome?"

"I think I'll feel better with a hot drink inside me, but this has all been such a shock. It's hardly the normal kind of thing I get caught up in." *Though you'd be shocked if you knew some of my past,* she mentally tagged on. *You might not think so kindly towards me then if you didn't bother reading the full details.*

However he said, "No," with a sympathetic smile, "I suppose it isn't. I'll come and find you if we need to ask you anything more." He could see that she was hardly going to be able to sneak back to her car and drive off when the patrol car was right behind it.

With relief, Kat went and grabbed her small cool-bag with the sandwich and chocolate bars in it, and her flask, and then headed for the garden. She'd spotted the curious round, stone-built gateway before, but the closer she got to it now the more disconcerting she found it. It wasn't just that it was an architectural oddity – she'd never seen a kitchen garden with quite such a huge fancy entrance before – there was something about the gateway itself that was tweaking her senses too. It wasn't a full circle – the bottom quarter, or as near as made no difference, would have been submerged into the ground had the brickwork gone all of the way – but Kat had the oddest sensation that in some way there was a full circle there, even if it was only one of energy, or some force or other, not physically. Why or what that force of nature was, though, she couldn't begin to guess.

Suddenly unable to face any more strangeness yet, she turned away and went and sat down on a wooden bench outside one of the stable cottages. With the late morning sun now having risen enough to shine over the roof of the main house, this sheltered spot was actually quite warm, despite the fresh breeze, and she settled her herself down. The sandwich was gone in no time, and only the heat of the coffee prevented her from gulping it down fast. But between them they restored some of her more normal equilibrium. Certainly enough for her to wonder, *why am I so affected by this?*

Come on, Kat, she thought sternly. *What's the matter with you? Obviously finding that blood was shocking, but it wasn't as though it was lying there in a big wet puddle. And you've seen much worse, albeit not affecting you quite so personally. But then Scott is hardly personal to you either, is he?*

She was recalling being the first person to pull in and try and help at the scene of a pile-up on the motorway a few years back. There'd been a lot of blood then, especially with people with quite bad cuts. And although the shock had set in later on, when she'd felt distinctly shaky, what she hadn't felt at all was the head-swimming faintness and nausea she'd experienced in the cellar, and had continued to have bouts of right up until she'd come to sit on this bench.

So why had it happened now? What was so different this time? She leaned back on the bench and tried to clear her head with some breathing exercises, just focusing on breathing in and out. It certainly helped, and she found herself feeling rather more 'present' than she had since they'd come up from the cellar. With that in mind, she then thought to kick off her trainers and put her feet directly onto the ground. 'Grounding' was a technique which some would have thought a bit hippy-ish and flaky, but Kat was a firm believer in there being a primal energy in the earth and in growing things, and that it was something everyone needed to reconnect with periodically. Whenever she felt she had spent too much time staring at computer screens and stuck inside without fresh air, she had found it beneficial to go out into the little garden area belonging to her miniscule town house, and to just sit beneath the small hawthorn tree she had in a large pot, hands on its trunk, and her feet on the bark chippings she'd put down beneath it and the seat beside it. Half an hour out there and she would normally be able to think straight again, and any tension gone.

So it was a shock to her to kick off the synthetic soled trainers and put her feet down with just her thick cotton socks between her and the ground, and to feel the swimming sensation rising again. Horrified, she opened her eyes and lifted her feet off the ground. The sensation went away. After some more calming deep breaths she tried putting her feet back down again. And again that weird swirling sensation came back again.

Tucking her feet up onto the bench, Kat now thought long and hard. In one way, just knowing that there was some kind of local phenomenon was reassuring. Seated here like this and disconnected from the ground, she could think perfectly normally, and that was a relief. So whatever it was, it wasn't that she was either sickening for something, or having some kind of odd breakdown. If she'd been losing it, she couldn't think that she would yoyo quite so crisply between clarity and fuzzy-headedness.

But if it was something localised that was affecting her, then what could it be? Going back over being out here with Scott, she recalled that she'd felt something odd out here in the courtyard back then, too. Something which had stuck with her from their visit to the cellars on that occasion as well. Back then it had vanished when they went into the stables cottages, so she pulled her trainers back on and went and tried one of the cottage doors. This time the door was firmly locked, as were the doors to the other cottage, which in one way confirmed her suspicions – Scott was not in the habit of leaving the whole place wide open. However, that made it all the more worrying that he hadn't had time to lock the big house up.

She was still standing thinking in the yard when she heard more vehicles coming up the drive. That would be the forensic team, no doubt. But what would happen after that? Presumably they'd just lock the place up and wait for the results?

You have to come back here! an insistent voice said in her head. *You owe it to Scott to investigate. Even if he's dead, are you going to let him be remembered as a wife-killer? You're the one who is feeling the real problem with this place, so you need to investigate.*

Quite where those thoughts were coming from, Kat wasn't sure, but they were enough to get her moving across to the laundry room door. They were going to find her fingerprints on it anyway, and she'd already told Miles that she'd come in that way, so she was hardly contaminating evidence anymore than she had. But inside either the laundry or the big kitchen, she had memories of seeing some keys hanging up when she'd walked through with Scott. He hadn't needed any back then, the place being open because of him working on it, but if she could grab them before the police found them, that would allow her back in without technically having to break in.

When she found them, the keys weren't in the modern kitchen itself, but hanging up outside the door in the hallway by the boiler room on a couple of hooks. Many of them were old, just the simple mortise lock types that must have been original to the house, but as Kat scurried back out, she tried them in the lock of the original kitchen door and found one that worked. So having already pulled out the key that had been on the inside, she put that on the laundry room table and then locked the door from the outside. Having told Miles that she'd locked the cottage for security, hopefully he would assume that she'd done the same here. There was a substantial old bolt on the door, and if the police shot that across then she wouldn't be able to get back in, but at least it was worth a try.

She was less bothered about accessing the back door to the cottage the Hawkesmoors had used. She'd felt nothing noxious in there beyond the foul atmosphere that Flora and Jeanette had created, and anyway, she presumed that would be somewhere the police would focus on more. Moreover, she really didn't want to hamper their investigation. If Scott could be found alive and well by normal means, then nobody would be more delighted than her. But there was something wrong with this house, even if it was something like a full psychic cleansing that needed doing, Kat felt a certain responsibility to do it, given that she was probably one of the very few to come here who was capable of diagnosing such a thing and doing it properly.

As she hurried to tuck the keys into her cool-bag under the old sandwich wrapper, it suddenly dawned on her that maybe what was wrong with this place was that somebody had tried to sort it out in the past, but had done totally the wrong thing. The knee-jerk reaction of a lot of folks would be to call in the local priest, and if, as Scott had told her, the owner-builders had been a Catholic family, then might they have demanded an exorcism? The big problem with that, Kat had discovered by talking with her grandparents and online with other 'sensitives', was that quite often it only muddied the waters. Not necessarily made something worse – although that had happened too – but could be more of the equivalent of giving a place a metaphorical emetic when what it really needed was its 'gastric ulcer' soothing.

Not every psychic oddity was evil, and not all needed violent expulsion. And the more Kat analysed her sensation of the place, the more she thought some sort of turmoil could be at the heart of the problem. For the sake of whoever might come to live here after this, she really ought to settle the whole place down, especially if there was a chance of someone bringing kids into here. They were always far more alert than adults, and could be more deeply affected.

So picking up the bag and her flask, she decided that she would go and have a look in the garden, but before she could get there, Miles appeared around the corner of the house with another man.

"Ah, I'm glad we found you," he said with a half-smile. "Can we get your fingerprints for elimination purposes? I presume you must have touched quite a lot in the house?"

"Not today so much," Kat clarified, "but when I was going around with Scott

Hawkesmoor, yes, I probably did. I was doing things like tapping on the panelling and plasterwork to see how sound it was, so my fingerprints are probably going to crop up in all sorts of odd places. ...Oh, and I know I used the loo up on the main floor then, too. That's the one marked for staff at the back of the house, and also the loo in the cottage when I was there talking over samples later on."

"That's really helpful," the forensic guy said, putting his equipment down on the bench. "This won't take a moment."

"No problem, I'm glad to help."

While the technician took her prints, Miles told her, "DS Rigby has just told me that what you said to him about the two different driving styles is very helpful. He wants to come and speak to you himself in a bit, but he's already got on to the traffic division to see if there are any images on the motorway cameras which might help."

That was a relief to Kat. She'd had the fear that if Scott had a spotless driving record, then checking the speeding cameras might have been a low priority otherwise. And DS Rigby was obviously both sharper and more energetic than Miles, because no sooner had the fingerprint man done with her than he appeared to question her.

His approach, though, was very different.

"Thank you for being so helpful, Miss Newsome," were his first words. "I've had a word with our colleagues over in Worcester on the way here, and they were telling me about your run in with your fraudster. My colleagues over there say that you may have been instrumental in closing several fraud cases by alerting them to this Peter Erdington character."

Kat blinked. "Wow! I wasn't aware he'd targeted that many besides me. But that does explain how he was so sure of what to do. But in that case, I think you'll understand what I mean when I say that I really needed this contract. I'm far from broke, but Peter's ensured that my cash-flow is decidedly the worse for wear. Normally I wouldn't remotely consider coming down to stop in a place to work, and obviously now I'll be going home again tonight, but when Scott asked me if I'd start work straightaway, I was only too glad to be getting such a big job so fast."

Rigby immediately nodded. "Yes, given that context, I can see why you would have grabbed this job with both hands. How much is it worth to you."

"Given the number of rooms, and the fact that he wanted me to consult on the whole house…" and the amount she gave him had him start in surprise.

"Bloody hell! That's a lot of money!"

"Yes it is, and in fact I under-quoted him because I need it so badly. My competitors would be charging half as much again."

"Christ! Well that certainly gives you a strong motive for wanting to keep Scott Hawkesmoor alive."

Kat flinched. She'd not thought of it in quite those terms, but yes, she most definitely needed Scott alive and well. It was just disconcerting to have her actions scrutinised in such a light.

He quizzed her some more about the family, Kat repeating what she'd told Miles about the acrimonious set-up, but also about Scott's intentions to come back here and try and make a go of this. "I honestly think he was happy at the thought of never having to go back to the house in Yorkshire," she told Rigby. "The conversation I had with him about it made me think there were too many bad memories up there. Far from wanting to inherit it, I believed he was looking forward to getting rid of it. And I certainly don't think he needed the money from the sale of the place to refurbish this house. He seemed to have all the costings for this already worked out, and at least allowed for. Scott was – is – an experienced builder, and even in his grief, I just can't see him being so woolly-headed as to buy a place like this and then suddenly realise that he hadn't the capital to work on it. That makes no sense."

"Interesting," Rigby mused. "And you say that there's a lot of land with this place too?"

"Oh yes! The wood behind us is all part of the estate, and so is the land going from here down to the Wye. Scott was talking about putting a golf course in on that." Well that wasn't exactly true, of course. The golf thing had been her idea, but Scott had agreed quick enough, and Kat wanted to impress on this detective that Scott was a hard-headed businessman who had no reason to just up and vanish.

"Big money in golf these days," agreed Rigby. "Hmmm, so lots of potential for someone with the right ideas. And you say that there's a garden behind these cottages too?"

"Yes, a big one. When you go up to the top floor you get a very good idea of how big this place must once have been. These two cottages were once the stable block, and they won't take much to turn into successful holiday lets."

"Have you looked in there for Mr Hawkesmoor?"

"No, they're all locked up – another point I was going to make to you about how odd it was to find the main house unlocked."

Unlike Miles, Rigby caught on straightaway. "Yes, that is odd. You'd expect him to be more security conscious about the most valuable building, wouldn't you?"

"Exactly!"

"Hmm, it's certainly starting to look more likely that Mr Hawkesmoor never left for Yorkshire. ...Is that the way into the garden?"

Kat felt a shiver run down her spine, but Rigby had already turned and was walking to the odd-shaped gateway, leaving her little choice but to follow him. If she didn't, how could she possibly explain to him how it gave her the jitters? As his hand closed on the old iron ring of the gate itself, Kat felt something shift. An odd kind of lurch in reality, as though the gate had somehow just realigned itself fully with this world once more. Or if not from an 'other world', at least with this here-and-now.

Rigby obviously hadn't felt a thing, because he swung the metal gate open and stood to one side to allow her through. But as Kat followed him through the gate of decorative, latticed metal within the stone archway, she got a definite tingle, something like a static electric shock. Nothing more, though, and then she was through and into the garden.

"Oh what a lovely place!" she found herself exclaiming without hesitation.

"I thought you said you'd seen it from upstairs?"

"I have! But the view from up there doesn't even start to do it justice. All those lovely old plant supports crafted out of iron – they're probably worth a fortune, because I've never seen anything half this good in the salvage yards I go hunting in. ...And look! All the original bed-edging terracotta tiles, too! Priceless! Restore this place and you'd have somewhere gardeners would flock to. It'd be like the Lost Gardens of Heligan all over again, and do you know how many people travel to see that place?"

Rigby snorted, but with good humour. "You sound just like my wife – and yes, I do know about Heligan. My boy and I got dragged around there on our Cornish holiday two years ago. The missus was in raptures! In the end we left her to it and went and raided the ice-cream stand."

Kat had to laugh with him. Again that was something so very normal in this odd place. Rigby and his son had probably been hoping to get a game of beach football in rather than admiring the camellias.

"Well you'll have to treat her to a visit to here, because if she loves gardens, then this place is a treasure trove even in its current state. I'm not much of a gardener myself – I don't have the space or the time – but my granddad was very keen, and he taught me enough for me to be able to appreciate what's here. Look at these espalier apples and pears along the wall. These look like they might be the kind of really old varieties you don't see any more. They all need a damned good pruning, mind you, but with the right person doing it, they could be productive this year."

They walked along the path to the end of the garden and turned to look back at the house.

"God, it is big, isn't it," Rigby observed. "And we're farther from the house itself at this end than I realised. Now I see it like this I can see what you meant about the potential for several holiday flats. And you're right – the back wall of the stable block must once have been just a garden wall, not with the windows and doorways in it."

Kat nodded, but was wondering rather more at the way that the odd sensations had vanished quite quickly after coming into the garden. Whatever was going on at Fownhope Priors, it wasn't touching the garden. All there was here was a sense of wholesome earthiness. But then something caught her eye beyond the trellis fencing demarking the patios.

"Oh my God! What's that? There, in front of the cottage French window!"

It looked like a coat fluttering in the breeze, or certainly cloth of some description, and she and Rigby ran down the second of the lengthways paths straight for it. As they got closer they could see it was someone lying on the ground. Someone lying very still, making them both put on an extra burst of speed. But as they both slithered to a halt, and Rigby bent down over the figure, Kat gasped. Whoever this was, they didn't have dark hair, so this wasn't Scott but some other poor soul!

Chapter 8

Rigby pulled out his phone and immediately called for an ambulance.

"He's breathing, but only just!"

"I'll go and tell the others," Kat offered and set off at the run, but shouting back over her shoulder, "That's not Scott Hawkesmoor, though!"

Several of the forensic team followed her back to Rigby, but not all to secure and process the scene. One woman had come into forensics from medical school and was soon bending over the man and inspecting him very thoroughly.

"He's got hypothermia, for a start off," she observed. "I'd say he's been out here overnight at the very least, probably longer. Thank God we haven't had any frosts these last few nights, and at least this spot is sheltered."

Rigby straightened up and asked Kat, "Did you come out here with Mr Hawkesmoor?"

Kat shook her head. "No, I only saw the patio from the inside, but I don't think we could have possibly missed him if he'd been here then." Then realised the other unspoken question that Rigby must have. "But that's also why I'd not really seen the garden, you see. If you turn around and look out from here, you can only see a small part of the garden because of the trellis marking out the patio, and from inside you can see even less of the wider garden."

She looked down at the man's face as he got gently turned over so that they could wrap him in what looked like a foil blanket, no doubt to try and warm him up until the ambulance arrived. He seemed to be someone in his late twenties, maybe a bit older but not much, with fairish brown hair and a beard, but then with beards being very much in fashion at the moment that signified nothing. It could be looking unkempt because he'd been face down in the residue of the autumn leaves which had blown into the little seating area, rather than being some derelict.

"Before you ask, detective, I have no idea who he is. I've never seen this man before. But if you ask me was he maybe in the garden when I was in the house? I honestly can't tell you."

Rigby sighed but nodded, acknowledging that he understood what she was telling him. If this man had been sleeping rough in one of the old greenhouses along the far wall, for instance, it could well be that nobody in the main house had known about him until he'd crossed paths with his assailant. He gestured Kat to step back out into the garden, and then after instructing others to now make a thorough search of the garden, led her back out to the bench where she had eaten her lunch.

"This is just getting odder and odder," he confessed. "The one forensic guy has just said that they think the blood you and Constable Miles found in the cellar is just a few days old –

so certainly a fit for the last time anyone saw or heard from Hawkesmoor. But as to where he is, we're no further forward than when we first got here."

"Will you be able to match it to his DNA from something of his from upstairs?"

Rigby shrugged. "That's up to the technical guys to decide. I wouldn't dare to say yes as yet."

"But are you still looking at Scott as the killer of his wife and mother-in-law?"

"Well that's not our case, so I can't say about that, either, but I will be ringing the Yorkshire lads to tell them what we've found. Let's just say I can't see how Mr Hawkesmoor had time to go up to Yorkshire, commit that murder, and then be down here to get knocked on the head himself, if it is his blood, and the timing gets confirmed."

There wasn't much else that Kat could do, and once Rigby was sure that she was okay to drive, and the ambulance had come to take the mystery man away, he let Kat go home. She had made a note of the fact that the mystery man was being taken to Worcester Hospital, because of a lack of beds available at Hereford right now. That might give her a chance to go and visit him if he woke up without having the sharp-eyed Rigby spotting her, because once again Kat's senses were twitching at her and prodding her to think of him as somehow significant. If possible, she'd like to have a talk with him in private and see if he'd seen anything odd in the garden – the kind of 'odd' that Rigby wouldn't know to ask about.

Once back at home, she prepared a meal and then settled down for the evening. Tomorrow she would go into work and see if any new jobs had come in, but for now she felt that she just needed to clear her thoughts. Lighting some candles in her fireplace, she spent an hour meditating, but although she felt calmer at the end of it, she still had no more of a clue as to what to do, if anything. One thing was for sure, there was something calling her back to that house that went far beyond what some might see as morbid curiosity over what might or might not be a crime scene. And she had a sense of urgency nagging away at her that refused all attempts for her to relax and forget about what had happened even for one night.

Come the morning, though, she was feeling more decisive. There was no way she should risk going back out to Fownhope Priors today, because even on a Saturday she was sure Rigby would be having the house and grounds thoroughly searched, if only to make sure that Scott's body wasn't lying undiscovered in the grounds somewhere. There was a fair bit of ornamental garden filled with huge shrubs that she'd not yet set foot in, but which Scott might have staggered out into. And if he was lying dead there, there was no way that Kat wanted to see him like that. He'd got under her skin enough that she cared, and her extra sensitivity to things already made visiting places like graveyards a trial, let alone viewing somebody she'd known and liked who'd come to a violent end.

What she did do was go into her office/showroom to check her emails and ordinary post. To her amazement, there on the mat was a letter with a Yorkshire post mark, and with a solicitors' heading on it. Disregarding everything else, and stuffing the inevitable junk mail straight into the recycling, she sat down at her desk and opened the letter. It was from Scott's solicitor and was a confirmation of his contract with her, but with the additional information that Scott had asked for this to be sent, because in previous instances he would have sent official letters of confirmation from his company, and he wanted this to be every bit as businesslike. That was both comforting and worrying, in as much as it proved that Scott had had every intention of being hands on with this project.

But that gave Kat an idea. She couldn't act on it today, because the chances were Mr Andrew Treadwell wouldn't be working in his office in Keighley on a Saturday, but come Monday morning she would ring him. If anyone could tell her what that contract was worth now, it ought to be him. That wasn't being merely mercenary. Kat had bills to pay, and moping around after Scott wasn't going to save her office if she couldn't pay the rent in the coming months.

However she was also hoping that he or his secretary might be the chatty sort, and she could find out more of what had happened to Flora and Jeanette. After all, she still didn't know what day they'd died on. It could have been anything between Tuesday and early Friday, because she couldn't imagine the Yorkshire police hanging about to try and find someone they saw as a suspect. So the calls to Hereford might have been instigated in the early hours of Friday. What was worse, and which Kat hated to have to think about, was that a lot might hang on who was deemed to have died first when it came to inheritance, and Kat was praying that either Scott was still alive and might yet turn up, or that he would be assumed to have inherited from his wife, which might give her plan a chance.

Because Kat had decided on two things to suggest to his solicitors. The first was that in the absence of a body, they had to give Scott a chance to reappear. After all, he could have suffered a terrible blow to the head, and be wandering around in an amnesiac state. That was what she was half hoping for, because firstly there'd be a chance of his recovery both for his sake, and also so she could proceed with the commission as they'd planned. But if the worst had come to the worst, she felt that she had to convince this solicitor that Fownhope Priors would take a long time to sell on again in its current state. Much better, she would suggest, to continue with Scott's plan to make the flats sellable, or at least rentable, if the legal procedures were going to take a long time. Part of her was cringing at the thought of taking advantage of Scott's misfortune like this, but bloody Peter Erdington had got her with her back against the financial wall and she didn't have many options right now.

It made for an uncomfortable weekend in limbo, not helped by a visit to the hospital to track down the mystery man from the garden. He was stable now, she was told, but still hadn't regained consciousness, and since she could hardly claim she was a relative when she didn't even know his name, she could hardly press the nurses for more. At least she knew which ward he was on, but that wasn't much of a salve to her frustrations.

So she was very glad when Monday morning rolled around and she could ring the solicitors.

"Could I speak to Mr Andrew Treadwell?" she said when the phone was answered.

"Who shall I say is calling?" the secretary asked.

"My name is Kat Newsome. I'm the interior designer Mr Hawkesmoor contracted. I had a letter from Mr Treadwell at the weekend."

"Oh right-oh, I'll put you through."

That was easier than Kat had expected. No argument there.

"Hello, Miss Newsome," a friendly voice said. "Andrew Treadwell, here. How can I help you?"

"Mr Treadwell, I'm so glad you wrote to me so that I had your phone number. Mr Treadwell, I'm very worried about Scott. Can you tell me anything of what happened to his wife? I've had the police asking me about their relationship in the light of their deaths, but I'm hardly the person to be answering their questions. And while I normally wouldn't be this concerned over a client, the fact that he was intending to keep in touch with me and now can't be found by the police is very concerning."

"Really? Scott can't be found down there, either?"

"No. He's not answering his phone and nobody seems to have seen him in days."

"Oh dear, what to say."

"Does it make more sense if I tell you that I was at the house yesterday, and with a policeman we found blood on the floor of the cellar which they think might be Scott's."

"Bloody hell!"

"Oh, not enough to think he'd been killed there, thank God. But I said to them that I was worried that he might have been attacked by Mrs Underhill rather than him being the one suspect in their death. She seemed a very aggressive woman to me."

There was a barked laugh. "Aye! She's that, alright! ...Or rather she was. I told the police up here when they came asking, Flora Underhill wasn't short of enemies. They didn't need to look just at Scott for that. In fact I said that Scott ought to be well down their list. That woman had upset pretty much everyone in Keighley Moor. There wasn't a person in the villages here who didn't hate her guts."

That sounded as though she hadn't been any too popular with him either.

"So what happened to her, Mr Treadwell? Did Flora Underhill take Scott's car and crash it on the way home? He told me that's what he was afraid of her doing."

That seemed to dissolve the last of any resistance.

"Oh please, call me Drew. And I'm not surprised he was worried about that. Bloody Flora was a law unto herself! She stamped over anyone and everyone, doing whatever she wanted when she wanted. I told the detective who came to me that Scott would never have knowingly let her drive the Jag', and that was because he knew what a maniac she was behind the wheel. So it's bloody preposterous to think that he'd have tinkered with the brakes on it and then let those two loose in it. Would never have happened. Not ever."

"But when and where did the accident happen?"

She heard Drew huff. "They think either late Tuesday or early Wednesday. Poor postie found them when he got out there late on Wednesday morning with his delivery. They must have been coming *out* of their lane. The police are saying that they've found the women's bags in the house. So they'd obviously made it home in one piece, though God knows how, and we can only presume they were heading out shopping, though there are no late-night shops in the village. There's a sharp steep turn with a long drop down to a stream on one side as you come up towards the main road – not that that's a busy road most of the time, so I doubt Flora would ever have needed to brake hard for that. I went up there on Saturday. Not a sheep in sight, and Flora wasn't one to worry about squashing the odd rabbit or even a roe deer. So I have no idea what happened. All I can say is that there was a very weird set of skid marks. Almost as if she veered one way and then the other. But no marks as if she'd braked hard."

A vision of Jeanette reaching over and grabbing the wheel as her mother drove hammered itself into Kat's mind, making her gasp aloud.

"Miss Newsome? Are you alright?"

"Ermm, yes. Look if I'm going to call you Drew, please call me Kat. So Drew, I've just had a worrying thought: do you think that maybe Jeanette tried to grab the wheel?"

"Christ! Now that's a thought and a half! And I hate to say it, but Jeanette was unstable enough to do something like that. In fact Scott's said she's done that to him twice since the boys have died. She gets in a right hysterical state where she doesn't seem to fully know what she's doing. Both times he was strong enough to hold onto the wheel until he managed to pull over, but would Flora have been? I doubt it."

"Will you be telling the Yorkshire police that?"

"I will now! To be frank I was just so knocked sideways by the news of their deaths and him being a suspect, because I regard Scott as a close friend, that's why I didn't remember that earlier."

"Great. So where, as his friend, do you think Scott might be?"

"I've no idea, but I'm worried sick about him now you've said he's not down your way either. I just assumed that he'd run out of battery on his phone having spent hours arguing the toss on it with Flora or Jeanette, or that it had been in the Jag' when Flora made off with it, and was somewhere in the stream below the crash."

"Only I'm not sure he ever left here. I've suggested to the police that Flora might have picked up a speeding ticket or three, and that the motorway cameras might prove whether someone was in the back seat or not, and they're looking into that. But he seemed to be determined to finish this project. And that's in part why I wanted to talk to you this morning. I think I ought to carry on with the work – or at least produce all the proposals he and I talked about.

"I'm not trying to take advantage, Drew. I want this to work out for Scott. I know I only met him for one day, but I really liked him, and I just think he's long overdue for something to go his way."

"You're not wrong there. I knew Charlie Underhill. My dad was his solicitor for years. And Charlie often said to Dad that he felt eternally guilty for forcing Scott into marrying Jeanette. No bloke deserved that fate. Charlie got away from Flora as often as he could, but her father had been the one with the money that let him get started. To divorce her would have cost him dearly. Mind you, in his boots I'd have taken the financial hit. But Charlie was a proud man. Too proud for his own good sometimes.

"But the realisation that he'd dragged a good man like Scott down into the same hell-hole got to him as he got older. That house up on the edge of the moor where the crash happened? That had belonged to Flora's family for generations. They'd been gentlemen farmers once upon a time, but most of their money was tied up in the land they owned by the time Charlie married Flora. It was Charlie who sold a chunk off and developed another chunk into a housing estate. That's what made him.

"And like many other men like that, he wanted a son to take it all on after him. The only trouble was that Flora wasn't a good breeder. They only had Jeanette, and so Charlie picked a son-in-law he thought he could work with. Well he was right about that. Scott made him as proud as any father could have wished for. But the cost to Scott was high – too high in my opinion."

"Poor Scott. I hadn't realised that it had been that bad for that long."

"Aye, well it had. But you can see why the coppers up here might think that he'd finally taken all he could."

"Yes, and I think they weren't wrong about that, just in how he'd resolve it. He was going to let Jeanette have everything up there. That's what he told me."

"Did he? That's good! That's very good. You see he told me to start the divorce proceedings up again, but we'd not signed anything as yet. So they've only had my word so far that Scott was intending to simply walk away from Jeanette. But him having told you that too, and in a totally unconnected conversation, that gives it a lot more weight. Would you sign a statement to that effect?"

"Absolutely. In fact it's probably part of the statement I gave to the police down here already."

"Even better."

"So the thing is, Drew, can we carry on as if we're expecting Scott to return at some point? Legally, I mean. I know both of us want him to come back, but where do we stand when it comes to inheritance, for instance? I don't want to put loads of work into this and then find that some relative of Flora's appears and sticks the place on the market leaving me out of pocket."

"Ah, I see why you're concerned. Well let me set your mind at rest there, Kat. Flora has no living relatives as far as I know. There might be someone very distant, but it's going to take some digging and a fair time to find them, so for the foreseeable future I think we can work on the assumption of Scott being the one to inherit. Not that we can do anything about that until he reappears, and also any charges get dropped. So for instance, I can't authorise the sale of Moorside House to finance any work."

"To be frank, Drew, I don't think we were ever talking about that much money being involved. The way Scott was speaking, he had sufficient funds available of his own. What I was thinking of more was, can we access those funds of his if I act as project manager on the ground, and you oversee things financially? Scott had already asked me to be very hands on down here, not least because I know the local suppliers."

"Oh, I see! Hmm. Well that would be a very different proposition."

"Yes it would. But Fownhope Priors had been standing empty for eighteen months before Scott bought it. Consequently I don't see another buyer rolling up any time soon with it in its current state, even if you do need to sell it at the end of the day."

"Hmm. I get what you're saying. ...Look Kat, I think I really need to see this place. Can I arrange to come down and meet you there?"

"Absolutely. In fact I'll undertake to have the basic designs ideas drawn up for you to look at so that you can see that I'm not going overboard on this."

"Great. What about Friday?"

"This Friday?"

"Yes."

Kat was rather taken aback. That was a lot of work to get through, but if that was what it was going to take to get Drew to work with her then she didn't have a lot of choice.

"Okay. But you do realise that it would just be rough designs at that stage? I won't have had time to do full costings."

However Drew seemed to realise that he too need to do some explaining. "Flora's solicitor must be the only one who gave a damn about her, so the dreadful man is holding a memorial service for her on Friday. As Scott and Jeanette's representative I ought to go, but to be frank I'd rather be flogged with a zombie's rotten legs than have to sit and listen to that sanctimonious old windbag wittering on about what a good woman she was. I might disgrace myself and puke in the parish church!"

"Oh dear," Kat laughed, "then I'd better give you a good get-out, hadn't I?"

"You've no idea how grateful I'd be."

"Then why don't you come down by train? Unless you know the area, Fownhope Priors is a sod to find. I'll pick you up at Worcester station, take you out to the house, then you can stay the night in one of the nice hotels in Worcester, and catch the train back on Saturday when the kerfuffle has all died down."

Drew followed his sigh of relief with, "I'm already seeing why Scott liked you so much. Give me your email and I'll send you the details of what train I'm catching and where I'll be staying."

With the exchange made, Kat rang off, but feeling much less at sea. All she had to do now was work her socks off in the next few days to get things ready for when Drew came down. But that also gave her a very good reason for going back to the house. She needed to take some more measurements, and with any luck DS Rigby need never know that she had been back there.

Chapter 9

For the next two days, Kat worked right through into the evening, getting basic drawings and computer models made of the kind of things she and Scott had discussed. In one way, because she needed to make the flats acceptable as public spaces, the simpler they were the better, and they were the part of the old house she thought should be tackled first. If Scott couldn't be found, then the house would be far more sellable with those flats all ready to let out, because who on earth would want something that large as a single house she couldn't imagine.

However, on Wednesday evening she went straight from work out to Worcester Hospital. She hadn't forgotten the mystery man, and she wanted to find out if he'd woken up yet. Whoever this poor soul was, there was a strong chance, to her mind, that he'd fallen victim to the same thing that had hit Scott – whatever that turned out to be.

Luckily visiting hour was in full flow, and so she managed to sneak into the ward as another visitor came out of the security doors, rather than announcing herself to the nurses. For a moment she stood back out of sight of the desk area, wondering which of the four small wards radiating off the central area he might be in. Then her luck turned and the nurses hurried into the one six-bed room to help someone, and Kat heard the screens being pulled around a bed. So she hurriedly looked into that room and decided that unless the man was the one they were attending to, he wasn't in here. He wasn't in the next room either, but looking into the third one, she saw someone who looked familiar. Even better from her perspective, he was sitting up in bed, all by himself, and looking very lonely compared to all the others who had family and friends clustered around them.

And so plucking up her courage, Kat went in, stood at the bottom of his bed, and gave him her best smile.

"Hello. You don't know me," she began, "but I was there when they found you. Would you mind if I sat and talked to you for a bit?"

He looked worriedly back at her. "Who are you? More police? A social worker? I'm not mad, you know."

That sounded very encouraging in one way, and Kat was quick to explain, "No, I'm none of those, but I might be the one person who believes you." She came and perched on the edge of the bed, all the chairs having already been taken. "My name is Kat, and I'm an interior designer. I was asked to go to Fownhope Priors by its new owner, but he's now disappeared and I'm very worried about him. It was him – Scott – who we were looking for when we found you."

She paused and looked encouragingly at him, but he offered nothing of his own, making her carry on with, "So can you remember who you are? What you were doing there? Honestly, anything you can tell me, anything at all, would be really helpful."

He gave a bitter laugh. "You think so? That detective thinks I'm barking mad!"

Kat forced the smile to stay. "Well I'm not him. Why don't we start with the simple stuff? What's your name? Can you remember that much?"

"I'm Ryan ...Ryan Edwards."

"Okay, Ryan, so what's your story? How did you come to be at Fownhope Priors?" He looked so upset she feared he was about to start crying. "Honestly, I'm not going to judge you. Please, all I'm asking is for you to tell me whatever you can remember."

He still looked dubious but began with, "You know today's date, right? Well I can't remember anything of the last two years." He paused again. "Or rather, the last two years as you know them." Again he waited, as if expecting her to say, 'what do you mean?'

Instead she said, "Go on, I'm listening."

"Well I can remember the things that happened to *me* in the last two years. It's just that nobody believes me, because they aren't what happened here."

There was another pregnant pause and Kat decided to try a different approach. "So do they believe you about things before two years ago?"

Ryan blinked in surprise. "Erm, yes, there's no problem with that."

"So what were you doing back then, then?"

"I was the general handyman at Fownhope Priors Nursing Home. I'd been there about a year and half by the time it happened. Trained as a carpenter, you see, but the building trade took a slump and I had to take what I could get in the way of work."

"You must have loved working on that old place. There's some fabulous old panelling in there," Kat encouraged him with, and was relieved to see him perk up a bit.

"It's great, isn't it?" he enthused. "I'd rig up any number of contraptions to stop them drilling holes in it to hang things off. Bloody Matron Harkness! Total philistine, that woman was. No appreciation for what a lovely old place it was at all."

"I'm hoping to restore it to its former glory," Kat admitted and actually got a smile out of him for that. "So carry on. You obviously loved working on the building even if you didn't like some of the people there."

"Yes, I did. The biggest project we had to deal with was when the roof started leaking. Luckily, with them having the top floor half full of patients, they had to do something about it, even if they didn't care that the nurses up there were getting drenched whenever it rained. So the insurance coughed up, and since Harkness was too bloody fat to get up into the roof space to see for herself, I managed to get the bloke on one side who came to inspect it up there, and got him to agree that it needed to be done in keeping with the house."

"Was it you who floored the loft?"

"Yes."

"Well you did a great job up there. I've seen some right sights up in attics, I can tell you, but that's a proper job." The compliment on his workmanship brightened him even more, and Kat saw that he was almost beginning to relax in her company. "Did you have anything to do with the garden? Because that's impressive too."

His face suddenly fell. "Not exactly. That was Josh's province, really. He'd been RHS trained, you see."

"And where's Josh now?" Kat asked, almost dreading the answer.

"I don't know. That's what's been so awful about all the questions the police have kept asking me. They think we ran off together in some kind of gay lovers' tryst. But we weren't and we didn't!"

"Okay, so you were neither of you gay, just friends?"

"Yeah. Like me, he'd trained for better than what we were doing, but they kept him on because he saved them a fortune by providing the fresh veg. And he loved working in that old garden as much as I did the house, though I helped him more than he did me, 'cause the garden needed care all the time. We got our keep too, so it didn't matter that the wages weren't great when we could share the one cottage for nothing."

Kat thought very carefully about how to phrase her next question. "So when did it all start to go wrong? I presume something did go wrong?"

Ryan gave a shudder. "It was just after Christmas – so a bit over the two years ago actually. Josh used to store things like the apples and root veg' down in the middle cellar because it was ideal – nice and dry, and dark enough that things like the spuds didn't start sprouting. So he'd gone down there to just check on them. You know, make sure that a bruised apple hadn't started to rot and then turned the others in the tray to mush as well.

"Well he came up to find me, really rattled. He said he'd heard voices down in the cellar. …At first I laughed. Thought he was taking the piss, 'cause Josh could be a bit of a joker when it was just me and him. But then I saw he wasn't joking.

"He said they were talking funny. He couldn't tell whether it was foreigners or what. But he was adamant that there were several of them and that he could hear them in the front cellar. He wanted me to come with him, you see, in case they turned nasty. We'd had a couple of unpleasant incidents with foreign casual workers off the farms trespassing and getting drunk in the gardens, and that front cellar has an iron grill leading down into it from the outside. Back in the day they used to drop the coal down into the cellar from there. So it wasn't so daft to think that somebody had cut the padlock off to try and get into the house and pinch the drugs."

"I'd say that was a pretty normal assumption," Kat agreed. "A big nursing home like that was bound to have lots of medication locked up. I've seen what they used to use as a pharmacy and it's a fair sized space."

Ryan looked faintly relieved that she believed him this far.

"That's what we thought. So Josh went and got the big pick-axe he used for hauling stumps out with, and I got my lump hammer. Seemed better not to go down there totally defenceless, just in case we were going to run into four or five blokes who might be drunk or drugged up. On the other hand, we could hardly call the police without any evidence, and out there they take forever to arrive anyway, even though we're not that far from Hereford itself. Not part of the city policing team's patch we'd been told the last time we'd called for help. And bloody Harkness had mainly Philippino nurses working for her by then. Wouldn't pay the going rate for English ones! So they were some lovely ladies, but dainty little things you couldn't ask to deal with a big aggressive bloke."

"So you knew it was down to you and Josh to deal with whatever this was."

"Yeah, we did. So we go down to the cellar. Couldn't hear anything specific in the first one where everyone dumped junk, but as soon as we got through to the old wine cellar that Josh used, I could hear them too. Real clear they were. I was sure they were on the other side of the door.

"So we took a good hold of our 'weapons', and then I threw the door open and we charged in…" He stopped.

"Go on. What did you find?"

But Ryan ducked his head and looked embarrassed. "This is the bit the coppers don't believe."

"Okay. They don't believe you, but I might. What happened?"

"That's the thing. We saw bright light where there shouldn't have been any ...I mean *sunshine*, not a light bulb... and then it was like I got hit by something."

"Like what?"

"I don't know!" he said through gritted teeth.

Kat reached out to him and squeezed his hand. "Steady. Take a deep breath in... Okay, and now breathe out. ...And in again... And out. There, that's better. I wasn't doubting you. I just wondered whether you meant someone hit you with their fist, or with a plank of wood, or something?"

Ryan drew in another ragged breath. "It was more like a blast of air. Have you ever turned a corner and been hit by a gust of wind? Well like that but much stronger. ...I don't know whether I went backwards and hit my head or what, but the next thing I remember is coming around and being outside by a campfire. I remember rolling over and seeing Josh sitting beside me and him looking all shook up. And then this odd looking bloke comes over and says, 'You have to do what they say. Don't try and fight them, whatever you do!' and I remember thinking his accent was odd.

"Maybe I fell asleep, or passed out again, I don't know, because the next thing I remember it was morning, and that was when I got a real shock. I realised I knew where I was. We were somewhere where the garden was supposed to be, and the wood was still there, but the house wasn't! And then this bloke comes along with a nasty looking sword – and I may not be some re-enactment nut, used to swords, but that thing looked seriously scary! It looked like it had been *used*! And used in anger, too. I wasn't going to argue with him. No way! And he starts yelling at people in what I wondered at first might be Welsh.

"On the other hand, I've got a bit of Welsh on account of my one grandma being from North Wales, and even so, I couldn't understand a word. You knew what he meant, though! He made that bloody clear! Get up and start moving, or that'd be it for us. And the old bloke who I recognised from the night before comes and helps me up, and I see his mate doing the same for Josh.

"Now him I could just about understand. He'd got the thickest local accent I'd ever come across, but he was local Hereford, very local. So he's telling us to just keep moving with them, and then we come around these bushes and I see it. Not the house. The house wasn't there! But they're building something, and by the look of it, the plan of it is the same as the cellars of the house."

He stopped and looked hard at Kat. "You haven't called me barmy yet."

She smiled at him. "No, and this is probably the point where I should tell you that my mum's parents were both descended from people with very strong psychic abilities. My much-loved grandfather, who I always called Papa Viktor, came from Siberian shamen on both sides of his family."

"Jeez! That's a bit exotic!"

Kat laughed. "I suppose so. But I never thought of it like that. I thought it was perfectly normal to have a granddad who could read animals and the natural world the way others read the newspaper. He taught me to keep an open mind about things. And the woman he married, my Grandma Valerie, might have come from the Welsh Valleys, but she was more true Romany than anything. She could read people as if they were transparent, but she always drummed it in to me that this was a gift which should only ever be used for good, or it was likely to do you as much harm as the person you used it against.

"So given that I spent every school holiday with them while Mum and Dad were away at work, you won't be any too surprised to learn that while other kids learned to play cricket or Monopoly, I was being taught how to use a tarot deck properly, and how to dowse. Many was the time I went with Grandma Valerie and Papa Viktor to do a house cleansing, for instance, and out on the Welsh border there are a lot of old, old houses that have links to many eras. And not all of them are quite as sealed off in their different layers as they might be, either.

"One old place was a right mess. They'd had priests in doing exorcisms and all sorts, and it took Grandma and Papa three visits before they got the place calmed down. It's no use sealing the top layer, you see, if there's this maelstrom of conflicting times and places bubbling away underneath. In the end they'll only break through again. You have to sort out where it all started and begin with that, gradually working your way forwards."

"Bloody hell!" Ryan was looking at her aghast.

"Well not quite Hell in the biblical sense," she said with a grin. "That'd be a bit too much. But when you read modern physics – or as much as any layperson can understand – and you find they're beginning to wonder whether time is quite as linear as everyone thinks, you can understand more how in certain places you might get a bit of what I prefer to think of as seepage coming through."

"So you don't think I'm barmy, then?"

"No, not at all. I think you've had a very traumatic experience, but I believe that it was also completely real for you. Somehow or other, you and Josh ended up crossing one of these liminal areas in time, and ended up some-*when* else. If you think of how the earth sometimes folds over itself when earthquakes happen, and then think of the same kind of thing happening with time, it starts to sound more of a natural phenomenon and a bit less flaky."

"Jeez, you don't know what a relief it is to hear you talking about it like that," Ryan said with a definite quaver in his voice. "Between the doctors and nurses, and then the coppers, all telling me I've been on a two year acid trip, I was really starting to wonder if I was losing my mind!"

"Well it helps no end that I felt a very weird atmosphere when I was in the cellars just over a week ago," Kat admitted. "And it's also the best explanation I've come across as to why my friend Scott would have vanished, as if he'd been wiped off the face of the earth. ...So come on, then. What happened next? You'd got as far as seeing what looked like the cellars being built."

Ryan cleared his throat, but now started talking with more confidence. "Yes, but I gradually learned that they weren't building cellars for a house. This was the undercroft for a church!"

"Ah! That explains the barrel vaulting!"

"Yes, it does."

"And why the house is so long and thin. If they were planning a church, then why wouldn't the footprint be the length of a nave?"

"Oh God, it's such a relief to talk to you!" Ryan gulped. "Yes! That's exactly it. And I'd not thought much about it beforehand, but the cellars only run under the rooms on the stables side. They aren't under the rooms which face eastwards."

Kat sat up straighter in shock. "No, they aren't. I never saw that as significant before, but that brings the proportions even more into line. But you just said something else that's weird."

"I did?"

"Yes. If they were building a church, a Christian church, then they would surely have orientated it east-west? Now I know that the current house doesn't sit squarely on the compass points. The back of the house is more or less to the north-east, and the front faces south-west. But that makes the stables' side facing north-west, and the drive side south-east. That's definitely not the orientation for a church, so what else happened?"

Ryan gave her a thin smile. "At least you're asking what else happened, not suddenly doubting my every word. And in a way you've given me part of the answer to the bit I didn't understand myself."

"I have?"

"Yes. We'd been working away on the place, and by then I'd discovered that a fair few of the other men working there were Victorian workmen. They must have been the guys the house builder brought in to do the labouring. There had been the stonework of the undercroft still standing, they said, and they'd started building the house around it. They said something about the owners buying that patch of ground off the Church, who said it had never been consecrated and weren't bothered about it if they could get some money for it.

"Those men had then fallen into the other place, but there weren't that many of them left by the time we got there. It was a weird place to be in, because it felt like time wasn't passing so fast there. They were old men, but not a hundred and twenty years kind of old! They said most of them had died since they'd been there, and that the few other men who were working with us seemed to have come through over the years. One chap, I discovered, had slipped while delivering coal to the big house in the 1940s, fallen into the cellar, and like me, the next thing he knew, he woke up in the past."

"This ought to be provable," Kat said thoughtfully. "Surely the local papers would have reported on missing workmen?"

"I suppose they might, but I've hardly been in a position to go checking – still aren't."

"Well as soon as you can get out of here, we'll go to Hereford library and do some research. It might never satisfy DS Rigby, but it'll stop you from wondering if you were imagining it."

"Thank you, but that might not be for a while. They seem to think I'm some kind of 'vulnerable adult'."

"Oh Lord, that's not good! I'll have to see if I can come up with a way to get you out, then. But what was it I said that made sense to you?"

"Ah, that was about the orientation. So we'd been there for what I'd now guess to have been about a year in this time, and then all of a sudden there's this horrible rumbling in the ground. The soldier types started going nuts, and the oldest guys told us that this had happened before. The ground shook, and then when they got up the next morning the undercroft had somehow kind of twisted sideways."

"A ground slippage! Oh my word! Yes, that would account for it, especially with the house being up on a shallow bit of an otherwise steep hillside. It wouldn't be enough to have the whole slope sliding, but it could be enough to move a particular patch several feet."

"And it had! When the morning came, we got herded back up to the building and found it wasn't where it had been any more. It was a little farther down the slope with some of the walls buckled and toppling over, and although the bottom end hadn't moved more than a yard, the upper end had come much further adrift.

"But then a really weird thing happened. This odd character appeared up on the hillside, and he's screaming and shouting at us. But this time I could recognise it as Welsh. Not understand it, mind you, but I knew what it was. Whereas the soldier types I was beginning to think were talking something that sounded a bit Scandinavian at times, but also had words that were almost French."

Kat's jaw dropped. "Those must have been Normans, Ryan! Proper Normans. Did you know that the first actual castles to be built on this side of the Channel were built here in Herefordshire? And that's because even before the Conquest of 1066, Edward the Confessor invited Normans he'd known while in exile in Normandy, to come over and help him secure his Welsh border. Not that you'd necessarily have had a castle right on your site – it's just that the castles were big enough for us to find the remains of them nowadays. But they must have built other places too. And I suppose it would be logical for them to want a church of their own, not to be praying in a wooden chapel with the locals. If you could get radar up on the hillside, I bet you'd find the remains of ramparts not too far away."

"How far back did I go?" Ryan asked worriedly.

"If I'm remembering what I read right, probably to about 1055."

Chapter 10

"1055?" Ryan gasped. "Christ! No wonder I didn't understand them!"

"No, I doubt even a modern Anglo-Saxon scholar would, because Normandy quite literally means the land of the Norsemen. It was the Vikings who settled there at the behest of the French king of the day, and so I doubt they spoke what would have been considered good French, even by the standards of their time. But that would account for your raging Welsh priest. I can't imagine the local Celtic Church was happy at having these foreigners coming in and deciding to plant a new church in their midst that they had no control over."

"He was pretty scary, I'll tell you that. And he also put the wind right up the soldiers. They obviously thought he was bringing some curse down upon them, because they all got down on their knees and started making the sign of the cross and praying. Our workmen friends said this kept happening over and over, same time every 'season' – although come to think of it he was a bit hazy about what that meant because we never quite seemed to hit proper winter back then – and every time, that Welsh priest appeared in the same place saying the same words. Yet when the soldiers would go up the hill in the morning to look for him, they could never find any evidence that he'd been there – not even if it had been throwing it down with rain earlier and the ground was soft. That's why they thought he was some devil come to torment them. He never left any imprint on the ground."

"But if he was equally as out of time as you were, then he wouldn't would he? If you were seeing him through another gap in time, one that opened up with the landslip, then there was no reason why he would leave footprints for the soldiers to find?"

"Oh! I never thought of it like that! No, I suppose not."

"And now you begin to see what my grandparents meant about things not necessarily being evil, just misplaced."

"That's a relief!"

"But I want to know what you meant about not knowing what happened to Josh."

"Oh." Ryan stopped and took a deep breath, looking miserable once more. "That was the same day as we saw the Welsh priest. With the soldiers distracted and us understanding what our fellow workers were saying better by then, George, the one old boy we'd made friends with, says to us to be careful, really careful. He points to a strange swirly spot where the cellar is and tells us that where they found us the previous time. And I can see it. I mean it's a kind of bluish shimmer, but everything on the other side of it is distorted and …and …well it didn't look right.

Not like here – the here and now I'd come from, I mean."

"Fascinating! I've never met anyone who's actually seen a portal."

"Oh, there wasn't one – there were two."

"*No*! Two? What was the other one? Ermm, I mean, what did the other one do? Did you find out?"

"Oh yes. George said that people only ever arrived through the cellar portal."

"Arrived?" The penny dropped for Kat. "So was the other one the way back? The way you took back?"

Ryan nodded miserably. "But the thing was, Josh had had enough the first time we saw it. He couldn't cope with life on the other side being so brutal. So when George said that the other, much brighter, swirly light only ever took things away, Josh thought it must lead back home. He started running towards it, even though George said they'd seen animals die that inadvertently ran into it. But Josh just screamed that he'd rather die than live like this."

Ryan had to stop and wipe his eyes, Kat fetching him some tissues from off the side cabinet.

"That was the last I saw of Josh. Him just vanishing through the blue light. We didn't find a body in the morning. Nothing. That's why I keep saying I don't know what happened to him, because I don't. But it puzzled George and the others that we didn't find his body, I can tell you that. That was what made me decide to risk it this time – that and having had enough myself.

But when I got here there was no sign that Josh had ever made it. Not that I was exactly thinking straight, mind you."

Kat felt her heart sinking. That didn't sound good news where Josh was concerned. On the other hand…

"Hang on, Ryan. Could it be that if this other light only went forwards, then the reason why the animals died was because they never existed beyond that time? Do you see what I'm getting at? You successfully returned because you genuinely belong here. You've always belonged to the future. In which case, Josh did, too. But if Josh came back a year ago, then the house would have been empty. And what's more the garden has had a whole year in which to cover any tracks of his. I'm not remotely surprised that you found no signs of him by then. There'd have been nobody there to help him like we did you, either.

"So if he came back exhausted and disorientated, he would have had to make his own way to a road or a farm. Not that I'm going to promise that he's got back here safely. I'm just saying that it might not have been the portal which killed him if he is dead. You nearly died of hypothermia, and so might he. That would explain why nobody's been saying words to the effect that your story doesn't match up with his. If his body was found outside somewhere, he would have looked like some poor bloke who was homeless and fell prey to the cold weather. He'd have been recorded as an accidental death, especially if they couldn't match his fingerprints, and that would have been that. But equally we can ask to see if some dazed and confused man was found in the area a year ago. Let's not give up hope just yet."

He nodded and sniffed into the handkerchief.

"Ryan?" Kat suddenly had an idea. "The courtyard by the stable block feels odd to me too, so was that where they originally started building the undercroft? I mean, is it likely that that's where the first footings went in before the landslips started?"

He looked up at her, bemused. "Umm, yeah, probably. Why?"

"It's just that it seems weird to me that a portal that's a slip in time should have an 'in' door and an 'out' one. Natural phenomena don't work like that. Think of the surface of a pond – you drop a pebble onto it and it goes straight through, it doesn't wander around. And thinking of other liminal places in nature, such as when you blew bubbles as a kid, where you might briefly dent the surface of the bubble but then it would burst, can you see that it really doesn't make sense for it to have always had this strange one-way system. So if we think of the portal coming into being through a freak of nature – however that might have been – then it ought to have been in just the one spot. In which case, what would alter it? Might it be that the landslip has been stretching it?

"Think of those corrugated tubes you use for the vents of things like tumble-driers. When you buy them they're practically just a hoop. But as you pull them they get longer and longer, and if you overdo it, they tear. Well I wonder if the portal is becoming like that? Getting stretched out of shape the older it gets? Particularly if there's this peculiar Groundhog Day thing going on where the landslip repeats in the past." Ryan was looking at her with owlish eyes as she went on, "So they're not two separate entities. They're just the two ends of the same thing. And that means we can get Scott back!"

"But when?"

"How long does this phenomenon last for? I suppose that's the key question. Is it just for one day?"

"The weird lights? About a month – or so George said. But only when the moon rises, according to him – I wasn't taking that much notice. They start at the new moon before the equinox, peak at the full moon and the equinox itself, and then gradually wane back to the new moon again."

Kat rummaged in her handbag and found her diary. "*Hmph*. The only good thing is that the new moon was right at the equinox this time, so we're only at the first quarter so far. That gives us about couple of weeks to rescue him in before he has to wait for another year. ...Have you any idea what actually makes the portal open, Ryan? Because I've been down into that cellar with the police and there was no sign of any blue light then."

But Ryan could only shake his head miserably, seeming to struggle now that she was asking him for independent input.

Sitting back in the chair, Kat thought hard for a few minutes. If the Victorian workmen had gone through the portal, had they all gone together? Or had they only come through one at a time? That didn't seem likely if several had died before Ryan had got there. So had that possibly been the point when the phenomenon had started? Had the workmen disturbed something they shouldn't have? She must look into ownership of the site, because if it had belonged to the Church, or at least some monastery in the past, it might have lain undisturbed for centuries, considered not worth the effort of redeveloping.

Or maybe the Victorian men cut into some primal energy strand? She wasn't entirely sure that she believed in ley lines, but was there some other energy which might have become disrupted? Right now she would have loved to be able to sit down and talk this through with Papa Viktor. He would have meditated upon it and given it his serious consideration, which was a lot more than she could hope for off any of the other men she had come into contact with of late. Not that she was blaming guys like DS Rigby – this wasn't his area of expertise or experience, and she wouldn't have expected him to have believed Ryan's story.

"Could you hear anything from the other side?" she asked him. "Only you said that you could hear the voices of the workmen and that was what alerted you to the fact that something was wrong. So with the other portal – the one you came back through – could you hear anything of this side?"

"Erm… No, not really, but then how would we have known the difference between the birdsong then and now?"

"So you didn't… No, of course you didn't hear any voices. Who would there have been here either when Josh came back or you?"

"Why does that matter?"

"Because I was wondering if I could call to Scott, and try and direct him towards the portal? You know, let him know that it's okay to come through this weird thing he's seeing."

"Oh. I hadn't thought of that."

Kat smiled at him. "There's no reason you should have. You were too busy trying to stay alive in that other time, and if Josh passed out as he went through the portal, even he wouldn't have called back to you. Do you have any recollection of the actual point when you came back, Ryan?"

"No, not really. I remember running at the blue spiral that seemed to be inside something, and then being cold, so very cold. And that's about it. I think my last thought was that I was dying. At that point I honestly didn't think that I was going to make it."

Kat was worried by this. What was it about this other world that was so terrible that it had made Ryan willing to effectively commit suicide? Because if he'd genuinely believed that Josh had died trying to get back, then he could have only ever had the slimmest of hopes that he would make it through alive. And that made her very worried for Scott. He was someone who had seemed to her to be hanging on by the thinnest of threads. What would he do if he found that other world to be even worse than what he'd been through here?

"Ryan, I have to ask you this for Scott's sake, what was so terrible about that other world?" she asked gently. "I'm not trying to make you relive your worst nightmares, but I need to know what he's facing back then."

She saw him squirm slightly in his bed.

"It was everything. It was so nasty, so alien, so brutal. If you dropped a tool – even a simple shovel – they'd lash out at you. And it was with their fists! They thought nothing of *hitting* you. Nobody had ever hit me before! And for nothing, too." He sniffed miserably. "Never a word of praise. They never told you if you'd got it right, and you just had to try and work it out why you'd got something *wrong*.

"…And the food! Oh my God, it was disgusting! Even the hospital food is better than that. At least I can recognise what it's supposed to be. If I see another root vegetable it'll be way too soon. No meat, just fish on Fridays if we were lucky, although I'd rather have not had the fish at all, because it was just thrown into the endless sloppy stew we had." He shuddered. "And they served that in these hollowed out chunks of horrible tough bread. It wasn't even edible, though men like George seemed to cope with it. I couldn't. I never got used to it. Josh and I used to fantasise about ordering pizza, or having a curry – you know, proper food."

And suddenly Kat had a wholly different perspective on things. It suddenly began to sound as though Josh and Ryan had been the kind of single lads who lived off modern takeaways – an endless diet of beige food that never saw a green vegetable, and where even potatoes were processed into mash or chips. So eating the kind of food most British people would have known on a daily basis up until the late twentieth century had been a shock to their system. Having grown up with grandparents who'd known what it was like to go without, Kat had eaten her share of vegetable stews, because they'd still lived frugally. Granted Grandma Valerie had been a dab hand with her herbs and stocks, so those stews had always been flavoursome in a way that basic camp food wouldn't be, but it wouldn't have been half the shock to Kat that it had to Ryan.

As for the bread, that sounded like they'd been using trenchers in the absence of pottery bowls, but the bread of the time would probably have been mixed grain and barely half wheat flour for the most part. And again, if Josh and Ryan were such products of modern life that they ate nothing but white bread, that would have tasted beyond strange. It might even have seriously upset their stomachs to start with. Yet the Victorian workers had managed to survive on the food for years, so it couldn't have been that lacking in nutrition.

But the real giveaway had been that bit about nobody ever having hit Ryan before. That sounded as though he'd never even had a slap off his mother if it was such an extreme shock to him. And his absolute horror at that wasn't faked. He genuinely couldn't believe that anybody would just lash out at *him,* even though he and Josh had probably blasted the living daylights out of things in video games, never for a second understanding that in real life such things hurt, and hurt badly.

Suddenly she wanted to ask Rigby what he'd found out about Ryan, if only because she was looking at his dejected expression, and was beginning to wonder if he was a bit of a fragile flower – not necessarily 'vulnerable' in the sense that the hospital might use the term, but definitely not one of life's survivors. Had Ryan really not been *able* to get work on a building site? Or was it that he couldn't find a job where he fitted in? Was it closer to the truth that although he was good at his job, that he couldn't cope with the all-male atmosphere of a large building project? Had he and Josh been content to hide away at the nursing home because they were already struggling to cope out in the wider world? Because in Ryan's case, building sites might have involved a lot of dirty jokes and innuendo and laddish behaviour; where someone a bit precious and sensitive might have come in for a lot of leg-pulling, even if it hadn't been meant maliciously.

"Ryan, have you got someone coming to fetch you?" she thought to ask. "Parents? A brother or sister?"

"Mum's dead and Dad thinks I'm a waste of space," he muttered. No siblings by the sound of that, so maybe he had been a very indulged only child?

"Well what about mates, then? Is there someone who could put you up for a week or two until you get back on your feet?"

She wasn't being nosy. At the start she'd half thought of offering Ryan a place to stay if he would help her sort things out. But the more they'd talked, the more her intuition had begun to throw up warning signals. Ryan seemed to be making no effort to help himself, and having been thrown the lifeline of Kat believing him, she would have expected him to be a bit more concerned for Scott as another victim trapped by the portal. Not that she was expecting Ryan to go back through to rescue Scott, but by now he could surely have offered her a bit more information of his own volition? Yet who did he get on with if his options were so few? Kat hardly had much in the way of family, but she at least had friends who would have come and got her from hospital, and been delighted that she'd reappeared after being lost for so long. They probably couldn't have put her up for long, but she'd certainly be welcome to come over for meals and the like. So where were Ryan's mates like that?

However, "Josh was my mate," was the only response she got, and he was increasingly sounding more like a teenager than a man in his early thirties.

"What? Not even someone from when you were at school? An old girlfriend you've stayed friends with?" She couldn't imagine someone being quite that isolated that nobody at all would lift a finger to help. Okay, not everybody would be in a position to have someone sofa-surfing for a few months, but surely there ought to be *someone* who could help him find somewhere to stay, or at least pick him up from the hospital?

And there it was again, that vacuous expression and shrug of the shoulders that he ought to have grown out of by now.

"Oh dear. Well I'm sure the social workers will find you somewhere to stay." Suddenly Kat wanted to get out of here before he got the idea that she might look after him. If Peter had been a liability in one way, Ryan was looking more and more as though he could be one of a different kind.

"Look I need to go now," she said firmly, "but I'll start making some enquiries about Josh, and I'll have a look at the old newspapers too. If I find anything I'll come and tell you, okay?"

"Okay." It was as if he realised that he'd put her off, and rather than trying to get back in her good graces he was accepting it as what always happened.

"You take care, Ryan, and I'll try and come and visit you over the weekend."

She paused, waiting for him to say something, but when he said nothing could only add, "Well that's what we'll do then, alright? Bye for now," and she scooped up her coat and bag and almost fled from the ward.

What a narrow escape that had been! But as she got into her car, the thought of Josh coming back to an empty house and garden wouldn't leave her. However much of a weak reed he might have been, he hadn't done anything to deserve being left to die alone.

And what of Scott? That was more pressing, because whereas Josh's fate had long since been determined, she might yet rescue Scott. Just how long had she got before this damned portal closed up for another year? Because in his current state Kat couldn't see Scott surviving that year, even if he was a much tougher character than either Josh or Ryan seemed to have been. He might yet cope with the heavy work and the rough company, but that wasn't a chance Kat wanted to take.

As she pulled away from the hospital car park she knew she had to go back to Fownhope Priors tomorrow come what may. She couldn't wait until Scott's solicitor got down on Friday, not least because she was far from sure what he'd say about going hunting for oddities like portals, and standing yelling through doors for his friend whom he thought was missing in a much more earthly sense.

Chapter 11

The following morning, Kat went into her office and finished off the layouts she would need for Drew tomorrow. But in thinking about him, and him being Scott's solicitor, she realised that she had the perfect reason to give to DS Rigby for returning to Fownhope Priors. Better to give him a plausible reason for her having been there than sneak around too much, just in case she inadvertently left some indicator behind and he and his men went in again. If they knew she'd been there on at least one day, then they wouldn't be questioning about the other ones she didn't tell them about.

Picking up the phone, she rang the number he'd given her, and when he answered told him,

"I just wanted to let you know that I'm planning to go to Fownhope Priors tomorrow with Mr Hawkesmoor's solicitor. I hope that's okay? We won't be hampering your investigation in any way if we go, will we? It's just that he and I agreed that we have to start making contingency plans for what will happen to the property if Scott isn't found soon. It's not helping matters that there's all this complication with Mrs Hawkesmoor and Mrs Underhill's deaths, so Mr Treadwell foresees it being a long and drawn out process, and he needs to know what he's dealing with."

She heard Rigby tapping computer keys, and guessed he must be at his desk even though she'd rung a mobile number. "Hmmm. He's not planning on putting the place straight on the market or anything like that?"

"No, not at all. In fact, because he knows it may be a long time before anything like that can happen – and even so, it might take ages to sell – he's thinking that it might be worth me carrying on with the plans I made with Scott, particularly if it will help get the property into a more marketable state." Not entirely true when she'd yet to convince Drew of that, but Rigby wasn't to know that. "We've certainly got the time to do stuff. And hopefully, if Scott comes back or is found before then, then we've not wasted time when we could have been getting at least some of the work done."

"Okay," Rigby agreed cautiously. "And what sort of work are you thinking of precisely?"

"Initially, simply decorating the top floor apartments that already exist, not mucking around with the main rooms. All they need is something doing with the plaster of the ceilings, where the old roof leaked and has made the plaster bubble. Then beyond that it's just getting a decorator in to brighten them up a bit, and even so that's going to take a couple of weeks or more even to arrange, because we'll have to hire someone and that will depend upon availability. So you can see why we want to get some preliminary decisions out of the way. We can easily leave the rooms Scott last used alone and locked up so that they aren't disturbed. And we weren't looking at doing anything with the separate cottages just yet."

Then she seized her opportunity. "By the way, about those cottages. Are you interested in the stables cottages? Only I went to the hospital to see the man we found – I just thought someone ought to make the effort, because I wasn't sure if he even remembered who he was for you to find his family."

"Oh he remembers," Rigby said dryly. "Not exactly the sharpest knife in the family drawer, though, is young Ryan."

Grinning and glad that Rigby couldn't see her reaction, Kat agreed, "No, he's feeling very sorry for himself."

Rigby gave a snort of disgust. "I reckon him and that equally drippy mate of his, Josh, were growing weed in the greenhouses and getting off their faces on a regular basis."

"Really?"

"Oh yes! Forensics found the dried up remains of marijuana plants in one of the greenhouses. Quite a few of them. And it turns out that Ryan got chucked off the previous building site he worked on for being off with the fairies so often that he was a danger to the other workers. ...*Hmph!* Probably shouldn't have told you that, so don't go spreading it about, but I didn't want you to get suckered in by his lost puppy act. If I'm any judge of character, he's brought whatever happened to him down on himself. We traced his father, and he doesn't want to have anything to do with him since he caught him trying to sell some of his late mother's jewellery to fund his nasty little habits."

"Ouch! That would sour you against someone."

"Well it's certainly soured his family against him. We found the father so quickly because he'd actually filed a report with us about the attempted theft. Neither I nor Social Services can find a single family member who's that bothered that Ryan's still alive, much less wants to take him in. So it's off to a B&B for him in a day or so's time since he's got nowhere else to live, and if you'll take my advice, leave him to it, because it won't be long before he's back to his old ways again."

"Thanks for the warning. I'll steer clear of him. But he said something about him and Josh having shared one of the stable cottages. So are you interested in them at all? Only as the second stage we were thinking of getting them habitable too."

"No. They'd long since been scrubbed clean of anything useful to us. I suspect the former matron was glad to see the back of the pair of them. When we tracked her down by phone in some place in Spain where she's retired to, she said that she was glad they'd gone, even though it left her a bit in the lurch, because it gave her somewhere for the nurses to sleep while they were having the last section of the roof done. So there wasn't much point in me sending the forensic people in, and running up another bill for the lab, when there wasn't going to be anything left of Josh and Ryan in there. If those nurses had any sense at all, I bet they went through the one those two shared with bleach and carbolic soap, because I doubt personal hygiene was high on those two's agendas – especially Josh's when he was outside all of the time."

Good grief! Kat thought, Rigby really had a pretty low opinion of the two young men – what on earth had he come across beyond what he'd told her? And Rigby hadn't seemed like the callous type. No pushover, but then that went with the job, but he didn't seem to have been that hardened by it when he'd spoken to her. So could it be that one or the other of them had had rather more of a police record? Then she realised that Rigby was saying to her,

"You'll need the keys, then."

God, she'd nearly dropped herself in it there!

"Oh, yes please, that was my next question to you. Can I come over to Hereford and collect them today? Only I'm meeting Mr Treadwell off the nine-forty train at Shrub Hill Station, so that we can get over to the house with enough time to do something useful. He's coming on the early train from Leeds, you see, so I'd rather not have to fight my way into Hereford city during a Friday morning rush hour if I can help it. I can drop them back to the main police station tomorrow evening, if that's okay?"

"Fine. Just don't go down into the cellars where we found the blood, the cottage where the Hawkesmoor's were living, or that courtyard where we found Ryan Edwards – but then if you have a solicitor with you, I'm sure he'll be quick to tell you to keep clear of anywhere that might destroy evidence his client might come to depend upon."

"I'm sure he will." Oh, so that's why Rigby was letting her back. It was because she'd have a solicitor with her, not because she was particularly trustworthy. That wasn't exactly flattering, but Kat was glad she knew where she stood now. "In that case, I'll pop over about four o'clock for the keys," and she rang off.

Best not to seem too eager for them by asking for them any earlier than that, though, because Rigby would start wondering why she wanted them with half a day to spare. That might get him wondering if she was hunting around on her own, and she definitely didn't want that. It was a bit of a pain, however, because it meant she wouldn't get to the house until closer to five o'clock, and she wouldn't have a lot of time to go searching until she lost the light. But then she thought back on what Ryan had said yesterday. Hadn't he muttered something about the old workman saying that the lights came, 'only when the moon rises'?

She sat back in her chair and thought hard. From spending so much time with her grandparents, she was familiar with looking up into the sky and sometimes seeing the moon up there even during the day, depending on its orbit, and she knew that moonrise could be very flexible time-wise. Some folk might think that the moon only came out at night, but Kat knew that in reality most people simply didn't notice it when it was in one of its phases when it rose during the daytime. At home she had a calendar of the moon phases already, but here in her office she would just have to go online and look it up, because the first thing she wanted to do was to look at the moon phases on last Tuesday or Wednesday when Scott had vanished. Would they match up?

When she brought up one of her regularly used websites, she was partially relieved to see that moonrise had been around six-thirty in the morning on the Tuesday, and about an hour later on the Wednesday. So far, that looked as if what Ryan had mentioned was viable, because she couldn't imagine that Scott would have been lazing in bed until mid-morning, and he'd probably have been up and about bright and early. That meant it was possible that he'd gone down into the cellar just when the portal was active, presuming the old workman had been right.

So what about today and tomorrow? She scrolled down the page, seeing that moonrise today had been at eleven in the morning.

"Damn, that's no use today," she muttered. "If I was too late to see it on Friday, when it came up at about half-past seven and I was there by not long before eleven o'clock, it can't last for very long. Maybe it only lasts for a couple of hours?"

However, tomorrow it would rise at around twelve-fifteen. "Just when I ought to be there with Drew. Now that could be useful, because if anything is going to persuade him that I'm telling the truth, it ought to be him seeing it for himself."

Stuffing all the things she would need into her laptop case, along with the laptop itself so that she could show Drew her computer generated images, she admitted defeat at trying to do anything more in the office for now. She couldn't concentrate on anything else, and she still had several hours before she could go and get the keys. So she decided the best thing to do would be to go home and have her main meal of the day. That way she wouldn't be running low on energy if she was out late rummaging around in the house. She also wanted to make sure that her pair of big flashlights both had new batteries in them, because she wanted to see what the house was like at night.

That was because one big question kept nagging away at her: why hadn't anyone seen these glowing portals before? The one in the cellar she could understand. In the years of the old house having coal fires, the servants had probably brought up scuttles of coal first thing in the morning, but wouldn't necessarily have lit fires until later on in the day, except in the worst of weather. Back then even the rich didn't have rooms as warm as modern houses in the winter months, they simply wore more layers. So the chances of servants being in the cellar at the exact point when the moon rose were already fairly slim. But even so, surely there must have been some coincidences? Even taking into account the possibility that the weather at the time of the spring and autumn equinoxes in most years might not have been cold enough to warrant fires, according to the workman they were visible for virtually the whole equinoctial cycles of those moons. And wouldn't an Edwardian housemaid scream the place down if there was a big glowing thing where the door to the cellar ought to be?

"There's got to be more to it than that," Kat muttered darkly, as she went into her kitchen and prepared a stir-fry. "Could it be super-moons? Is it *only* when an equinox coincides with the moon being closer to the earth? Indeed, is it even that linked to the equinoxes? That would make a bit more sense. Ryan said they never seemed to go fully into winter, so were the two key shift points in the seasons as relevant in that place/time, especially if the autumn one never really came around before the Groundhog Day thing started again?"

She shredded some precooked chicken to go into the pan with her vegetables and then put some rice on to cook. Then while she was waiting for that to simmer before putting the veg' and cooked chicken on, she sat at her laptop at her tiny kitchen table and looked up super-moons. Yet even that couldn't wholly be the answer, because in most years there were actually about four times when the moon was close enough to the earth to be classed as a super-moon, and those usually in successive months.

"What the hell is the trigger for this portal thing?" she fumed aloud as she began sizzling all the stir-fry ingredients. "There has to be something. Something *specific* which sets this thing off. It can't just be lurking there every time the bloody moon comes up, or people would have been shouting their heads off about it even if it was only four times a year – that's far too many coincidences to have remained totally unnoticed. And the same goes for the equinoxes – surely to god, if the damned thing opened every spring and autumn like clockwork, someone ought to have seen it? Come on, woman, think! You've got to get your head around this if you're going to go poking around up there. The last thing you want is to get caught by this thing yourself, or even lose Drew Treadwell in it – because if he goes missing when you're around, the police really will start looking at you sideways!"

Nothing came to her until after she'd eaten and washed everything up, but then it came to her that possibly the moon's actual distance might be a factor. Going back to the astronomical charts she looked at them more closely.

Right, let's start with this year, she said to herself. *Oh! That's interesting!*

The full moon that was coming next Tuesday would be the one when the moon was at its closest for the whole year. It was only a difference of roughly four hundred kilometres – absolutely nothing in astronomical terms – compared to the full moons on either side of it, but was that enough? Was it sufficient that its gravitational pull did something which affected this portal? If so, it was the first halfway sensible thing she'd found about it, because despite what many would think, her shamanic grandfather had had his feet firmly planted on the ground, and he'd impressed upon her that natural things responded to natural rhythms.

How to test the theory, though? Then she thought of something else that Ryan had said. A coal delivery man had fallen through in the 1940s and become trapped. Could she pinpoint his exit from his own time? She brought up a different chart for the twentieth century and scrolled through until she got to the 1940s. In 1940 itself, the closest super-moon distance-wise had been in March and the next year it had been in April, both months being chilly enough for the house to still have been having coal delivered for fires – and at least close-ish enough to the equinox if that really was a vital link. But thereafter, right through until 1946, the super-moons had come in the summer months, and Kat guessed that it would be unlikely that there would have been coal deliveries in those months, meaning the man would have had no reason to be there anyway.

Making a note of the six years in the 1940s when they happened in the winter months, when it was more likely that the man might have been delivering coal, she looked at the actual distances again more closely, and compared them to this year. This year the distance was around three hundred and fifty-seven thousand miles, but in 1947 it had been closer to three hundred and fifty-eight, so maybe not then. 1948 and 1949 looked more promising though, because then the figure was even less than now. With specific months in those years to search with, Kat began to feel a bit more hopeful of finding her missing coalman in articles in the local newspaper archives.

And then it dawned on her that Ryan had described the portal only opening once a year, yet those he was with couldn't seem to predict it. That was bizarre, given that there were two equinoxes in any year. Surely even an urban workman of the Victorian era would have caught on to that and begun to predict them? So had it in reality been very little to do with the equinox – and she had to admit at this point that Ryan was far from being a reliable witness – and more about when the super-moons came? That would make it much more unpredictable in past years, because Kat felt sure that even in the eleventh century somebody would have known about things like equinoxes, especially the spring one, when most people were tied to the agricultural year and would look for signs such as that to plan things like ploughing and sowing seeds. Unlike Ryan, she wasn't going to write them off as stupid just because they didn't live and think the same way as herself. These men would have worked with a purpose and a timetable of their own, for a start off, and Kat thought they would have noticed something that was regularly occurring once a year long before Ryan and Josh had stumbled into their world.

So if she was looking at something which would only occur once a year but seemingly randomly for most people, then it was starting to be a bit more plausible that it would have gone unnoticed for some of the time. Then knock out the years when this occurred in the summer months – such as 1905 through to 1909 – and you could start to see how this might have been something which only got spotted once in a decade.

Hmm, Kat mused. *Then take out those times when the family would be likely to be away socialising, and also the two world wars when the houses might have stood empty, and for a fair chunk of the first half of the twentieth century you can see how this might have got overlooked.* What would be interesting would be to find out how often in later years the house had also stood empty, because again, that might remove a good many years from her list. Huge Edwardian houses had often stood vacant for years if not decades, many becoming derelict and collapsing without any other intervention, purely because nobody could afford to run a place like that once the years of cheap servants had vanished.

But what of the portal that Josh and Ryan had come back through? Why had she and Scott not spotted that – aside from it being too late in the day, that was. What of the odd shimmer Ryan had described of the incoming portal? Why hadn't they seen that? Or was it because it hadn't been dark enough at the time to see it?

Well you did have a very odd sensation about that garden gateway, she thought as she grabbed her stuff and headed for the car. *You must have been picking up on the residual energy from that garden portal opening when you were there on Friday, even if you didn't see it.* Then she stopped in her tracks as another thought came to her. What if the portals were only visible on the way in? Ryan hadn't said anything about them seeing a blue light at the cellar once he'd arrived in the past, aside from a slight shimmering, and could it be because that was the primary portal? The one which had been created by whatever had been disturbed?

That makes more sense, she thought triumphantly, *because in that case, gardeners could walk into the garden through the arch of the physical gateway without any issue, because they were in effect still on the outside of the portal's wormhole in time. And they could walk back out again, because the portal there only brought people forwards, it didn't take them backwards in time. So they wouldn't have had access to it in the here-and-now.*

That's far more like it! she decided with satisfaction, as she set off to drive to the police station. *Nobody saw the garden one because it wasn't visible and didn't do anything from our side of it. That makes the cellar one the only one that has ever been visible in this time, and that would have been out of sight for many of the years. Okay, I can live with that as a passable starting theory.*

At the police station in Hereford she was relieved to find that Rigby had left the keys at the front desk, and although she had to provide proof of identity and sign for them, she'd expected them to take such precautions. Keys in hand, she left and was secretly delighted, once she'd got into the car and looked at them more closely, to see that Rigby had given her fewer keys than she had on the ring that she'd picked up on the sly. That might be really useful, because if rooms were locked, and Rigby didn't have a key, then that gave her opportunity to go and investigate as long as she locked up after herself so as to not give the game away.

"Right!" she said resolutely as she turned the car towards Fownhope Priors. "Time to go and do some investigating!"

Chapter 12

As she drove in down the long driveway, Kat couldn't avoid having the odd shiver. In the lowering light, and this early in the year, there weren't even any birds singing so late on, and an eerie silence lay over the place. The old Land Rover sat forlornly on its own, forgotten about and looking even more dilapidated than Kat remembered it being on that fateful day when she'd travelled here from the station in it.

Pulling up beside it, Kat had to steel herself to get out. Something was seriously tweaking at her senses, and if it wasn't exactly active danger, then it also wasn't pleasant.

Come on, you've got to do this, she lectured herself sternly. *There're things you can't really do with Drew here with you tomorrow – or at least not unless he turns out to be a very sympathetic and empathetic kind of guy.*

Just because he'd sounded pleasant on the phone, it didn't mean that he'd be comfortable with her dowsing over the place, for instance. He might be quite hard-nosed when it came down to it, because after all, he was a solicitor and he must have had his share of dodgy clients. Although he wasn't on the criminal law side of the profession, it didn't preclude him having had dealings with people who were skating on very thin ice legally, and amongst them Kat was thinking of Charlie and Flora Underhill. 'You don't make money without stamping on people,' her Grandma Valerie used to warn her, and by the sound of it Charlie had made quite a bit. She thought Scott was probably straight, but then Charlie might have cleaned his act up a bit by the time Scott was senior enough in the company to be taking part in the decisions. And belatedly Kat realised that she didn't know how old Drew was. He could be easily ten years older than Scott, and have taken over from his own father a lot earlier than Scott had from Charlie – and that could sway him a lot with his decisions on Fownhope Priors. Might he be more of the Charlie type than Scott? In which case, a quick profit might govern his decisions.

The thought of some late middle-aged solicitor dogging her steps tomorrow was enough to get Kat out of the car and moving towards the house, at which point she decided that she'd try going in through what was now the utility and laundry room first via the original old kitchen door. That would tell her whether the police had bolted that door or not. If they had, then she would have to go in and out through the front door – something she was reluctant to do on any subsequent visits she might make, if only because it being unlocked would signal that someone was in the house should somebody like Rigby come along; and for no good reason she could put into words, Kat really didn't want to be locking herself into this place either. Or at least not until she'd had the chance to give it a really good cleansing.

Mercifully, the key turned in the former kitchen door, and when she turned the knob it opened easily. She'd made a point of putting latex gloves on for now, although she'd take them off when she came to dowsing. Another thing she'd realised was that she must not leave fingerprints about the place aside from where she would go tomorrow with Drew. That would be another telltale she wouldn't be able to explain away easily if it was somewhere he didn't recall visiting if asked. Yet that also meant that for now she didn't hesitate to reach out with a gloved finger and flick the light on.

As the strong light bulbs bathed the laundry room in reassuringly modern light, Kat huffed, realising that she'd been holding her breath, although what that would achieve was plain silly, she scolded herself. There'd been that odd sensation lingering as she'd walked up the cobbled courtyard past the stables, and it was a considerable relief to get inside the house and close the door on it. At least here in the laundry room there wasn't anything prickling at her senses, although in the cellar below it would be a different matter, she knew.

Right, where to start? Maybe upstairs? Be methodical, Kat, she told herself firmly. *If the cellars are going to start battering at your senses, you don't want to start with them, because then you won't feel a thing when you come back up.* So she headed for the main stairs, glad that for now she wouldn't need to put the lights on, and turning the laundry room lights out as she went out into the hallway by the other switch. It would be best to assume that there might be somebody out walking a dog in the woods who, although they would be kept at bay by the estate fence, might call the police if they suddenly saw the place lit up like a Christmas tree.

Going right up to the apartments, Kat opened all of the doors, noting that every one of them had been closed by the police, which made it easier for her since she wouldn't have to try and remember which ones had been opened, and which closed. At that point she then stripped off the latex gloves and brought out her pendulum and her crystal wand, which was nothing like what a child would think of as a wand and more a long, thin pointed piece of crystal. She had debated with herself long and hard about which ones to use, since she had several of each, knowing that her choice might affect the outcome and how effective she might be.

Part of her had wanted the protection of black obsidian or black tourmaline crystals in the pendulum, but the pendulums she had of those stones were simple single wands attached to a chain. This time, though, she felt that the issue was much more complicated, and had chosen to start with an amethyst pendulum she had created herself. The main stone was a beautiful deep purple amethyst sphere, but it hung from a solid silver cap with a loop on it onto which she could clip different chains, and a matching lower cap with a quartz tip was fixed beneath the amethyst. A goodly length of chain was necessary to allow the crystal to move independently, and Kat always liked a heavier crystal and chain which wouldn't be prone to being moved just by the odd finger twitch or breeze.

So this time she'd put on a chain she'd created herself, which had seven other crystals in it, albeit much tinier pieces than the main one. They started with a ball of smoky quartz – a good stone for protection and grounding, which was something Kat wanted right now. She needed to be sure that she wasn't just jumping at shadows all the time and was keeping her head firmly in the game. Next, after seven links of chain, came a ball of amethyst, though paler than the main stone, and then after another seven links one of lapis lazuli, a stone with a reputation for healing properties. A small piece of the rarer green tourmaline came next – another stone which Grandma Valerie had always said guarded you against negativity and emotional harm, and in this instance Kat was glad that she'd built this stone into the chain. She wanted to make sure she wasn't going to suffer some unpleasant backlash in the process of searching. Yellow jade came next bringing extra protection but also healing, and then a lovely warm orange piece of carnelian to boost energy levels. The final stone was a beautiful red garnet, not good enough to be classed as jewellery quality, but still with its own warm fire inside, ensuring that the end of the chain both anchored and grounded it, and bringing positivity to the search. At the end was a goodly sized loop which Kat could slip over a finger if she felt the need.

Such precautions with the protection might have seemed silly to some, but Grandma Valerie had taught Kat that you treated the energies with respect, and that only a fool would leave themselves unprotected when using their senses. That was how people got frightened when messing around with things they didn't take the time to understand. The other thing to understand was to ask questions which could be answered by a basic 'yes' or 'no', because the pendulum could only swing in certain directions and still be clear in its response.

And so Kat began going through the rooms asking three simple questions. 'Is this room dangerous?' was the primary one, followed by, 'does this room link to the portal in any way?' The final one was, 'can Scott hear me from this room?' because just at the moment her priority was to try and find a way to communicate with Scott, wherever he was.

She wasn't expecting to get any positive answers from up on this floor, but it was reassuring to find that as near as she could tell, the top floor was divorced from anything that was going on down at the lower levels. At this stage she wasn't using the wand she had brought with her. That was another composite piece she had made many years ago with Grandma Valerie, and it had clear quartz points at both ends, but with a lovely wand of Merlinite in the centre. That stone in that shape was incredibly hard to find, and it had been a gift to her from Grandma Valerie which she treasured, knowing that it brought protection but also healing from the past, and peace and harmony to the present. At the two joints of the stones they had put smoky quartz chips as extra balancing and protection in a fine net of sliver wire. This would be what she used to try and seal the gateways once she'd worked out more how they operated, but for now, once she'd finished dowsing she simply stood the wand on its lower point and said a blessing at every window, and at the top of both sets of stairs. With luck that should stop anything leaking upwards, but she also went through the rooms with a smudge stick she had made for the purpose. Hopefully the scent of the pungent white sage base wouldn't still be lingering tomorrow when she came here with Drew, but just in case she cracked the windows in the two front bedrooms and also in the two back kitchens to get a bit of a through draft.

Feeling rather better when she had finished, Kat put her gloves back on and closed the top floor up once more. On the next floor down where the main rooms were, she repeated the process and again got firmly negative answers to her questions. She was astute enough to know that she couldn't consider her dowsing to be absolutely accurate, but she'd had enough successes using it in other situations to feel that it was as good an indicator as she or anyone else was likely to get.

The only place where she got a glimmer of a twitch out of the pendulum was outside of the dining room. That baffled her for a moment until she went to what looked like a cupboard door next to it, and discovered the shaft of an old dumb waiter. Back in the days when the house had been full of guests, this would have been the fast way to bring dishes up from the kitchen on the ground floor to the dining room on the first. But Kat guessed that the shaft for it might well lead right down into the cellars to accommodate the mechanisms. Therefore it wasn't so odd that some of the weird energies might be leaking upwards just here.

Here she decided that stronger measures were needed, and after smudging the hallway, brought out the spray of holy water. Ideally it ought to have been from a proper church, but Kat had always struggled with organised religion, finding it too quick to judge people like Papa Viktor and Grandma Valerie. And so she had resorted to the home-made version, though in her case the three versions of the Lord's Prayer said over it came from three different eras – the first was the Old English version from the tenth-century Exeter Book; the second was from the Wycliffe translation of 1380; and the final one was the well-known version from the King James Bible of 1611. Kat had been very careful to pick these early versions as she'd prepared the spray bottle back on Tuesday night, and the three times three repeating of the prayers should make it even more potent. Those eras ought, she hoped, to bracket the past time that she was dealing with, and if anyone on the other side could hear her, hopefully they might join in if it sounded familiar – the King James Version being the one that had still been in regular use in parish churches throughout the land when this house was built. The spray bottle itself was a purpose-bought one, of the kind used to mist plants with, but she had a large spare thermos flask of the water with her in case she needed to be fairly liberal with its use.

Even so, she stood at the open top of the dumb waiter and began reciting as she sprayed.

"Fæder, þu þe on heofonum eardast,"
she began,
"geweorðad wuldres dreame. Sy þinum weorcum halgad,
noma niþþa bearnum; þu eart nergend wera.
Cyme þin rice wide, ond þin rædfæst willa aræred under rodores hrofe, eac þon on rumre foldan.
Syle us to dæge domfæstne blæd,
hlaf userne, helpend wera,
þone singalan, soðfæst meotod.
Ne læt usic costunga cnyssan to swiðe,
ac þu us freodom gief, folca waldend,
from yfla gewham, a to widan feore."

That was the Old English done.

"Oure Fadir that art in hevenes,
halewid be thi name; thi kyndoom come to;
be thi wille don in erthe as in hevene:
gyve to us this dai oure breed over othir substaunce;
and forgyve to us oure synnes, as we foryyven to ech man that owith to us;

and lede us not in to temptacioun, but delyvere us fro yvel."

That was the Wycliffe Middle English version said, and then the King James,

"Our Father which art in heaven, Hallowed be thy name.
Thy kingdom come. Thy will be done, as in heaven, so in earth.
Give us this day our daily bread.
And forgive us our sins, as we forgive every that is indebted to us.
And lead us not into temptation, but deliver us from evil:
For thine is the kingdom, and the power, and the glory, for ever, Amen."

Standing back she gave herself a moment, and then dowsed over the spot again. Would she need to repeat the process twice more to give it the power of three times three even in the anointing? To her great relief the pendulum was now showing no signs of picking up anything, and that Kat found encouraging, because she'd not been entirely sure that she was strong enough to do this. The only cleansings she'd ever done on her own had been far lower grade stuff than this, just removing the residue of the odd troubled teenager from a couple of friends' houses. But this was the kind of thing she'd seen Papa Viktor and Grandma Valerie working on together, and she was by no means certain that one person alone would be enough for the task.

Of course they could have been working on it together because they were such a close couple that it would never have occurred to them to go alone; but firstly as a child and then barely into her teens, Kat had never thought to ask them at the time whether it had been out of necessity too, though now she wished she had.

At the top of both sets of stairs, she then took the time to repeat what she'd done on the floor above, but after that she had a decision to make. By now it was getting very dark in the house. Dare she put the lights on? This time she wasn't so much worried about being seen from outside, because the ground floor was largely hidden from sight at the rear by a high earth bank which led up to the woods. Rather, she was concerned that the modern energy might skew her readings. Never having attempted something this complex before, she didn't want to blithely switch all the lights on, go around getting negative readings, and then turn up tomorrow with Drew and feel the hairs on the back of her neck standing up when she walked in. On the other hand, she really didn't want to trip over in the dark and end up with something stupid like a sprained ankle, which would make driving home a nightmare of a different kind.

In the end she decided to put the hall lights on. They would give her enough light to work by, and to not fall over the odd bits of wood Scott had left about the place, yet once she was within the individual rooms, their effect ought to be minimal. And this time she decided on a rather different tactic. Remembering her talk with Ryan, and how the cellars were only under the one part of the house, she decided to eliminate the rooms which sat on solid ground first, and one at a time.

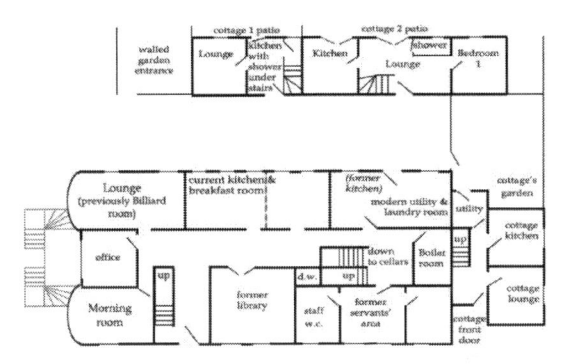

So her first call was to the former morning room. Although it was right by the main stairs, they didn't carry on downwards from there, and so effectively the morning room was cut off from below. As best she could tell, the cellars must start beneath the adjoining office, but only about halfway across it, so she'd leave that until later on.

Therefore it was with some relief she was able to dismiss the morning room as totally harmless, and moved onto the former library which also faced out onto the driveway. On the whole this too gave off negative signals, but the corner where the shaft of the dumb waiter butted it up to it had her pendulum jittering all over the place. So that corner got a dousing with the holy water and the prayers said over it as well as the blessing and smudging, which seemed to do the trick. And by the time she had bent down and put the wand to the floor where she had felt things were worst and repeated her blessing, that room was also as safe as she could make it.

I pity the poor old folk who slept in here, though, she thought as she picked up her bag and moved back out into the hallway. *I bet they had some strange and very frightening dreams, especially whoever drew the short straw and had their bed in that one corner,* and she shivered as her imagination filled in the gaps. Was that partly why she had got such strange readings just there? Because several old souls had passed on laden by troubled spirits due to the effect of the portal beneath?

Out in the hallway she debated whether to tackle the dumb waiter yet. Of anywhere, that was going to be the source of the worst leakage, but she hadn't looked into the other rooms at the back yet, and she had no idea how good or bad they might be. And so she went down the hall, skirting the servants' stairs, and went to dowse over what had become the staff toilets. To her astonishment, the pendulum was all over the place in both the ladies' and men's toilets, and was more than a bit jittery in the old boiler room too. What on earth was making these places so bad? They weren't over the cellars – or at least only half of the boiler room might be, and she had her doubts about that, because that far back at below ground level, it ought to be cutting more into the solid slope of the hillside.

Perplexed, she went into the utility and dowsed in there. Nothing! Not as much as a twitch from the pendulum there. And so steeling herself, she opened the door to the cellars and went down, flashlight in hand. For now she simply wanted to see where the cellars ended, that was all.

At the bottom step, she opened the door into the cellar, and trying to ignore the way every hair on the back of her neck seemed to be standing on end and goose-bumps were running up her arms and legs, played the flashlight around to her right. Sure enough, there was nothing but a solid wall there, and as she turned and went back up the stairs, she estimated how far she was going. At the top she then paced the same distance out, and realised that the original kitchen had never been over a cellars because they didn't cut this far back into the bank of the hillside. The modern kitchen-breakfast room was, though. And as soon as she went into there, she could feel it, although not as badly as in the staff loos. That was really odd given that they were on the other side of the house, albeit next to the dumb waiter's shaft, and she went back out and returned to the laundry room so that she could think clearly.

Had the toilets always been there? That might explain things if the original workmen had dug deeply to lay in sewer pipes. Had they cut into the moving edge of the phenomenon? Was that why in the past the same point in time now seemed to keep repeating itself? And if they hadn't, would the Victorian house at some point have developed a structural fault and begun to collapse? She presumed that Scott had not been so stressed as to fail to have had a structural survey done before he bought the place, so for now it was almost certainly physically sound, but had there been a point when that might not have been the case?

Oh bother, that's too complicated for me to worry about now, she mentally sighed. *The question is, which bit do I try and seal first? The loos and boiler room, or the new kitchen-diner along with the lounge and office at the front? I don't want to muck this up by sealing them up in some way that allows leaks around my wards.*

In the end she dowsed over the question, feeling that if there was enough connection in the pendulum to cleanse the rooms, then that higher energy ought to know which sequence it needed to be done in. Papa Viktor had regarded this as speaking to the ancestors, while Grandma Valerie had said it was tapping into the energy of the Earth itself. Whichever it was, the pendulum definitely wanted her to start at the office and work her way back through the lounge and kitchen-diner, and she wasn't going to question that.

Moreover, that seemed to work well, and not once in those three rooms did she feel the need to resort to spraying any part of them. Going back into the laundry room and sitting at the table in there for a short break, Kat had a drink from the flask of hot herb tea she had also brought with her. As the chamomile and mint refreshed and soothed her, she felt more able to tackle what remained, for this was what was going to test her hardest.

Starting with the boiler room, that ended up needing just the smudging and blessing, and the same went for the old servants' room which had been recently been used as a locker room by the nursing home staff. The two toilets, though, were an altogether different prospect. Just as Kat felt that she had one part calmed down, another seemed to flare up. Up until now the pendulum had simply swung moderately in circles for 'yes', and back and forth for 'no' in answer to her questions, but in here the question of whether they linked to the portal had both yes and no going on, and so vigorously that the pendulum several times swung hard enough as to lose control and crack Kat sharply across her knuckles.

"Sod this!" Kat swore furiously as she had to stop and rub her bruised hand again. "Right! This is getting a dousing in holy water!"

She went out and topped her sprayer up from the prepared flask in the laundry room, then went into the gents' first. This was the toilet adjoining the boiler room, and once she had sprayed it from top to bottom while repeating the three versions of the prayer in triple sequences, it calmed down. Doing a quick check back in the boiler room, all was quiet in there still, and Kat wondered whether the only reason the boiler room had seemed so off kilter was because of its proximity to the toilets next door.

On that basis, it was probably no surprise that the ladies' was worse given that the wall opposite the window formed one of the walls of the dumb waiter. And so with that in mind, Kat first 'sealed' the door back into the locker room. She didn't want the energy swirling and finding a new route, given that the head of the servants' stairs down to the cellar was also right outside the locker room's door to the hallway. Then starting from the window, she repeated the total spraying she had done in the other room. Please God, Drew wouldn't want to use the gents' while they were here, because he might be shocked to find the place quite so damp! If he did, she'd have to send him to the loos up on the main floor. And with that in mind, Kat cleansed the window and 'sealed' it, then cracked the top windows a little to let fresh air in.

Yet thinking of the other loos upstairs, Kat was now surprised to realise how clear they'd been. But then the sewer and water drainpipes to them were on the outside of the building, and the water supply pipes had probably been replaced more than once since the toilets had been installed. That must mean that it was the original disruption to the ground which was making these two ground floor toilets quite so toxic. And again, Kat was aware that they weren't over the cellars at all, so of themselves they didn't connect to the portal in the way that the dumb waiter's shaft did.

However, by the time she had finished the ladies toilet, Kat was starting to feel drained, and she knew it would be foolish to carry on. She still had to drive home and get there in one piece, and even though it was only just after nine o'clock, she felt as if she had run a marathon in the four hours she'd been here. So for now she just went and sprayed the door to the dumb waiter, and smudged and blessed the top of the stairs going downwards.

She was just about to pack up and go when another thought came to her. Ryan had described opening the cellar door to the front cellar and seeing the light, but with that also being the point when he lost consciousness. Had that been because he had naturally leaned forwards with the door as it had swung open, thereby actively taking him into the portal? If that was the case, then she couldn't risk that happening to her or Drew tomorrow!

So she decided to go down to the cellar and see if she could open the door now. This late in the day it shouldn't be any more active than it had been when she and Scott had come down together, but even so she proceeded with caution. After all, Scott passing through might have opened the way up more for all she knew. Therefore she went and found a length of wood that was heavy enough to lodge into the ring of the door handle. If she could stand to one side and twist and push, she ought to be out of the way of the portal if it flared as the door opened.

Feeling her stomach fluttering with nerves, she went down into the cellars and put the lights on in the first two. Then standing well to the side, she worked the piece of wood into the iron loop of the handle and tried to twist it. It was far from easy. She hadn't got the right angle on it for a start off, and she ended up having to push it in a bit further, and also crouching down herself to get sufficient pressure on the lower part of the ringed handle in order to turn it. Even so, she ended up getting far closer to the door than she would have liked, but with an extra sideways shove, she finally got the door to at least come off the latch.

At that point, though, she couldn't manage to pull the piece of wood out.

"Bugger, sod and damn!" she swore. "Well that's a bloody big sign for Rigby that somebody's been down here! How the hell do I get that out now?"

Taking a wide loop around to the other side of the door, she shone her flash-lamp into the other room. All was dark, all was quiet.

"Oh well, here goes nothing," she sighed and reached out to tug at the piece of wood. By working it upwards, she managed to get it back out, but still used it to give the old door a good hard push rather than going in herself. Luckily the hinges were stiff, and so once fully open as far as it would go, the door was in no danger of swinging shut again.

"Right, well let's see if when I bring Drew down here tomorrow there's a big flashing blue light – and hopefully not of the police kind!"

And with relief, she went back upstairs, switching the lights off and putting the piece of wood back where she had found it.

After that it was just a case of locking up after herself and then making the drive back home. Once there it was all she could do to pour herself under the shower, and then fall into bed exhausted, just about remembering to set the alarm so that she'd be up in time to meet Drew off the train.

Chapter 13

The next morning, Kat was at Shrub Hill Station ready for the train. Although she had feared the house might invade her dreams, she had in fact slept like a log, struggling to surface when her alarm had gone off. She couldn't have said that she was actually still tired after the house cleansing of last night, but she was definitely glad that she wasn't going to be repeating the exercise today. If there was any nastiness still lurking about the upper floors, then it was going to have to wait until another day for her to do something about it, because today wasn't going to be the day to wade in with crystals and smudging sticks. Heaven knew what this Drew Treadwell might make of her burning a bunch of white sage and other herbs under his nose!

When the train pulled in, she scoured the passengers getting off for a man in a smart business suit, yet nobody quite like that seemed to be looking around for their lift. As the scattering of people headed out of the station, she suddenly found herself being approached by a man carrying a large leather satchel over one shoulder, and an overnight bag in the other hand. This had to be Drew Treadwell, yet he wasn't what she'd been psyching herself up for at all, and in a nice way. As he got closer she could see that the Barbour jacket he was wearing was original – not some cheap knock-off – but looked well-worn, and under it he was wearing the kind of leaf-green jumper she'd seen the hunting and shooting types wearing, along with the similar cream open-necked shirt with a faint checked pattern on it. Glancing down, she saw he was wearing jeans, obviously very good quality but equally not brand new, and the shoes were sturdy walking shoes, not office brogues. *Not what I was expecting,* she thought, *not what I was expecting at all.*

"Hello!" he said cheerfully as he got up to her. "Kat Newsome?"

"That's me," and she found herself mirroring his grin. "Come on, the car's this way."

More than a little thrown, Kat led the way, because Drew Treadwell was definitely worth a second glance if not a third. He was probably only around the six feet mark, but closer to seemed a much bigger man because he was chunky with it. Not fat. There wasn't an ounce of excess on him going by the way he was striding out. It was just that he was broad-shouldered and solidly built. All in all she'd have put him down as some well-to-do Yorkshire farmer's very fit and active son, used to being out in the fresh air, not a solicitor cooped up in courts and offices. His closely cropped mid-brown hair had the look of being wildly curly if it had been much longer, and already he was starting to have the tanned look of someone who'd been outside a lot, even though spring was only just getting going. And it wasn't a sun-bed tan, either, unless she was very mistaken. That coupled with hazel eyes which positively sparkled with energy, and Kat had to admit that if Drew was far from classically handsome, he had the kind of charisma that probably made him very popular with his female clients.

Don't go making a fool of yourself, she cautioned herself firmly. *For all you know, he's got a wife and tribe of kids back up north. Blokes like him don't hang around on the shelf until they're well into their thirties to get snapped up.* And unless she was wildly astray, far from being in late middle age, Drew was probably only a few years older than her at coming up to forty. But then that would put him at about the same age as Scott, which might explain why they seemed to have been friends as well as having a working relationship.

At the car, Drew threw his overnight case into the back of the VW, and then shrugged off the Barbour too.

"Why is it that every station in Britain is bloody freezing at six a.m.?" he said with a laugh. "I've never been on one where they open up the waiting room at that hour – certainly not outside of London anyway. And the wind always whistles through those places like there's a tornado on the way, even on the quietest of days." He flexed his shoulders as Kat shut the tailgate. "Ach, that's better! Felt like I was muffled up like Scott of the Antarctic!"

Watching him stride around to the passenger side and get in, Kat had the feeling that by the

A Gate to Somewhere Else

end of the day she might be utterly drained after keeping up with this human whirlwind.

"Can we stop somewhere for coffee?" was the next question as she got in behind the wheel. "I brought a thermos mug with me, but that went a long time ago, and the tiddly cups you get on the train service didn't last more than a couple of mouthfuls," and as if to illustrate the point his stomach gave a pointed growl.

Resisting the urge to giggle, Kat told him, "If you can hang on until we get out of town, there's a Costa out on one of the retail parks. Will that do?"

"Great! Costa is my favourite of the various chains – you clearly know your coffee."

"While I was in college I shared a house with an Italian," she explained. "Let's just say I got educated about coffee very quickly. At home I tend to make tea, because I don't always have time to make proper coffee, and I'm not a fan of instant anymore."

"You're a girl after my own heart," he agreed. "Much easier to make good tea quickly."

This was going remarkably well, Kat thought, but felt she ought to clarify something before this got too chummy. "Have you booked anywhere for tonight?"

"Aye, I've booked in to the Premier Inn by the cricket ground."

Of course he had. He probably came down for every game between Worcester and Yorkshire, because Drew had the look of a man who would love sport. But his answer had made her next words easier.

"Oh good. I'm sorry I couldn't offer you anywhere to stay myself, but I only have a tiny one bedroom townhouse, and to be frank, my sofa isn't fit for sleeping on under any circumstances."

"What? An interior designer without a luxury pad to show off?" he quipped, but the cheeky grin robbed his words of any offence.

Kat laughed. "An interior designer with a plan is what I am. I bought my little place because at the time I'd not long left college, and I had next to nothing to put down as a deposit. So getting somewhere bigger really wasn't on the cards. But then I decided that I'd stick with it for ten years, and in that time try and pay off as much of the mortgage as I could. I don't particularly like living as close to the city centre as I do, but I reckoned it would always be sellable, and it'd appreciate in value quite quickly – which it has.

"The longer-term plan is then to sell it and get enough out of it to be able to buy a decent house without having a crippling mortgage. That in turn means I've focused on keeping it in good decorative order rather than splashing out on fancy furniture, especially since I don't know what will fit the next house I buy. In this one everything has to be extremely compact! So every year I've been paying myself a respectable bonus out of the business, which I've used to pay a chunk of the mortgage off with. That's what's so bloody infuriating about what's happened to me. That thieving little shit, Peter, has cleared off with what I would have used for that – or rather what I would have used once I done my yearly accounts, and ploughed a bit back into the business." Hopefully that would quell any doubts he had about her business sense after having to reveal just how badly Peter had defrauded her.

"A woman with a plan, that's good," Drew complimented her. "So I presume there's also a plan with this 'decent house' you want?"

"Very much so. I want a place with a garage that I can convert into an office-showroom. That way I can dump the one I have in town and save myself the rent on that, too. I don't want to convert a front room, because that makes it too invasive of my personal life. Too easy for client to ask to use the loo and get a good look at the rest of the house and judge you on that! I'm no domestic goddess, and if I want to leave stuff scattered about, I don't need that impacting on my work life. Anyway, I think it's healthy to be able to shut the door at five or six o'clock and walk away from your job."

"Couldn't agree more. By five o'clock I've had it with ninety percent of my clients. The ones I would ever want to see outside of work, like Scott, are few and far between. That's why I don't live in Keighley, but about ten miles away nearer to Leeds."

"Ah, I wondered why you got the train from there."

"That and better connections."

They chatted generally until Kat pulled in to the car park by the Costa coffee shop, and then was quietly amused at the way Drew went in and grabbed not only an egg muffin, but also both a sausage and a bacon panino, and then a croissant as well. It was worryingly like watching a jet plane taking on fuel, especially when he ordered the largest size of Americano with two extra shots of coffee in it.

"Can I get you anything?" he asked, as the muffin and the panini got whisked away to be heated up.

"I'll join you with an almond croissant," Kat decided, thinking that her modest morning bowl of porridge wasn't going to last her very long at this rate. "And a medium latte, if you don't mind?"

"One almond croissant and a medium latte coming up!" and he handed over a well-used loyalty card to the girl at the till, his broad smile drawing one in response from her.

At this time of the morning there were only a few pensioners sitting nursing cups of coffee and cakes, and so they were able to go and find a window seat away from everyone so that they could talk freely. For a while conversation was halted while Drew devoured the food, but as he sat back with a contented sigh and wiped the ketchup from his mouth, he admitted,

"I'm bloody worried about Scott. This isn't like him. It's not like him at all. I can say to you what I wouldn't dare to the police, and that's that while Scott may have hated Flora's guts, he'd never have raised as much as a finger against her."

"What was all that about the brakes having been tampered with?"

Drew grimaced. "God knows! I've finally managed to get an admission that the brake cable might have become severed when the Jag' crashed down through the undergrowth. Bloody hell, Kat, it was a mess. They ploughed down through a bunch of saplings growing up the side of that gully, and it's a steep drop, so they went through a fair few of them before they hit the bottom and the stream. And they must have been going at an insane speed for that back-road to go down with such force.

"I think that's partly why everyone was so quick initially to assume that the brakes had been deliberately cut – there were no signs of skid marks, you see. No sign that Flora had even tried to brake for the bend. But then they've had to admit that the cut isn't clean, and as they've gone over the car in more detail, it's come out that what they thought was just debris around the cut from *after* the crash, might instead be what's left of the sharp end of a broken branch that did the cutting. And I kept telling them, you're not seeing any evidence of braking because I doubt Flora ever braked for that turn in her life! The only difference this time was that she wasn't in her piddling little Mazda sports car, but Scott's Jag' with twice the engine power."

"You don't have to convince me," Kat said with feeling. "I felt like I aged five years in that journey I took from the station with her. I've never been so terrified in my life!"

Drew smiled at her. "And I think you telling your local coppers that, and it getting passed on to our local lads, made them think again. So thank you for that. Having someone with no personal involvement saying that Flora drove like a lunatic all the time helped to convince them that I was telling them nothing but the facts."

"Well I'm glad I could help. I really didn't like Flora at all, which it's probably wicked of me to say, given that she's now dead, but I was more worried that she'd done something like whacking Scott over the head than the other way around."

"Not wicked at all," Drew said with a wrinkle of his nose in disgust. "Flora Underhill was an evil old besom. If she gets a good turnout for this memorial service today, it'll only be because most of them want to be sure that she's finally gone. Some might even come back and piss on her grave when it's filled in! Honestly, Kat, I've never known anyone with such a talent for trampling over people's feelings, and for causing trouble where none should have existed. I don't think there was a single family in Keighley Moor who she hadn't rubbed up the wrong way at some point. And that, I think, is why Scott continued to feel sorry for Jeanette even if he never loved her much. He said to me that she hadn't stood a chance with a mother like Flora.

"And it's why it took him so long to decide on the divorce. He'd been trying his best to mitigate Flora's influence on his boys, you see, but when it was clear that the only way to do that was for him to live totally apart from the family, so that he could at least have young Martin come and live with him, I think that made his mind up for him. Kevin was a lost cause, I'm afraid. It's sad that he inherited Scott's good looks, but he was all his mother inside – neurotic and selfish – and he used his looks to charm his way out of trouble. Martin was the other way around. Poor little bugger looked like a younger male version of Flora, but he was much more his dad's personality." He sighed and scrubbed his fingers through his short hair. "How the bloody hell Scott will take knowing that Jeanette's dead, I do not know, especially since she died in his car even if he wasn't at the wheel."

He looked so genuinely worried that Kat reached over and caught his hand as he put both of them back on the table. "We've got to find him first," she reminded Drew. "There's something very odd going on up at that house," and she told him all about finding Ryan Edwards after being lost for two years, but at this stage omitted the part about the portal. She wanted to gauge Drew's reaction to that first.

"Two years!" he exclaimed. "And he used to work at this nursing home? Wasn't he reported missing? Did the police look for him back then?"

However Kat rocked her hand and winced. "That's another thing. You see it turns out that Ryan and his mate Josh had their own marijuana plants going in one of the greenhouses, and Ryan already had a record for both being a druggie and for not being exactly reliable. I suspect he only lasted as long as he did at the nursing home because he knew he was onto a good thing. I doubt there was that much work to be done on the place, truth be told, so he was probably out in the garden with Josh a fair amount of the time. And I don't think the nursing staff would have had time to keep tabs on what they were doing out there. So as long as they kept the supply of fresh fruit and veg' coming, and saving the home a fortune in that way, they could virtually live for free there, doing as they liked, since there was nobody to watch them even if they weren't being paid much. But then why would they need much money if they had their own supply of weed ready and on hand? All they were funding was a diet of takeaway curries and pizzas!

"So when they both seemingly left, I'm sure the nursing home reported that they'd upped and gone, but I doubt that anyone thought much more of it. Why would they? Two guys in their late twenties, with already unreliable reputations, and who then walk out of stable jobs, aren't going cause the police or anyone else to look that hard at them. And to be frank, I can understand why DS Rigby seems to think that they just went off somewhere, got stoned until the money ran out, and then when something went badly wrong, Ryan came crawling back hoping to get his old job back. It's me who is thinking, in the light of losing Scott, that there was something altogether more untoward about Ryan and Josh vanishing like that."

Drew nodded. "I see what you mean. Yes, I can easily see that the police would think that in the first place Ryan and Josh were a low priority. And also that now, they don't necessarily think that they are connected to Scott, unless Ryan's brought some kind of trouble back with him which they haven't spotted yet. But then given that Ryan's showing no signs of having been beaten up by some drug gang he's crossed, you can forgive this detective for thinking as you've said, and that Ryan crawled back but came unstuck because the house was empty. And if he's as hopeless as you described, then finding him crashed out and suffering from hypothermia isn't that strange – in fact there's almost an inevitability about it if you look at it from Rigby's point of view."

"There is, and I think he's just dismissing it as a coincidence, because having searched the house and garden, he can't see any sign of Scott having been dragged off by force. Nor has Scott obviously come to grief by falling down the stairs, or the like. The only thing suggesting foul play in any way is the blood stain in the cellar. And to be frank, I fear Rigby is thinking the Scott just tripped, got a nasty knock on the head, and wandered off in a confused state – presuming he didn't go back to Yorkshire. I really wish I knew whether they found anything on those motorway cameras to prove he wasn't in the car."

Drew gave her a wan smile. "That was a smart bit of thinking on your part. It was only after you'd said it that I realised how significant that could be. They don't need to see who it is in the back, do they? Just the fact that there must have been three people in the car is enough."

"It really hit you hard, didn't it? This news about Scott?"

"Too right. Scott's one of my closest friends."

"Where did you meet?" Kat ventured to ask. "I'm guessing it wouldn't be at school, because Scott said he grew up in Cheshire."

"No, that's right, I didn't meet Scott until after he'd married Jeanette. But we both played on the local cricket team, and we discovered that both of us were as miserable in our marriages as one another. It gave us a pretty potent starting point for a lot of conversations. I was the lucky one of the two. My ex had come up with me from London where I'd been at university, but she hated Yorkshire with a passion. So I was soon suspecting that she was having affairs all over the place."

"Ouch!"

"Yeah …well at least we didn't get as far as having any kids, unlike poor Scott. Mine just cleared off back to London one day ten years ago and left me a free man, albeit considerably more wary after that bruising. God, but the divorce cost me dear! And I think seeing how I'd only been saved by virtue of the business still being in my dad's name, and me just getting paid a small salary, was sadly part of why Scott held off from getting divorced himself. At that stage, Charlie had already brought him more into the company than ever my dad had me, so he had a lot more to lose. He said he was scared stiff of ending up with no job, no home, and being stung for a massive alimony payment he couldn't hope to meet; and to be fair, knowing Flora, he probably wasn't wrong in that. And then later on, he'd got so used to just staying away for as much of the time as he could manage, he was as good as separated from Jeanette anyway, and at least with that set-up he could see the kids whenever he wanted. He often stayed at my house, you know, if he was working in the area, but didn't want to go home every night. My one spare room still has all of his stuff in it – though I didn't tell the police that! They'd have no doubt found something suspicious in that."

Kat managed to cover her delight that Drew was clearly single by saying, "I'm glad that Scott had someone who supported him. I got the impression he was far more on his own."

Yet Drew looked sad as he explained, "But in this last year I'm afraid he was. Once he'd stepped down from the company, he had no reason to be able to get away from the house for days on end. And Jeanette was in such a fragile state after the boys died, he mostly only spoke to me on the phone, because he was scared to leave her. He said that Flora acted like nothing had happened, and was so callous with Jeanette it only made her worse. But I was getting very worried about what all of it was doing to him. It was like all the fight went out of him."

"That's been what's been worrying me," Kat confessed. "I know I only met him for a few hours, but I don't think I've ever had a client where I've felt that my work was throwing them such a much needed life-line. Honestly, Drew, he was practically hanging onto my every suggestion, not debating with me as most people do. And the way he just came out and told me all about his sons, it was as if he was desperate for someone to confide in. I suppose if he'd been obnoxious I wouldn't have been so drawn in, but he came across as a thoroughly nice bloke who'd just had the worst time ever."

"You had him right, there."

"But his state of mind at the time is also what's had me so worried about his disappearance. In a way, I'm almost less worried about what's happened than how he's coping with it." *And how the hell do I tell you that he's possibly the thick end of a millennium in the past?* she thought desperately. *Please God that portal is still active when we get there today, because that's going to save an awful lot of convincing if it is.*

Chapter 14

Luckily Drew wasn't for lingering in the coffee shop, and so with two more coffees to take out with them, they got back in the car, and Kat turned towards Hereford. It was infuriating that traffic was heavy on the main road towards there today with it being Friday, and every pensioner in the shire seemed to be out and driving at twenty miles an hour, but as she glanced at the time, at least Kat could be sure that they'd still get there for when the moonrise happened at twelve-fifteen. And if she was honest, there was a part of her that wanted to be there when it happened to see if she could sense the portal opening. Would it happen all at once, and be that strong? Or would it fade in more gradually?

What she wasn't expecting was Drew's reaction when she finally pulled out of the tree cover of the drive and he saw the house for the first time.

"Oh what a great old place!" he exclaimed, genuinely enthusiastic. "Oh wow! I can see why Scott fell for it!" Then her saw her surprised expression. "Didn't you expect me to like it?"

Blushing, Kat had to admit, "I was prepared for you to be a chrome and glass wall kind of person. Someone who had an ultramodern office, with IKEA conference desks and wall-to-wall white. I've certainly done enough commissions like that in the past."

"Christ Almighty!" he laughed. "That's my idea of hell! My office is upstairs in one of the old places on East Parade, and I live out on a farm cottage that dates from the 1870s. That's another thing Scott and I had in common, a love of old buildings."

By now he'd got out and was wandering across to the horseshoe stairs leading to the first floor French windows. "God, I'd love to live in a place that had something like these. Aren't they great? I could just imagine standing out at the top of an evening enjoying a well-earned drink."

Kat laughed. "I'd agree that the old folks who used that room as their lounge had some spectacular views. You can see right down to the River Wye from up there."

"Can you?" and he was instantly bounding up the steps to see for himself. "Oh yes, now that's a view and a half," he approved, standing there and drinking in the fresh air. "Oh yes, I can totally see why Scott wanted this."

"Well come on down and I'll show you around," Kat said, feeling that this was rather like keeping some over-excitable Airedale puppy on a tight leash. On the other hand at least he was being enthusiastic, which was way better than she'd hoped for.

This time she went in through the front door, not wanting to give Drew the idea that she'd been sneaking around as yet. She wanted to gauge his reactions more before she did that.

And as he switched the lights on to get a better view of the original floor tiles and wood panelling, Kat grabbed a moment when his back was to her, closed her eyes and opened up her senses. All clear! Thank heavens for that! The cleansing from last night seemed to be holding this far.

She'd only paused for a moment, but as soon as she opened her eyes she realised that Drew had vanished from view, and his voice then came from the direction of the morning room,

"Oh very nice!"

Trotting after him, Kat found him questing about the room like a hound on the trail.

"Nice mouldings, no sign of rot in the skirting boards, and these windows won't take much to put right."

Valiantly pulling herself together, Kat began her sales pitch. "When Scott and I conferred about this being a wedding venue, I thought that this might be one of the rooms we could make into a ground floor apartment," she began. "I was thinking that not everyone would manage the climb to the second floor ones, and although this room doesn't have the spectacular views of the front bedrooms at the top, it would still make a nice place for someone like the bride's parents or grandparents to stay in. The steps block the view to the front a bit, but if you're only here for a couple of nights, that's not going to be the end of the world."

She held the door open and then led the way into the office. By going in first, she got a sense of the room, and once again all felt calm. That was a really good thing, but then she looked at her watch and realised that it was still half an hour off moonrise. Whether the air would suddenly start tingling then was another matter.

"I thought this office would either stay as one, or could be turned into a bathroom for one of the rooms on either side," she said. "As you can see, there wouldn't be a problem with privacy, because the window is largely obscured by the stairs anyway. So some frosted glass would be all that was needed." *That and closing that bloody portal underneath here. Dear God, I hope that driving drainage down in this spot doesn't rake up something else, or I'll be cleansing this place ten times over!*

"Yes it is a bit dingy in here," Drew agreed with a frown. "I think anyone wanting to use an office much would want better daylight these days. Otherwise you'd be paying a fortune in lighting."

"Quite. ...Now this room," and she opened the door to the nursing home's other lounge, "used to be the gentlemen's billiard room, according to the old plans that Scott saw."

She saw a grin spreading on Drew's face and he mimed taking a shot. "Yeah! Lots of room to manoeuvre a cue in here." He strode over to one of the side windows. "And what's that out there?"

"Ah, that's the former stable block. That's what got converted into the two cottages where I was telling you Ryan and Josh lived while they were here."

"Oh right. And these are the ones you were

saying you and Scott thought might make good holiday cottages?"

"Yes, not least because they're totally separate from the house itself. You wouldn't need to open up the whole place out of the main season to carry on letting them."

"Sensible," Drew approved. "I've got to say, I'm with you all the way so far."

"Then come and have a look at this kitchen. When the house was first built, it looks as though these were just two more reception rooms – maybe a smoking room and something like a study – but the nursing home made them into a modern kitchen." She opened the door with a flourish. "You could easily ask a caterer to work in here. Look at all the work-surface space you've got. And it's nice and bright, and with all the windows it's easy to ventilate. No nasty cooking smells lingering about the place. This room doesn't need anything beyond a damned good clean and some fresh paint."

"No it doesn't." Then Drew wrinkled his nose. "But talking of nasty smells, what the heck is that? It smells like something died in here! Has some bird fallen down a chimney and died?"

Kat had caught a whiff of it too as he spoke, but it was clearly not in this room. What worried her more was that Drew was out of the door ahead of her and, following his nose, was going across the hallway into the former library. As he flung the double doors open, her heart skipped, dreading what he might be walking into. Yet he stopped in his tracks.

"Oh, whatever it is, it isn't in here," he said, puzzled, looking at the empty grate.

"No it isn't," Kat said, slipping past him and making as though looking around her in general, but in reality casting a few hard glances to the corner she'd had to work so hard on last night. She couldn't be sure, but it looked as though there was something that looked like dead mould on the floorboards down there now. Whatever was that? Some ghastly residue she'd killed off? No time to look closer now, however.

"Nice room, though," Drew was saying as he went and inspected the mullioned windows looking onto the drive. "Did you have plans for this room? Shame the plaster isn't in such good nick in here."

"No it isn't, but I think that's because it used to be the library, and some heathen ripped out the built-in bookshelves."

"Nooo!" Drew groaned. "Sacrilege! And I bet they were lovely old ceiling-to-floors ones with lots of carving on, too. What a terrible shame."

As much to stop herself from jumping at shadows as anything, Kat confessed, "I was thinking that it might be interesting to go back into the archives in Hereford Library and see if any of the magazines of the day did a feature on this place. By the time this was built there were plenty of them about, and featuring the new builds of the rich if not famous, nor of noble birth. The Victorians and Edwardians were great ones for self-aggrandisement – no different to the celebs who want features in magazines like

Hello these days, really. You never know, there might be some old photos of it in its glory days. If nothing else, it might be a nice thing to have some of those framed and in the entrance hall. It does tend to lend a bit of gravitas to the place to be able to show its history."

"I think that's a great idea, and if you find any I'd love to have a look." He was running his fingers lovingly over the original iron latches which were still on the windows, even if they were also secured by more modern bolts. "Places like this fascinate me. So much craftsmanship in them." Then he wrinkled his nose again. "*Phwar!* That smell isn't getting any better, though. It's actually getting worse."

"Yes it is," Kat agreed, looking worriedly at her watch. Ten past twelve. Shit! Was this another effect of the portal opening up? It wasn't sulphurous, which would just have been too Hammer Horror film for words, but it was of something decayed and rotting. Oh God, please let it not be another body! And especially not Scott's!

"Are you okay, Kat? Only you've gone quite pale. I must admit it's quite a stink now. Where is it coming from?" and Drew was off again, and before Kat could stop him, he was opening up the door to the ancient dumb waiter.

Even as she called out, "No…!" he had shut it hard again, coughing deeply at the smell.

"What in God's name is that cupboard?"

"It's not a cupboard, it's the shaft to the dumb waiter. They would have loaded the dishes from the kitchen into it and sent it up to the dining room upstairs. Much quicker than having people carrying the platters and serving dishes all the way around via the servants' stairs. ...Oh lord, Drew, are you okay?"

He'd gone distinctly greenish and was gulping convulsively.

"This way!" Kat yelped and ran with him to the toilets where he disappeared inside and was very sick.

She didn't want to say it to him, but she was rather glad about that. Whatever he'd taken in, his body was repelling it vigorously, and with any luck he wouldn't take any permanent harm. Luckily she had brought a small water bottle with some fresh holy water in it with her, thinking more of herself when she'd made it at breakfast this morning, because she'd thought it wise to have some protection to hand just in case the house got to her. Crystals and smudge sticks might have looked weird, but someone just taking a swig out of a water bottle with a famous brand name on it wouldn't register on anyone's radar as odd. Now, though, she offered it to Drew as he emerged looking rather shaken but a better colour.

"Water?"

He shook his head and reached into a pocket, coming out with a hip flask from which he took a good swig. Whatever it was, it was strong enough to make him cough, but then he managed a wobbly smile, saying,

"Malt whisky. Strong enough to kill anything! If that was a mouthful of something noxious I got, that ought to sort it." He wiped the top and extended it to her. "Want some?"

"No thanks," she said with a smile, taking a swig of her water. "Although when we stop for a meal tonight I might take you up on the offer. I've still got to drive us back, yet."

He shrugged but nodded to indicate he understood, and took another swig himself before turning to look at the dumb waiter again. "So does that go all the way up and down?"

"Not as an open shaft. The actual dumb waiter only ran between this floor and the one above, but of course there had to be space above and below it for its mechanism. That's not a problem on the floor above, because there was plenty of room beyond its opening for the rest of the shaft to be fitted in just within that room because of these high ceilings. But it must go down into the cellars a way even though you can't see it from in there."

"Right, let's go and have a look."

"DS Rigby wasn't keen on us going down there, because that's where they found Scott's blood, but if you don't say anything to him, I certainly won't."

Drew looked suddenly serious. "If that's where my best mate came to grief, I want to see it. Lead on."

And so Kat led the way around to the cellar steps and opened the door, half expecting to be assaulted by the smell again. To her relief there was nothing but the general mustiness of any old cellar, and that gave her the confidence to lead the way down, flicking the light on as she reached the bottom. Standing out of the way, she let Drew come down to stand beside her.

Again his first reaction was one of delight. "What glorious old barrel-vaulting! And in stone, too. This can't be original to the house. I've never heard of a Victorian house having anything like this."

"You're very knowledgeable about old places," Kat said curiously, earning her a roll of his eyes and a shake of his head as he explained,

"I never wanted to be a solicitor. Never really wanted to go into the law in any form, to be honest, although if I'd managed to go into criminal law, I might have felt I was doing something a bit more worthwhile. But with a father and grandfather in the business, and me being the only son, I wasn't given a fat lot of choice. As soon as I was born it was mapped out for me that I'd go to university and take law, and then come and take over the family business.

"And I know this is going to sound awful, but unfortunately both my father and grandfather have lived to very advanced ages. So although my parents had almost given up hope of having children, and I arrived when they were a bit over my age now – so old parents by the standards of their generation – my dad only went into a nursing home two years ago. That's when he finally surrendered the business wholly to me. But then his own father had lived to ninety-four, and only let go of the reins at eighty-five, so I suppose I did well to get let loose on my own when Dad was eighty."

"Good grief!"

"Yeah! You can say that again. And so right up until I had to point out to Dad that unless he let me become the owner of the business, on what he was paying me I wasn't going to be able to help pay his carers, I've just been getting a junior partner's pay." He shook his head in disgust. "So between Dad and my ex wife, I've never had the chance to throw in the towel and go and do what I really wanted, which was to go into business with Scott and learn to be an architect. It's not as though our firm has been making a fortune doing the conveyancing on the sales of farms that have gone bust – we don't compete with the big firms in the cities for the prestige properties – and besides that it's just wills and stuff. Nothing to get excited about."

"That's so sad. I wasn't terribly close to my mum and dad because they were travelling all over the world with Dad's job, but they've settled in the Scilly Isles now, and if I don't see them very often, they were always supportive of me doing what I wanted." Not the whole truth, but the version she told to people and the one Drew would get until she was surer of him. "I suppose it helped that I had a fair idea of what I wanted even before I went to university, and it wasn't something that had no practical application – I might have had more of a fight on my hands if it had, I suppose. And my grandparents were very proud of me graduating. I'm just sad they haven't lived long enough to see me make a success of the business. So I can't imagine what it must be like to be so trapped in a job you don't want."

Drew gave a wry smile. "Well not for much longer, with any luck. Dad's got very befuddled in the last couple of years, and now I don't think he'd know if I sold the business. He doesn't even recognise me anymore, but then there wasn't much love between us for him to hang onto. Even Mum had a problem showing any real affection. It was their housekeeper, Maud, who was far more of a proper mum to me. She's the one who I really miss. Her son, Tommy, was my closest friend while we were growing up, and like Scott, he's been one of my best mates in later years too. But nowadays he's happy working on his cousin's family farm up in the Dales – gone into partnership, they have. I drew up the contracts for that."

He looked up at the curve of the vaulted ceiling again, adding, "But as for this place ...I've read everything I can get my hands on about old buildings, and if I'm not mistaken, this is genuine medieval stonework. What a find!"

Whatever he might have said beyond that, however, was halted as through the open doors there was a sudden blast of air, as if a large door had been flung open in the wind. It made them both stagger, and as they did there was a flicker and then suddenly a bright blue light appeared at the entrance to the front cellar.

As Kat instinctively reached out and grabbed Drew's arm, the initial flash subsided, but they could both see the light starting to swirl. It was like watching water going down a plughole, and there was a faint sucking sensation even from back here.

"What the fuck is that?" Drew asked in horror, but Kat could only stare open-mouthed at it, for the portal had opened.

Chapter 15

"What is that?" Drew asked again, though not expecting Kat to be able to answer.

"Don't go near it!" Kat warned, tugging at his arm. "That's what Scott went through!"

That halted him in his tracks and he turned to her appalled. "What do you mean, 'what Scott went through?' How do you know? What do you mean?"

"Please, Drew, come upstairs. …Please! …I'll do my best to answer all of your questions as best I can, but you need to come away from here. Now!"

Almost shoving him up and through the brick arch on the stairs, Kat just remembered in time to turn the light off, and then followed Drew to the top of the stairs, where she shut the door and leaned against it with relief.

She could see that Drew was angry, and she couldn't blame him. "Come on through to the laundry room. We can go and sit outside and I'll tell you everything I know," she said, feeling both wobbly from the effects of the portal, but also because she didn't want Drew to think she had plotted Scott's disappearance. In just the short time she'd been with him she'd come to like Drew as much as she had Scott, and there weren't many people who she ever took to like that.

When they had both got out to the bench where she had sat eating her lunch last week, Kat began by saying. "I'm going to tell you it all in the order I experienced it, okay?" And she began by her coming and meeting Scott, and having the odd feelings about the place. At which point she had to digress and tell Drew about Papa Viktor and Grandma Valerie, because otherwise he wasn't going to understand why she'd taken so much notice of her gut feelings. But then she went on to tell him about coming to meet Scott, as she'd thought, and then the police turning up and the discovery of Ryan in the garden.

"At that point," she said, having taken another swig of her water, "I honestly didn't have a clue about that thing down there in the cellar. I swear on both my grandparents' spirits, Drew, that I'm telling you the truth about that. All I knew was that I was very worried about Scott in the light of Ryan turning up in that state."

Drew was looking at her very sternly, but not, she hoped as an out and out liar. "So when did you decide to ring me?"

"After the letter arrived that Scott asked you to send to me. Honestly, Drew, I wanted to speak to someone who knew Scott, in part because it just never rang true with me that Scott either went on some homicidal rampage and killed Flora and Jeanette, or just threw in the towel and went off on some weird walkabout. Finding that blood stain down in the cellar right where we've both now just seen that portal open up was worrying me sick. That was the point when I honestly thought that Flora had whacked him over the head, and the police were going to find him flaked out in the grounds somewhere where she'd left him to rot. I know all my talk about having a Siberian shaman for a grandfather must sound ridiculous to you, but Papa Viktor taught me well, and I was getting a very bad vibe off Flora in the short time I encountered her."

Drew leaned back and huffed. "Well I'm bloody glad I'm never going to have to present this in any court of law. And to be frank, if I hadn't just seen that thing downstairs, I'd be thinking that you'd been at the wacky-baccy or the magic mushrooms yourself. But what I saw …shit, I can't explain that in any logical terms." He paused for a moment and Kat let him think. It was a huge amount to take in, and to stretch his credibility over, and she didn't want to seem like she was rushing him onwards to cover herself in case he asked awkward questions. "So when did you start suspecting that there was this portal thing? I presume you did suspect it, because you were too quick with that as an explanation otherwise."

Kat sighed, and went into recounting her meeting with Ryan. "He's everything that Rigby says he is," she concluded, "almost certainly unreliable and a complete waste of space as an employee. But what made me start thinking that he really was telling the truth was that it was so off the wall, I couldn't believe that someone with his limited intelligence and imagination could have made it all up – or at least not without there being an awful lot more holes in his story than there were. After all, he wasn't the one with the pair of high-ability psychics as grandparents, so how would he have come across such stuff other than by reading fantasies or watching films? If he'd got the idea that way, it should have sounded more Hollywood, not like something Papa Viktor would have talked about. And it fitted worryingly too well with Scott's disappearance, as well. Right from the start I'd been feeling that Scott hadn't reappeared because he *couldn't*, not because he didn't want to."

Drew's expression was distinctly pained, but he nonetheless asked, "And did your grandparents ever tell you about these portal things?"

"Specifically? No. But Papa Viktor always impressed on me that there's a natural order to the world. So for instance, if you look at the heart of a sunflower, the way the seeds spiral out from the centre is the same shape as that portal was making. Did you notice it was swirling just as water does? You get whirlpools that do that which have no weird connections at all. So it's a freak of nature to be sure. I wouldn't pretend that it's anything else. I certainly don't think it's manmade, or that anyone or anything has control over it, and it certainly doesn't have a mind of its own – that would just be beyond weird! But as best I can understand it, you might divert it, as you would a stream, or a current in water. Or maybe seal it up, like you could with a sinkhole in the ground."

Drew looked at her sceptically. "And you think that the other end of that thing is where?"

"There," Kat said, pointing to the circular gateway into the old walled garden. "That's the way Ryan came back, and I'm hoping and praying that that's the way that Scott can come back."

"So why aren't we seeing that swirly blue light, then?"

"Because we're behind it, in effect. It starts in the past, where we can't see it, but the people back then can see the same effect we just saw down in the cellar."

She suddenly had a bright idea. "Look, down between that double flight of steps at the front which you so admired, there's a grating leading down into the front cellar – or so I'm told. Let's go and look for it and see if we can move it enough to see down into there. If my theory is right, we shouldn't be seeing a thing."

Grateful to at least have some way of trying to prove something, Drew got up, and together they went around to the front steps. Shifting the couple of large pots of dead plants which shielded the office window from view, Drew led the way into the arch under the balcony above and over to the window.

"Ah, you mean this?" he said, tugging aside a tatty old piece of carpet which had no doubt been put over the old coal chute to stop the drafts whistling underneath and into the office. There lay a sturdy iron grill, and a few tugs by Drew soon had it lifting up. It may have been padlocked in the past, but these days it had been forgotten about.

"Well that proves the coalman's story," Kat said hopefully, "because I don't know about you, but I wouldn't have looked for that there if I hadn't been told about it. And with that ratty old bit of carpet being covered in moss, I would have just thought it was solid ground there."

"You've got a point," Drew admitted, brushing the soil off his jeans where it had flown up from his tugging of the carpet. "Okay, let's see what's down here," and he knelt down, carefully put one hand on either side of the coal chute and leaned in. "Black as the inside of a cow's belly down there!" he declared, his voice echoing in the empty cellar. "But is that because the light's gone out?"

He heaved himself up and brushed himself off, then set off at a brisk stride to the back door, Kat hurrying in his wake. Without hesitation he went to the cellar door and down the stairs.

Oh shit, Kat thought, *I don't want to go down there, but I daren't let him go down on his own. What if he decided to poke that thing? I've no way of knowing how strong it might be, and if it might suck him in.*

Yet as she hurried down the stairs she bumped into him where he'd stopped in his tracks.

"Fuck me!" she heard him swear softly, and peering over his shoulder from a couple of steps further up, she saw that the swirling blue light was still there, and if anything was even brighter.

He turned and gestured her to go back upstairs. Once they were back outside, he jogged around to the front of the house and peered in through the coal chute again.

"Well it looks like I have no choice but to believe you," he said worriedly as he got back to his feet, dropping the metal grill back and tugging the old carpet back over it. "Christ, but that's the weirdest thing ever!"

"I won't argue with you over that. But do you now begin to see why we can't see the returning portal in the walled garden?" She gestured to the old gateway. "Come on, come and have a look."

Together they walked up to the ornamental stone circle, but paused a short way back from it.

"All the hairs on my arms are standing up," Drew said with a shiver.

"That's exactly how I feel, and it was the same when I was here with the police," Kat confirmed. "I think that was the first time I thought that there was something really supernatural going on here – and I mean that in its more literal sense, not just ghouls and ghosts. This is something natural above and beyond our normal experience."

"I won't argue with you over that. So can we go through the gateway?"

"I did with Rigby, and when I did, once I was on the other side, that sensation of ants crawling over my skin stopped."

Drew looked down at her, then surprised her by taking hold of her hand firmly and marching through the gateway, the gate having been left open by the police. As they got into the garden Kat experienced exactly what she had before, the lessening of the odd creepy-crawly sensations over her skin, but so, apparently did Drew going by his sigh of relief. He turned and looked back at the gateway, shaking his head in amazement.

"Nothing! Not even so much as a shimmer," he said softly.

"Can I suggest something?" Kat ventured. "Would you be willing to go up to that gateway as close as you feel comfortable doing, and then call Scott's name? He knows your voice, doesn't he?"

"He bloody well ought to by now."

"Well then he'll be more likely to heed you than me. I'll just sound like some shrill spirit if he's disorientated, but you've got a deep voice. There's no way you're going to sound unearthly, and unless he's really had a nasty whack on the head, you should sound familiar, too."

Drew looked down at her. "It's a good job there's only us here, because I'm going to look a right pillock, you know that, don't you?"

"Better to look a pillock than stand on your dignity if it saves your friend's life," Kat said gravely, not even close to laughing at the thought, and that finally convinced Drew that however barmy he might think this, Kat was at least sincere in her beliefs.

Walking up to the gate he took a deep breath, then bellowed, "Scott! Scott! Can you hear me mate? Come towards my voice! ...Scott? If you can hear me, come to the blue light. It's okay mate! It's the way home! ...Scott? Scott!"

Yet nothing happened. They waited and waited, but if Scott was on the other side, then either he wasn't believing it, or he couldn't come through for some reason.

"I wonder if they're that busy hammering away at the old basement that they can't hear you?" Kat wondered, and told Drew about her super-moon theory. "So the full moon is on Tuesday coming, but moonrise is also at six in the evening by then. Hopefully that would mean that they'd be finished working for the day and at the camp which, if Ryan is to be believed, is somewhere where we are now. That might make all the difference as to whether Scott can hear you."

"It's possible," Drew said thoughtfully, "but I'm wondering if I can send him a different kind of message?"

"That's a great idea," Kat said sadly, "but I'd already thought of that. The problem is, whatever we write and send through, it won't exist in that past time. Do you see? It's the same principle as the animals from the past that Ryan saw going into the light and then dying. They weren't meant to exist beyond that point in time, but anything we send back written on modern paper wasn't meant to exist in the past, either. Why people like Ryan, Josh and Scott are surviving I can't explain, but even if they get our message, how would we know when they can't send anything back?"

However Drew was shaking his head as he began to search the ground. "Find me stones!" he instructed her. "As round as you can get, and preferably about the size of a cricket ball."

"A cricket ball?"

"I'm a mean fast bowler, and Scott knows that. What's more, he knows the normal intervals between balls in a match. I want about half a dozen I can take downstairs and send through that hole-thing. If they're stones, they've always been here, haven't they? Old as the hills, people say, well now's the time when we prove that!"

Cricket balls, Kat thought, amazed. *Well I can't argue with that, so pebbles it is.*

After half an hour of searching, they had four which Drew thought were suitable, and so they trekked down to the cellar once more.

"I wouldn't go to close to that thing," Kat warned, as they saw how brightly the portal was glowing right now.

"Don't worry, I've got no intention of!" Drew declared. "Right, here goes," and he hefted the first of his stones in his hand. Then standing as far back as he could, he made a short run across the first cellar, and about halfway across the second let the stone fly. He had to be as good as he'd said, because the stone flew from his hand and straight through the centre of the wormhole.

"Good shot!" Kat congratulated him as he came back for the second one.

"Practice," Drew said with a cheeky wink, then after a pause, sent another stone down the wormhole with a shout of "Howzat!"

For the briefest of instants, Kat could have sworn she heard someone yelp in pain, but she wasn't certain enough to tell Drew.

The rest of the stones followed, with Drew keeping the intervals as near to the same as he could.

"Right, quick! Back up to the other side!" he shouted, already bounding up the stairs so fast that Kat had no chance of keeping up with him. By the time she caught him, he was back in the garden shouting Scott's name again, but standing to the side of the gateway. As Kat came through it, he grabbed her arm and hauled her out of the direct line, and not a moment too soon. Out of the blue, a stone came flying out of the gateway and skittered down the gravel path. It was a distinctive one that Drew had picked out, white with pink veins in it and some greenish spots on it, and seeing where it had landed, Kat could see that another one had already come back before it. And now Drew seized them, belted off with them in his hand, and then returned minutes late without them. Only seconds after that, the pink stone reappeared, again coming out of nowhere at speed, and one of the others following it.

"I think he's got the message," Drew said with a grin.

"Thank God for that!" *Who would have thought something as simple as that would work,* Kat thought, torn between amazement and relief.

Yet although they waited and waited, there was no sign of Scott coming back.

"I think we have to recognise that the men in charge might not be letting him move about easily," Kat finally said with a sigh.

"But we need to be here when he does come back," Drew said passionately.

"Yes, we do," Kat said, putting a reassuring hand on his arm. "But that will get easier as the moonrise gets later on in the day. We have to trust that Scott will try if he can. But there'll come a point today when the portal on his side will disappear."

"And when will that be?" Drew demanded.

"Well, maybe into the night," Kat admitted, "or at least that's when the moon will set, but going on when I was here with Scott, I don't think the portal lasts more than a few hours after moonrise."

However Drew was shaking his head. "I'm not leaving here. Not now. Not now that I know he's alive and might need my help." He pulled out his phone. "I'm going to ring and cancel that booking at the hotel for tonight. You can go home if you want to, but I'm not leaving this place."

Kat sighed as he walked away, and then began speaking to the hotel reception. Drew had a change of clothes with him, she didn't. And what was more, there was nothing to eat here. One of them was going to have to leave and get supplies if nothing else, and that looked as though it was going to be her. Worse, she'd promised Rigby she'd take his set of keys back to him this afternoon, and that was something she dared not fail to do. What she didn't want, though, was to leave Drew on his own for long, or at least not yet, not until he'd calmed down a bit.

So when he walked back to her, she said, "Look, I get that you don't want to leave, and of the two of us, you're going to have more success at calling to him. So why don't I go and get us some food and take Rigby his keys back? You must be starving by now," and as if to prove her point, once reminded, his stomach began growling hollowly. "I only need to go into Hereford, not all the way back to Worcester. There are plenty of small stores on the outskirts where I can pick up stuff to see us overnight. Then first thing, before the portal opens up again, I'll go home and get some spare clothes and some more supplies."

She saw him blink in surprise but then nod his agreement. That was great, at least he wasn't fighting her over that.

"There's still furniture in the cottage Scott was using," she added, "and as far as I know, there are two beds there that we can use." She didn't want to add that she'd be bringing stuff to wipe the place down with back with her. If the worst came to the worst and they didn't get Scott back this month, then the one thing they mustn't do would be to leave their fingerprints all over the cottage for Rigby to find. What she wasn't expecting was for Drew to say,

"Get some jacket potatoes then, and some burgers and sausages. I can get a bonfire going and we can cook them up out here while we keep watch."

"Drew, no! We can't do that. Or at least not the cooking outside bit. A bonfire to keep warm by we might just get away with, but Rigby's not an idiot. He'll have us both hauled away for questioning if he comes here and finds too much evidence of interference. Please, think about this! I nicked the main key ring for the house, but I've still got to take the keys I got off him back tonight or he'll come looking. And even so, he might send someone out to make sure I've locked the place up securely. We have to be careful! You believe me now, but how would we ever explain this to the police?"

Her words gradually sunk in, and he nodded wearily. "Okay, get what you think best. Sorry… I just got carried away at the thought of rescuing Scott."

"And there's nothing wrong with that," Kat consoled him. "We just have to do it in a way that doesn't have Rigby thinking we've both been at the remains of Ryan's weed."

That made Drew laugh. "Point taken."

"I tell you what, why don't you come with me to the cottage? If Scott was as organised as you describe him, I bet he had some kind of portable heater with him. If it's one of those things that run off bottled gas, there's no reason why we can't use that outside. All we'll need to do is make sure we hide it away during the day. I suspect tomorrow is going to be the one where we have to be most careful. If we can get away with it that far, then we can stay as long as necessary."

That convinced Drew, and together they went around to the cottage at the back of the house. As Kat has suspected, in the cottage's utility room, they found a portable heater, and also a couple of paraffin lamps, but then Drew surprised her by asking,

"What about the stables' cottages? Is there anything in there?"

"I have a feeling there were a couple of beds left in there. Why?"

"Well if we're being sneaky, it's going to be a lot easier to hide away in those when they don't have any windows onto the courtyard beyond the old doorways. And also, I'd feel a lot better if we could camp out in the one nearest the gateway. That way, if Scott does stumble through when we're not expecting him to, we're more likely to hear him."

Kat didn't want to burst Drew's bubble of hope by saying that by about six o'clock the chances were that the portal would have shut up again, but his point about staying hidden more easily was a good one. And so she helped him to carry stuff across to the cottages, and to also find the fuse box which turned the electricity back on to the two cottages. Then leaving him sitting out on the patio on one of the garden chairs, watching the path from the gateway, Kat drove off in search of food.

Chapter 16

At a local convenience store, Kat picked up plenty of microwavable food since that would be easiest to heat up, but also, they could take the containers away with them, and she added bin bags to her shopping for that. Things like pieces of proper meat would take more cooking, and they wouldn't be able to disguise a hot oven if they had to leave in a hurry. It meant eating the kind of cheap food she normally avoided like the plague – microwaveable bacon rolls for breakfast didn't thrill her, but would be better than nothing.

Had she known it, she was shopping at the same store that Scott had used, and remembering Drew's hip flask, she looked at the shelf behind the cash desk and bought a bottle of the same single malt for Drew, plus a couple of cans of ready-mixed gin and tonics for herself, and then thought to add a couple of bottles of red wine, too. If Drew preferred white that was too bad, but she'd tried to cover all options. Tomorrow, after she had been home and changed, she would go to somewhere where there was a better selection of food and stock up, but for tonight these would have to do. A couple of plates and knives and forks liberated from the main cottage might serve for now, but if possible Kat was hoping that they would be able to eat out of the dishes the meals came in, thereby saving on the need to heat water up to wash up with.

With her supplies carefully stashed out of sight in her boot, she then drove to the police station, surprised to find Rigby waiting for her.

"How did it go?" he asked. "You look a bit dishevelled."

Kat instantly decided to keep to as close to the truth as possible. "Oh my God, that Drew Treadwell is a one man whirlwind! Honestly, I'm knackered from just trying to keep up with him."

"Oh? Not some older bloke then?"

Kat shook her head. "No, nothing like I was expecting. I think he probably plays every sport going and does marathons over the Yorkshire Dales for a bit of fun at the weekends. Considering he must have got up about five o'clock this morning, I don't know where he still has the energy coming from. I'm beat!"

Rigby laughed. "So has he agreed to your plans?"

"In principle," Kat said cheerfully, and hoping she wasn't showing her dismay at the fact that Rigby had just put the keys into his pocket, not over the desk for safe keeping. "We've still got a few details to iron out about the use of a couple of the rooms, but I'll keep you informed if we find a tradesman who can start fairly soon."

"Great, well I'll let you get off. Have a good weekend, Miss Newsome," although he put a strange emphasis on her surname.

"And you," and Kat managed a casual stroll out of the station, and even kept her cool as she walked off down the road. What had that been all about? Had he been digging into her past? Please God not that, not now when she needed to get Scott home safely.

Then looking back at the station under the pretext of crossing the road, she was horrified to see Rigby come out and get into a car which he'd obviously pulled around ready to leave in. As he drove past her, she had a terrible premonition that he was going out to the house to check that she'd locked up properly. And so once he was out of view, she frantically dialled Drew's mobile number.

"Come on, answer, for God's sake!" she muttered as it rang out. And when he did finally pick up she cut across him with, "Get out of there! Get out now! Rigby's on his way to the house! He was waiting for me to bring the keys back, and I saw him put them in his pocket and then drive off with them. You've got about ten or fifteen minutes, depending on the city traffic, that's all!"

"Fuck! Why's he doing that?"

"I don't know. Maybe he just wants to make sure his crime scene is secure? But get your bags out of the cottage and hide them somewhere, then make sure the back door is locked on both the house and Scott's cottage, and get yourself out of there. ...Oh, and don't hide in the greenhouses! He'll probably look in there! Now go!"

Feeling her heart racing, Kat now had to decide what to do. She dared not go back too close to the house because there weren't that many places where she could pull in and not be seen. And she knew that her covert skills probably weren't anything like a match for Rigby's observational ones. Probably the best thing to do would be to pull her car into the station car park. That way, if it was spotted she could always say that she'd felt too tired to drive home, and had caught the train. She just hoped that Rigby didn't think her suspect enough to check the CCTV at the station for her boarding a train. Damn it! She'd thought she'd finished with having to sneak around like this years ago, even if it hadn't been the police she'd been hiding from back then.

Yet knowing she had to keep things seemingly convincing, once she'd done that, she went in search of a café where she could sit and while away some time without looking suspect. Luckily she found a pub with a smoking area outside, and settled down with an orange juice and lemonade to wait, hoping against hope that she would spot Rigby's car if he came back into Hereford this way. Otherwise, all she could do was pray that Drew got clear in time, and then would ring her when the coast was clear. Failing that, at some point she'd have to take a chance and go back to the house in the hope that he'd gone. Even her keys were with Drew, and she didn't fancy the idea of sliding down the coal chute into that cellar in the dark just to get back into the house, if Drew had got hauled away by

Rigby – although such a visit would be very much in the future in that case, because if Rigby started questioning Drew, he'd certainly be calling her back to the station. That made her shudder; she'd had enough of police stations for one lifetime even if none of it had been her fault.

* * * * *

At the house, Drew sprang into action. Luckily he hadn't got around to unpacking his overnight bag yet, and the blankets they'd brought over from what he thought of as Scott's cottage were still neatly folded on the two beds. So shoving those under the beds out of sight, he grabbed his two bags and went outside, casting about for somewhere to hide them.

Then he saw it, a section of the old walled garden on the wood's side where a tree had come down and broken the top of the wall in the process. Some of the rubble would make that an easy climb, and so he ran over to it and dumped the bags behind the remains of a large old cold-frame nearby. Running back to the cottage, he slipped out of its front door, locked the two back doors and then relocked the garden cottage door from the inside, and not a moment too soon. He'd just got out of the patio door and was locking it when he heard the distant sound of a car engine struggling up the rough drive.

Bloody hell, Kat was right! he thought as he sprinted for the fallen wall. *Rigby's come to check on us! Good job she was on the ball and realised what he might be up to or I'd really be in the shit. I know I wanted out of the law, but getting arrested wasn't part of the plan. ....And why has he come? Is he that suspicious of Kat? Or of us? Or is it that it's the weekend and he just wants to make sure that the place is secure in case any of the local kids come exploring?*

Whatever the reasons, he'd only just grabbed his bags once more, thrown them over the wall, and then got over the top of the wall himself before the car engine suddenly came louder and then stopped, the next sound being of its door being shut. Listening hard, he thought he heard what was probably the front door of the house being slammed shut, then remembered that Kat had said that on Rigby's key ring, there wasn't a key to the laundry room door or the French windows. So Rigby would have to walk around the outside to check on the stable cottages, and that made him appreciate all the more Kat's words about not having any bonfires. What an idiot he'd nearly been! If it had been left to him he'd really be in the shit by now.

But what was Rigby going to do? Would he go and look in the cellars? Drew looked at his watch. It was already five o'clock. So had the portal closed like Kat suggested? Damn! Had they left the cellar stairs door open? That would be a terrible giveaway. But then he remembered how careful Kat had been to always close that door, telling him the last time that she had done something to it, and that as long as it stayed closed, she believed that nothing of the portal would leak out that way. Well whether that was true or not, her caution was going to be the saving of them in that sense.

Yet was he safe here? Just how much of an eager beaver was Rigby? And thinking of that, Drew realised that he could see the back top windows of the house from here, and if he could see them, then someone up there might well see him. Thank heavens he'd worn this green sweater, because its muted colour blended in with the undergrowth, but it might be as well to get around the outer corner of the garden wall and well out of sight.

Luckily last year's dead undergrowth at the moment had been flattened by the winter' heavy rain, so he wasn't going to leave as visible a trail as if he'd had to forge through fresh growth, and he looked up, then with his bags in his hands, made a quick dash for the corner. He was very glad he'd done that moments later, when he heard a sash window being opened. Bloody hell, that had been too close for comfort too!

Risking a peek around the corner from crouched down low behind the skeleton stalks of last year's rampant willow-herb, Drew saw a figure at the top end window leaning out and looking around. *I suppose it makes sense,* he thought as he eased back and leaned against the bricks. *If he wants to get a quick overview, that's one of the best places to do it from. Hopefully it'll mean he doesn't come into the garden.*

Yet he waited and waited for what seemed like forever. He heard another window opening and then closing minutes late, so guessed that Rigby had gone to another viewpoint. Then there was briefly the sound of what he thought might have been the front door shutting, but the car didn't start up, and so Drew stayed put. Suddenly realising that if Kat phoned him, the ringtone would give him away, Drew quickly put it on to silent with just the vibrate to alert him, and not a moment too soon. Just as he was sliding the phone back into his pocket, he heard the distinctive sound of footsteps on the gravel paths. Had he left the large stones lying around? No, he'd put those down on the patio, but then there was an artistic heap of cobbles in a little water feature in the corner, so hopefully, if Rigby noticed them, he'd think they'd just been disturbed and rolled from there.

The other thing he didn't know whether to pray for or not was if Scott suddenly appeared now. In one way, Scott stumbling out of the past to be discovered by the very copper who was coordinating the hunt for him down here might be a good thing. No awkward questions for Drew or Kat about where they'd found him. But on the other hand, Drew thought Scott deserved to have the chance to catch his breath and prepare a story before he got the inevitable grilling from the police, because nothing about his reappearance was going to be normal.

The footsteps came right around the garden, indicating that Rigby was walking the perimeter path. Good job, then, that Drew hadn't thought leaving his bags behind the cold-frame would be sufficient to hide them. *Damn, I'm no good at this sneaking around,* Drew thought ruefully. *I suppose one good thing about Kat having to be careful who she tells about all that woo-woo stuff is that she thinks a lot more of how things will appear to people. She obviously believes all this guff that her grandparents told her, and to be fair, if she's seen more of this weirdness like what's down in the cellar, she might even be justified in that. And she does seem awfully pragmatic about it all. Not what I expected someone like that to be, not even remotely. So I suppose if her grandparents were as down-to-earth and sensible, it's not surprising that she believed them.*

Then with Rigby's footsteps having gone from the garden, but with the car still not having started up, Drew mentally fumed, *What's the matter with the bloody man? Hasn't he got a home to go to? For the love of God, it's Friday night! If he's not on duty, why isn't he down the pub with his mates, or watching the telly with his missus? …Ah! At last!* The car engine turned over, and Drew heard it starting off down the drive. But even so, he erred on the side of caution. Rigby might be sneaky enough to drive down a way and then walk back if his instincts were telling him that somebody was about. And so Drew fought his way through the dead undergrowth along the far wall of the garden, and began making his way along the side nearest to the drive. This was a lot easier, because this side of the garden wall had been used to train ornamental plants up against, and so there were some huge old camellias along this stretch, their branches heavy with flowers just at the moment so that they drooped down low, affording plenty of cover and deep shade beneath them.

When he'd got as far forwards as he dared, Drew squatted down behind the dead fronds of a huge old fern and listened. Yes! He could still hear the car making its way down to the road.

That was one blessing of it being so very quiet out here and the drive being so rough, he could hear everything. If they'd been a bit closer to civilisation, the sounds of other cars would have made this impossible, but even the drive only came out onto a little used country lane. He hung on even so, wary of Rigby maybe coming back for another lap of the drive, even if he didn't go into the house, but thankfully the detective seemed to have satisfied himself that nothing was going on at the house and left.

Breathing a sigh of relief, Drew pulled his phone out and called Kat.

"All clear, you can come back now," he told her.

"Did he search the place?"

"Yes, he bloody-well did! Thank God you warned me, because I'd have been well and truly caught otherwise."

"Okay, I'll be back in about half an hour. I want to give Rigby time to get off the roads to the village as well. He has to think I'm headed back to Worcester by now. It's a good thing I only gave him my mobile number and I don't have a landline in my house. He won't bother with my office, hopefully, because he'll know I'm not there over the weekend, but I'd better sound as though I'm at home with my feet up if he rings later on."

Drew sighed. "You're way better at this than me. I'd not got that far, either – about the lanes leading to here, I mean. I hadn't thought about him driving past you coming this way. So yes, give him plenty of time to get away from the area."

"I had got some microwave meals, but there's a chippy along the way. Do you fancy fish and chips?"

"Fancy them? I could mangle the biggest portions they do!" and he heard Kat laugh on the other end of the phone.

"Okay, one deep-fried whale and a sack of chipped spuds coming up, then."

"Cheeky bugger! But yes! The bigger the better!"

By the time Kat pulled up with the fish and chips, Drew had got his bags back into the cottage and had put the electric fire on to warm the place up. Now that the sun had gone down it was remarkably chilly, which he'd not expected this much farther south than his native Yorkshire. And so they sat in the two armchairs on either side of the fire, eating the food out of the paper, and drinking the wine out of mugs.

Suddenly he laughed, making Kat look up quizzically.

"Sorry," he said with a grin, "but why is it that fish and chips out of the paper always tastes so much better? I know it's only psychological, but that's just taken me back to being a kid and being allowed fish and chips when I was away on a camping trip with the scouts."

"Didn't you have fish and chips at home?"

Drew shook his head. "*Tsk!* No, far too common for my parents. What would the neighbours have said if they'd got a strong whiff of salt and vinegar coming over the garden fence? ...Not that we had any neighbours that close, but even the bin men looking askance would have been the social gaff of the century."

"Gosh, you did have a deprived childhood," Kat said sympathetically. "Fish and chips were a treat when I was living with my grandparents, but I'm talking about once a month or so, not once or twice in my entire childhood."

"That's what Scott said when I first told him. After that, if he was stopping with me, he'd turn up every so often with a couple of packets from the local chippy. I think he missed having them, to be frank, because Flora and Charlie were as pretentious as my folks were."

"Well then when we've got Scott back, we'll have to go and do what I did with Papa and Grandma."

"Oh? What's that?"

"A day trip down to the north Somerset coast. It's not that far. We used to go down there, and then go and get fish and chips, and a big bottle of Vimto or Coca Cola, and then we'd go and sit on Dunster beach to eat and watch the stars coming out. If it got a bit cold, Papa would build a driftwood fire, and then we'd sit around telling stories until we fell asleep – or they would ...the story-telling bit, I mean."

"God, that sounds magical."

"It was. That was when Papa would tell me the old legends of the stars, and if it was warm enough to sit out without a fire, and we kept really still, there might be a seal come up on the beach, or a deer come down on it. If it was a deer, in the morning, Papa would get me to track it back as far as I could. Usually that ended when we got to an electrified cattle fence. The deer could jump it, especially if it was one of the big red deer stags that had come down off the moor, but of course we couldn't."

Drew sat staring at her in amazement. "I've never met anyone whose childhood was like that. No wonder you could believe in magical stuff, you had a head start on the rest of us."

Kat laughed. "Oh yes! I wish you could have met Papa. He never lost his sense of wonder at the natural world. Despite having had quite a hard life, especially his childhood in Russia and then early on when he first arrived here, he never got embittered or soured by the world. I think that's such a blessing." And she found herself thinking, *yes, and I wish you could have met Papa for other reasons too. I'd love to know what he thought of you, and whether he thought I was right to be so attracted to you. You seem such a nice guy, but the more you talk about your past, I'm wondering whether you're really strong enough to cope with the whole truth about mine.*

However, Drew was already changing the subject, saying, "I think it might not be a bad idea if we used the shower here tonight rather than in the morning. That would mean we were up and ready to make a run for it in case Rigby rolls up again tomorrow."

"Do you think he will?"

"I don't know, but he was being very thorough today. I'd rather him not see anything like soapsuds in the drains if he comes around, and I think he's sharp enough to notice."

"I'd agree. And in the light of that, how do you feel about making one last trip across to the cellar now? Would it set your mind at rest that the portal doesn't last long if you see it all quiet now? Only I think it might not be a bad idea if you come back to Worcester with me tomorrow morning, and we leave the place genuinely empty for a while. When we come back, if I put my hiking shoes on, we can leave my car somewhere farther away and walk up. That way, if Rigby is here, we can dive into the bushes out of sight much more easily."

"I think that's a good plan," Drew agreed, still slightly disconcerted by Kat's familiarity with sneaking around.

And so, armed with the flashlights from Kat's car, they went across. However, the portal was now totally dark. Moreover, the dreadful smell had completely gone from by the dumb waiter.

"Do you know," Kat said thoughtfully, "I think that dreadful stench might be an indicator that the portal is about to open. It certainly got less the later it got. And each day that goes by, the portal will open a good hour later. So tomorrow we've got the whole of the morning before Scott would have any chance of coming through. Does that make you feel any better about leaving here for a while?"

"Yes it does," Drew replied as he locked up after them. "I tell you what, though, I'm going to use that time to ring my secretary at home, and ask her to clear my appointments for next week. Not that I had that many, but I'm not going back until I know Scott is safe. Thank goodness I got rid of the old harridan my father had as his secretary! She'd have been down to the nursing home and telling him that I was skiving off the moment I put the phone down!"

"Gosh, he kept you on that tight a leash?" Kat asked, feeling increasingly sorry for Drew, but also a twinge of alarm that he'd not had the strength of will to break free of this domineering parent.

"Too right he did. He hardly ever took a holiday himself, so he couldn't see why anyone else would want to. That was one of the attractions of playing sports for me – if we had an away match, I could legitimately ask to leave early to travel to a game, and he allowed that because otherwise I was letting other people down. I tell you, if ever I have kids, I am *never* going to be like him!"

Don't worry, you won't get the chance to, Kat found herself thinking, then was glad Drew couldn't see her blush in the dark. Where the heck had that thought come from? She'd only known Drew for a day and her subconscious was planning on a family with him? *Down girl!* she told herself sternly, *Good grief! Get those hormones under control! You've got some serious baggage and so, by the sounds of it, does he, and that might scupper any relationship before it's even had a chance.* But at the same time thinking, *It's not just my hormones that need a slap. I wish his bloody pheromones would give me a break too!*

Chapter 17

It was a weird sensation going to bed with somebody else in the same house, and although Kat could soon hear Drew's soft snores coming from the other bedroom across the galleried landing, it took her a while to get off to sleep herself. Part of that was the feeling of disconcertion which she couldn't shake off at the depth of her attraction to Drew. And that was all the odder since he wasn't the kind of man she was normally attracted to. Her type, as she would have told her female friends upon due consideration, was definitely the quieter, more cerebral sort, and not such an obvious sportsman. She also needed someone who would be prepared to keep quiet about things, and Drew struck her as the scrupulously honest type who might be a stickler for the truth at all times. Yet somehow, Drew Treadwell had got under her skin in a big way, and she wasn't quite sure how she felt about that.

When she woke up, it was because she could hear someone whistling rather tunelessly down below in the kitchen, and for a moment she struggled to remember where she was and who that might be. Then when reality kicked in, she found herself scrambling to try and find a hairbrush so that at least she wouldn't end up going downstairs looking like Cousin It from the Addams Family.

God in heaven, look at you! she found herself thinking in despair, as she scrutinised herself in the tiny mirror still nailed to one of the exposed beams in the bedrooms. *When did you ever get into such a tizzy over some bloke seeing you less than perfect? For pity's sake, get a grip, Kat! You've got your mum and dad to think about, because it's not just your secret to tell him, so don't go making these foolish plans …yet!*

Having tamed her pillow-ruffled hair into something resembling decency, she went downstairs to find that Drew had already found a teapot and had a brew on the go.

"That's a welcome sight," Kat sighed, gladly taking a mug-full off him and adding a splash of the milk she'd bought. "I'm no use to man nor beast until I've had my first cuppa."

"Not a morning person, then?" Drew teased.

"God, no! A thorough night-owl, me!"

"Tut! I'd have been up and going for a run an hour ago on a lovely morning like this."

"A run?" She stared in horror at her watch. "It's not even eight o'clock yet!"

"Well it's not like I've had much in the way of an incentive to stay in bed," he riposted, then turned bright red as it dawned on him what he'd said. Quickly turning back to the kitchen counter he asked, "Any preference on which of these delicacies you have for breakfast?"

Kat laughed. "No, I can cope with any. You choose what you want and I'll have what's left. I just saw how you fell on your breakfast yesterday and thought I'd better bring something to hold body and soul together until I could get something better." Then thought, *Thank heavens it's not just me, then. He's feeling this strange attraction between us too. ...It's actually rather reassuring that he's turned such a lovely shade of red. Makes him seem less of the habitual Casanova.*

With breakfast out of the way, they piled into Kat's car and she drove back to Worcester. For a fair bit of the journey, Drew was on the phone, thereby avoiding the need for any awkward conversations, and by the time she had pulled up outside of her house, the strangeness of the morning conversation had passed.

"That's next week organised," Drew told her with a sigh of relief. "I feel I can focus on Scott now without any worries."

What he was less prepared for was for her to have a large sleeping bag of good quality, which she hauled out of the top of the capacious cupboard which lay under the stairs.

"Here, that should be fine for you," she said, then pulling out something far more homemade and ethnic looking.

"Whatever is that?"

"This? It's the sleeping bag Papa made for Grandma. Honestly, Drew, it's really warm and comfortable."

"So why have you got this one, then?"

"Ah ...You remember I told you about the Italian who taught me about good coffee? Well he was my boyfriend."

"Was?"

"Oh yes! I haven't seen or heard from him in years! He's back in Catania in Sicily, teaching in one of the local primary schools – or at least he was the last time I saw him, when I got an invitation to go over to his wedding."

"And you were okay with that?" Drew asked warily.

"Oh my God, yes! We were just kids when we got together. In uni', I was one of the few who understood what an Italian family might truly be like. You know, all the family obligations and the like. But after we'd graduated, it became clear that we didn't really have that much in common, aside from being the odd ones out amongst the rest of the students. We went our separate ways very amicably, and now he has a lovely wife and three kids who send me photos every Christmas."

"Oh …right…"

Clearly Drew hadn't ever come across someone who'd had quite such a peaceable break up before. And in a way, that made Kat sad on his behalf. What had his life been like that he expected stress at every turn? Or was it she who had been unusually lucky despite her mum and dad's problems? It sounded as though, like Scott, Drew was due a substantial dose of good luck to redress the balance, and with that in mind, Kat quietly slid several of her considerable supply of small candles into the bag she was packing. A few candles with some essential oils in them at full moon wouldn't do any harm, she decided, and if Grandma Valerie was right, might even do some good.

What she also had were some Ordnance Survey maps of the local areas, and she fished out the right one for Fownhope Priors.

"Before we go," she suggested, "why don't we have a look and see if there's another way we can get to the house on foot? It would be good if we can find somewhere that's not right on the drive to leave my car out of sight."

She spread the map out on her lounge floor, and they both looked at it carefully.

"Well those black lines have to be the drive up to the house, and those squares must be the house itself and the stable block, plus the bits and pieces of the garden," Kat declared, "though it's not marked as anywhere of consequence on the map."

"But isn't that an Iron Age camp, or at least a fortification, up on the top of the hill within the wood?" Drew observed. "I know my map reading skills are a bit rusty, but that's what those dashed lines mean, don't they?"

"Yes, they do, and that makes a bit more sense of things. It was probably always regarded as a special place, even in prehistory. If it then got seriously disrupted by the building of the house, that might explain why the portal appeared, though I have to say I've never heard of anything like that happening elsewhere."

"So can we get to the house from the other side of this hill?" Drew wondered. "I can see footpaths, but nothing that looks like we might get a car up it."

"No," agreed Kat, "nothing we could drive up from that side. But look at the road the drive goes off. There's that viewpoint a bit further on. I wonder if there's room there where we could pull the car in and hide it from sight? It can't be more than half a mile from the house as the crow flies, and even if it's two or three times that on the ground, it's still not an arduous walk."

"Let's try for the viewpoint, then," Drew agreed, and loading up the car, they set out for Hereford once more.

This time, however, they made a point of stopping at a major supermarket along the way and getting a good supply of food in. They had also brought along Kat's Moka stove-top coffee maker and coffee, and other equipment that they could then take away with them later. That way they wouldn't be leaving quite such a conspicuous trail behind them.

They drove through Fownhope village itself, instead of taking the direct turn off for the house, and carried on to turn down a small road towards the church at Brockhampton.

"I must admit to being curious about this place," Kat admitted. "There's a Brockhampton Estate that's owned by the National Trust, but this isn't it. That's closer to Bromyard. What *is* here is an amazing Arts & Crafts Movement church."

"Really?" Immediately she had Drew's attention. "I thought all the churches around here would be really old?"

"Well you'd think that wouldn't you? And in the main you'd be right. That's why I find this Brockhampton so curious. I looked it up while you were fighting the sleeping bag into its bag, expecting it to be twelfth or thirteenth century, but it said that it was built in 1902. So that's after our house. But the people who commissioned it were another nouveau rich family, this time with American connections. They had taken on another estate that was pretty close to derelict, by the sound of it, and that makes Fownhope Priors far less of an oddity at the time. In fact it was almost normal for these up and coming families to find old estates which had fallen into disrepair due to lack of funds, and to buy them and do them up. It gave them a kind of *faux* respectability, if you like."

At the church, Drew had to get out and have a look around, but in the end he didn't linger long.

"Beautiful though it is, it doesn't have the atmosphere of a really old place," he said with a disappointed sigh as they got back into the car. "I can truly admire the artistry of those turn of the century craftsmen, but their work doesn't tug at me the way something genuinely old does."

That statement did nothing for Kat's inner turmoil, because it told her that even if Drew didn't recognise it as yet, he had a natural feeling for the old which she could teach him to tap into. He was closer to her way of looking at things than he might realise at the moment. For now, though, she simply handed over the map and asked him to tell her when she was close to the viewpoint.

In the end they found that the viewpoint wouldn't be suitable to leave the car at, but a bit farther on they saw an old gateway almost by the turn to the drive. It looked as though it hadn't been used in years, because the gate itself was barely hanging together. Yet a bit of careful lifting by Drew got it open, and Kat was able to ease the VW in through the gap, and then turn it so that it was parked alongside the hedge under the shade of the woods which the gateway led into.

"We'll leave all the bags and stuff here," Kat decided. "There's no point in lugging it all with us when we can drive up if the coast is clear."

"Dare we walk up the drive?" Drew wondered, but Kat had already turned into the trees.

"Why bother? The drive does a loop around the slope of the hill to avoid it being too steep. They must have made that back in the days when carriages had to get up it. But we've only a short sharp climb here, and then we should be at the other edge of the wood looking down at the garden. I know the wood is fatter farther west, but here it's quite thin according to the map. Come on!"

Given that she had the map, Drew couldn't argue with her. He just hoped that her map reading skills were as good as she thought they were, or they could be fighting the undergrowth for a long way. So he was pleasantly surprised when after only five minutes he could start to see the trees thinning out ahead. What he was rather more shocked at was seeing Kat produce a pair of wire cutters from her pocket.

"Kat? What are you doing?"

She turned back to him in surprise. "Didn't you see the height of the fence around the estate when we were in the garden? It's one of those square construction ones meant to keep deer out, so it's far too high to step over, and it won't be strong enough to climb. Blimey, Drew, I'm not going to cut it to ribbons, just snip a few strands so that we can slide through!"

"Oh."

Kat inwardly groaned as she saw the worry on his face. So this was when the solicitor part of him came to the fore. Not ideal timing, but it could be worse.

"Drew, we need to see if Rigby is there, don't we? We can't see the drive from up here, so we've got to get down somewhere where we can go and hide if he is. How else do we explain why we're back there when – as far as he knows – we don't have a key to the place?"

"Looking around the garden again?" Drew said faintly, but obviously knowing what a daft thing that was to say even as the words were coming out.

"I'll twist the strands back together once we're through," Kat said as she turned and pushed through the last of the undergrowth to reveal the fence, and wishing that she'd managed to keep the exasperation out of her voice more. "Don't worry, the deer won't shove their way through this little gap."

The fence was exactly as she'd described, and Drew realised that one of the things which kept wrong-footing him with Kat was her acute observations of the natural world. He was used to being outdoors up on the moors or dales, and thought of himself as quite the outdoors man, so his pride was a little dented at finding that this young woman could read signs he didn't even notice were there. She also snipped the stiff wire with ease, releasing just enough of the fence so that she could slide through. When Drew tried to follow, she had to cut two more strands to allow his bulk through, but then was as good as her word in pulling the strands back and making at least one twist in the wire to hold it, for which he noticed she'd also had the foresight to bring a pair of pliers.

"You're a regular little burglar," he teased, then was shocked at the way she whipped around to glower at him. Why had that made her so angry? And she was suddenly very angry, of that he was sure.

What they might have said next, however, was overtaken by him taking a step forward and hearing something going crunch under his foot. Whatever it was, it certainly wasn't just some twig snapping, and he looked down to see what it was.

"Fucking hell!" he yelped, making Kat turn back to him demanding impatiently,

"Now what?"

"Look!" and he pointed shakily to the ground. There, exposed by his foot nudging it, was the skeletal remains of a human hand.

"Oh bollocks," Kat sighed. "I've a nasty feeling we've just discovered Josh. He must have known this was the short cut to the road, but perhaps the fence wasn't here when he left?" She turned and looked at it again. "This section is certainly clean and fairly new. Maybe the nursing home had it put in after he and Ryan left? Wouldn't have done to have deer coming down and raiding the veg' patch."

"Never mind that!" Drew spluttered. "We've got to call the police!" He used his foot to nudge a bit more of the fallen leaves away and winced as he saw that the hand was still attached to the bones of an arm. He looked at Kat standing calmly to one side. "What's the matter with you? This is a dead body! We *have* to report it!"

"Yes we do," Kat replied evenly, "but think for a moment, Drew. If we do that, we can hardly keep coming back here for Scott, can we? The moment you ring that in, there'll be coppers all over the place. The house and the grounds will be crawling with them, because by finding Josh's body we'll be giving Rigby a good reason to order a much more comprehensive search for Scott as well."

To her horror, Drew was already shaking his head and backing away as he fished in his pocket for his phone.

"Drew! For God's sake! Think of Scott! He's still alive, whereas Josh has been dead for two years already. Things can't get any worse for him than they are, but they could for Scott!"

But she could see it was no use. Confronted with the reality of Josh's death, Drew's belief in what he'd seen yesterday was crumbling to dust. She'd seen it happen all too often before. When Papa Viktor and Grandma Valerie had cleansed a house next door to where they'd been stopping on holiday the one year, only two days later the couple were telling everyone that it had just been the old plumbing making noises and that they'd got it fixed now. Quite how the plumbing could have been responsible for pictures being torn off the walls and thrown across the room, or for rugs being rucked up and then spoiled with raw sewage far from the bathroom, was something Kat found harder to believe than the disturbed entity which had been unable to leave the house, and which her grandparents had put to rest. But that hadn't been how the owners had recalled things the moment it had all been resolved, and it looked as though Drew was another such as them.

"You'll always be on the outside," Grandma Valerie had told her sadly when she'd been indignant that the couple hadn't even said thank you properly, "but you have to make the choice: fit in and deny what you are and what you can do. Or be true to yourself and accept that very few people will be able to cope with seeing the real you."

And now she was seeing it again in Drew's expression. He was already doubting her, that much was obvious, and Kat found herself not wanting to hear how he was explaining away the blue light, or the way the stones had been thrown back at him yesterday. It was too painful when she'd thought she might just have found someone special. And there he was, dialling on his phone before she'd had the chance to dissuade him any further as if he'd not even heard or respected her reasoning. So as she heard him asking for the police and then starting to describe what they'd found, she turned back to the fence and began untwisting the wires so that she could get back through. Thank God she'd put her gardening gloves on against being cut by the wire, so there'd be nothing but traces of soil and plants on the wire for the police to find.

"Where are you going?" she heard Drew say in horrified tones as turned back to her while she was twisting the wires back together on the other side.

"Covering your arse, genius!" she snapped. "One of us has got to go and bring my car up here now ...*haven't I!* Because unless you want your reputation sullied even further, you don't want to be telling Rigby that we've been sneaking into the place by the back way to avoid him. You're going to have to hope now that he buys your story about us coming to have another look at the garden. I'd go with us coming up here to get a better view of the grounds in the light of thinking to put a golf course in, but then I'm not the bloody solicitor here, am I? You'd know better what will stick with the coppers," and with that parting shot, she turned on her heels and ran.

She didn't want him to see the tears streaming down her face, didn't want to have to explain her complicated past to him right now. But when she'd got her car out from behind the gate, with much struggling and swearing, and had pulled it round and up the drive, she got out and made a phone call of her own.

"You aren't going to believe this," she said. "I'm so sorry, DI Scathlock, but I'm going to have to ask for your help again. You were good enough to keep things quiet over Peter, but I've gone and fallen into something even worse, and I'm going to need rescuing from your colleagues in Hereford."

Chapter 18

Kat had managed to splash some water onto her face and calm down a bit by the time she heard the police coming, and forced herself to get out of the car and walk over to where she could see Drew standing dejectedly in the courtyard. He'd obviously found the path she'd already seen coming down to the garden, which must have been cut into the bank by the original gardeners so that they could get up to keep the wilderness at bay. In fact it was probably how Josh had got up there too, because to Kat's eyes, there wasn't more than a couple of years of unchecked growth on the bank – there weren't any saplings making a bid to colonise it, for a start off, and left much longer they would have.

"Mr Treadwell, nice to meet you at last," said Rigby as he led his men across to them. "Miss Newsome," and his nod to her was considerably cooler than before.

Oh Christ, he's looked me up and started digging, Kat thought miserably. *And he's going to start making the same wrong assumptions the first detective in Worcester did until Bill Scathlock stepped in. Why did my dad have to have such a devious bloody family? Why couldn't they have been as law-abiding as Mum's? Papa and Grandma were positively normal by comparison.*

But there was no further time for reflection as Drew began leading Rigby back up the sloping path to where the body was. He was talking as he went, and suddenly exhausted, Kat went and sat on the bench in the courtyard and left them to it. It was only as she heard Rigby calling the forensic team up that she woke up to the fact that she might very well get taken into custody. In which case, she must not have the house keys on her if they asked her to turn out her pockets. Firstly, her taking them would make the situation worse, but secondly, at some point she wanted to be able to come back and rescue Scott. So she got up and stretched, then ambled to the corner of the garden wall, pausing to sniff the scent of the camellia that was growing there. As she reached up to pull a branch towards her, she saw what she was looking for – the stub of a branch where the camellia had been pruned in the past. And so blessing the fact that the keys were in her left pocket, and so on the other side to where Rigby might see, she slipped them out and hooked the large old ring over the spur. Once she'd let go, the riot of heavy, waxy blooms completely obscured the hanging key ring, and she could only hope that all Rigby might do was check to see that she hadn't dropped anything on the ground.

She was still calming herself by admiring the plants and the view when Rigby and Drew came back to her.

"Mr Treadwell is coming to the station to make a full statement," Rigby said a tad too smugly for Kat's liking. Then said what she'd been fearing. "But you Miss Newsome, you haven't exactly been honest with me, have you? Or should I say Miss Robarts?"

"Whaaa...!" she heard Drew gasp.

"It is Newsome," she told Rigby coldly, "and perfectly legally too. I changed my name for reasons you can seemingly guess at."

"Oh I can fill in the gaps quite well enough," Rigby riposted coldly. "But you should have told me about that when I first spoke to you. It would certainly give you more credibility now."

"Credibility?" Kat snapped. "Why would I need more credibility? I've done nothing wrong."

"Nothing wrong?" Rigby parroted. "Your ideas of right and wrong really do need sorting out if you can say that," and as he spoke, Kat could see Drew's expression becoming more and more appalled. "As Caitlyn Robarts you had quite a run doing burglaries to your father's order. Especially the one where you knifed that poor unfortunate shop owner who was just acting as a front for 'Big Alf' Robarts' main rival."

"Kat?" she heard Drew whisper as she turned and walked away with the constable, who was holding on to her arm rather tighter than needed.

But what was the point of arguing here? The more she seemed to protest the less he'd be convinced once they were back at the station, and Kat was just praying that DI Bill Scathlock would be on his way already, because it was going to take a more senior detective than Rigby to convince him that Kat wasn't Caitlyn, and never had been.

It was a frosty journey to Hereford, and Kat was just glad that Drew was taken in a different car. She couldn't have faced his accusing looks, or worse, his questions. Then at the station, while he was treated with civility and respect, she was marched into an interview room and left there with just a WPC watching over her.

Rigby finally came in, dropping a file with various print-outs in it onto the table in front of him with an aggressive thump. Interview rooms were supposed to have been made less threatening in recent years, but Rigby's whole attitude and body language was a massive threat all by itself.

"So, Miss Robarts, what's your interest in Mr Hawkesmoor and Fownhope Priors, eh? Hoping to fleece him of his money, were you? Or was it you who did the deed with Mrs Hawkesmoor's car?"

"Oh for pity's sake!" Kat was stung to snap back. "The Yorkshire police are saying that was an accident! I had nothing to do with that, and good luck trying to pin that on me. I have several contacts who I face-timed from my office with regard to sourcing products for Mr Hawkesmoor – and they know my office well enough to be able to swear I wasn't somewhere else."

"Ah, but the Robarts gang had a lot of contacts, didn't they?" Rigby said nastily. "And even with your daddy banged up inside for the rest of his natural, I'm sure that there are a few of his old mates you could call upon?"

"He's not my 'daddy', and I'm not Caitlyn Robarts."

"Oh come on, Caitlyn. Pull the other one." And Rigby pushed a photograph across the table of a woman who was a dead ringer for Kat. "Are you really going to tell me that that isn't you?"

"No, it isn't me," Kat said firmly.

Then to her intense relief she heard raised voices outside, one of which she recognised as DI Scathlock's. Thank God for that, her saviour had arrived. She heard someone saying,

"Sir! You can't go in there, he's interviewing the suspect!" and Scathlock's far from polite response, before the door was flung open and Scathlock's bulk filled the doorway.

"DS Rigby, a word! *Now!*" Scathlock snapped.

"Who the hell are you to come barging in here?" Rigby demanded, going rather red in the face.

"DI Bill Scathlock, and if you don't want to end your days pounding the pavements in Hereford, I suggest you let Miss Newsome go and pin back your ears. You've got it wrong, Rigby! And what's worse, you've disregarded all the alerts that are on our records about Miss Newsome."

"Don't you mean Caitlyn Robarts?"

"No I sodding well don't! Caitlyn Robarts is another woman altogether. Now stop being an idiot and let her go."

Footsteps came from behind, and then another voice said furiously,

"What the hell is going on here? This is *my* station, I'll have you know!"

Turning on his heels, Bill took the two steps needed to take him to within close range of a furious man who turned out to be the uniformed inspector in charge, and proceeded to speak rapidly but very softly to him, obviously conveying in terse sentences some very pertinent information.

When the inspector winced and said, "Oh bloody hell," Kat saw Rigby begin to lose his smug expression, and when the inspector snapped,

"Rigby, my office, now!" the penny fully dropped that somehow he was in the shit.

"Miss Newsome, would you come too, with DI Scathlock?" the inspector asked more politely.

"Thank you so much," Kat managed to whisper to Bill as he stood aside to allow her to leave the interview room. Then felt much better as he winked at her and said,

"Not a problem, but you do stop my life from getting boring."

In the office and with the door closed, the inspector glared angrily at Rigby.

"I know I'm not your direct superior, but you've dropped this in my lap, and that gives me some authority in the matter! So which part of you decided to ignore all the warnings to leave well alone when Miss Newsome's name came up?" he demanded of the detective sergeant.

"What warnings?" Rigby demanded, but with very little conviction.

Scathlock stepped around to the inspector's side of the desk and asked, "May I, sir?" with a nod to the computer. As another inspector, Bill was of equal rank with the uniformed man, but in reality the two halves of the police didn't trample on one another's territory, and therefore he was being far more courteous than he would have been with Rigby's own detective inspector.

"Be my guest," the inspector said with a wave of his hand, scooting his office chair out of Scathlock's way.

With rapid tapping on the keys, Scathlock was clearly bringing up records for the inspector to see, and the way his expression was becoming more pained as each new one came up, made it only too clear that Rigby must have been ignoring the blindingly obvious.

As Scathlock stepped away from the desk and resumed his seat beside Kat, the inspector said in measured tones, "I know we commend enthusiasm and keenness, Rigby, but we do also expect you to temper that with some common sense, and the wit to know that if there are as many warnings scattered over files as I'm seeing here, then you ought to leave it *bloody well alone!*"

"Sir."

"Don't just 'sir' me, man. What explanation do you have for this?"

"But she's obviously Caitlyn Robarts," Rigby protested bullishly. "There's a longstanding arrest warrant out on her."

"Yes there is," Bill growled, "but there are also warnings all over both her record and the record in the name of Kat Newsome, that this mistake has been made before." He glanced to the uniformed inspector then back at Rigby as he added, "I'm going to tell you this now, in the sanctity of this office, but if so much as a whisper of this gets out, I shall be after you like the wrath of God. Do I make myself clear?"

"Take note, Rigby," the inspector warned, "because I'll be passing this on to your own inspector, too."

Bill cleared his throat. "You are right in that 'Big Alf' Robarts was one of the nastier gangsters in Birmingham in the late sixties and seventies, but what you won't have heard is that he has a brother who's only a year younger than him. But whereas Alf Robarts followed his mum's brother into the family gang which then took his name, *Archie* Robarts wanted nothing to do with them. Now the family wasn't any too pleased with that, especially Alf, and he did everything possible to force Archie to join him. Archie found a way out by joining the army, and that worked at first. But then he came out and got married, and that's when things really started to get bad.

"Now if there's anything swimming around between your ears, you should have guessed by now that it's Archie and his wife who are Kat's parents. Kat's mum's people were living well away from Birmingham, so they never really came within the gang's radar, but Archie and his family had to move around a lot to stay one step ahead of the gang. In the end, Kat got to spend most of her childhood with her maternal grandparents, while Archie and Elena took jobs out in various holiday resorts around the

Mediterranean, just about managing to keep one step ahead of Alf's search for them until one fateful day sixteen years ago. Note that time, Rigby, because you should have recognised it as about the time big Alf got sent down."

Suddenly Rigby's eyes began to widen, and he started to look rather sick.

"Yes, you see it now," Kat said bitterly, wishing she could enjoy this more, but actually just wanting it to be over. "My mum and dad had a scooter that they travelled to the hotel on, on the little Greek island they were working on at the time. Some thug of Alf's spotted them and decided to give chase in his hired car. Unfortunately he clipped the back wheel of the scooter, Mum and Dad went off the road, and Mum got thrown down a ten feet drop onto the rocks on the shore. She's never walked again.

"So that's when I decided enough was enough, and I was old enough to make that decision for myself. I'd heard the family talking over the years, but now I went out and sat my dad down and had a good talk with him. And I got enough out of him to be able to go to the police with. *I'm* the one who got 'Big Alf' sent down. But it also meant that I had to change my name. Luckily, Alf and his dim-wit of a wife had never realised that my proper name is Ekaterina – they thought it was Catherine to copy their Caitlyn, who's just eighteen months older than me. Arrogant bastards. So I've kept my real first name. I just picked Newsome because it was the name of my favourite teacher at school. That's why you couldn't find any link from me to any real Newsomes – I deliberately did that so that there wouldn't be anyone who 'Big Alf' could send someone out to pressure me by threatening.

"My mum and dad lived for a while in the north of Scotland, but then when the cold and damp started to get to Mum, they moved down to the Isles of Scilly – somewhere remote enough, and with a close enough community, that they would get word if anyone ever came looking for them. It's been tough on all of us, because they never got to come and see me graduate, for instance. But 'Big Alf' isn't getting out any time this century – not with five murder convictions hanging over him – and his daughter's been smart enough to leave the country, though where she is now I genuinely have no idea.

"But I'm exactly what I told you I am, DS Rigby. I truly am an interior designer and nothing more than that. And I am still deeply worried over the safety of Scott Hawkesmoor – in fact I hope you can understand why I would be more worried than most people now that you know my story. I always have to have one eye looking over my shoulder, just in case my idiot cousin comes back and starts making trouble for me. She may not know my name these days, but we always looked like twins as little girls, and so she probably has a fair idea of what I look like now. So when Scott vanished so unexpectedly, you ought to be able to understand that there was a little bit of me that was worried it might just be because of Caitlyn. I'm pretty certain now that it's not, if only it's because you've been looking so hard at me, you should have noticed my double wandering around a place as small as Hereford."

Rigby looked glum, knowing that he dropped himself right in the shit, but still had the gall to ask Bill Scathlock,

"So how the hell did you know all of this?"

"Because I read the bloody file, you idiot," Scathlock said with a weary shake of his head. "Kat's had some trouble with a nasty little shit breaking into her work computer, and my DC spotted her file and brought it to me, wondering much the same as you. The difference was, she didn't go in feet first, and we had time to find out the truth and not go flinging accusations around, and drawing attention to Kat that she really doesn't need. Her witness protection needs may no longer warrant her to be in hiding, but that doesn't mean that we want her identity broadcast to all and sundry; and that includes a piece in some local newspaper congratulating a rural DS on being eagle-eyed and apprehending someone he thought was a known big-time villain."

The way Rigby instantly went beetroot red at the mention of newspapers confirmed to everyone else that he'd had visions of being crowned with glory in the local press if nowhere else. The inspector got up, holding out his hand to Kat,

"Miss Newsome, you're free to go, and please accept my sincere apologies for all of this. DI Scathlock, thank you for your prompt intervention. Normally I wouldn't be keen on someone from both another division and CID coming barging into our station unannounced, but you seem to have saved us from having a considerable amount of egg on our faces, so thank you for that. ...Rigby, you stay there, I haven't finished with you, and I'll be back as soon as I've shown these two out!"

The inspector left them at the corridor, but as Bill escorted Kat out, she saw Drew sitting in the outer part of the station, and his expression of surprise as he saw her walking free.

"Would you mind if I went and spoke to him for a second?" Kat asked Scathlock. "I think he's got the wrong impression of me, and I'd like to set the record straight."

"Be my guest," Scathlock said, "I'll wait for you outside and then take you back up to get your car."

Walking over to Drew, Kat sat down on the bench-seat beside him.

"Caitlyn Robarts is my cousin," she said softly. "She and I happen to look alike, and this isn't the first time I've been mistaken for her. Rigby's been warned to keep his mouth shut, and I'm going to have to ask you to keep quiet too. You see, I was the one who turned my uncle in – that's the 'Big Alf' who Rigby mentioned – and because of my testimony in court as to his attempted murder of my parents amongst other things, he's doing life with no hope of parole.

"I wanted to explain that to you because you asked why I was so used to sneaking around, and that's it. After the trial I had to change my name to stay safe, and that's why I was so worried about getting involved with the police again.

Even going into a police station has its risks for me, because although the gang my father's family were involved with were all in Birmingham, it would only take one elderly old conman coming in to bail out his grandson to recognise me, and I could be in serious trouble. That's why I'm good at keeping under the radar – I've had to be – but it's not because I've been doing anything illegal. And my mum's parents really were the Papa Viktor and Grandma Valerie I've talked so much about. They were the ones who brought me up a lot of the time, because Mum and Dad had to keep moving around all over Europe to avoid getting dragged into his brother's gang."

Drew looked at her in shock. "Oh my God, I'm so sorry, Kat. I feel awful now for having doubted you."

She gave a bitter little laugh. "Well if you want a quiet life, I'd suggest you go back to Yorkshire and forget you ever met me, because my life isn't normal and despite my best efforts, it refuses to be quiet."

Chapter 19

On the drive back to Fownhope Priors, Kat told Bill Scathlock as much of the full story as she could, which meant just leaving out the bit about the portal. He'd been good enough to come all this way at speed and at very short notice, and that meant that she felt she owed him that much at the very least. Strangely enough, he was the one person she had ever met who had hinted to her that he might have had an 'unusual' experience himself. It had been when he'd come to her house to talk to her, and the subject of Papa and Grandma had come up. Far from being sniffy about Papa's shaman heritage, Bill had astonished her by wanting to know all about it and taking it seriously, and he had then dropped a hint that he'd had more than one case in the past which had had something about it of what might be called the supernatural.

"Some of my colleagues would be marching me straight off to the police psychiatrist if I told them what I thought had really happened," he'd confessed with a rueful grin. "On the other hand, I wish I'd known your Papa Viktor, because it sounds as though he'd have been able to give me a lot more specialist advice than anyone else I had to call upon at the time."

And so it was as Bill's big Subaru took the lumps and bumps of the drive far more in its stride than Kat's VW that he said, "So what do you think has really happened to Scott Hawkesmoor?" and Kat felt able to reply,

"I can't say outright just at the moment. But do you recall our conversation about Papa Viktor?"

"Clearly."

"Then would you accept for now that I'm wishing that I had him here to consult with?"

"Oh, I see. Okay, so by that I'm guessing that it's something that would have Rigby laughing like a drain in his ignorance?"

Impulsively Kat reached across and squeezed Bill's hand. "You're a very special person, do you know that? And I'm not just throwing that in as a random compliment. You're one of the rare people who goes through the world with your eyes properly open. ...And I also appreciate your tactfulness, but yes, Rigby would probably have me dragged off to the nearest psychiatric ward if I told him the truth."

"Do you need any help?" and Kat knew that he meant something beyond his normal police work.

"Not at the moment, but thank you for the offer. I think I have everything in hand as long as your forensic people don't hang around the house too long. Let's just say that there's a time element to getting a really successful conclusion to this."

Bill gave her a sideways glance and a half smile. "Anything to do with the coming full moon by any chance?"

"Everything!" Kat said with a nervous laugh of relief at finding someone who truly got the picture.

"Fine. Well I'll make sure that I keep Tuesday night free, so if you need me, give me a call."

"I certainly will," Kat promised, not least because she knew he meant it. Someone who already knew when the full moon was without having to look it up was clearly no amateur in such things.

By now they had pulled up on the drive outside of the house, and they could see that Kat's car was blocked in by both the forensics team and the pathologist.

"Oh dear, I'm not going to get to move that any time soon," Kat sighed.

"I tell you what," Bill said, getting out of the car, "the pathologist is an old pal of mine. I'll go and have a chat to her and see what she thinks," and he ambled off towards the bank, where Kat could see a host of white-suited figures combing the ground and kneeling around one spot.

Relieved that nobody else was around, Kat went and retrieved the keys from the camellia, feeling much better once they were safely in her pocket again. Then she went and flopped down on the now familiar bench. What a day! She felt utterly drained by it all, as she always did when she had to go back into the hell that was her dad's family.

Was that ever going to leave her in peace? And was she ever going to find someone who could accept all the chaos that went with her association with the Robarts gang? It had been what finished her relationship with Peppino, her Sicilian boyfriend of long ago. Not that she could blame him. Of the few boyfriends she'd had which had gone beyond a casual date, he'd known what it was like to live with the threat of the Mafia, and with Sicily finally dragging itself free of the stranglehold of organised crime, Kat had truly understood why he couldn't face the prospect of a girlfriend who had ties to the English equivalent, however much more small-time the Robarts gang had been by comparison.

What she needed was someone who could applaud her taking a stand against them, and without her finding them looking at her with that question in their eyes which asked the unspoken question of, 'but how dirty did you have to get to do that?' The truth had been 'not much', because it had been her dad who had given her most of the information. She had just been the one who had stood up in court and testified. And that was what was hurting her so much at the moment about Drew. He'd been far too quick to assume her guilt

Well sod him, she thought. *I was set to rescue Scott on my own before he turned up, and I'm sure I can do it now without him. He's done the one thing I couldn't do, which was to send Scott an unwritten message he would understand.* But that made her wonder about the portal again and she looked at her watch. She and Drew hadn't got back here until nearly one o'clock this afternoon, thinking that they had plenty of time and that it was better not to come too early in case they'd bumped into Rigby. But then the whole nonsense of being taken back to Hereford and Bill having to come and get her, meant that it was now well after five o'clock. That put it nearly four hours after moonrise, so would the portal even still be open?

At least Scott hadn't come stumbling through today, because if he had, they would surely have had a frantic phone-call while they were still at the station. But dare she try taking Bill Scathlock down to the cellar to show him? She looked up and saw him coming back down the slope towards her.

"Sylvia says they'll be here for another couple of hours," he said cheerfully, "but that's just because they want to lift the skeleton tonight. Interesting, though, it looks like he was killed by a crossbow bolt through the back."

"Oh no!" Kat gulped. That was a risk she hadn't factored in. What if the soldiers saw Scott making a run for the portal and let loose with a crossbow? She'd not thought of them actually shooting at someone they probably thought of as their servant or maybe even their slave – because there had still been slaves in Anglo-Saxon England even if they were few and far between by the eleventh century.

"Are you okay, Kat?" she heard Scathlock saying. "You've gone awfully pale."

"Would you come with me?" she asked him. "I'm hoping that something is still there and hasn't faded, and if it is, I'd like you to see it. It might explain something to you better than I can in words."

She saw his eyebrows rise in surprise, but equally he didn't object. And so she led him around to the front of the house, unlocking the door with the excuse of,

"I had keys left me by Scott," though even Bill Scathlock didn't need to know that Scott himself had never got that far.

She led him into the hall and along the hallway to the cellar steps.

"Mind your head," she warned him as she led the way down, "The sergeant cracked his head on the ceiling the first time. I think the servant classes in the days when this was built were a good bit shorter than us. I'm okay, but you guys are way taller."

She heard him chuckle behind her and then he was standing beside her in the cellar. With the first cellar lights on, the blue of the portal was far fainter than it had been yesterday, but it was still just about visible.

"Oh my word," Bill breathed. "Is that what I think it is?"

"If you think it's a naturally occurring portal to another time, then yes it is."

"Bloody hell, do you know to when?" he asked, going forwards but much more cautiously than Drew had.

"Going on what Ryan Edwards told me, my best estimation is somewhere in the years just before the Norman Conquest of 1066. The language he described sounds very like Norman French, and there were men from that area in this part of the world in Edward the Confessor's reign."

Scathlock had paused at the doorway between the first cellar and the wine cellar and was scrutinising the portal but without any fear. "Why do you think it was then? After all, there were Normans here after the Conquest too."

"It's this," Kat said, waving her hand at the barrel-vaulting. "I checked when I went back home, and there's no record of anyone trying to establish a church here after the Conquest. Whoever the lord was who originally wanted to create a church on this land, he failed and his family either didn't care or got moved on in the reshuffling during the years after 1066. You've only got to look at the dates of the lovely old churches which still survive around here to get a feel for that…"

"…Like Kilpeck or Kempley…"

"…Exactly! By the time the Normans who came over with King William felt secure enough to start building churches nearly a century later, everything was settled enough that they at least lasted for a while – and you certainly wouldn't have had the Welsh throwing fits over it, because by then they had Norman abbots and priors, too. But this place? This failed to even get beyond the undercroft. There's not so much as a mention of it in Domesday, but then we can only ever infer the presence of a church if a priest gets mentioned attached to a settlement that was worth taxing."

"Hmm, my archaeologist friend tells me that Domesday Book is wonderful for giving us a snapshot in time in 1086, so we get lots of oblique references to churches that either no longer exist, or which we might not otherwise have been able to date," Scathlock said knowledgably.

"God, you do know your stuff," Kat said with relief. "You've no idea what it's like to be able to talk to someone who doesn't think I'm mad."

"So what do you think happened here?"

"To the church or here as in Scott disappearing?"

"Hmph. Both I suppose."

"Well in terms of the church, I had a dig around in the records as best I can, and I reckon that whoever the family were who owned this manorial estate – if it was even as much as that – at the time when the undercroft was begun certainly weren't in power by 1086. And then the only other thing I could find was some passing references to it as having being used as a store by the monks who had a small priory nearby. But that's all a bit fuzzy, because we're talking about an account by a local Victorian historian, not anyone modern or qualified, and he was writing about a priory which had got snapped up by one of the local landowners during Henry VIII dissolution of the monasteries. All I could get out of it was that the 'fine stonework' of the monks' actual buildings got carted off to build a house which itself no longer stands. So all we've got as a clue is the name of Fownhope Priors, and that doesn't tell us much."

"But then that's not exactly abnormal, is it?" Scathlock sympathised. "Minor monasteries, which probably never had more than a handful of priests, getting shut down and the building robbed out for equally minor landowner's homes is a tale which repeats itself out all over England. ...And what about 'here', as in Scott Hawkesmoor?"

"Ah, I left that door to the front cellar open because I didn't want anybody else to get caught by that thing. But I think that Scott came down here in genuine ignorance of it being here, and when he opened that door because he heard or smelled something odd, he was pretty much hit by the full force of that thing. It's waning now, but when it first opens it's much brighter and you can actually feel the pull of it from where you're standing now."

"Yes, I can see that might be the case," he agreed. "It's already fading from when we came down here. When I first stood here, I could feel it prickling at my skin, but that sensation's now gone. ...Oh, and there you go, it's vanished for the night."

"Right, come on upstairs and I'll tell you the rest of it," Kat promised, and as she led him out to the walled garden, she explained her theory about the portal getting stretched out.

When she'd finished, Scathlock turned and stood looking at the gateway. "And you say these stones came back out here?"

"You'd have been hit by them if you were standing where you are now, so yes."

"Interesting. And good thinking by Mr Treadwell. That's something I might have come up with eventually, but not as fast as that."

"Well I think it helps that he's been friends with Scott for many years, and they know how each other thinks."

Scathlock looked down at her and smiled sadly. "But now, thanks to Rigby and his hefty size twelves trampling all over you, Drew Treadwell doesn't trust you anymore?"

"No, I don't think he does."

"Would it help if I had a word with him?"

"It might. As another policeman, and one more senior than Rigby, he might believe you."

"Have you got his number?"

Kat found Drew on her phone and passed the number on to Scathlock, after which he said,

"I'll give him a chance to get out of the station at Hereford and catch his breath, and then I'll give him a ring later on tonight. But what are you going to do, Kat?"

"To be honest, I don't really know. The portal won't open up until at least three o'clock tomorrow afternoon, so there's not much I can do here. I shall want to give that cellar a good cleansing at some stage, but there's no point in doing that until I've found a way to close the portal for good."

"Then if you'll take my advice, go home. Go and get a good night's rest – I won't say 'sleep' because you've had an upsetting day, and sleep might not come so easily. But go home and do whatever it is you usually do to restore your equilibrium. I'll get the forensics guys to move their van so that you can get your car out, and then I'll tail you home to make sure you don't end up in a ditch somewhere."

She was feeling so drained that Kat was very grateful for that offer. Drew Treadwell was old enough and capable enough to sort himself out. She had enough on her plate without running around after him, and if she was being honest with herself, a night alone to sort out her feelings was probably exactly what she needed at the moment.

And so once she could get into her car, she drove back to Worcester, glad of the presence of the big Subaru following behind her until she turned into her parking area. Then with a toot of the horn and a wave in her direction, Scathlock left her to her own devices.

What a tactful man, she thought with relief, as she closed her front door behind her and slide the chain across on it. Despite whatever they had said, she'd known some men who would nonetheless have expected to be invited in for a coffee at the very least. And so the first thing she did was go and run herself a deep bath, then with some soft music on and candles scattered about the bathroom, she had a long and relaxing soak. By the time she emerged she realised that she was ravenously hungry, but rather than hang around waiting for something to cook or a takeaway to arrive, she put on some pasta, microwaved a packet of frozen vegetables, and then stirred them through the pasta with some sauce. By the time she'd grated some fresh parmesan over it, it felt like a feast fit for a king, and she devoured it with relish.

For the rest of the evening she sat with just her candles lit in her dinky conservatory, so that she could look out onto the minute courtyard garden that was outside the windows. A random selection of classical music made for easy listening, and by the time she went to bed she was relaxed enough to sleep well. And if portals and Drew Treadwell invaded her dreams, it was not enough to wake her up, or for her to remember come the morning.

By the time she had got up and made her breakfast, though, she knew she had to decide what she was going to do in the coming days. With it being Sunday there was no need for her to go into the office, since nobody would be expecting replies from her to any queries she had sent out and had responses to. On the other hand, if she did that today, that would mean that when she went out to Fownhope Priors later on today, she wouldn't have to rush back tonight, but could stay on for at least one more day. Yet today she felt that there were higher priorities than curtain fabric.

For no reason she could pin down, Kat felt sure that if Scott didn't make it back by Wednesday, then with the moon waning from then on, he probably wouldn't be able to get through the portal. *I've got to get you back tonight or tomorrow, if possible,* she thought. *I really don't want to be waiting until after the full moon. After all, what if it changes after then? What if that end of the portal that leads forward as the moon rises, then turns and goes back even farther once it starts waning? That's a worrying thought, isn't it? That Scott could end up even farther in the past than he is at the moment? Oh heck, I really need to warn him that that might be the case. So what symbols could I scratch onto one of those stones to convey that?*

She sat at her kitchen counter, sketching ideas out on a rough pad she had until she was fairly sure she had something intelligible. At that point she copied it out onto a post-it note which she could stuff into her pocket, and went to dig out her engraving kit. That needed a mains electricity source, but by now Kat was confident of getting into the cottage she and Drew had stayed in or the main house, and being able to plug it in there. Actually engraving seemed a better bet than trying to write something, although she did take an indelible marker with her, too, to go over the lines with to make them stand out more.

Then around two in the afternoon, having made herself a substantial lunch and retrieved some of the food she'd bought what seemed a lifetime ago, she set off for the house once more. *This is starting to feel like a Groundhog Day all of my own,* she thought, as she drove along the quieter roads with only a few Sunday motorists out, rather than the usual busy traffic heading between Worcester and Hereford. *Please let me be the only one out there today, I feel I need to be able to focus on Scott, not have my feelings being yanked around all over the place.* It wasn't that she didn't want Drew to be there, but after yesterday she wasn't ready to have another emotional bruising from him not quite believing her all the time.

So it was with great relief that she pulled up to the house to see the battered old Land Rover once more standing in splendid isolation again.

"Hello, old friend," she said, going to give its bonnet a friendly pat. "Just you and me again today, so let's see if we can get your boss back, shall we?"

And past being worried about Rigby, she went in through the front door, but this time locked it after her. In the old laundry she opened the back door, went across to get the most distinctive of the pebbles, and then came back in, again locking the doors after herself. She then spent some time with the engraver, carefully scratching the symbols she had worked out into the stone, finally inking them in with the black marker pen.

When she was satisfied that the ink had dried, and alerted by the strong smell once again rising through the old dumb waiter, she made her way down to the cellar. Sure enough, the portal was open and glowing brightly. Now should she attempt to copy Drew's fast bowl of the stone through? The trouble with that was that if she missed – and she was realistic enough to know that her aim would be unlikely to be true – then there was the risk that if it hit the old stonework it might shatter. That all by itself might be dangerous to her because of flying shards of stone, but she was also relying on Scott recognising the distinctive patterning on this particular stone.

In the end she decided on an under-arm throw that was more like someone playing bowls than cricket. But at least it would roll through to the other side, rather than being in danger of knocking someone out, and that might give Scott a better chance of getting hold of it if the guards weren't wondering whether they were under attack. And so she lined herself up, tried to remember what it had been like bowling for games of rounders at school, and let the stone go.

With a grace she wouldn't have believed she could achieve, the stone went neatly through the middle of the spiralling light and vanished.

"Gotcha!" Kat chortled in delight, then ran for the stairs. If Scott got the message, then she needed to be up in the garden ready to welcome him back.

Chapter 20

In the past on the Friday, Scott saw the first stone come flying out of nowhere and was shocked by its sudden appearance. But when the second one came through only a minute or so later there was something very familiar about the way it sailed through in a perfect arc. When the third one followed, he was certain. He really hadn't been imagining it that he'd heard Drew's voice. But not here, not at this portal. Somewhere over… he turned and stared around him, suddenly picking up on the sight of the other portal back by the camp.

As another stone came through and hit one of the guards squarely in the midriff, Scott seized his chance, and scooping up two of the stones, he ran towards the other portal. Even as old George called out, "No, Scott!" he let fly with the first stone, then backed off and ran to throw the next one. Both stones vanished back the way they had come, and Scott managed to send two more back, sure that at least one of them had already come through already. But then Scott found his arm being caught by one of the guards before he could send any more back. At least the guard wasn't truly angry, though, having realised that Scott was only sending these strange missiles back at whoever had thrown them.

That meant that Scott was soon back at work on the construction, yet now he was faced with a dilemma. Because in truth, Scott wasn't sure he wanted to go back. Yes, this was a tough life, and if the food wasn't great, it was edible, and compared to Flora's cooking it was actually not bad. And Scott had found a real sense of peace in working with his hands again. He had blisters everywhere from the unaccustomed rough work, but he'd done his training doing hands-on stuff like this. This was familiar, and what was more, it was satisfying.

Even in the few days he'd been here, he'd been able to help the others, identifying the reason why the keystone at the top of the second barrel-vault would not stay put. Now that four-ribbed arch was stable, and today they had taken down the wooden supports, the mortar having dried out. But what had given Scott a real surge of pleasure had been the way all the men had held their breath as they stood back, and then when it had held, had all cheered and come and slapped him on the back, congratulating him. Scott couldn't remember the last time anyone had done that to him, and it created an instant bond between him and these other workers from who knew when.

Because of having worked with men from all over the country, Scott had become a dab hand at working out heavy accents, and by now he'd managed to communicate with most of the workers, even if he couldn't understand a word the soldiers in charge said. For that he had to rely on old George and a few key men. But in talking to the men in camp at night, he'd quickly worked out that, however unbelievable it might be, that somehow he was in a past era, and these men had all arrived here from various points in the late nineteenth or twentieth centuries. None of them had expected to be here anymore than he had, but they were very quick to warn him that the guards were really angry that one of them had managed to escape through the blue light at the same time as he'd arrived, and not to try it. That they also told him that they thought those men had died in doing so had been a huge disincentive to even consider trying that route – that was, until today when he'd heard Drew's voice and the 'cricket balls' had come flying through.

Yet it went even further than that. The first night when Scott had slept soundly he'd put it down to exhaustion and the smack on the head. But when three nights later he was still sleeping like a log and waking up feeling refreshed, which was a first in more years than he cared to count, he began to wonder why. He ought to have been feeling stressed and lost, and probably a whole host of other emotions too, but he wasn't. If anything, he was experiencing a surge of what he could only describe as relief. And it was at that point that it dawned on him that it was because all responsibility for Jeanette had been removed.

Here in this other time there was nothing he *could* do for her. And with that gone, it left a blessed sense of peace behind it; which, he had to admit, was very sad. What an awful legacy to be left with after all those years. Just the knowledge that he might never have to deal with one of Jeanette's moments of wild hysteria, or one of Flora's screaming rages ever again, was so liberating as to practically make him want to cry with happiness.

Moreover, he was genuinely happy being back in this all male company. This he knew, this he understood. No dancing around trying to make sure his every move wasn't misconstrued. No worrying whether he should have smiled at that lady in the office in case it was misread – because heaven help him, being a good-looking man had had its serious drawbacks. Twice he had found himself skating perilously close to accusations of having behaved improperly, just because someone had read way more into just a casual comment than had ever been intended. And that was something his two closest male managers hadn't had to contend with, since Stu had had a face like a bag of spanners, and despite having good bone structure Tim was covered in scars from teenage acne. Nobody ever accused them of anything, but Scott had only had to walk through the main office when a new woman had arrived, and he could practically feel her eyes drilling into his back as he passed. As if he'd have wanted an affair! Living with Jeanette took so much energy out of him he hadn't had anything left for an office fling. So no, he wasn't missing his old life at all, except for the knowledge that he might never see a few close friends like Drew ever again.

All of which meant that he spent the rest of that day feeling worried for the first time since he'd got here. Would Drew do something reckless, like coming to look for him? Because Scott knew that Drew wouldn't cope so well here. Drew might love working on projects at the weekend with Scott, but that was a far cry from getting up with the sun and putting in eight or ten hours of hard labour. Drew's kind of sporty fitness wasn't geared up for that. And so there was a brewing concern for his friend.

Also it finally bore in on Scott that in his own time, somebody would be asking questions like where had he gone? Why had he gone? And was somebody else responsible? At which point he remembered Kat. What if she was blamed for his disappearance? Because remembering Jeanette's screamed accusations as he'd left the cottage on that last night, it would be horribly typical of her to throw all of the suspicion onto Kat, instead of wondering whether maybe Kat wasn't to blame at all, but that she herself was. And Kat most certainly didn't deserve that.

Even so, that night, as he sat and watched the blue light of the portal from a distance, he couldn't quite bring himself to move towards it. He wanted to see this building project here finished. In truth, wanted to know that it had been *his* hands which had created that lovely barrel-vaulting which would last for a thousand years. One old cellar might be all that it was, with the church never getting built above it, but even that was one heck of an achievement. How many other people had ever had the chance to know such a thing for certain? If he went back, he would never have that again because there was no way he could live that long. It wasn't ego. It was simply the joy of knowing that what he'd done had *worked,* was good, and would last. Because George said they'd lost count of the number of times the arch at the end of what in the future was the first cellar had fallen down, and with no apparent reason why. And it had been Scott who had identified the stresses caused by the slope of the hill as the culprit, and helped them put it right.

However, things changed again when he was working on the next vaulting two days later, and the now familiar tingling of the portal opening began. This time, when Kat's stone rolled through, Scott was quick to pounce on it and stick it into his pocket. That it had something written on it had been obvious, but he didn't want to stop and try and read it now, not when the soldiers were watching them. It would have to wait until they were back in camp, and he could look at it properly.

He didn't have long to wait. As the afternoon came to an end, a fine but persistent drizzle set in, and for once the guards had had enough too, letting them go back to where the makeshift tents were and to kick the cooking fire back into life. With a little light left, Scott went and sat on the edge of the group of men with his back half turned, and pulled out the stone.

It seemed to have symbols on it rather than writing, the first being a tube with an arrow pointing in at one end and out at another. Well that was easy to understand. It meant the portals. The next row of symbols was rather more worrying, though. There was a circle which clearly meant the full moon, and the half moons on either side of it. Under the full moon was a caricature of a Viking-like figure, and Scott thought that maybe the man who'd made a run for it on the day he'd arrived might have told someone about the time he was in now. That made sense, because although his guards weren't Vikings, they probably weren't that far off that period, either.

What he had to think rather harder about were the other symbols. From beneath the full moon image, arrows pointed both ways, the one before the full pointing to a symbol of a car. Okay, that was clearly to the future he'd come from. But why did the one pointing the other way seem to have a child's drawing of a dinosaur on it?

"What do that mean?" George asked, coming and plonking himself down beside Scott.

"I'm not entirely sure. Someone's trying to send me a message, and an important one, of that I'm sure. It's just deciphering it that's a bit hard."

George peered at the stone. "Whoever done that ain't bad with a chisel, I tell 'e that."

Scott laughed. "I think it was probably done with an engraving tool, but you're right, someone has an artist's eye," and that made him think again of Kat. Yes, she would have the both the skill and the right kind of imagination to make something like this.

"Whoever it be, they done well to work around the stone," George added admiringly, as Scott rolled the near sphere in his hands to look at the symbols again.

"Yes, they have. There's a lot crammed onto here. Look at this last bit. That looks like a spring to me – you know, coiled, like you would have seen on carts and things."

"Oh aye! It do, don't it!"

"Then look at this next version of it next to it. See? It's like it's being stretched out? I think that means that as time goes on, these 'things', whatever they are, are being stretched farther and farther apart. Which is why I've now come through more than a hundred years after you came through, even though at this end things don't seem to have changed that much."

George looked surprised but nodded. "Aye, now that makes sense. 'Tis the first time anyone have given an explanation that actually makes sense to me."

Scott gave a wan smile. "Unfortunately it makes sense to me too. But that means that if I'm going back, I have to do it soon. And this middle bit with the moons? The more I look at it, the more I think it means that if you go through as it's coming up to the full moon, in other words as the moon's pull is rising, then you go forward. But if you wait until the moon is waning, then instead of going forwards, you end up going even farther back in time."

He looked up at George and saw understanding breaking over his elderly friend's face.

"What is it, George?"

"Those men years back, that died when they ran into the blue light? I thinks they might have gone after the full moon. I can't be sure. My memory ain't what it was. But could it be that they hung on too long? And that they died 'cause they went back to when they d'ain't belong?"

Scott sighed. "Oh bugger. That really does mean that I have to go within the next few days." He looked up at the thick clouds covering the sky. "No telling where we are tonight, but as best I can recall, we're only three or four days off the full moon by now."

George looked at him quizzically. "Don't 'e want to go back?"

Scott reached out and squeezed the old man's hand. "There's a lot in my old life I don't want to go back to – a nagging wife for one!" and George gave a wry laugh. "But until these messages started coming through, it never occurred to me that me disappearing might have made a lot of trouble for some people. I don't think I can live with the thought that I've brought someone a lot of trouble with the police, for instance. And there was a lady …no, not like that, George! She was someone who was going to do some work for me – helping me with things like what curtains to put in the house when the work was done." That was the best description he could give to someone like George of what an interior designer would do.

"I was thinking of making the house that you were building in 1890 into a kind of hotel, you see, and she came to advise me. Well she's a really nice lady. Someone I could make a very good friend of, I think. But my dreadful wife was making nasty accusations before the first day was out. And now I'm thinking that if she said those things to the police…"

"Oh Lord, yes I sees what 'e mean. Could mean a heap of trouble for her what she don't deserve."

"Exactly. …So the thing is, George. Now that I've shown you how to reinforce the base of the ribs on the vaults, do you think you can carry on without me?"

George had no doubts about that. "With that and the other stuff you been telling us at night? Yes, no doubt about it. It all made sense once you explained it. We just didn't have the learnin' to work it out ourselves."

"Well it took me a lot of studying to learn about things like stresses," Scott admitted. "I'm not that clever on my own. But I have used that knowhow a few times since, too, so it's really stuck in my mind."

"Then I'm glad it did. It's saved us a lot of beatings from the soldiers, I can tell you. As it's fallen down time after time, they've been getting more frustrated with us, like it was our fault and we was doing sommat deliberately. O' course we weren't, but how could we explain that? So that vault holding up for the first time has made our lives a lot better already."

"I'm glad about that."

George looked at him sadly. "So I thinks you have to go, my friend. Go and make sure this nice lady what sent you this message don't get stuck in the clink by the coppers."

Scott looked around him. The guards were definitely in a more relaxed mood tonight, possibly even cheerful, and there seemed to be some kind of booze being passed around amongst them, even if none of it was coming the workers way. And the ten men who made up the other workers were eagerly clustered near their cooking fire, waiting for the night's meal to be ready, also relieved that the guards were in a good mood. So if he was going to go, he'd not get a much better chance than this.

"Don't run at that thing, though," George cautioned him, as if seeing his resolve. "If'n you do that, they'm still got their crossbows ready by their sides. They shot at that first other lad what ran. Don't know if they hit him or not, but I could swear I heard a scream as he vanished. I don't want that to happen to you."

Scott looked around. "If I head off to the latrine pit, they won't suspect anything. And in this drizzle they won't see far anyway. I should be able to creep around the back of that clump of hawthorns and get closer to the thing before I have to get up and make a run."

He reached over and handed George the engraved stone. "Hang onto that. Just in case some other poor sod falls through, eh?" Then gave George a hug. "Take care, my friend. It's been good knowing you. And if you can get this project finished, maybe you can go home too."

He didn't want to say that they only had to get a couple more of the vaults done and then they wouldn't be building any more. What would happen to George and the others then he didn't want to think too hard about. After all, in their own time they would have died years ago anyway, but it was hard to think of it like that when he'd taken such a liking to the old man sitting next to him. It would be more like losing a much liked elderly neighbour rather than just someone anonymous in a history book. But then if that happened, might he die here with them too? That made his mind up for him faster than anything, because however grim life could get, Scott wasn't ready to die just yet.

With studied calm, he got up and made a gentle jog towards the latrine pit. If he walked too slowly, any of the men watching him would wonder why he was willingly getting soaked on an evening like this by taking his time. So he had to make this seem normal.

At the latrine he was glad to see that none of the guards had felt the need to use it too, but gave it a moment or two just in case somebody had been following him. After all, he could hardly have looked behind him on the way without having someone wonder why he was so bothered about it. It wasn't as though anybody had shown signs of sneaking off with another man for any assignations, so he couldn't even have covered his behaviour by saying he'd been watching out for a specific somebody.

After a count of ten, nobody had appeared, and Scott thought he was clear to start creeping around the back of the small knot of stunted hawthorns. They'd been heavily coppiced over the winter for firewood, and so he had to crouch down as he crept along. At one point he even had to get down and do an army-style crawl across an open stretch, because that got him beyond the hawthorns to a large tangle of wild blackberries. Those at least were a much taller cluster, last year's long canes waving gently in the breeze and constantly breaking up anyone's view, which allowed him to stand up, albeit bent over, and to flex his legs well.

He was going to have to make a sprint for it over the last few yards, but he glanced around both sides of the clump and decided that if he ran in line with it, he could get a lot closer to the blue light before he needed to swerve to go through it. Did he need to hit it square on? That was something he didn't know. If he dived in at a tangent and came out of the side of the spiralling light, would he come out in the 1950s, for instance? Was it even possible to come out part of the way through?

That was a worrying thought, because aside from the risk of dying here, the reason he was going back was to help those he knew in his own time. If he couldn't do that, then he'd rather stay here and take his chances until it became clearer whether his life was in danger on this side. *So hit the bloody thing straight!* he told himself nervously.

Taking a few deep breaths to steady himself, and to get his breathing right for the run, Scott took off like a scalded cat, running at an angle to the light at first while keeping the blackberries between him and the camp. But then as he came up on the light, he turned and tried to come around in a curve so that he was more lined up with it. It didn't help that now he was instinctively crouching lower, all too aware of George's warning of the cross-bow bolts which might start flying about his ears any second now.

As he got up to the light he could feeling it tugging at him with every stride, which at least was helping his own momentum. And as his leading foot hit the edge of the spiral, he found himself toppling forwards, even as he heard a cry going up behind him. Something whistled past his head and he felt it snag in the sleeve of his fleece as he instinctively whirled his arms to try and regain his balance. But then the world went blank.

Chapter 21

Up in the garden Kat made sure she was well out of line of the gateway, and then settled down to wait. *Half past three,* she told herself, looking at her watch. *So I reckon I've got until about six o'clock before the portal starts seriously fading. Maybe, just maybe, if the light starts dimming in that past world that Scott's in, especially if he's under one of those vaults, he might have finished labouring with the others and be at the camp by then. I don't know whether to pray that he tries it tonight if the portal is close to closing, or to hope he hangs on until tomorrow night when he's got another hour to play with.*

On the other hand, tomorrow was Monday, and would the forensics people be back then, scouring the ground for clues? It was an old murder case, so she wondered whether there was quite as much urgency to making a thorough search as there would have been if it had just happened? After all, all concerned must have to take into account that more than a year had passed, and that even if the ground had lacked human interference, then there must at least had been a fair few foxes and badgers who'd conducted their twilight foraging over the ground in that time. How often did cases like these end up with the smaller bones never getting found because they were down some creature's burrow? And would that mean that there was a point when the investigating team accepted that what they had was all they were going to find?

She went and fetched a garden chair and sat on the first of the two crosswise paths, nicely out of direct line of the portal, but close enough so that she could leap up and help him should Scott come through hurt in some way. The sleeping bag she'd unearthed for Drew's use she now unzipped and draped around the plastic chair, keeping the chill of the breeze off her back and legs, her coat protecting the rest of her. It had been a nice weekend so far, but this early in the year it still wasn't sitting outside in the evening kind of weather from choice. After which it was just a case of settling down to wait.

Sitting there in the peace and quiet, she found her thoughts once more turning to Drew. How did she feel about him now? It was a real problem for her, because there was no doubting the attraction between them. But if he couldn't trust her not to be the out-and-out criminal her cousin was, there didn't seem to be much hope for them. After all, Rigby had blurted out that bit about Caitlyn's violent assault record, and that ought to have sounded just plain *wrong* to him, even on such a short acquaintance.

Yet was she basing that assumption on her own knowledge of what Caitlyn was like? The explosive temper, the overt racism, and the unwavering belief that she had the right to take whatever she wanted in life? Was that skewing her own view of things? Had other people initially seen Caitlyn for what she was, or had she been able to put on the charm and fool folk – if not wholly, then at least enough that the mistaken identity between the two of them wasn't so ridiculous for a stranger? Would she have reacted so very differently if it had been Drew who had been suddenly accused by Rigby, and taking into account a life for herself where she hadn't been already familiar with unjust accusations like that? Maybe not.

However even taking that into consideration, Kat couldn't help but feel that he had been too fast to dismiss his own instincts about her, and to metaphorically feed her to the wolves. Comparing his reaction to both Bill Scathlock's and to his DC's, both of whom had quite rightly started off suspicious, but who had rapidly revised their opinion of Kat right from as soon as they had seen the warnings, and before they had had chance to read them in detail, Drew seemed to not have given her much of a chance to explain herself.

Oddly enough, she had no such qualms about Scott. If he came back safe and sound, then Kat could foresee a long and happy friendship, and maybe even a good business partnership. Romance in such an imagining, however, never came into that equation, and she didn't think it would for Scott, either. Theirs had been a meeting of minds and to some extent of souls too, yet even without any physical buzz between them, Kat couldn't imagine him being quite so quick to judge her.

It didn't do much for her equilibrium as she sat there waiting, and then the peace and quiet was shattered by the sound of a car coming closer. It was still a long way off, the quiet of a late Sunday afternoon making the sound travel, but Kat had a horrible sense of foreboding that said it was heading here. Running out to her car, she took the handbrake off and shoved it hard. Luckily, with there being a bit of a slope in her favour, it began rolling at a gentle pace, and she managed to steer it as it went, until it had slid back off the drive under a huge rhododendron with massive leaves. Putting the handbrake back on, and pulling the branches of the shrub back into their original place, Kat could only hope that the VW's grey would blend it in with the shadows. There wasn't time for her to get back into the garden, though, and so she crouched down deeper into the foliage, glad that the police vans had churned up the gravel of the drive sufficiently that it wasn't obvious that she'd been here.

To her horror, it was Rigby's car which pulled up outside, and to make matters worse, Drew got out of the passenger side. What the hell was he doing here with Rigby? Hadn't either of them taken any notice of what DI Scathlock had said? And Kat had enough reason to trust the big Worcester detective to know that having promised he would ring Drew, that Scathlock would have made good on it.

"And you say it's in the cellar?" she heard Rigby saying as they headed for the front door. "I have to say, I'm shocked at you getting taken in like that Mr Treadwell. I'd have thought you'd have come across enough con-artists in your time to not be so easily fooled. They all have their sleights of hand."

Even as Kat felt her blood starting to boil at the insult, Drew was starting to say,

"Well if I hadn't seen it with my own eyes, I would have thought it all some con."

"*Hmph!*" Rigby snorted. "And it never occurred to you that she might have just set up some digital projector and a strong fan? After all, by your own admission, she seems to have got another set of keys from somewhere."

Oh damn you to the deepest levels of hell, Drew Treadwell! Kat silently fumed. *Really? You had to tell him that? Why?* But then it made her wonder whether Rigby wasn't smarting from the dressing down he must have got off the uniformed officers' inspector, and would also be dreading what his own superior would be saying to him on Monday morning in the light of that? So was this some desperate attempt on Rigby's part to prove that he'd been right all along, in order to avoid the potential disciplinary action he might be facing? Kat thought that might be close to the truth, especially since her impression had been that he'd built his hopes up that he'd be getting a commendation, maybe even a promotion, out of catching a woman who was a notorious criminal.

That might mean that he'd dressed up what Kat had told Drew in very different terms in some subsequent conversation between them. Had he said words to the effect that Kat was actually being taken back to Worcester by

Scathlock because the Worcester detectives had a prior claim on her? And would Drew believe that? Possibly, since by his own admission he wasn't that up on criminal law, having dealt with commercial cases for all of his career.

By now both men had reached the front door and had gone inside.

Do I follow them, or do I stay well away? Kat wondered.

She squinted hard at the downstairs front windows which were looking her way. As best she could tell, they hadn't gone into either of them, nor up into the big hall, and so she risked a quick sprint back across to the garden gate. Going back into the garden, she grabbed the chair and sleeping bag, and took them back to the patio of the cottage. The sleeping bag she rolled up quickly and stuffed under a chair in the next patio, hoping that if Drew was daft enough to lead Rigby back here, then it would be to the cottage they had shared for the night, and not the other one.

But then what to do herself?

She crept back up to the stone circle of the gateway and stood very still. What was disconcerting to her was that standing here, the portal was setting all of her senses on edge, and that was doing nothing for her ability to hear where Drew and Rigby were. The damned thing was practically humming like a swarm of small insects all of a sudden.

Get back you idiot! her senses screamed at her, and as she retreated several paces, suddenly the portal flared. The only way she could describe it afterwards was that it was what it must be like to be underwater and see the effect of something being thrown in – that reverse of a splash. But then all thoughts of anything else were driven from her mind as she saw Scott emerge, stumble, and trip to go flying on the gravel path.

"Scott! Oh thank God! You made it!" she exclaimed, as she ran to help him to his feet.

"Kat?" he looked up at her, dazed but far from as befuddled as Ryan was even now.

"Yes, it's me. Am I ever glad to see you back safe and sound!"

"Have you been here waiting for me all the time?"

"Well not the entire time you've been gone. It took a bit of working out at first as to what had happened. But yes, I've been coming here as much as I could. ...But let's get you inside into the warm and something to eat. There's a whole heap of news I've got to tell you, and there's someone here who I think you're going to want to see."

"Drew?"

"Good grief, you guessed that?"

"Not so much guessed. I thought I heard his voice, but then also thought I was imagining it. Or at least I did until those stones started flying through the portal. Was that your idea?"

"Using the stones like cricket balls? No, that was all Drew. He came up with that all by himself."

By now she had her arm around Scott and was helping him hobble back to the cottage patio. The gravel had done some damage to his hands, and she guessed that when he came to have a shower he'd be well and truly scraped on his forearms, knees and shins too, after the way he'd landed. But for now she just wanted him to be able to wash the dirt out of the scratches on his hands, and so she dug in her pocket for the keys and unlocked the French window. If Rigby came in now it was tough luck. He'd have a hard time prosecuting her given that the man he thought she'd done for was alive and well and back here.

There were a lot of hissed intakes of breath as the water ran over Scott's hands, and more than a few winces as he used the soap Kat gave him to clean them thoroughly. The cut on his head where he had fallen in the cellar was already scabbing over well, so she didn't try to do anything more than dab some disinfectant on that. In the here and now it would probably have had stitches, but she knew that while scalp wounds bled like fury, they also tended to heal quickly, and so she wasn't worried about that anymore now that it had closed up. Consequently, while he was scrubbing himself as clean as possible, and picking the gravel out of his hands, Kat unlocked the front door to the cottage and made a quick run across to her car for the kettle and tea, and having grabbed them paused on her way back to call,

"Hey there! Drew! Scott's back!"

There was no answer.

Oh screw you, she thought, bitterly. *Some friend you are!* Then hurried into the cottage with her bag of supplies and set about making Scott a hot drink and microwaving something for him to eat as well. Mr Drew Treadwell could come across in his own sweet time if that was the way he was going to be.

* * * * *

From Drew's point of view, the last couple of days couldn't have got any stranger. He'd been very disturbed by Kat's reactions up on the bank, and he had to admit that at the time he'd been seriously disappointed in her. Weren't there any decent women left in the world?

Then at the police station, that big detective from Worcester rolling up and seemingly giving Rigby a bollocking had been another unexpected turn. And to then see the inspector escorting the detective and Kat out in the friendliest of fashions had only confused him further. Yet the way Kat had seemed so angry with him in that briefest of conversations before she left had also left him feeling more than a little bruised. How could he possibly have known that she would have such a dark secret in her past? With all the people he'd met over the years professionally, he'd never once come across anyone with that kind of past – and here he had to admit that of anyone, it was he himself who had the dangerous past. Moreover, there was a big part of him that was wondering whether he could ever be comfortable living with someone like that? How would you ever know whether they had told you the truth, for a start off?

And although he'd not got as far as telling Kat this, he'd had enough issues with people endlessly pulling the wool over his eyes in his own life to be very wary of getting back into such a situation again. Therefore much as it saddened him, he was coming to the conclusion that it would be better to forget that he'd ever felt such a strong attraction to Miss Kat Newsome – if that's who she really was. *Sort this out and then go back home to Yorkshire,* he'd begun telling himself. *You've just got to the point where your father has nothing more he can hold over you anymore. So go home and get your life back on track. Get rid of that bloody albatross of a business and decide what you want to do with the rest of your life. You've got time to change, for God's sake – you're only thirty-nine! People have started alternative careers much later than that and made a go of it. Maybe if Scott ever comes back, you and he could start up something together? Who knows what possibilities are out there until you look? And Kat Newsome doesn't have to play a part in any of them.*

Except that that resolution had been fine up until he'd had the phone call from DI Scathlock. By the time that had finished, he'd got the impression that the detective thought Kat little short of heroic for making such a stand against her uncle's crime syndicate. And if the Robart's gang had hardly been on a par with the Mafia – whether in Italy, New York, or even London – he'd got the impression that 'Big Alf' had been a substantial and dangerous criminal for Kat to risk crossing. Even worse, there had been the underlying hint from Scathlock that he would take a very dim view of it should Drew leak such information to the press, or indeed to anyone who might make it public, thereby endangering Kat's life.

Kat as the silent heroine was something Drew hadn't even thought of up until then, and so his feelings had still been bouncing around all over the place when Rigby had called him on Sunday morning. The Hereford detective put a rather different spin on things, implying that the Worcester lads wanted to keep the kudos for apprehending Caitlyn Robarts all for themselves, and Drew wasn't such an innocent that he didn't know how much of a boost a detective's career might get by such an arrest. And so when Rigby had asked if he could meet Drew to discuss the case 'in calmer circumstances', as he put it, Drew felt that that would be very welcome.

As a result, having booked in to one of the hotels in Hereford for the night, since nobody seemed inclined to give him a lift to Worcester, Drew met Rigby at Sunday lunchtime in one of the quieter city centre pubs.

"Thanks for coming," Rigby said, as Drew walked over to the corner table. "I picked this one since it's out of the way and we can talk freely. Can I get you a drink?"

Feeling the need to keep a clear head, but already awash with coffee from breakfast, Drew requested just an orange juice, and got a nod of approval from Rigby, who he noticed was also on a soft drink unless that pint of what looked like lemonade had gin or vodka in it as well. When Rigby came back, he politely asked how Drew was, sympathising that it must have been quite a shock to find Josh's body – or what was left of it.

"I don't imagine you've been out to many crime scenes," he said soothingly.

"No. they don't tend to crop up in property sales or will making," Drew conceded, even so shivering at a memory from his own past.

"Miss Newsome – if that's truly who she is – seemed to take it much more in her stride," Rigby craftily added. "Seems to me you can't be part of a family like that and not have seen a few things that would give other people sleepless nights."

And there it was. The very thing that had been lurking away in Drew's subconscious. Why had Kat seemed so unfazed by the sight of Josh's skeleton? That wasn't normal, was it? Even with those odd grandparents of hers, she surely hadn't seen that much of death? Or was it rather that she was just so hardened to everything that she was incapable of feeling much for anyone? He hoped not, but then nothing else seemed to fit what he'd witnessed, and so he found himself inclined to agree with Rigby.

Over the course of the next hour, Drew found himself revealing more and more of what had gone on in that strange couple of days since he'd met Kat. Part of him was telling himself to shut up, and that he was being naïve if he thought that Rigby wasn't going to use this against Kat. But another part of him was feeling very hurt that this seemingly nice woman, whom he'd been so attracted to, had been using him all along. And that part of him wasn't such an angel that he didn't want her to get her comeuppance for that, excusing it to himself that he'd be saving some other poor guy from being suckered by her.

Yet even so, a quiet voice inside of him was saying disgustedly, *Really Drew? You'd stoop so low? She's done nothing to you, nothing at all, so why are you being such an arsehole about this? You do realise that you're shooting any chance you had with her down in flames, don't you? But then you do this every time a woman comes along who you might have a chance with. For God's sake, you've got to get over your past or you're going to end up some sad old bloke propping up the end of the bar all on his own, while your friends are at home with their wives and families. Not everybody's family is going to be as warped and twisted as yours.*

But it was no good. By the time he'd blurted out about the portal, and faked laughing at the ridiculousness of such a thing to cover his embarrassment, he found he'd talked himself into going up to the house right now with Rigby. And so as they got into the detective's car – parked rather too conveniently close by for Drew to be able to have second thoughts – he found himself quietly praying that Kat wouldn't have been daft enough to go back to the house today.

By the time they got there, Rigby had talked Drew into thinking that DI Scathlock had been more than a little self-serving in trying to convince him of Kat as the heroic witness, risking her all. And so there was a part of him that wanted to go into the cellar and see nothing more than dust and cobwebs. Something that would be all perfectly normal and sane. On the other hand, that irritating little voice of his conscience was still nagging away at him, and wanting the portal to be active so that Kat would be proven right.

And so Drew let Rigby witter on as they went into the house and around to the cellar steps. Perhaps he should have taken the lead then, he was to think later, because if he'd been in front, things might have been very different. Instead, he let Rigby go down ahead of him, and it was only when he nearly barged into the detective at the bottom of the stairs that he woke up to what must be happening.

"Nooo!" Rigby spat savagely. "Hey you! ...Yes you, whoever you are! Cut it out! Game's over! Switch that bloody projector off and come out where I can see you!"

"Rigby, that's not..." Drew started to say, as Rigby snapped on the first cellar's lights and started to walk forwards. "No, Rigby, please! Don't go any closer to it."

Rigby turned around to him, a belligerent expression on his face. "Don't do what? For fuck's sake, Treadwell! Grow some balls! This is nothing but some bloody prank. Some bastard's playing games with us, and I bet I know who, too! It's that bloody woman!" he was picking up speed towards the portal even as Drew was trying to reach out to catch his arm. "God, I hate those bloody smart-arsed women!" Rigby was continuing to fume, but his words struck a chill into Drew. "Think all men are bleeding stupid, they do. Think they should get preferential treatment all the time just because they're women. *Pfhaa!* Getting all the promotions and recognition…"

And there it was, out in the open, Rigby's personal beef with any capable professional woman, making Drew feel such a fool for having been swept along by him. Rigby wasn't the reasonable one. He was as far from having a 'reasonable' view of this situation as it was possible to get. Blinkered and prejudiced, he wouldn't see the truth even when it was staring him in the face, and to Drew's horror he was reaching out saying,

"Look! Just a bloody blue light!"

"*Noooo!*" Drew yelped, diving forwards with the intension of knocking Rigby to one side.

Instead, Rigby was already waving his arm into the portal as Drew made contact with him, and even in its waning state, that close to, its pull was strong. So far from knocking Rigby away from the portal, Drew found himself sucked forwards and into it, with the last thing he heard being Rigby's scream echoing his own.

Chapter 22

By the time Kat had got Scott fed and several cups of tea inside of him, there was still no sign of Drew or Rigby, and now Kat was really seething inside at the pair of them, because the one thing that wouldn't wait any longer was breaking the bad news to Scott. What kind of friend wouldn't want to be there for his mate when he got the news that his wife had died? And yet here was Kat, stuck on her own, and having to break the worst possible news to Scott without any back-up, when in truth he barely knew her. Nor could it wait, because as he recovered his equilibrium, Scott was starting to ask her questions she dared not answer with lies.

"Scott, please come and sit down here," she began, patting the seat of the armchair where Drew had sat previously. "There are things I've got no choice but to tell you, and it's not good news, I'm afraid."

Coming to sit by the fire with her, Scott was with it enough to already guess, "It's to do with Jeanette, isn't it? You've not answered one of my questions about her."

"Yes it is. God, I'm so sorry to have to break this to you right now, Scott, but you were right to be worried about Flora taking your Jag'."

"Oh shit, no!" Scott groaned, burying his head in his hands. "Are they dead?"

"I'm so sorry, yes, they are. But not on the motorway going back to Yorkshire – though heaven only knows how they got away with that. The police found their bags in your house, so they know that they got that far. But for some reason they were driving back out again. From what I was told, there's a sharp bend just before you get to the proper road, and with a steep drop down to a stream?"

Scott looked up at her, his face white and with an appalled expression. "Oh no! They didn't go down there, did they?" then took in Kat's regret-filled nod. "Oh bloody hell, they wouldn't have stood a chance. Not an earthly. I presume Flora was driving?"

"I gather so. At first the police thought that the brakes must have been tampered with, because there was no sign of Flora having braked for the bend. They were even chasing after you because they thought you might have done it."

"*What?*"

"I know. Drew and I both independently told them how terrifying Flora's driving was, and then after forensic inspection of the car, they decided that the brake cables being cut had been part of the crash, not the cause of it." She took a deep breath as Scott sat staring blankly into the fire. "Can I add something else? You may not believe this, but after what you've just experienced you might. You see my maternal grandparents were a bit ...unusual," and she told him about Papa Viktor and Grandma Valerie.

"Now the thing is, just occasionally I 'see' things. I don't mean hallucinations or anything dramatic like that. It's more like a very strong image comes into my mind that I'm not expecting, and it goes way beyond normal imagining. It's more like I'm being shown something very real."

"Okay, I might not have believed this a fortnight ago, but I'm with you now."

"Well I told Drew about what I 'saw', and he said this had happened before with you. You see, I saw Jeanette reaching over and grabbing a car steering wheel."

There was a strong huff of breath from Scott as he leaned back in the seat. "Holy crap. So she finally did it. …Yes, he's right, she had done that to me. Three times in fact. Every time I took her back to the doctors and they upped her antidepressants, but I don't think they did much good." Tears were starting to run down his cheeks, even though he wasn't sobbing as Kat had expected, and he began scrubbing them away as he added. "It was another reason why I tolerated her verbally shoving the blame for what happened to Kevin and Martin onto me all the time. I knew, you see, that deep down inside she couldn't forgive herself. She knew that I'd been right about them not having the bike. And that I'd told her time and again that if Kevin wasn't doing as he was told – both about wearing the crash helmets, and about not having Martin on the back – then she was to take the keys off him."

"Except that she didn't."

Scott nodded sadly. "Except she never did.

And so that crash really *was* on her and Flora for not being the adults in the situation. In her heart of hearts she realised that, Kat, and it was driving her mad – almost literally, I'd say. I was scared to death to leave her because I knew she wanted to commit suicide, that she couldn't live with herself anymore, and my one hope was that over time the pain would start to dull for her. But if anything I think it got worse. The loss of the boys she might have got to a point where she could live with it, but her own guilt? No, that just seemed to be getting worse month on month, I suspect because she had nothing to distract her from seeing what she'd done for the first time in her life."

"That's part of why you wanted to divert her attention by bringing her down here, isn't it?"

"Oh yes, very much so. And why I wanted to leave Flora behind, because that bloody woman never had a guilty moment in her life, nor an ounce of compassion. But Jeanette seemed to need her like some religious flail to her soul, and once she'd rejoined us down here, it was obvious that Jeanette was never going to heal." He sighed heavily again. "But to go like that? Bloody hell, that's cruel."

Kat felt she had to offer him something more, and so said, "I think it must have been very quick, though. Honestly, Scott, the police showed me a photograph of the Jag' to identify it as the one you'd had down here, and it was virtually unrecognisable – I think back then that they wondered if you'd hired another to confuse the issue, you see, although that soon changed.

The force of the impact must have been incredible. No airbag could have cushioned that, but then that's one mercy, because they'd have been here one minute and gone the next. There was no lingering in pain for Jeanette, of that I'm sure." And she was, she realised, and offered up silent thanks to her grandparents for that psychic nudge too.

"Yes, that would be a blessing," Scott decided, seeming to pull himself together a bit. "Sorry, Kat, you've had the rotten job of telling me. But in truth, I'm feeling more than a bit guilty myself. You see while I was on the other side, I was in two minds whether to even come back, and a lot of that was to do with the burden Jeanette had become to me. To suddenly find myself free of her, and in a situation where there was nothing I could do to help her, was so weirdly liberating and such a relief."

"I think that's a very understandable feeling," Kat sympathised. "Especially as it was never just Jeanette you were carrying the load for. Even in the short time I knew them, Flora came across as someone who'd be very good at shoving her problems off onto someone else. And *that* you never deserved to have to carry."

"No, Flora was a burden of a wholly different kind, and God forgive me for this, but in her case I wish that she had suffered more."

"Oh she won't get away with it," Kat said with a weak smile. "Grandma Valerie didn't believe in Hell in the biblical sense – you know, the old fire and brimstone stuff – but she said that once in the afterlife we have to account for our actions in this one, in as much as we're made to understand the implications of what we've done. If you've caused nothing but distress and misery, I suppose you could consider that a kind of hell of your own making. In which case, Flora is in for a very long period of spiritual discomfort."

That actually cheered Scott enough to wring out a wan smile. "Then I hope your Grandma Valerie is right. ...By the way, you said that Drew was here? Did you mean here at the house right now?"

"Ah, that's a bit harder to explain," Kat sighed, and had to go through all that had happened with Drew and herself, so that he would understand why she hadn't rushed out to greet Drew when he'd arrived today.

"Good Lord, that's a tale and a half," Scott declared when she finished. "Well I'm very sorry for that lad Josh. To get all the way back home and to still die from an arrow from the past is just rotten luck. But don't be too hard on Drew, either. You're not the only one with a messy past, unfortunately."

"Really? But Drew seemed so ...well, normal, for want of a better word."

Scott grimaced. "And that's the trouble in a way. His father put in a lot of effort keeping a façade up in town, and so people make assumptions about what the family home life was like. So poor old Drew doesn't get cut much slack, I'm afraid, especially by women – though that's not criticism of you, but rather of previous girlfriends. Let's go and find him and see if I can persuade him to tell you his story himself."

"Okay, if you feel up to going into the house again?"

Scott heaved himself to his feet. "Ah, but don't forget, the past wasn't the traumatic experience for me that it was for those two lads – who do sound a right pair of snowflakes, to be frank, both from what you've told me, and from what old George said, too. So come on, let's go and find Drew and this pain in the arse copper."

Yet when they went across to the house, though they called and searched, there was neither hide nor hair of either man. And once down in the cellar, they found the lights on, no sign of the portal, but a dropped warrant card from Rigby.

"Oh no!" Kat gulped. "Surely not? Drew must have had enough sense not to go anywhere near that thing?"

"Drew might, but what about Rigby? Drew's a good sort, you know. He wouldn't let even a bloke like Rigby come to grief without trying to stop him."

"Oh bugger. Then we're going to have to hope that they manage to come back tomorrow night or the one after, because otherwise they're going to be stuck there for a whole year!"

Scott looked at her, horrified. "A year?"

Kat winced. "Come on back across to the cottage and I'll explain further. Oh, and leave that warrant card where it was dropped. As far as the police are concerned, I was never back here, and we'll have to come up with some way that I found you away from here, too."

"You did get a bruising off Rigby," Scott said sympathetically, realising now why she had put gloves on to go back into the house, and had insisted that she be the one to open doors and switch on lights.

"That's putting it mildly," Kat admitted, coming to a stop in the courtyard. "I don't know what I'd have done if I hadn't had that contact with DI Scathlock. I could've been looking at packing up my life and going into hiding just as my mum and dad have had to do, if Rigby had splashed my name across the papers. And the whole point of doing what I did was so that we'd all be able to have some semblance of a normal life. Not be forever looking over our shoulders. I think that's what's set me so against him – his blind bashing on even when all the warnings were there for him to see.

"And speaking of that. I'm sorry, Scott, but I think you need to come home with me to Worcester. I truly don't think it's wise for either of us to stay here tonight. For a start off, I don't know if Rigby had any close buddies who he might have told what he was planning. If he did, and they don't get his triumphant crowing that I've been proven a lying bitch, they might come looking."

"In which case we certainly don't want to be found here," Scott agreed regretfully. "Damn, I wanted to be here when he got back."

"Well unlike you, he knows the way home," Kat pointed out.

Scott suddenly smiled. "Yes he does. I left your stone with old George – just in case some other unfortunate got sucked in. God, I never thought it would be Drew, though, never in a month of Sundays."

"But it does mean that he knows what he's got to do. ...So I'm sorry, Scott, but we need to clear every trace that we were here and get away. He can't come back now until late tomorrow afternoon, and a lot might happen between now and then. At this point we need to cover our own backs. It would be a bitter pill to swallow if having found your way home, you then got accused of harming Drew."

That really made Scott blink, but it got him helping her to pack what little she'd got out of her car back into it, and then they made a brief foray into the cottage to grab some clean clothes for him. After which, Scott helped Kat to push her car out of the undergrowth so that she didn't churn the ground up too much trying to drive it off the softer earth. Once they were back on the road towards Worcester, though, Kat explained her theory about the super-moons and why the portal had been missed in the years since it came into existence.

"Hmm, and you say that this isn't absolutely regular, like the equinoxes are?" Scott asked thoughtfully.

"No, certainly not in a way that would have been easily anticipated in the past," Kat told him. "If you're up for it, tomorrow morning we could come as far as Hereford Library and have a look through the old newspapers? We might find some reference to those men who went missing, especially given that you have a bit more of an idea about who some of them were. I have to admit it would set my mind at rest a bit if I could pinpoint those disappearances to the times of the super-moons, because that's about the only kind of proof we're going to find.

"But even before that, tonight we have to come up with a reasonable explanation for your being missing for so long, and how I've managed to find you. I know this might go against your better instincts, Scott, but in this instance the truth isn't an option – and heaven help me, I've had lots of practice at 'adjusting' the truth to what people will comfortably believe, and like now, with more than my own neck in the noose if they don't."

Pulling up outside her tiny house tucked into the lee of three large tower blocks, Kat led Scott inside, and for the first time he saw how frugally she'd been living. As she prepared a meal for them both in the little galley kitchen at the back, she told him the same as she had Drew about her plans to get a larger house. However Scott saw another side to this, and as they sat at her little dining table, squeezed in under the upper part of her stairs and landing, he ventured to say,

"But that's not all, is it?"

"What do you mean?"

"Oh come on, Kat, how long would it take you to pack all of this up and move? Not even a day, I would have thought."

Kat had the grace to look sheepish. "Fair cop, governor, you've caught me out. Ever since the trial I've had trouble settling down. I'd never thought about it before, you know. Perhaps because I'd been living with Papa and Grandma, and then doing the normal off to uni' student thing. But after that trial it really made me think twice about stuff. That was why I changed my name by deed poll while I was still at uni. They understood, and I wanted to graduate under the name I'd be using in the future." She gave a sad shake of her head. "Even so, I felt so ashamed that I wasn't using my mum and dad's name to graduate with. It felt like a betrayal of all the effort they put into me having the best possible childhood possible.

"You see, they could have carted me around Europe with them. They were my rightful parents, after all. But they quickly decided that I needed stability and a proper home, and with mum's parents having no associations with Birmingham, let alone the part where the Robarts gang held sway, they were the obvious ones to ask. Even then, if they hadn't been willing it would have been a different matter, and I suppose I might have ended up in some European boarding school. But I didn't, and I'm eternally grateful for the sacrifice my mum and dad made to give up their time with me so that I could have a normal childhood. With the perspective that's come with me getting into my thirties and thinking about having a family myself, I've come to realise what a huge thing that was for them to do, because it certainly wasn't that they didn't want to have me with them."

Scott was regarding her gravely as he said, "As one who's had kids, I have to say that I, too, admire what your parents did. As you say, it was no small thing for them to do, because they must have known that they'd be missing all the landmark moments. Dear God, I missed enough with the boys because of working away, and because of Flora's malignant influence, and that was hard enough. But to do what they did, and when they must have wanted to have kids…?"

"Oh yes, they did. Mum's said since that they'd hoped to have a large family, but by the time I was a toddler things had started to get bad. I can just about remember my pre-school years being in Italy and then Croatia, and it seeming idyllic to me then. All that sun and sand, and always having either Mum or Dad with me – because I now know that they deliberately worked opposite shifts at the hotel so that one of them would always be there.

"But of course, as I got closer to school age, and Dad's brother got more and more frustrated that he couldn't pressure Dad into coming to work with him, Mum says that they realised that the dream of a big family was going to have to stay as that – just a dream. They knew her parents would take me on, but at their ages to ask them to take another two or three on just wasn't sensible or kind. And bless Papa and Grandma, they gave me the most wonderful childhood. I don't think I'd be anything like as sane or stable if they hadn't. And although I care about my parents deeply, it's Papa and Grandma who I loved and now miss terribly, and it was them who gave me the strength to go to the police with the evidence of Dad's brother."

"You're not referring to him as 'uncle'."

"No, I'm not, and it's because he's never earned that. An uncle ought to be someone who looks out for their family, not who drags them into their own personal hell. Poor Dad, he was never able to quite dissociate the man his brother became from the boy he shared his childhood with. Even after my mum got crippled, he still couldn't quite believe that his own brother would sanction something like that. And it was close to murder. But Papa and Grandma had said all the way through my childhood that Alf Robarts was evil incarnate, and consequently I was never even slightly emotionally torn on his account."

Scott sat back in the chair and handed Kat his plate as she got up to clear away. "You know you have far more in common with Drew than you would believe."

"Me and Drew? Seriously? Mr law-abiding-solicitor-man who doesn't give anyone the benefit of the doubt? I find that a bit hard to believe."

Scott winced. Bloody hell, Drew really had mucked this up if Kat thought that of him. Why couldn't he have gone with his gut instincts just for once on this one? Because of every woman he'd met, Scott felt in his heart of hearts that Kat was the one woman who might truly understand what Drew had been through.

Chapter 23

After they'd finished eating and moved into Kat's tiny lounge, the first issue was what to tell the police about Scott's reappearance.

"Keep it simple," Kat warned. "Don't over complicate things. If you had a knock on the head, as everyone already thinks, then you've every reason to be very fuzzy about a few days if not a whole week."

"So where do I say I've been?" Scott asked worriedly. "I can hardly have gone back to Yorkshire, can I? Especially as the police up there have been looking for me with regards to the crash."

"No, definitely not Yorkshire," Kat agreed. "I think you need to have been down here somewhere. Possibly sleeping rough because you couldn't remember where you were, or *who* you were. If I take you on a drive around some of the lanes tomorrow, they'll be vaguely familiar enough to you to be recognisable if the police ask you to go out with someone to see if anywhere strikes a chord. Nothing clear will be far more convincing than crystal sharp memories. The big thing we're going to have to come up with is what you've been eating and drinking since then, unless you say you had quite a bit of money on you to buy stuff without using a traceable card; and in that sense, the fact that you've been drinking the water in the past – which will hardly have been pure – will probably mean you pass any medical examination they want to give you. That and the fact that you're now sporting that rather ferocious beard."

Scott laughed. "So is that why you didn't want me to shave it off?"

"Yes! You have to be convincing as a man who has spent the last week or so living rough. If necessary, say that you stole food from farms. There are enough around that part of the world who sell produce at the farm gate, and have vegetables and fruit in store. You could easily say that you can't remember where, but that you got some raw stuff from a farm shop that was locked up for the night. Maybe stole it from the bins out the back? Customers are very picky about the slightest bruise on an apple, or a carrot that's a bit past its best, so we're not implying you were eating stuff only fit for the pigs. And the good thing is, nobody but me saw you before you went missing, so if we say you've lost weight too, we might get away with it."

Scott grimaced. "My clothes will bear that out without any lying on my part. Over the last year I've lost a lot of weight." He eased the buckle on the belt and put two fingers into the waistband of the clean jeans he'd put on after he'd gratefully piled into Kat's shower, and tugged at them to show how much room there was now. "Look at that! I could go down a full size, maybe two, without any trouble. The only reason I hadn't bought any new clothes was because I really didn't care anymore."

Kat looked at him appraisingly. "Gosh, I never noticed that before, but of course you were wearing a fleece, so the fact that that was a bit loose didn't register as odd with me. I just thought you were one of those men who's broader in the shoulder compared to the rest of you, and so that's why it was baggier lower down."

Scott shook his head. "No, by the time I gave up my job, the business dinners had begun to take their toll on my waistline. If not actually porky, then I was a far cry from the slim lad I used to be. But now? Now I'd say I'm getting back to the size I was in my twenties, and that might be a shock to anyone who hasn't seen me in a while."

"Then that's all to the good," Kat decided, "because if the police show your photo to people in Yorkshire now, they'll notice you've lost weight."

In the end they decided that any more than that would depend on Rigby's frame of mind when he came back with Drew. If the detective was determined to be belligerent, then Scott might have to do some fast thinking. But if the trip through the portal shook him up as much as Kat thought it might, he could as easily be willing to accept Scott's story at face value, just glad to not have to revisit his own nightmare. Yet just as they were about to spread the sleeping bags out for Scott on Kat's floor, with the addition of the sofa and chair cushions for a bit more padding,

Kat suddenly clapped a hand to her forehead, exclaiming,

"What an idiot I've been!"

"Kat? What? What 's wrong?"

"DI Scathlock. He told me he's had a few 'odd' cases, and he wasn't a bit fazed by seeing the portal. If anyone can help us create a story that the police will believe, it's him. I'm going to give him a call right now, because if we can go and see him first thing in the morning, that would be great."

Yet when she rang Bill Scathlock's mobile and explained Scott's reappearance and their dilemma, without hesitation he said,

"Come down to the main police station right now! I'll explain once you get here, but you might be able to help us as much as I can you."

"Gosh, that's a bit cryptic."

Scathlock gave a grunt. "Just come down. I'll meet you at the front desk."

At that time on a Sunday evening it was barely a five minute drive to the police station, and as they walked in through the door, sure enough, DI Scathlock was waiting for them.

"Quick, down here," he said, guiding them through to an interview room. Once inside, though, he made no attempt to turn on the recording equipment.

"Now listen," he began, "I'm on duty, and we've just done a sting on a nasty piece of work who's been human trafficking. We've been after this bastard for months, but because he keeps buggering off home to Latvia, it's taken us ages to catch him.

"What this evil little scrote does is transport his fellow countrymen over here to work as little more than slave labour on the less reputable farms. We've known we've been making a dent in his profits, because on his last two runs he's had to dump his 'cargo' out in the countryside when he's realised we were on his tail. Sadly, those poor sods were so frightened of his gang back home, they won't testify. We got DNA matches the last time for some of them from the inside of his wagon, where there's a secret compartment, and connected that evidence to those who we managed to catch stumbling around in the dark. But even so, none of them will actually point him out in a line up and say, 'that's him.'

"Well we've got uniformed officers out trying to round up the half dozen he dumped on the roadside near Ledbury a few hours ago, but I'm betting that they'll be the same as the previous ones we've brought in. They're as frightened of us as they are of him, and that doesn't help, either. But when you said you needed some help, it occurred to me that this might help us both out."

"In what way?" Scott asked, more than a little perplexed.

Scathlock gave a disgusted grunt. "This charmer thinks that because we're English, we're too soft, and going to be a pushover. The outright lies we've caught him out over – like the mother he told us had died one time and whose funeral he *had* to go back for, suddenly being in the land of the living sufficiently to be 'seriously ill' as another fake reason why he *had* to go back home the next — and yet he still thinks he's going to get away with this because this is England and nothing really bad could possibly happen to *him* here. But the thing is, we don't just want him, we want the evil bastards who are behind him.

"...Oh, don't get me wrong," he added hurriedly, seeing the slight confusion on Scott and Kat's faces, "I want to nail him, and I want to do it legitimately so that he can't wriggle out of anything. There's a nineteen year old girl in Worcester Hospital who's just miscarried at six months thanks to the way he treated her, and that makes me bloody angry! We knew we'd buggered his plans the last time he was over — which was when we found the girl — and that was only last week. And so when the border police contacted us to say that this time he'd been reckless enough to come back in the same truck, we knew we'd got him on the hop. He's come in different registration units each time before, you see, which also made it harder to pin anything onto him, even though most of them were fake plates. But he and his masters are greedy, and we hoped they'd want to make one more run to recover their money's worth before giving it a rest.

"Well we were right, and this time they got careless — either that or desperate. But the icing on the cake would be if we could pin this bastard not just for the transporting — which, by the way, he claims every time he knew nothing about, though how you could not hear a girl screaming her head off in pain in the back beggars belief —

but as someone actively doing the trafficking. And it's got to everyone on this case with the way he just sits there smirking at us, and lawyering up the moment he gets in here."

"I still don't see how I can help," Scott confessed.

However Scathlock held up a cautionary hand. "Don't worry, I'm not going to ask you to falsify evidence or anything. I'm merely thinking of scaring the shit out of him, that's all. If we move him from the interview room to a cell, and in the process he happens to pass you in the corridor, what I'm hoping you'll do is say very loudly, 'That's him! That's the bloke who shoved me into his van with those other people,' or something similar – whatever you're comfortable with."

He saw Scott's raised eyebrows and hurriedly clarified, "I'm never going to put that in writing. Your name will never go onto any tape or paperwork connected with this case. It's just that I've got this griping feeling in my gut that this sod's a total coward deep down. And it's not just me. We've all said that if he thinks someone's going to finger him in a line-up, then he'll turn on his bosses in a heartbeat to save himself from doing serious time. It's just that we've never been able to make that line-up because all of his victims are too scared to even do it from behind the glass.

"So if you two will go and sit by the coffee machine while we tell him we're whipping up a line-up, we'll get you and him to pass one another. He won't know that subsequently there's nobody on the other side of the glass when he goes into the line-up, although I doubt we'll even need to get him into the room by then. All we're going to do is feed his fear a bit and let his own imagination do the work for us. And from your point of view, having several Worcester lads able to say that they've seen you here in our nick on the day that you were found ought to silence a lot of questions for you."

Scott thought for a moment. "A nineteen year old girl, you say?"

Scathlock opened a file and pulled out a photo. The waif-like girl in it looked nearly as white as the hospital pillow she was lying on, white that was except for the patchwork of dark purple bruises mottling her face, and the split lip which marred her looks even more. Her nose would never be straight again, and neither would the one cheekbone, but it was the past caring look in the one eye she could open which was most upsetting.

"Point him out to me," Scott said, instantly seeing why this had bugged Scathlock so badly.

Scathlock grinned at Kat. "I'll even make the call to Hereford for you, if you like. Say that Scott's turned up dazed and grubby, but generally unharmed, even if he can't remember where the hell he's been since he got whacked on the head."

That seemed like a fair offer, and as Kat and Scott concluded in a hurried but quiet discussion as they sipped their coffees, inevitably whatever they were going to do was going to necessitate lying to the police in some form or other.

Nobody was going to take it seriously that Scott had spent a week in a different millennium, and might even get very nasty if they thought he and Kat were trying to pull the wool over their eyes. And so as long as Scathlock made nothing of this ruse official, they decided they would go along with his plan.

Not long after, Scathlock appeared out of one door and came to stand beside them, "He's on his way with two of my colleagues, who've told him that we've got a line-up waiting for him, so come and stand here in this interview room doorway. I can tell you that although he's putting on a lot of bluster, just the thought that we're going through with this identification has got him jittering. His leg was jiggling like he'd got ants in his pants when they went into the cell to get him."

Moments later another door open and there was no mistaking who the trucker was. Slicked back greasy hair, lurid tattoos on his hands, tatty fake designer clothes, and a strong reek of cheap tobacco made him a stark contrast to the two accompanying policemen. He strolled through with an arrogant swagger, and a sneer on his lips as one of the policemen said,

"Down here to the line-up."

"You got nothi..." he was starting to say, when Scott made as if to shove past Scathlock, who played his part nicely, catching hold of Scott's arm as he cried out,

"That's him! That's the bastard who shoved me in his truck! Thought I was some tramp!

Whacked me over the head again, he did, like it wasn't enough he ran into me!"

"Eh?" the Latvian yelped, all the fight going out of him like a pricked balloon. "Who you…?"

"Oh come on, Gatis," the other policeman cut him off with, both of them tightening their hold on him as they hustled him onwards. "You keep telling us you can't remember who these people are. Are you suddenly going to expect us to believe that you know just one man? Pull the other one!"

"Is he the one?" they heard Gatis squeak in terror. "Is he the one who's going to finger me?"

"Finger you?" they heard the one constable say innocently. "…Oh, the bloke back there? …Don't know. Think he's just in on a drunk and disorderly."

The trio vanished through another door, but they could hear the man Gatis' protestations of,

"I not going in there! …You can't make me!" rising in panic even as they faded away, but not before they heard his squeal of,

"Okay, okay, I talk. …I help, you make deal, yes?"

"Perfect!" Scathlock said happily. "He'll be giving us chapter and verse within half an hour. We'll never have to do any actual line-up going by the way he's panicking. And as far as he and his solicitor will be concerned, you're just someone disorientated and dehydrated from your days living rough, and he's jumped to the wrong conclusion out here. Now then, come up to my office and I'll make this call to whoever's on duty over at Hereford, and then you can go home and get some rest."

* * * * *

"I can't believe that went so well," Kat confided to Scott the next lunchtime as they drove once more towards Fownhope Priors. "DI Scathlock certainly had that trucker read right," for the errant Latvian was currently singing like the proverbial canary now that it had finally sunk in that he was going to carry the full weight of the prosecution. The result of that was that in return for a reduced sentence, he was giving the anticipated chapter and verse on the gang he was working for, and the police were confident of making a series of arrests in conjunction with other forces, hopefully dismantling the whole English end of the gang's operations. And best of all, even the trucker's solicitor didn't believe him about the strange man he'd passed in the station during the night. Gatis had cried wolf so many times already that he'd lost all credibility.

What was more, there had been a phone call to Kat's mobile in the morning from the Hereford detective inspector – Rigby's boss, and who of course had never met Kat – but who had obviously spoken to Scathlock already, and was merely checking that all was well. Clearly the force didn't have the spare manpower to worry too hard about a grown man who had gone missing, but had turned up in one piece and with no claims of kidnapping or forcible restraint to be followed up on. Indeed the only troubling moment was when he asked Kat if she'd seen DS Rigby, since he hadn't reported in for work, nor was he answering his phone. Yet nobody so far seemed to be thinking that he would have gone back to Fownhope Priors, because Kat had a feeling that they might be questioning her and Scott a lot harder if they did.

At the house they went through and down into the cellars. With it being not much beyond midday as yet, the portal hadn't opened, but Kat had wanted to be absolutely sure of that, and also to reassure Scott that Drew couldn't have come through as yet.

"Right, then let's go and have a look in Hereford Library," Kat suggested. "With us having the years and months for when several of those men went missing, it surely can't be that hard to find any newspaper reports of the time."

Once they had found the right part of the library, Kat was proven right, for missing people weren't that common an occurrence out in the countryside.

"Here we go," she said, pointing to the article which lay in the second column of the newspaper page. "Oh how awful! George and his friends are made out as common thieves! And all because they took their tools with them."

Scott sighed. "I suspect as common labourers, this man the paper's talking to who hired them probably supplied a good many of those tools. You can't really blame him for being cheesed off that, as he must have seen it, the men made off with his property. After all, they never reappeared in his lifetime, did they?"

"No, I suppose not," Kat admitted, "But it does seem very unfair that someone who was as nice as you described old George as being should have been thought of like that. It says here that some of them were from the Rhonda Valley. I do hope that news of this never got back there. I remember Grandma telling me that back in those days the chapels ruled the Welsh valleys with a rod of iron. An awful lot of Bible thumping and 'thou shalt not's got handed out. One hint of a member of your family being a thief would have been enough to tarnish the reputation of the whole family. Bad enough if a family was unlucky enough to have a genuine rotten apple amongst them, but for men like these, who in truth were wholly blameless, it does feel horrible unjust if this freak of nature ended up harming their families too."

"Hmmm, I hadn't thought of it rebounding on their families," Scott admitted, "but then after so long, I don't think the four original men had much of a memory of their families anymore. They certainly never talked of them. What of Eli the footman and his brother Enoch? They went through in December 1920. They really had my sympathy. Just back from the Great War, thought they were lucky to get any sort of job with the big depression coming on, and then only months later they're shovelling coal and end up in a different kind of hell."

Kat scoured the newspapers until she found the right month. "Oh, here we go …Reported missing …oh no! That's so sad! They'd already been described as suffering from shellshock and only ever talking to one another. This butler the paper talks to sounds really worried that they might have lost their minds and gone wandering off."

"They weren't in great shape when I saw them," Scott admitted. "In fact I asked about them once I'd got my ear in to the others' accents, because they stood out as being so switched off. George said it was to do with a war, but of course for him in the 1890s that was unknown."

"What about the other men?"

However Scott now shrugged. "I didn't have long enough to get to know them. And to be frank, I think that at least one of them might have fallen through the portal at a time when the house was empty."

"Okay, let's see if we can find anything out about that."

An hour's search only turned up a couple of articles in the glossy magazines of the day, but it seemed that once the Second World War came around, the house was too remote to have been used as a hospital, as some other grand houses had been, and had been empty more often than lived in for the whole of the second half of the twentieth century.

"Well I think that answers that," Scott sighed when they finally gave up their search. "Poor Dai the coalman didn't even warrant a mention, and the other blokes must have been semi-derelicts who got into the house to try and find somewhere dry and warm to live. The cellars would have been the obvious way in and out for them, because it would have left the main doors securely locked, meaning if anyone came looking it would all seem undisturbed." He looked around for a clock. "What time is it?"

"Half past three. We've just got time to go and grab a coffee and a sandwich and then get out to the house. Moonrise is around half four today."

Chapter 24

In the past world, Drew was having a whole other kind of nightmare. He and Rigby had tumbled through together, and if their arrival hadn't been with the brutal thump that had knocked Scott out, nonetheless it was a disorientating and stomach-churning landing. But whereas Drew had staggered dazedly to his feet and then held his hands up in the universal gesture of surrender, as he took in the deadly crossbows pointing at them, Rigby had gone on the offensive. Screaming like a maniac, he had dived at one of the soldiers, and though by some miracle the crossbow bolts loosed at him missed, in his hazy state he tried to land several punches, though he was no serious threat to the soldiers while that befuddled.

A swift thump to the jaw had had Rigby reeling even more, and then with callous disregard, the soldier had simply reversed his crossbow and thumped Rigby on the head with the solid wooden butt. At that point Rigby had been dragged, and Drew walked, across to the workers' camp. Yet to Drew's surprise the guards left them to it, instead going around the camp as if looking for someone. That allowed Drew the chance to call out softly,

"Scott? Are you here, Scott?"

"Scott's gone," a wizened old man said, coming hobbling up to him, and pointing to where Drew suddenly realised another blue swirling light lay.

"Oh bloody hell! Kat was right!" he gulped.

"Yes!" the old man said, and then said something which Drew thought might be, 'Scott spoke of someone called Kat,' and then thrust something into Drew's hand.

For a moment Drew didn't realise what it was, but then his vision cleared and he realised it was the distinctive stone he had thrown back and forth with Scott. Except now it was more than that. When had those markings been put on it?

"Kat," the old man said, tapping the stone, and suddenly Drew knew what he meant. Kat, the woman he had metaphorically thrown under the wheels of Rigby's car, had kept her head together and had come up with a way to help Scott, while he'd been no bloody use at all. Why hadn't he trusted his instincts? Why hadn't he believed the evidence of his own eyes? The portal had been there right in front of him, and what had he done? He'd believed Rigby's self-serving excuses and disbelief over the woman who, even before today, had been proven to be right.

And why was that? Because of his own past. Because when you can't even trust your parents anymore, how do you trust someone else? Yet even that wasn't enough to excuse his behaviour, he was forced to acknowledge. That came down to his lack of courage to try at another relationship. He'd made a mess of things with his ex-wife, Meg, and since then he'd made a run for the hills every time he'd found himself confronted with a woman who he was really attracted to. *Which makes you a fucking idiot!* he told himself sourly. *With what you've now been told of her background, of any woman you've ever met, she's the one who might just understand what a horrible position your parents put you in back when you weren't old enough to argue back.*

That had left him sitting miserably in the drizzle until the old man had come and chivvied him closer to the fire, but when Rigby woke up later in the evening, the verbal fireworks started again. Seemingly unable to come to terms with the fact that, even if he couldn't accept that he was in the past, that he was somewhere beyond anyone coming to rescue them tonight, Rigby began bawling and shouting. Drew knew that the soldiers watching them wouldn't have a clue as to what he was actually saying, but they weren't stupid, and they knew full well when they were being threatened.

"For fuck's sake, shut up!" Drew hissed at him, when Rigby paused to draw breath. "You're not achieving anything by antagonising them like that!"

"I'm a member of Her Majesty's police force!" Rigby fumed. "How dare they? How bloody dare they!"

"It doesn't matter how they 'dare'," Drew threw back at him. "If you don't want another smack on the head, keep your mouth shut!"

But it was no use. Rigby kept on and on, and in the end the inevitable happened, with him not only getting another whack on the head from the butt of a crossbow, but a damned good kicking thrown in for good measure. All Drew could do was to keep his head down and hope that the guards would think him the placid one. He had no desire to join Rigby in getting that kind of beating. Getting trampled on while playing rugby was one thing, but these men knew what they were doing and were going for maximum pain with minimal damage, and Drew knew that they would still expect Rigby to get up and start working in the morning, if only because he'd seen the half finished barrel-vaulting and had worked out what that meant. For now, though, all he could do was to huddle down with the other men and try and get what sleep he could, because come tomorrow he had a feeling he was going to need it.

When the watery dawn came around, Drew hadn't had a lot of sleep, and so while others got the fire going for the sloppy oatmeal brew he suspected was all they were going to get in the way of breakfast, he used the brighter daylight to scrutinise Kat's stone. Damn, but she'd crammed a lot onto it! Like Scott, he was initially confused by the dinosaur, but it didn't take him that long to work out what she meant. Yet that brought with it a whole new problem, because Drew wasn't any too certain when the full moon was. Could it be tonight? Tomorrow night? Or had it been last night? Last night wasn't the end of the world, because as he tried to force his brain to work rationally, if he went through tonight and it was just one day after the full moon, then he was unlikely to end up anything more than a day adrift. And that might prove awkward but not impossible to cover. Anything beyond that, though, and he could find himself in serious trouble. He had no desire to end up in the 1800s or even further back.

But what to do? He looked across to where Rigby was coughing and spluttering himself into a waking state. Dare he tell him? Probably not. If he was any judge of Rigby, he'd walk up to the guards and demand that they be let back through the portal – and that was never going to happen!

It didn't help that Scott wasn't here, and if he'd understood the old chap correctly, that Scott had gone through to the future just as they'd fallen into the past. And Scott being Scott, he'd probably been of far more use than anyone else they'd had who'd arrived over the years, so no wonder they were pissed off about him leaving. So how was Drew himself going to get back?

I'll crawl on my bloody hands and knees through the grass if I have to, he thought, *if that's the only way to get to that other portal unnoticed*, and with the dread knowledge that that might be exactly what he'd have to do.

That day was the longest Drew could ever recall. Never in his life had he had to do such back-breaking labour for hour upon hour. No tea breaks. No lunch break. Just keep on shifting those damned great lumps of stone into the place which would eventually become the middle cellar. And something had recently changed, he began to realise. As he laboured on, he kept hearing the name 'Scott', and it didn't take him long to realise that Scott had identified some problem these men had been having and had set them right. Certainly they were now working with a confidence and assurance that meant that they couldn't possibly have been working at this pace and still not have finished what would become the three cellars. Something – though he couldn't have begun to say what – had been holding them up, and that something had now been removed or changed by Scott's time in this era.

What was worse, throughout the day Rigby kept on drawing attention to himself, and twice more Drew saw him getting a beating, although this time it was with leather whips which must by now have been making a mess of Rigby, even through the heavy tweed jacket he'd been wearing when he'd fallen through the portal. The only good thing that Drew could see about that was that the guards had no time to look at himself, and so he kept doing what he was told by the other men and tried to melt into the background. Even so, that tore at his conscience, because as the hours ticked away, it was becoming ever clearer that if he was to have any chance of escape, then he was going to have to leave Rigby behind. There was no way that he could risk saying a word to the detective about his plans to creep up to the portal tonight, none at all.

So when they finally were allowed back into their camp, Drew made a point of sitting well within the group of other men as the revolting stew got slopped out for them. *It's just for tonight*, he reminded himself, *so keep your face straight and eat the bloody stuff.* And it was as he was forcing himself to force down another spoonful that it happened. The portal flared up again.

Yet for no reason that Drew would ever understand, Rigby stood up, shrieking like a steam engine about to blow up, and tried to make a charge towards the cellars where they'd come through from. *What are you doing?* was Drew's first thought. But then as Rigby began trying to batter his way past the guards, admittedly using some unarmed combat techniques that they'd probably never had to counter before, Drew realised that this was his chance. They were all looking the other way. All of them trying to deal with this idiot who, against the odds, had managed to lay out two of the guards already, one of them with a vicious chop to the throat which had that man lying on the ground fighting to breathe, and maybe even dying.

As if reading his mind, the old man suddenly tugged at Drew's sleeve, pointing away to the one side to where Drew now knew the latrine pit was. Of course! That must have been the way that Scott had got close to the portal. And so Drew carefully shuffled along the ground until the main tent was between him and the guards. Then standing up, he made a fast sprint to the latrine pit.

So far, so good. But now he had to make a crouched run for as far as the bushes would give him cover, and it was at this point in the failing light that he saw the signs of somebody having crawled onwards from beyond here. So that was what Scott had done! Well if it had worked for Scott, then there was hope it might work for him, and without any hesitation, Drew got down on his hands and knees and started crawling.

Unlike Scott, though, he got to the bramble patch and looked back to see the guards still wrestling with Rigby. And so instead of making a run for it, which might have caught their eye, he stayed down and hoped to God that all of those charity assault courses he'd completed in the past for good causes might now save his hide. In the fastest crab-like scuttle on all fours he could manage, Drew sidled up to the portal, all the time trying to stay in the darker patches to the side of where the blue light was shining across the grass. Only at the very last did he check behind him, see that four of the guards were now carrying Rigby's limp form between them towards the camp, come up into a crouch, and then make a dive for the portal.

He came at it low and at an angle, yet its energy seemed to be sucking him towards the centre, which he could only hope and pray would be enough. And in a not dissimilar move to the awkward stumble with which he'd arrived in this place, Drew flung himself into the portal with a last prayer that if he was going to die doing this, then let it please be fast and painless.

* * * * *

When they pulled up onto the drive, Kat didn't know whether to be happy or not that Rigby's car was still there. Part of her had been hoping that his colleagues would have twigged where he might have gone and come looking for him. It would certainly have made her and Scott's lives a lot easier, especially if someone could have said that they'd searched the place and found neither hide nor hair of him there. The last thing she wanted was to be accused of spiriting away a detective sergeant!

Scott's thought were obviously echoing her own, because as they walked past the car he said, "Rigby can't be very popular with his colleagues. Otherwise you'd have thought by now that someone would have come up here and found that."

"I saw a fair few women when I was at the police station," Kat mused. "And if the way he spoke to me was typical of his attitude to other women, then I can well imagine he wouldn't be the most popular bloke in the station. It does bother me that nobody's come looking, though, if only because it leaves us with another story to fabricate that will be plausible," and she sighed heavily. "Honestly, Scott, I'm so sick of having to try and keep track of who I told what. If it wasn't for Mum and Dad needing me to keep tabs on what goes on here in the Midlands, I think I'd go and live on Orkney or somewhere. Some place where I could be Kate Smith, or something equally as bland, and where nobody would ever know my past."

"You've certainly had to shoulder more than your share of burdens," Scott sympathised, thinking that if Jeanette had been his albatross hanging about his neck, then Kat had had one equally heavy if of a different kind. Maybe that was why he felt such a kinship with her? And at that moment he resolved to tell her about Drew's past. If nothing else came out of this, if she was seeing Drew in a better light when he came back – and please God he would come straight back – then that would be something good to come out of this mess.

They went into the house and down to the cellar, but stopped at the bottom of the stairs. There was no need to go any farther. The portal was shining brightly down at the far end, and even from where they stood, they could feel it tugging at them.

"Right, let's get up to the garden and pray that Drew and that idiot Rigby make it through," Kat said. "I'd feel a lot happier if we could bolt the cellar stair door, but that would look even more dodgy to anyone searching the place."

Out in the garden, they grabbed a couple of the garden chairs off the patio, then went and sat close enough to watch the gateway, but without being in line with it, Scott being only too aware of the dangers of crossbow bolts following someone through. The one which had snagged in his sleeve was currently hidden in Kat's car, but it had taken some getting out and in the process they'd found out just how sharp the iron head was. One brush with one of those was quite enough, he thought.

As they settled to wait, Scott plucked up his courage and began, "You know I said that Drew had a past...?"

"Yes. You said you'd try and get him to tell me."

"Hmph. Well I've been thinking, and if I know Drew, he'll still be cagey about telling you anything. But of anyone, I think you'll understand why, so I'm going to take a chance and fill you in." He sighed and leaned back in the chair. "I'm not sure if he'd have even told me if he hadn't been so desperate the one time, but this is his story as I heard it.

"You wouldn't think it talking to Drew, but his parents were members of one of those small very fundamentalist Christian sects – you know, the sort who don't believe in medical intervention and stuff. That might be partly why his dad didn't get on very well in the area, because you know what rural communities are like, church on Sunday is pretty much compulsory. Well Drew's dad might have been Christian, but he certainly wasn't rolling up at the parish church on a regular basis like his competitors were.

"But of the two of them, I think Drew's mum was even more fanatical. Drew's dad had to at least be able to keep some semblance of normality going because of meeting people in town. His mum, though, only ever came in to do the shopping, and to my knowledge, she never socialised with anyone – even Flora never managed to find anything out about her, and that was damned near miraculous!"

"Poor Drew. That can't have been easy. Having thoroughly pagan grandparents set me apart, but mine were so caring and helpful to people that they were generally well-liked. But it isn't easy being the kid in the class with the weird family."

"I knew you'd understand. But like your uncle's side, there was something much darker in Drew's family closet."

"Oh?"

"The thing was, Drew's parents had bought this rambling old former farmhouse out on the edge of the moors. Kind of understandable if you thought everyone around you was a heathen being tempted by Old Nick himself, and I think that's why they got away with it. You see Drew isn't – or wasn't – an only child. He was their eldest, but then Mrs Treadwell got pregnant again within a year, and I don't think she was the healthiest of women to start off with. Well Drew had been born at home, and so the next child was too. Whether there were complications with the birth, or whether the damage had happened much earlier in the pregnancy, we'll never know, but Lionel wasn't right. In fact Lionel should have spent a fair bit of his childhood in hospital, by the sound of it."

Horrified by what she feared might be coming, Kat asked, "Just how bad was Lionel?"

"Both physically and mentally disabled to a pretty severe degree, I suspect," Scott sighed. "Yet the really weird thing is, Drew never knew that he had a brother for most of his early childhood."

"Eh? How was that possible?"

"Like I said, one of those rambling old farmhouses, with two separate stairs leading to separate parts of the upper floors. He was always told that his mother was 'delicate', and that's why he never saw her for most of the day. She and Lionel had a set of rooms upstairs on the one side, which Drew was forbidden to ever go near. And the one or two times he did dare even venture onto the stairs, he got such a thrashing off his father that he didn't try too hard again."

"He beat him?"

"Yes, and badly, considering Drew was still pre-teens on both occasions. I don't know how any parent could be that heavy-handed with their child, and God knows my two pushed me hard enough at times, but I couldn't have left marks on them the way Drew's dad did with him."

"Poor Drew!"

"Oh, it gets worse. Obviously someone had to look after Drew while his father was out at work, and so they hired Maud Presley. She only ever came in the morning to get Drew's breakfast and him ready for school, and stayed to clean the downstairs and cook the evening meal. But she never ate with them. Old Mr Treadwell wasn't having that. And he made sure that he was the one who did the dishing up of the meal too. Drew was made to sit at the table saying his prayers with his eyes closed, so he never saw that his father was plating *two* meals up and taking them upstairs. And he was genuinely scared stiff of his dad as a child. Old Treadwell was definitely of the 'spare the rod and spoil the child' kind, and if Drew had been even a generation younger, I think his teachers at school would have been a lot more alert to the problems. But we were amongst the last kids who went through school where nobody questioned what parents did at home too closely.

"When he was eleven, Drew got sent as a weekday boarder to a local boarding school. I think old Treadwell had begun to realise that as Drew got older, it was going to be harder and harder to keep the secret."

"What about school holidays, though?" Kat wondered.

"Oddly, that was easier, because he used to go and stay with Maud Presley and her family right from when he was little. I think she must have guessed that something wasn't right at that house, but with Treadwell being a solicitor, I think she thought she'd never be believed if she tried to tell someone. That's why she did her best to give Drew some sort of normality in his life. Maud was a kind woman, and going and helping on her brother's farm was heaven for Drew. So much so that by the time he got sent to boarding school, I don't think he missed his mother, because he could hardly have ever seen her.

"But in those years Lionel got sicker and sicker. Maybe he would have survived if he'd got proper medical help, but one day when Drew came home for the weekend when he was only just fourteen, his father told him he had a special job for him. He sent Drew out into the field behind the house with a shovel and told him to start digging a hole…"

"…Oh no! Not a grave?"

Scott shivered, even though the late afternoon was far from cold. "Yes, a bloody grave! Then he got Drew to go upstairs to those rooms he'd never been allowed into before, and they carried Lionel's body down between them. Drew's since said that he was sure that Lionel had died days before, but that his father had had to wait until he came home, because Lionel was too heavy for his father to shift on his own. Mrs T was no use, apparently. Just sat sobbing in the rocking chair she must have spent years sitting in beside Lionel's bed.

"But what was worse for Drew, she even asked his father who Drew was. Didn't recognise her own son now that he was growing up. And then when his father told her, she said she wished it had been Drew they were burying and that she could have her 'lovely Lionel' back."

"Jeez, that's harsh! No kid should ever have to hear that, not from anyone, much less their mother."

"No, and Drew was to hear it a lot more over the following years. By then his mother was as mad as a box of frogs. Didn't know what year it was or where she was. Maud Presley was let go – no need for her to keep Drew quiet now – and Drew was threatened with all sorts if he ever told anybody. I mean, when you're still a kid and your dad is a solicitor, and he tells you that the police will have you *hanged* if they find the body, you'd be bloody terrified too, wouldn't you?"

"His dad said *that*?"

"And more! And of course later on, when Drew went to study law himself, he found out what the reaction would be to concealing a body, especially for so many years. He thought he'd never be believed that he hadn't known what was going on, you see. By then his mother had died and been given a normal burial, so it would be just his word against his father's – the upright holier-than-thou pillar of the community, or as near as made no difference."

"Hang on, though. Why did the mum have a proper burial and not Lionel?"

"Because they'd never even registered Lionel's birth! They'd registered Drew, because he was perfectly normal, but not Lionel. They saw his deformities as a judgement upon them from God, and a burden they alone must carry. And of course the longer the deception went on, the harder it would have been to come clean. I think by the end, old Treadwell knew that he and Mrs T would be in serious danger of being charged with criminal neglect of Lionel if a post-mortem was done, maybe even more, such as outright abuse. Well he couldn't stand even the thought of the shame that would bring on him, let alone the actual consequences, and he was one of those desiccated, tall, stick-like men with not a shred of humour, full of pride."

"Good grief, what a horrible mess," Kat sighed, feeling very sorry for Drew now. "So how did you get to know all of this?"

"Because we had to move Lionel!"

"Oh crap! Really?"

Scott nodded. "Bloody stupid really. They buried Lionel in the field beside the house, but they didn't own that, and then one day – years after I'd got to know Drew – he came to me shaking like a leaf and telling me that the field had been sold for a housing development. Of course he then had to tell me why he was so upset, because nobody gets like that at the thought of a few semi-detached houses being put up down the road, do they?"

"Oh good lord, all those deep excavations to put sewers in and stuff!"

"I don't need to draw you a picture do I? The weirdest thing was that old Treadwell wasn't fazed by it. I think with his wife gone, he'd somehow removed it from his mind, made himself think it had never happened. Wouldn't take it seriously. Wouldn't even admit to Drew that he'd coerced him as a child. Wouldn't even permit himself to see what was so blindingly obviously going to happen when the diggers went in. But Drew was in bits. He knew full well that the chances of Lionel going undiscovered were nil. And he had visions of his father ending up in front of the police and him with him, if not actually pointing the finger of blame directly at him in his cockeyed way – you know, my child the spawn of Satan who wrecked the chances of the child which followed him in his mother's womb, and all that crap – which was why Drew confessed to me and begged me to help him."

"So what did you do?"

"We waited until there was another funeral about to happen at the parish church in one of the villages. I was the one who spotted the gravediggers at St Mary's, as luck would have it. So that evening we went out and started digging. Bloody hell, Kat, what a game! Drew had been so knocked sideways at the time of the original burial that he couldn't remember exactly where Lionel was except that it was close-ish to the big old oak tree. In the end I took a day off work, went and hired a mini-digger, and practically took the top layer off that whole corner of the field! We'd never have found him in time otherwise, but it did mean that nobody was going to say, 'ooh, why's that one grave-sized plot been dug up?'

"But I tell you, Kat, the way Drew reacted when we finally found Lionel, I thought he was going to have a heart-attack or something. Right up until that moment I don't think I'd realised how traumatic it had been for him as a boy. It made me go away afterwards and look up what state a body would have been in after four or five days, and after that I could cheerfully have wrung old Treadwell's scrawny neck for him."

"I'm guessing the words 'rank' and possibly 'oozing' apply?"

"I fear so. But of course twelve years on, and with Lionel only having been thrown in wrapped in an old cotton rag-rug, there wasn't anything left by then but bones. Yet it was like some black comedy, because as we lifted what remained of the rug, bits of him started falling out. ...Awful. Just awful."

But Kat was thinking of something else entirely. "So that's why he totally freaked out when we found Josh's bones! Oh my God! It makes so much more sense now!"

Chapter 25

"Ah yes, I'd forgotten you'd said about that," Scott sighed. "Yes, he would have freaked. That would have taken him right back into his personal hell."

"And no wonder he thought I was …well, whatever he thought I was. I couldn't understand why he was being such a drama queen, because while discovering a body isn't nice, by the same token, all we saw were clean white bones, nothing gruesome, not even the skull. But if his parents had demanded he cover up the death of his own brother, well I can totally see why now."

Yet at that moment the portal flared and Drew himself came stumbling through.

"Drew!" Scott called, leaping to his feet and running to help his friend up.

They helped a staggering Drew to one of the chairs to let him catch his breath.

"Where's Rigby?" Kat asked worriedly after a moment or two. "Wasn't he with you?"

"I think Rigby might be dead," Drew said hoarsely.

"Dead?" Scott gasped. "How? Did he have a heart attack going through the portal or something?"

"He kept fighting the guards," Drew croaked, gratefully accepting Kat's mug of tea off her, and gulping it down.

"Oh no," Scott groaned. "They wouldn't have stood for that."

"They didn't. I saw him being carted back to the camp by four of them just before I came through, but he was awfully limp. I didn't dare linger, though, in case I missed the chance to get back myself. I kept telling him to keep quiet, honestly I did, but he would keep banging on about how he was a policeman and they shouldn't be doing this to him. Why he couldn't believe what he was seeing with his own eyes, I don't know. He was acting like it was some horrible prank being played on us, instead of being for real."

However Kat put a consoling hand on his shoulder. "I don't think Rigby was ever capable of believing such a thing might happen," she said gently. "I heard you telling him about the portal as you went into the house, you know. If he didn't believe it then, he should have when you two went through it. Were you trying to stop him? Was that how you got swept in?"

"Yes, I was," Drew said regretfully. "If only I'd gone down into the cellar first, I might have managed to stand in his way – but then having seen what he was like later on, maybe not." Then it suddenly seemed to dawn on him that Kat was being awfully nice and understanding. What had changed? "After the way I've behaved towards you, you must think me an absolute arse for leaving him, though," he apologised.

"No, I don't," Kat replied gently. "Rigby was his own worst enemy. How we cover our tracks with this I'm not sure, but we'll have to come up with something, though, because we can hardly take any more coppers down into the cellar."

"Erm, about that," Drew said shamefacedly. "I'm really sorry, Kat, truly I am. It was only when I got back here with Rigby that it all came out. How he's held a grudge against all the female officers who've got promoted ahead of him. He was a bigot and far from truthful, and I should have trusted you given that you showed me the proof of the portal. I can only hope you'll forgive me. There are… Well my past is… Oh, never mind, it's not an excuse."

"Oh but it is!" Kat exclaimed. "Look, please don't shout at Scott, but he told me about your brother."

"Scott! No!"

But Scott reached out and put a restraining hand on his friend's arm as he struggled to sit upright in the chair. "It's okay, Drew, she understands. All of it. She gets it."

Kat was nodding vigorously. "I certainly do. It makes so much more sense of why you were so freaked out up on the bank, and I'm so sorry that I was so wrapped up in my own worries that I didn't think hard enough of why you were so suddenly all over the place."

Drew blushed. "But that was why you were so angry about my crack about you being a burglar when you cut the wire, wasn't it?"

"Oh, very much so. A jab right on the tender

spot, though you couldn't possibly have known it."

They stopped as they heard Scott's chuckle. "God, you two, you make a right pair! Before you start trying to out-apologise to one another, don't you think we should get Drew inside and another cup of tea or something into him?"

"Tea? God I'd kill for more tea and a sandwich," Drew declared longingly, allowing himself to be helped up, and then led into the first stable cottage.

Yet once they'd got him settled in the armchair with a mug in his one hand and a plate with two doorstep sandwiches balanced on his knee, Kat realised that she was going to have to present them with another uncomfortable truth.

"Look guys, before we move on, there's something we have to think about. If you're certain that Rigby may never come back, Drew, then we're stuck with a big problem, and that's his bloody car sitting out there on the drive. As far as the portal goes, it's only a day or so and then it'll be gone for another year. We don't have to worry about that."

"Won't it be visible for days longer than that right now?" Drew asked worriedly.

Kat scrunched up her nose. "*Meh*... Maybe not. You see, if the change from waxing to waning alters the garden end of the portal, wouldn't it make sense for it to change the cellar end too? In which case, mightn't this become the way back from the future? Although I'll confess I'm far from convinced about that, because that ought to mean that the garden portal changes too. All I can say is that this weird event can't have hung around for too long in previous years, otherwise it would have got spotted a lot sooner."

However, Scott now got up and went to look out of the window at the garden, saying, "I had a thought about this while I was in the past, you know. What happens when they finish the cellar in the past? Do you see what I mean? I asked old George if they found any other foundations when they were first digging the footings for the big house in his Victorian time, and he said not. So those three cellars really are it – the full extent of what gets built in the past. And now that I've put them right about the construction, how long do you think it's going to take for them to complete it?

"So that's now making me wonder whether the original builders had to get part of the way through that building of the cellars before the portal got disturbed at their end? Maybe they were using local labour, and those men got killed when the portal came into being? That would make it all the more likely that they would take the arrival of George and his mates as a fair exchange for the labourers they'd lost. And it makes the soldiers' frustration with them understandable too, because from their point of view, they'd lost men who'd been making good progress, and got in exchange this bunch of numpties for whom nothing seemed to stay up."

"Oh my goodness, that does make a kind of sense," Kat agreed, and even Drew was nodding thoughtfully, adding,

"So if they get that cellar done before the super-moon of next year, then you think there might be a chance that the portal might never open? Is that what you're saying?"

"I think it's a strong possibility," Scott concluded. "George said the problems started at our end when they bored down to put the sewers in for what would be the toilets. It's like the two disruptions in the same spot caused them to link up. It's around the same spot where they were having so much trouble getting the barrel-vaulting to stay up when I went through to the past, you see. So if they don't keep disturbing that spot in the past, by keeping on trying to dig deeper and better foundations in order for the thing to stay up, might that not settle everything down again?"

"That would be a blessed relief," Kat ageed, "because I have to tell you, I've been cudgelling my brain trying to think how on earth I could seal something as forceful as that portal, and I've been coming up empty every time. Going around with my crystals and smudge sticks and holy water might have worked for dissipating its energy upstairs, but getting rid of the thing itself was something I've been thinking would be beyond me."

"Then let's pray that Scott's right," Drew said hopefully.

"But," Kat cautioned them with a warning finger, "that means that Rigby will effectively vanish forever, doesn't it? He's not likely to come staggering through next year, even if he's not as dead as you thought already, Drew. So I'm sorry, guys, but we need to get rid of any evidence that he came back here with you, Drew. Because without even the portal to show anyone – even if we dared to do such a thing given Rigby's reaction – we haven't a damned thing to show that might stop the police wondering if we'd done something to him. Or at least, they might not think it of you, but two men vanishing when I'm around, and with my past, even if one of them has come back, might mean that the Hereford police look a good deal more sideways at me than they are at the moment. And sooner rather than later, someone's going to wonder just how dirty I had to get to have Big Alf locked up."

Drew grimaced. "And in truth, I don't want anyone digging into my past, thank you very much. I was just thinking I'd got shot of that once and for all. I don't want it suddenly rearing its ugly head again."

"Speaking of your past," Kat mused, "you didn't quite finish the story, Scott."

"How far had you got?" Drew asked his friend.

"Us having to move Lionel before the diggers went in."

Drew gave a shudder, making Scott come and put a comforting hand on his shoulder and recommence with,

"So we got all of Lionel together, and then went over to St Mary's in the depths of night. All we had to do was dig a bit deeper down into the already cut grave."

"Or rather you did," Drew said with a wan smile. "I was no fucking use at all that night."

Scott patted his shoulder. "He was your brother, mate, even if you never knew him. And what your dad made you do as a kid would scar anyone for life. ...So we put Lionel down into the grave and tamped the earth down as much as we could so that it wouldn't look too disturbed. Drew and I then bunked off work the next day and went and watched the funeral from a distance. Even his old man couldn't argue once he told him what we'd had to do – or rather, Drew left me out of it because he didn't want his father having that kind of hold over me as well. Thank God it was pissing down come the morning, and nobody at the proper funeral wanted to linger at the graveside. The coffin went in without a hitch, and so Lionel's remains are now under a genuine burial and not likely to come to light ever again."

He gave Drew's shoulder another squeeze of solidarity. "But all that secrecy before then really buggered up your marriage didn't it?"

"Oh God, yes!" Drew said with a huge huff of breath. "While I was at university down in London I could forget all about it. I even married Meg, thinking I could live a normal life. But then I qualified and the old man started pressuring me to come back. The miserable old sod soon remembered then that he had a hold over me. Threatened to tell the law society that it had been me, in a teenage fit of rage, that had done for my poor handicapped brother."

"*Nooo!*" gasped Kat, appalled. "How could he do that? To you? His own son? That's dreadful!"

"Pretty bloody easily if it got him what he wanted, I suspect," Scott grunted disgustedly. "And it was a threat that Drew couldn't tell anyone about, and would have had a hard time refuting."

"Hang on, though," Kat protested. "Surely there'd have to be signs of violence on Lionel's remains for an accusation like that to stick? I mean, I got what you said earlier, Scott, about there being legal problems and possible charges of neglect on Drew's parents' behalf, but there's a world of difference between that and murder. And I know all about that from having to sit and hear that shit of an 'uncle' of mine try and wriggle out of what he did to my mum. You couldn't have had any motive that would stick, Drew, at least not without a lot of other evidence."

Then she took in how sick Drew was starting to look.

"Oh no," she gulped, "please don't tell me that that 'spare the rod and spoil the child' violence got extended to a child who couldn't possibly know any better?"

Scott's expression was very bleak as he answered for Drew, "That was the new nightmare that he dropped on Drew to get him to come back from London. So Drew and Meg moved back to the house by the moors. But that changed how Drew behaved – well you can understand why, can't you. I saw Meg a few times in later years when I went to London, passing on documents and stuff for Drew, and every time she's said that it was the way he became so secretive and gloomy that upset her. She wanted them to have a home of their own, but any time she and Drew made plans to move out, something would happen and suddenly Drew would be frantically insisting that they stay put. One winter in that old house was all she could stand and then she was off."

Kat looked quizzically at Drew. "I thought you said she had affairs?"

He went scarlet. "Easier to explain away. Meg was never going to set foot in Yorkshire ever again, so I was hardly maligning her to people who would never dream of going down to London. And how was I going to explain to people why I behave like a complete arse towards her with no apparent reason, or at least not without letting the cat out of the bag?"

Something else dropped into place for Kat, too. "Oh! And that's why you said that about your father going into a care home had given you the chance of freedom! If he says anything now, they'll just think it's the dementia talking, won't they? *That's* why it's taken you so long to get away from him!"

"It is," Drew said sheepishly. "Weak and stupid of me, you'll think."

However Kat shook her head. "No, not at all. I watched how his evil sod of a brother warped and twisted all of my dad's feelings for him for years. It's not like some outsider doing that to you. When it's been going on from childhood, you're in a very different position to someone who just has something happen when they're already an adult — as a kid you're programmed to do what your parents tell you. I'm just glad that you're going to have the chance to break away now. Like my family, you've got a chance of a fresh start now, and that's all the more reason why we don't want anything upsetting the apple cart down here.

"You may not like this, guys, but this is what I think we have to do. We need to go and get all of Rigby's stuff from out of his car. Anything that will identify to him in person. And then we need to take it down to the cellar and throw it through the portal. After that, we drive that car of his out to somewhere remote and set fire to it."

"Christ! That's a bit drastic!" Scott protested.

"Is it?" Kat demanded. "You've only just been cleared of bumping off your wife and her mother; Drew's quite literally got a skeleton in his cupboard; and I've got connections to a family who made more than one person vanish in Birmingham in the sixties and seventies. Do you want to bet on our chances if someone decides to drag us through the courts?"

Drew snorted. "Bloody hell! Saying it like that, we look like the kind of suspects nobody would look much beyond. We're the trio most likely to do the deed, put like that."

"Exactly," Kat said dryly.

"Okay," Scott said with a sigh. "But can we temper this a bit? I can see the point of sending his personal stuff through, but burning the car is going to be risky. Once the petrol tank goes up, it'll be like a beacon. You can't guarantee that someone won't call the fire brigade. So is there somewhere on this estate where we could hide it? If Rigby never comes back, then we'll have to do something about it, I suppose, but I'd rather be very sure before we start making ourselves look too shifty. Let's try and make it look like something Rigby himself might have done, rather than us, eh?"

Kat nodded, "Fair enough. Let's go and get all of his stuff into a bin bag. Something we can swing at the portal without getting too close to it."

Thankfully Rigby hadn't bothered locking his car, and it was easy to clear out, all of them breathing a sigh of relief that he'd obviously used his own car and not one owned by the police. They also decided to let the portal calm down a bit before attempting the disposal, though Drew found a couple of half bricks to put into the bag to give it enough weight to swing. After that they moved into the cottage Scott had always used, if only because all three of them could sit down in the lounge in comfort there because of the sofa and armchairs. They would also be able to spend the night there, Scott declaring that he was quite happy for Drew and Kat to have a bedroom each, given that the sofa had been his bed for so long anyway.

After they'd had something to eat, they went back to the cellar and lobbed the bagful of stuff through the portal. As it vanished, Kat found herself breathing a sigh of relief, though she didn't want to say anything to either of the men. Rigby had been a bit too fanatical in his pursuit of her for her to have ever have been happy with his return, though she was hoping that in some way he would survive in the past and create some sort of life for himself. She just didn't want him anywhere near her.

"Why don't we go for a walk around the wider gardens?" Scott suggested as they locked up the big house once more. "It's a nice evening, and we might find somewhere we can just roll Rigby's car to."

Drew pointed to the path beside the walled garden where he had watched for Rigby what felt like a lifetime ago. "That looks like it leads somewhere. Why don't we have a look along there?"

His choice proved to be a good one. The path was wide and sturdy, but even better, led downhill to where some derelict old garden buildings lay. Only ever made of wood and with corrugated iron roofs, they had largely collapsed in on one another, but there was one doorway which was just about standing which looked as though it might have been where things like mowers and other equipment had been taken in and out of. When they managed to get close enough to look inside without leaning on anything too wobbly, at the far end of what had been a fair sized shed, they could see the front of an old tractor from something like the 1930s poking out from under the collapsed far end roof.

"Well if they got that in, I reckon we can get the car in," Drew decided, and so covering the driver's seat with bin bags, he carefully drove Rigby's down until it was just outside of the doorway.

"Don't drive in!" Scott had warned him. "One vibration too many and you'll be buried in there with it!"

And so once he'd got it down there and lined up, they all put on plastic gloves and pushed it. With a gentle roll, it slid inside, coming to rest with a soft thump against the ancient tractor. However Scott's assessment had been right. Even such minor bump as that was enough for the beam over the doorway to give an asthmatic groan.

"Watch out! It's going!" Scott called in warning, and with a couple more creaks, the doorway leaned sideways, the roof metal turned into a shower of rust, and the whole thing sank in on itself like an old lady giving her final curtsy. As the dust settled, not a thing could be seen of the car buried beneath the detritus.

In the morning, though, they had to decide what to do beyond that, and in the end they settled on giving it one more night at the house, just to see if Rigby would reappear. When he didn't, though, between them they decided that Scott and Drew must go back up to Yorkshire. If nothing else, Scott needed to make the arrangements for Jeanette's funeral, and now more than ever, Drew wanted to put his father's business on the market or wrap it up altogether.

"You carry on with the designs for the house, though," Scott reassured her, having told her of his plan to live in the stable's cottages. "Nothing's going to dispel questions about this place quicker than us getting it up and running as a successful business."

"I'll come up for the funeral," Kat promised when she dropped them at the station to catch the train back up north, and then wondered who she was going to miss most of the two, Drew or Scott, because both of them had become important to her.

Chapter 26

The funeral for Jeanette and Flora was every bit as grim as Kat had feared it might be. She made it a point to sit with Drew, just in case anyone got the wrong idea about her and Scott, but she needn't have worried – they were the only ones there aside from Flora's solicitor. He'd been a thorn in Scott's side, insisting on a full funeral service in the local church, before heading off to the crematorium, but Scott said he'd had to give in or have the damned man starting to spread the news all over town that Scott Hawkesmoor hadn't cared about his wife.

Because of that, Kat had been quick to return to Worcester the day afterwards, glad that Drew had decided to simply wind up his father's practice rather than try to sell it as a going concern. That would be a much faster process in getting to the point where he could come back to the Midlands, simply sending paperwork back and forth. Scott, too, was moving fast, getting a remover in to put what little he wanted from the family house into storage, and then getting a house clearer in to get rid of the rest.

"If I never see that place again it will be a decade too soon," he told Kat, as they gratefully escaped to the sanctuary of a country pub after the services were over. "I've already moved out into a hotel room."

"And what about you, Drew?" she asked, rather concerned that he seemed very deflated at being back here.

"Hmph. It turns out that a sizable chunk of what we can get for the business and for my parent's house will go to my bloody father's nursing home fees," he said gloomily. "Unlike Scott, I'll be coming out of this with not much more than some bits and pieces and my clothes. I hadn't appreciated how the old bastard had wrapped everything up so tightly. God! He never intended me to be able to walk away from him, you know, or at least not without losing everything."

"Can't you contest that?" Kat asked worriedly.

However Drew shook his head. "If he was dead it would be easier, but with Social Services on his case, it's almost impossible to get out of how much will go to him, certainly when he's staked his claim to so much over me."

"Ah, cheer up," Scott said with a wink. "We know of a nice place down in Herefordshire that's just waiting for you."

Yet Kat wasn't wholly convinced that Drew would shake off his past and come and join them. Whenever she'd spoken to Scott on the phone, he'd been increasingly enthusiastic about his return to Fownhope Priors, whereas Drew sounded so bogged down in the present he couldn't even think about the future. For that reason if no other, Kat didn't want to linger in

Yorkshire. Pinning her hopes on Drew was still too unsettling, not helped by her rising attraction to this new version of Scott that was emerging out of the dust of his old life. *See who comes and stays,* she kept telling herself, not because she would have ruled out moving up to Yorkshire herself, but because she didn't want to find herself weighed down by somebody else's past. For the most part, she could put her own past on the back-burner, only looking at it when it was forced upon her, as had happened with Rigby. And if she was going to share her life with someone, she wanted it to be with someone who was looking forwards with her.

As for Rigby himself, there hadn't been any sign of him. The portal had continued to flicker on past the full moon, but looking increasingly unstable, making Kat think that maybe Scott had been right – once the cellar was completed in the past, the portal would remain closed for good. And when the next full moon came and went without any signs of it, Kat knew that the only remaining confirmation she was going to get of the portal's demise would come with the super-moon next year.

Beyond that, a public announcement had been made by the police expressing concern about the whereabouts of DI Garry Rigby, who, according to the press release, had been suffering from stress and had become worryingly unstable. And once the DI from Hereford had become convinced that Rigby hadn't shown up and made a pest of himself with Kat, to her surprise she was left in peace. Even better, her involvement with Peter got rather taken over by the other fraud cases he was accused of, and it transpired that he'd stolen far more off other people, putting them higher on the prosecution's list of crimes to be thrown at him than Kat. There were also plenty of others willing to come forward and testify as to his thieving without Kat having to take to the witness box herself – something which she detected DI Scathlock's tactful touch over.

* * * * *

Therefore when mid-summer rolled around, and Scott announced that he was about to rejoin her at Fownhope Priors, Kat felt able to make the offer of selling her house in order to put some capital of her own into the venture, and to suggest that she might then use some of the big house to run her design business from. The fact that Scott agreed at speed made her very happy, especially when he offered her the three front rooms on the ground floor for the purpose. They would give her a wonderful space in which to display samples, and best of all to her mind, there'd be no need to disturb what lay beneath.

It resulted in Kat taking on the cottage Scott had originally used, and the two of them spending many happy hours of an evening and at weekends in the walled garden, bringing it back to life. So the only down side was that there was still no sign of Drew moving down to join them.

"Is he ever going to come, do you think?" Kat asked Scott one night, as they sat enjoying a large glass of chilled Pinot Grigio each after a long day weeding and planting.

Scott sighed. "I don't know, Kat. I spoke to him on the phone again, and he's now living out of a hotel room like I was, because the sale of the house and the office suite has all gone ahead. That's all moved faster than mine has. But the thing is, Kat, he's talking now about going down to London and putting things right with Meg. I've told him to leave well alone. That Meg's remarried and is happy as she is, but I think he feels he owes her some sort of apology. It's making me wonder whether he's ever really got over her, you know, and maybe that's why he's not had a relationship with anyone else. But he's a fool if he thinks she's going to go back to him."

"That's worrying," Kat admitted, while feeling faintly glad that Drew had stayed away if his feelings were like that. Better that she didn't see too much of him if he was going to prevaricate, not even knowing what his own feelings were. "And what does he think he's going to say to her? He can hardly tell her the truth now any more than he could in the past?"

Scott shrugged. "I think he's thinking of something along the lines of, 'my father was blackmailing me, and I couldn't tell you why.' But if he thinks he's going to be able to be fuzzy over it now, he's very much mistaken."

"He is," Kat agreed. "If I was in Meg's place, I think I'd be asking some very probing questions that Drew's not going to want to answer. And sadly, if he doesn't answer her, I'm afraid she's going to be even more pissed off at him for coming to see her and raking the past up."

"Changing the subject," Scott said, chinking his glass against Kat's. "It was a great idea of yours to get that wedding planner woman on board. We've got our first booking for a wedding next year."

"Yay! I told you we'd be better off farming that side of it out. It's a specialist thing, wedding organising, and like I said at the time, I don't have the temperament to deal with neurotic brides, stressed bride's mothers, and bride's dads who are getting ever more worried about how much everything is going to cost them. Aoife's Irish charm works much better on them than mine, and as she's already got an established business, she wanted another venue on her books. And she had the vision to see what the hall would be like even before the first coat of fresh paint went on. All we've got to do is get the front gardens in a fit state for photos to be taken out there, and we've nearly done that."

The top floor had had the two front bedrooms made into a bridal suite with the middle room made into its bathroom, and with an additional spare bedroom up there for anyone else who wanted to stay, that had made it an attractive proposition. As Kat had proposed from the start, the other three top floor apartments were now all set up for the arrival of their first tourists next year. But already Aoife was telling Kat to keep the weeks of the weddings free for other guests, and so Kat and Scott were confident of having the house full for a fair run even in their first trading year, which was very encouraging.

Scott had taken great delight in remodelling the stables cottages himself, leaving the two separate sets of stairs in so that he now had a three-bedroom house, but taking out the shower room under the stairs of the one cottage to allow access between the two. The far downstairs bedroom had now become his office, and the tiny lounge which Ryan and Josh had once shared had become a luxury bathroom. The kitchen had had a total makeover, and in a few days' time, a conservatory company were coming to put in one that would run almost the full width of the cottages' backs, thereby vastly increasing the sitting space. Kat had even been surprised at Scott's choices of colours, glad that he'd avoided playing safe with magnolia throughout, and had gone for some daring and interesting tiles and warm Mediterranean colours downstairs, making it feel like some Tuscan farmhouse transported to this corner of Herefordshire.

As a result of those changes, Kat found herself spending more and more time with Scott over here in the evenings, because as summer had come around, it was just nice to be able to sit out on the patio and watch the sun going down. And it wasn't lost on her that she and Scott never seemed to run out of things to talk about, but could also sit in companionable silence. There'd also been lots of close hugs, but nothing more than that as yet, making Kat wonder whether both of them were subconsciously waiting for

Drew to make up his mind what he wanted. Scott because he was a good enough friend to not want to stand in Drew's way if he was truly smitten with Kat, and Kat because she wanted to be sure that she wasn't messing Scott around after all that he'd been through, and needing to confirm just what her own feelings were.

"How long do we give Drew?" Kat now finally dared to ask Scott, knowing that it was a very loaded question for both of them.

Scott sighed. "Hard to tell. If a visit to London and Meg sorts him out, then I think we'll know pretty quickly whether he's coming to join us or not. But to be frank, Kat, I think there's a part of him that can never be fully comfortable here. He's mentioned finding Josh's body a few times, you know, and that makes me wonder whether he's frightened that some other skeleton isn't going to emerge out of the undergrowth."

"Good grief!" Kat snorted. "They're not going to be popping up like rabbits! The portal wasn't active enough for long enough for *that* many people to get caught in it."

"Maybe not, but it's still playing on Drew's mind, I fear. And there's the matter of Rigby. Drew's mithering that he's the last person to be with Rigby here."

"Oh dear, that's not good. But Scott, if he was under any suspicion at all, the police would have spoken to him long before now. I honestly don't think Rigby told anyone what he was up to, and I certainly don't think that out here anyone saw Drew in Rigby's car on the way over."

Yet when a year rolled around, and despite the super-moon of the year arriving with no evidence of the portal opening, Drew still hadn't moved down. In fact his phone calls had become increasing sporadic, and the last Kat and Scott had heard, he'd done a course and was now heading out to Japan to teach English out there for a year.

"Lord knows what he'll make of Japan, and they of him," Scott had laughed. "He's going to struggle to get a hearty meat pie out there!"

But at least that had settled things in their minds, especially as Kat had moved in with Scott in the autumn. The cottage at the back of the house they had been keeping in case Drew wanted it, but now felt that they could let that out as a holiday rental for the coming season too.

"There's just one last thing I have to ask, though," Scott said, as they ended the call with Drew, who'd rung from the airport to say he was flying out within the hour. "How do you feel about changing your name again, Kat?"

Her smile was answer enough, but he laughed with her as she said, "I think I shall be glad to see the back of Miss Newsome. She's got into far too much trouble. Hawkesmoor has a much nicer ring to it!"

THE END

Thank you for taking the time to read this book. Before we get on to the author's notes, I would like to invite you to join my mailing list. I promise I won't bombard you with endless emails, but I would like to be able to let you know when any new books come out, or of any special offers I have on the existing ones.

If you sign up I will send you free material to read, which includes free books and other offers.

Also, if you've enjoyed this book you personally (yes, *you*) can make a big difference to what happens next.

Reviews are one of the best ways to get other people to discover my books. I'm an independent author, so I don't have a publisher paying big bucks to spread the word or arrange huge promos in bookstore chains, there's just me and my computer.

But I have something that's actually better than all that corporate money – it's you, my committed and loyal readers. Honest reviews help bring them to the attention of other readers (although if you think something needs fixing I would really like you to tell me first!). So if you've enjoyed this book, it would mean a great deal to me if you would spend a couple of minutes posting a review on the site where you purchased it.

Thank you so much.

Author's Notes

The hamlet of Fownhope Priors is fictitious, but in the Wye valley there are many tiny places like this, all laden with history. Fownhope is a local place name, and of course many places had the appendage of Priors to their names to signify their original affiliation to a monastic institution. What many might not realise is the genuine pre-Conquest associations with Normandy in Herefordshire. While virtually every other castle in Britain dates to after the arrivals of the Normans in 1066, King Edward (the Confessor) really did invite some Normans over to help patrol his western border against the potential invasions of the then still-powerful Welsh princes. The castle in Hereford itself is one of those, and there are plenty of histories of the city which give a good description of what it must have been like, although nothing remains of it but the motte (a large earth mound) on which it once sat.

As far as early churches in the area are concerned, as mentioned in the story, the Welsh Church had the historical claim to founding many of them. The area that was once known as Archenfield has some very ancient churches, many predating the Norman conquest of 1066 and possibly having their origins in the first conversion to Christianity, but as part of the Welsh conversion not of the English. That's a hotly contested field of study, though, and whole

PhDs have been written about the ancient origins of churches mentioned in the ancient *Book of Llandaff*! So I'm not getting embroiled in that argument, but have just created an ancient church foundation of the period which didn't survive for long after that – also not unique by any means. However, there are real rural churches which once had their own priories, and if you want to go exploring, the Churches Conservation Trust has in its care the lovely church of St Cuthbert at Holme Lacy, and like my church, it is set in one of the loops of the River Wye, which (when in flood) can almost make an island of it.

Similarly, a monastic foundation simply vanishing after the Dissolution is nothing out of the ordinary. In some cases the church part survived to serve as the parish church – as at Deerhurst (Gloucs) – while others vanished altogether, robbed of all the building materials in order to create a fine house for a local nobleman. Even in the medieval ear, not every reference to a priest in the Domesday Book could be positively pinned to a later building, and so it is nothing uncommon for a place name to contain a word like 'Priors', and yet there be virtually nothing left to hint at why that might be.

I'd like to thank some very switched on friends of mine for introducing me to the necessity of 'cleansing' spaces, but also for talking about spiritual matters in the very down to earth way that I've borrowed for Kat. Whether or not you believe in ghosts or spirits, it's not so hard to believe in natural phenomena that we have no logical explanation for as yet, and people who live a lot closer to the natural world than many of us do in this modern life also have a way of looking at those phenomena with greater acceptance. I was particularly inspired for this book after reading about the survival of shamanism in Siberia despite the best efforts of the Communist regime to wipe it out, which is where Kat's Papa Viktor came from. If you want to find out more, *The Shaman's Coat: a native history of Siberia* by Anna Reid is worth reading.

DI Bill Scathlock has his own adventures in other books, as well as making the odd cameo appearance, as here. And finally I must apologise to the West Mercia Police for the creation of DS Rigby! I'm sure none of the current serving officers are anything like as blinkered or prejudiced as he is. However, this is a work of complete fiction and I needed a bad guy!

About the Author

L. J. Hutton lives in Worcestershire and writes history, mystery and fantasy novels. If you would like to know more about any of these books you are very welcome to come and visit my online home at www.ljhutton.com

---

Also by L. J. Hutton:

Time's Bloodied Gold – the first Bill Scathlock novel

Standing stones built into an ancient church, a lost undercover detective and a dangerous gang trading treasures from the past. Can Bill Scathlock save his friend's life before his cover gets blown?

DI Bill Scathlock thought he'd seen the last of his troubled DS, Danny Sawaski, but he wasn't expecting him to disappear altogether! The Polish gang Danny was infiltrating are trafficking people to bring ancient artefacts to them, but those people aren't the usual victims, and neither is where they're coming from. With archaeologist friend Nick Robbins helping, Bill investigates, but why do people only appear at the old church, and who is the mad priest seen with the gang? With Danny's predicament getting ever more dangerous, the clock is ticking if Bill is to save him before he gets killed by the gang ...or arrested by his old colleagues!

House of Lost Secrets

Some people keep secrets, this house hides them for generations. Can Cleo dig back in time to save the present?

When genealogist Cleo is asked to investigate the family of Upper Moore House as a favour to her estate agent friend, it's a different commission to the ones she's used to. And right from the start she feels there's something not quite right about Mrs Darcy D'Eath Wytcombe. What is Mrs Wytcome's real motive for digging so deep into her late husband's family? What secrets does she think Cleo will uncover? And is she prepared for what else might be revealed?

As Cleo discovers increasing numbers of old letters, some of which have been buried for over a century in hiding places within the house, a strange web of deceit begins to appear. What was the family's connection to Georgian and Victorian Croatia and Italy, and just how closely related to one another were some of the Wytcombes? More urgently, who have been the real heirs to the house down the generations, and have others been willing to resort to blackmail or even murder to keep it from them?

With Mrs Wytcombe pushing for a swift sale of the house, Cleo must work against the clock to find the true heirs to Upper Moore House and prevent a terrible miscarriage of justice.

Spirits in the Oak

Jenna needs a fresh start and a new job house-sitting might be it. But these houses aren't normal, and nor is what's inside them!

With her old wounds recently reopened, Jenna is in desperate need of a new start, and her friend Tiff thinks she's found just the thing when her company needs someone to watch over a trio of houses. Set in an idyllic location in the Shropshire Hills, the houses lie empty, tied up in a legal battle, but from the outset Jenna knows there's something wrong with them – and it's not just down to the vicious wrangling between the owners, either! Why does it feel like the houses are talking to her? And who is the mysterious ex-soldier in the only other house on the hill? Why does he hate the owners so badly, and does he know more of what's going on than Jenna has been told?

Join Jenna as she unravels the secret of the houses while she struggles to heal her own inner scars, and in the process finds unexpected friends and inner reserves she didn't know she had.

Printed in Great Britain
by Amazon